DORA LIVINGSTONE,

THE

ADULTERESS:

OR,

THE QUAKER CITY.

BY GEORGE LIPPARD, ESQ.

LONDON:

PUBLISHED BY G. PURKESS, COMPTON STREET, SOHO; E. LLOYD, 12, SALISBURY
SQUARE, FLEET-STREET; AND SOLD BY ALL BOOKSELLERS.

THE REVEL IN THE OYSTER CELLAR.

CHAPTER I.

THE WAGER IN THE OYSTER-CELLAR.

"I SAY, gentlemen, shall we make a night of it? Let's toss up for it—which shall have the night—brandy and oysters, or quilts and feather-beds?" And as he spoke, the little man broke loose from the grasp of his friends, and retiring to the shelter of an awning-post, flung his cloak over his shoulder with a vast deal of drunken dignity, while his vacant eyes were fixed upon the convivial group scattered upon the pavement.

"Byrnewood, d'ye hear?" exclaimed the tallest gentlemen of the party, gathering his frogged overcoat closer around him, while his moustachioed lip was wreathed in a drunken smile. "Look yonder at the church—sing—singular phenomenon! There's the original steeple and a duplicate. Two steeples, by Jupiter! Remarkable effect of moonlight! Very

—doesn't it strike you, Byrnewood, that yonder pump is walking across the street, to black the lamp-post's eyes for for making a face at him?"

The gentleman thus addressed, instead of replying to the sagacious query of his friend, occupied a small portion of his leisure time in performing an irregular Spanish dance along the pavement, terminating in a pleasant combination of the cachuca, with a genuine New Jersey double-shuffle. This accomplished, he drew his well-proportioned figure to its full height, cast his cloak from his shoulders, and turned his face to the moonlit sky. As he gazed upon the heavens, clear, cold, and serene as death, the moonlight falling over his features, disclosed a handsome though pallid face, relieved by long curling locks of jet black hair. For a moment he seemed intensely absorbed amid the intricacies of a philosophical reverie, for he frequently put his thumb to his nose, and described circles in the air with his outspread fingers. At last tottering to a seat on a corner post, he delivered himself of this remarkable expression of opinion,—

"Miller the prophet's right! Right, I say! The world—confound the post, how it shakes—the world is coming to an end—for, d'ye see, boys—there's two moons shining up yonder this blessed night as sure as fate."

The scene would have furnished a tolerable good subject for an effective convivial picture.

There, seated on the door-way step of a four storied dwelling, his arms crossed over his muscular chest, his right hand grasping a massive gold-headed cane, Mr. Gustavus Lorrimer, commonly called the handsome Gus Lorrimer, in especial reference to his well-known favour among the ladies, presented to the full glare of the moonbeams, a fine manly countenance, marked by a brilliant dark eye, a nose slightly aquiline, a firm lip clothed with a moustache, while his hat tossed slightly to one side, disclosed a bold and prominent forehead, relieved by thick clusters of rich brown hair. His dark eye, at all times full of fire, shone with a glance of unmistakeable humour, as he regarded his friend seated on the corner post directly opposite the doorway steps.

This friend Mr. Byrnewood, as he had been introduced to Lorrimer, was engaged in performing an extemporoneous musical entertainment on some aare railings with his fingers.

While continuing his performance, let us not forget our other friends, Col. Mutchins, in his snow-white overcoat and shiny hat; and Mr. Sylvester J. Petriken, in his glazed cap and long cloak, as leaning against opposite awning posts, they gaze in each other's faces and afford a beautiful contrast for the pencil of a Cruikshank.

Col. Mutchins' face, you will observe, is very much like a picture of a dissipated full-moon, with a large red pear stuck in the centre for a nose, while two small black beads, placed in corresponding circles of crimson tape, supply the place of eyes. The colonel's figure is short,

thick-set, and corpulent; he is very broad across the shoulders, broader across the waist, and very well developed in the region of the hands and boots. The gentleman, clinging nervously to the opposite awning post, is remarkable for three things—smallness of stature, slightness of figure, and slimness of legs. His head is very large, his face remarkable for its pallor, is long and square—looking as though it had been laid out with a rule and compass—with a straight formal nose, placed some distance above a wide mouth marked by two parallel lines, in the way of lips. His protuberant brow, faintly relieved by irregular locks of mole-skin coloured hair, surmounted by a high glazed cap, overarches two large, oyster-like eyes that roll about in their orbits with the regularity of machinery. These eyes remind you of nothing more than those glassy things which, in obedience to a wire, give animation to the expressive face of a Dresden wax-doll.

And over this scene of quadruple convivialism, shone the midnight moon. The long shadows of the houses on the opposite side of the way, fell darkly along the street, while in the distance, terminating the dim perspective, arose the crowd of buildings, with their pinnacles shooting upward into the clear blue sky.

"That champagne," hiccuped Mr. Petriken, clinging to the awning-post, under a painful impression that it was endeavouring to throw him down—"that champagne was very strong; and the oysters—oh, my——"

"As mortal beings we are subject to—sudden sickness," observed the sententious Mutchins, gathering his awning-post in a fonder embrace.

"I say, Byrnewood, how shall we terminate the night? Think how many bells are to be pulled, how many—curse the thing, I believe I'm toddied—knockers to be wrenched. Come on, boys?"

"Aye, come on, boys. Let's go round to Smokey Chiffin's oyster cellar, and have a cozy supper. Come on, I say. Take my arm, Byrnewood, there; steady here Petriken, never mind the awning-post, take this other arm—now Mutchins hook Silly's arm and let's travel——"

But Mutchins—who, by the way, had been out in a buffalo hunt the year before—was now engaged in an imaginary, though desperate fight with a Sioux warrior, whom he belaboured with terrific shrieks and yells.

"D—n the fool, he'll have us all in the watch-house;" exclaimed Lorrimer, who appeared to be the soberest of the party by several bottles. "Fun is fun, but this thing of cutting up shines in the street, after twelve, when it —keep steady Silly—amounts to yelling like a devil in harness is—un-un-der-stand me, no fun. Come along, Mutchy, my boy!"

And arm in arm, linked four abreast, like horses very tastelessly matched, the boon companions tottered along the street, towards the well-known oyster cellar, where they arrived, without a single interruption.

Descending into the subterranean retreat, our

friends were waited upon by a very small man, with a sharp face and a white apron, and a figure so lank and slender, that the idea involuntarily arose to the spectator's mind, of whole days and nights of severe training having been bestowed upon a human frame, in order to reduce it to a degree of thinness quite visionary.

"Come my 'Virginia abstraction,'" exclaimed Lorrimer, "show us into a private room, and tell us what you've got for supper."

"This way, sir—this way, gents," cried Smokey Chiffin, as the thin gentleman was rather familiarly styled, and the host disappeared from the refectory proper, through an obscure door into the private room.

These oyster cellars are queer things. Like the caverns of old story, in which the giants, those ante-diluvian rowdies, used to sit all day long, and use the most disreputable arts to inveigle lonely travellers into their clutches, so these modern dens are occupied by a jolly old giant of a decanter, who too often lures the unsuspecting into his embrace. A strange tale might be told, could the stairway leading down into the oyster cellar be gifted with the power of speech. Here youth has gone down laughing merrily, and here youth has come up, his ruddy cheek wrinkled, and his voice quavering with premature age. Here wealth has gone, and kept going down until at last he came up with his empty pocket, turned inside out, and the gripe of grim starvation on his shoulder. Here hope, so young, so gay, so light-hearted, has gone down, and come up transformed into a very devil, with sunken cheeks, bleared eyes, and a cankered heart. Oh, merry cavern of the oyster cellar, nestling so snugly under the ground, how great the wonders, how mighty the doings, how surprising the changes accomplished in your pleasant den, by your jolly old giant of a decanter!

It is here in this oyster cellar, that we open the fearful tragedy which it is the painful object of our narrative to tell. Here amid paint, glitter, and gilding, amid the clink of glasses and the roar of drinking songs, occurred a scene, which, trifling and insipid as it may appear to the casual observer, was but the initial letter to a long and dreary alphabet of crime, mystery, and bloodshed.

In a room, small and comfortable, lighted by gas and warmed by a cheerful coal-fire, around a table furnished with various luxuries, and garnished with an array of long-necked bottles, we find our friends of the convivial party. Their revel had swelled to the highest, glass clinked against glass, bottle after bottle had been exhausted, voices began to mingle together, the drinking song and the prurient story began to pass from lip to lip, while our sedate friend, Smokey Chiffin, sat silently on the sofa, regarding the drunken bout with a glance of quiet satisfaction.

"Give us your hand, Gus," cried Byrnewood, rising from his seat, and flinging his hand unsteadily across the table; "damme, I like you, old fellow. Never—never—knew—until to-night —met you at Mutchins' room—wish I'd known you all my life. Give us your hand, my boy!"

Calm and magnificent, Gustavus extended his hand, and exclaimed, in a voice which champagne could not deprive of its sweetness, that it gave him pleasure to know such a regular bird as Mister Byrnewood, great pleasure, extraordinary pleasure.

Gentlemen, I will give you a toast!" exclaimed Lorrimer, as he stood erect, the bold outline of his manly form, his handsome face, the high forehead relieved by thick masses of brown hair, the aquiline nose, the rounded chin, and the curving lip darkened by a moustache, all shown to advantage in the glowing light. Gentlemen fill your glasses, no heeltaps! Woman!"

"Woman!" shrieked the other three, springing unsteadily to their feet, and raising their glasses on high. "Woman! Three times three, hip-hip-hurrah!"

"Women!" muttered Sylvester Petriken. "Women for ever! when we're babies she nusses us, when we're boys she lathers us, when we're men she bedevils and bewitches us!"

"Woman," muttered Colonel Mutchins— "without her what 'ud life be? A dickey without a 'plete,' a collar without starch!"

"We can't help if we fascinate 'em?" exclaimed Byrnewood. "Can we, Gus?"

"All fate, my boy—all fate. By-the-bye— sit down, boys. I've got a nice little adventure of my own to tell. Smokey—bring us some soda to sober off with—It's a story of a sweet girl, my boys—a sweet girl about sixteen, with a large blue eye, a cheek like a ripe peach, and a lip like a rose-bud cleft in two. There's this material difference, boys, between a ripe peach or a cleft rose-bud, and a dear little woman's lips or cheek. A ripe peach won't throb and grow warm if you lay your cheek against it, and I never yet heard of a rose-bud that kissed back again. She's as lovely a girl as ever trod the streets of the Quaker City. Noble bust—slender waist—small feet and delicate hands. Her hair? damme, Byrnewood, you'd give your eyes for the privilege of twining your hands through the rich locks of her dark brown hair———"

"Well, well, go on. Who is this girl; uncover the mystery!"

"Patience, my boy, patience. A little of that soda, if you please. Now, gentlemen, I want you to listen attentively, for let me tell you, you don't hear a story like mine every day in the year."

Half-sobered by the combined influences of the soda water and the interest of Lorrimer's story, Byrnewood leaned forward, fixing his full dark eyes intently upon the face of Gus, who was seated opposite; while Colonel Mutchins straightened himself in his chair, and even Petriken's vacant face glowed with a momentary aspect of sobriety.

"I see, boys, that you expect something nice. (Smokey put some more coal on that fire.) Well,

Byrnewood, you must know I'm a devil of a fellow among the girls—and—and d—n the thing, I don't know how to get at it. Well, here goes. About two weeks ago I was strolling along Chestnut-street towards evening, with Boncy (that's my big wolf dog, you know,) at my heels. I was just wondering where I should spend the evening; whether I should go to the theatre, or take a turn round town, when who should I see walking ahead of me, but one of the prettiest figures in the world, in a black silk mantilla, with one of these saucy kiss-me-if-you-dare bonnets on her head. The walk of the creature, and a little glimpse of her ankle excited my curiosity, and I pushed ahead to get a view of her face. By Jupiter, you never saw such a face! so soft, so melting, and damme—so innocent. She looked positively bewitching in that saucy bonnet, with her hair parted over her forehead, and resting each cheek in a mass of the richest curls, that ever hung from the brow of mortal woman——"

"Well, Gus, we'll imagine all this. She was beautiful as a houri, and priceless as the philosopher's stone——"

"Byrnewood, you are too impatient. A pretty woman in a black silk mantilla, with a lovely face peeping from a provoking bonnet, may seem nothing to you; but the strangest part of the adventure is yet to come. As I looked in the face of this lovely girl, she, to my utter astonishment, addressed me in the softest voice in the world, and——"

"Called you by name?"

"No. Not precisely. It seems she mistook me for some gentleman whom she had seen at a country boarding-school. I took advantage of her mistake, walked by her side,——

"Became thoroughly acquainted with her, I suppose?" suggested Byrnewood.

"Well, you may judge so, when I mention one trifling fact for your consideration. This night, at three o'clock, this innocent girl, the flower of one of the first families in the city, forsaking home and friends, and all that these sweet girls are wont to hold dear, will seek repose in my arms——"

"She can't be much," exclaimed Byrnewood, over whose face a look of scornful incredulity had been gathering for some few moments past—"pass that champagne, Petriken, my boy. Gus, I don't mean to offend you, but I rather think you've been humbugged by some nymph of the kitchen."

A frown darkened over Lorrimer's brow, and even as he sate, you might see his chest heave and his form dilate.

"Do you mean to doubt my word, sir?"

"Not at all, not at all. But you must confess, the thing looks rather improbable. (Will you smoke, Col.?) May I ask whether there was any one in company with the lady when first you met her?"

"A miss something or other—I forget her name. A very passable beauty of twenty and upwards, and I may add, a very convenient one,

for she carried my letters, and otherwise favoured my cause with the sweet girl."

"And this 'sweet girl' is the flower of one of the first families in the city?" asked Byrnewood with a half formed sneer on his upper lip.

"She is," answered Lorrimer, lighting a cigar.

"And this girl, to-night, leaves home and friends for you, and three hours hence will repose in your arms?"

"She will—" and Lorrimer vacantly eyed a column of smoke winding upward to the ceiling.

"You will not marry her?"

"Ha, ha, ha! You're a-head of me now. Only a pretended marriage, my boy. As for this 'life interest' in a woman, it don't suit my taste. A sham marriage my boy,——"

"You would be a d——d fool to marry a woman who flung herself in your power in this manner. How do you know she is respectable? Did you ever visit her at her father's house? What is her name? Do enlighten us a little——"

"You're 'cute, my boy, mighty 'cute, but not so 'cute as you think. Her name? D'ye think I'm so particularly verdant as to tell it? I know her name, could tell you the figure of her father's wealth, but have never been inside of the threshold of her home. Secret meetings, secret walks, and even an assumed name, are sometimes wonderfully convenient."

"Gus, here is a hundred dollar bill on the bank of North America. I am, as you see, somewhat interested in your story. I will stake this hundred dollars that the girl who seeks your arms to-night, is not respectable, is not connected with one of the first families in the city, and more than all, has never been any better than some fair and frail ladies of our acquaintance."

"Book that bet, Mutchins. You heard it, Silly. And now, Byrnewood, here is another hundred, which I will deposit with yours in Mutchins' hands until the bet is decided. Come with me, and I'll prove to you that you've lost. You shall witness the wedding—ha, ha—and to your own sense of honour will I confide the secret of the lady's name and position—"

"The bet is booked, and the money is safe," murmured the sententious Mutchins, enclosing the notes in the leaves of his pocket-book "I've heard of many rum goes, but this is the rummest go of all."

"If I may be allowed to use the expression, this question involves a mystery. A decided mystery. For instance, what's the lady's name? There is a point from which Hypothesis may derive some labour. 'What's in a name' as Shakspeare says. I say, gents, let's pick out a dozen names, and toss up which shall have it?"

This rather profound remark of Mr. Petriken's was received with unanimous neglect.

It was observable that during this conversation, both Lorrimer and Byrnewood had been gradually recovering from the effects of their debauch. Lorrimer seemed somewhat offended at the distrust manifested by Byrnewood; who, in his turn, appeared to believe the adventure just related with very many doubts and modifications.

Lorrimer leaned over the table and whispered in Sylvester's ear.

"Well, well, as it is your wish I'll do it. A cool fifty, did you say? You think a devilish sight of the girl, do you then? I must provide myself with a gown and prayer book? I flatter myself I'll rather become them—three o'clock, did you say?"

"Aye, aye," answered Lorrimer, turning to the rubicund face of Col. Mutchins, and whispering hurriedly in his ear.

A pleasant smile overspread the face of the benevolent man, and his pear-shaped nose seemed to grow expressive for a single moment.

"D——d good idea? I'll be your too-confiding uncle! Eh? Stern but relenting! I'll bless the union with my benediction, I'll give the bride away?"

"Come along, Byrnewood. Here, Smokey, is the money for our supper. Mark you, gentlemen, Mr. Petriken and Col. Mutchins, the hour is three o'clock. Don't fail me, if the d——l himself stands in the way. Take my arm, Byrnewood, and let's travel. Then 'hey for the wedding.' Daylight will tell who wins!"

CHAPTER II.

MARY, THE MERCHANT'S DAUGHTER.

LEANING gently forward, her shawl falling carelessly from her shoulders, and her bonnet thrown back from her brow, the fair girl impressed a kiss on the cheek of her father, while the glossy ringlets of her hair mingled their luxuriant brown with the white locks of the old man.

The father seated on the sofa, his hands clasping her slight and delicate fingers, looked up into her beaming face with a look of unspeakable affection, while a warm glow of feeling flushed over the pale face of the mother, a fine matronly dame of some forty five, who stood gazing on her daughter, with one hand resting on the husband's shoulder.

The mild beams of an astral lamp diffused a softened and pleasing light through the parlour. The large mirror glittering over the mantel, the curtains of crimson silk depending along the windows, the sofa on which the old man was seated, the carpet of the finest texture, the costly chairs, the paintings that hung along the walls, and in fine all the appointments of the parlour, designated the abode of luxury and affluence.

The father, who sat on the sofa gazing in the face of his child, was a man of some sixty years, with a fine venerable countenance, wrinkled by care and time, with thin locks of snow-white hair, falling along his high pale forehead. In his calm blue eye, looking forth from the shadow of a thick grey eyebrow, and in the general contour of his face, you might trace as forcible a resemblance to his daughter, as ever was witnessed between an old man just passing away from life, and a fair young girl, blooming and blushing on the very threshold of womanhood. The old man was clad in glossy black, and his entire appearance, marked the respectable merchant, who, retiring from active business, sought in the quietude of his own home, all the joys, that life, wealth, or affection united and linked in blessings, have in their power to bestow.

The mother, who stood resting her hand on her husband's shoulder, was, we have said, a fine matronly dame of forty-five. A mild pale face, a deep black eye, and masses of raven hair, slightly sprinkled with the silver threads of age, parted over a calm forehead, and tastefully disposed of beneath a plain cap of lace, gave the mother an appearance of sweetness and dignity combined, that was eminently effective in winning the respect and love of all who looked upon her.

"Mary, my child, how lovely you have grown!" exclaimed the merchant, in a deep, quiet tone, as he pressed her fair hands within his own, and looked up in her face.

"Nonsense! You will make the child vain," whispered the wife playfully, yet her face flushed with affection, and her eyes shone an answer to her husband's praise.

The girl was indeed beautiful.

As she stood there, in that quiet parlour, gazing in her father's face, she looked like a breathing picture of youth, girlhood, and innocence, painted by the finger of God. Her face was very beautiful. The small bonnet thrown back from her forehead, suffered the rich curls of her brown hair to escape, and they fell twining and glossy along each swelling cheek, as though they loved to rest upon the velvet skin. The features were regular, her lips were full, red, and ripe, her round chin varied by a bewitching dimple, and her eyes were large, blue, and eloquent, with long and trembling lashes. You looked in those eyes, and felt that all the sunlight of a woman's soul was shining on you. The face was lovely, most lovely, the skin, soft, velvety, blooming and transparent, the eyes full of soul, the lips sweet with the ripeness of maidenhood, and the brow calm and white as alabaster, yet was there no remarkable manifestation of thought, or mind, or intellect visible in the lines of that fair countenance. It was the face of a woman formed to lean, to cling, to love, and never to lean on but one arm, never to cling but to one bosom, never to love but once, and that till death and for ever.

The fair round neck, and well-developed bust, shown to advantage in the close fitting dress of black silk, the slender waist, and the ripening proportions of her figure, terminated by slight ankles and delicate feet, all gave you the idea of a bud breaking into bloom, a blossom ripening into fruit, or what is higher and holier, a pure and happy soul manifesting itself to the world, through the rounded outlines of a woman's form.

"Come, come, father, you must not detain me any longer," exclaimed the daughter in a sweet and low-toned voice. "You know aunt Emily has been teasing me these two weeks, ever since I returned from boarding-school, to come and stay with her all night. You know I was always a favourite with the dear old soul. She wants to contrive some agreeable surprise for my birthday, I believe. I'm sixteen next Christmas, and that is three days off. Do let me go, that's a good father."

"Hadn't you better put on your cloak, my love?" interrupted the mother, regarding the daughter with a look of fond affection; "the night is very cold, and you may suffer from exposure to the winter air."

"Oh, no, no, no, mother," replied the fair girl, laughingly, "I do so hate these cloaks—they're so bungling and so heavy—I'll just fling my shawl across my shoulders, and run all the way to Aunt Emily's. You know it's only two squares distant in Third-street."

"And then old Lewey will see you safe to the door!" exclaimed the mother. "Well, well, go along, my dear child, take good care of yourself, and give my love to your aunt."

"These old maids are queer things," said the merchant with a smile. "Take care Mary, or Aunt Emily will find out all your secrets."

And the old man smiled pleasantly to himself, for the idea of a girl, so young, so innocent, having any secrets to be found out, was too amusing to be entertained without a smile.

A shade fell over the daughter's face so sudden and melancholy that her parents started with surprise.

"Why do you look so sad, my child?" exclaimed the father, looking up in his daughter's face. "What is there in the world to sadden you, my Mary?"

"Nothing, father, nothing," murmured Mary, flinging her form on her father's bosom, and twining her arms round his neck, as she kissed him again and again. "Only I was thinking—just thinking of Christmas, and——"

The fair girl rose suddenly from her father's bosom, and flung her arms hurriedly around her mother's neck, imprinting kiss after kiss on her lips.

"Good bye, mother—I'll be back—I'll be back to-morrow."

And in an instant she glided hastily to the door and left the room.

"Lewey isn't it very cold to-night?" she asked, as she observed the white-haired negro servant waiting in the hall, wrapped up in an enormous overcoat, with a comforter around his neck, and a close fur cap surmounting his grey wool and chubby round face. "I'm sorry to take you out in the cold, Lewey."

"Bress de baby's soul," murmured the old negro, opening the door; "habbent I nuss you in dese arms when you warnt so high? Lewey take cold! Debbil a cold dis nigger take for no price when a waitin' on Missa Mary."

Mary stood upon the threshold of her home, looking out into the cold starlit night. Her face was for a moment overshadowed by an expression of the deepest melancholy, and her small foot trembled as it stepped over the threshold. She looked hurriedly along the gloomy street, then cast her glance backwards into the entry, and with a wild bound she retraced her steps, and stood beside her father and her mother.

Again she kissed them, again flung her arms round their necks, and again bounded along the entry, crying laughingly to her parents,—

"Good night—good night, I'll be back to-morrow."

Again she stood upon the threshold, but all traces of laughter had vanished from her face. She was sad and silent, and there were tears in her eyes—at least the old negro said so afterwards, and also that her tiny foot, when resting on the door-sill, trembled like any leaf.

Why should her eyes grow dim with tears, and her foot tremble? Would not that tiny foot, when it next crossed the threshold, bound forward with a gladsome movement, as the bride sprung to meet her father and her mother once again? Would not that calm blue eye, now filled with tears, grow bright with a joy before unknown, when it glanced over the husband's form, as for the first time he stood in the father's presence? Would not Christmas Eve be a merry night for the bride and all her friends as they went shouting merrily through the luxuriantly furnished chambers of her father's mansion? Why should she fear to cross the threshold of her home, when her coming back was to be heralded with blessings and crowned with love?

How will the future answer these trembling questions of that stainless heart?

She crossed the threshold, and not daring to look back, hurried along the gloomy street. It was clear, cold, starlight, and the pathways were comparatively deserted. The keen winter wind nipped her cheek, and chilled her form, but above her, the stars seemed smiling her onward, and she fancied the good angels, that ever watch over woman's first and world-trusting love looked kindly upon her from the skies.

After traversing Third-street for some two squares, she stood before an ancient three-storied dwelling, at the corner of Third and B—— streets, with the name of Miss. E. Graham, on the door plate.

"Lewey, you needn't wait," she said kindly, yet not without a deeper motive than kindness to the aged negro, who had attended her thus far. "I'll ring the bell myself. You had better hurry home and warm yourself, and remember, Lewey, tell father and mother that they need not expect me home before to-morrow at noon. Good night, Lewey."

"Good night, Missa Mary, Lor' Moses lub your soul," muttered the honest old negro, as, pulling his fur cap over his eyes, he strode homeward. "Dat ar babby's a angel, dat is widout de wings. De Lor grant when dis here ole nigger gets to yonder firmeyment—dat is if niggers gets dar at all—he may be 'pinted to one ob de benches near Missa Mary, so he can wait on her, handy as nuffin, dats all. She's a angel, and dis here night is a leetle colder dan any night in de memory ob dat genel'man de Fine Col'ector nebber finds—the berry oldest inhabitant."

Thus murmuring, Lewey trudged on his way, leaving Mary standing in front of Aunt Emily's door. Did she pull the bell? I trow not, for no sooner was the negro out of sight, than the tall figure of a woman dressed in black, with a long veil drooping over her face, glided round the corner and stood by her side.

"Oh, Bessie, is that you?" cried Mary, in a trembling voice. "I'm so frightened I don't know what to do. Oh, Bessie, Bessie, don't you think I had better turn back."

"He waits for you," said the strange woman, in a husky voice.

Mary hurriedly laid her hand on the stranger's arm. Her face was overspread with a sudden expression of feeling, like a gleam of sunshine, seen through a broken cloud on a stormy day, and in a moment, they were speeding down Third-street towards the southern districts of the Quaker City. Another moment, and the eye might look for them in vain.

And as they disappeared the State House clock rung out the hour of nine. This, as the reader will perceive, was just four hours previous to the time when Byrnewood and Lorrimer closed their wager in the subterranean establishment along Chestnut-street. To the wager and its result we now turn our attention and the reader's interest.

CHAPTER III.

BYRNEWOOD AND LORRIMER.

LINKED arm in arm, Byrnewood and Lorrimer hurried along the street, their figures thrown in lengthened shadows by the beams of the setting moon.

The tall, manly and muscular figure of Lorrimer, presented a fine contrast to the slight yet well-proportioned form of Byrnewood, which now and then became visible as the wind flung his voluminous cloak back from his shoulders. The firm and measured stride of Lorrimer, the light and agile footstep of Byrnewood, the glowing countenance of the magnificent Gus, the pale solemn face of the young merchant, the rich brown hair which hung in clustering masses around the brow of the first, and the long dark hair which fell sweeping to the very shoulders of his companion, all furnished the details of a vivid contrast, worthy the effective portraiture of a master in our sister-art.

"Almost as cold as charity, Byrnewood, my boy," exclaimed Lorrimer, as he gathered Byrnewood's arm more closely within his own. "Do you know, my fellow, that I believe vastly in faces? "And now my fellow, you may think me insincere, but I tell you frankly, that the moment I first saw your face, I liked you, and resolved you should be my friend. For your sake I am about to do a thing which I woul l do for no living man, and possibly no dead one——"

"And that is——" interrupted Byrnewood.

"Just listen, my fellow. Did you ever hear any rumours of a queer old house down town, kept by a reputable old lady, and supported by purses of goodly citizens, whose names you never hear without the addition of 'respectable,' 'celebrated,' or—ha, ha,—'pious' most pious! A queer old house, my good fellow, where, during the long hours of the winter nights, your husband, so kind and good, forgets his wife, your merchant his ledger, your lawyer his quibbles, your parson his prayers? A queer old house, my good fellow, where wine and women mingle their attractions, where at once you sip the honey from a red lip, and a sparkling bubble from the champagne? Where luxuriantly furnished chambers resound all night long with the rustling of cards, or the clink of glasses, or—it may be—the gentle ripple of voices, murmuring in a kiss? A queer old house, my dear fellow, in short, where the very devil is played under a cloak, and sin grows fat within the shelter of quiet rooms and impenetrable walls——"

"Ha, ha, Lorrimer, you are eloquent. Faith, I've heard some rumours of such a queer old house, but always deemed them fabulous."

"The old house is a fact, my boy, a fact. Within its walls this night I will wed my pretty bride, and within its walls, my fellow, despite the pains and penalties of our club, you shall enter."

"I should like it of all things in the world. How is your club styled?"

"All in good time, my friend. Each member, you see, once a week, has the privilege of introducing a friend. The same friend must never enter the club-house twice. Now I have rather overstepped the rules of the club in other respects, it will require all my tact to pass you in to-night. It shall be done, however, and mark me, you will obtain a few fresh ideas of the nature of the secret life of this good Quaker City."

"Why, Lorrimer," exclaimed Byrnewood, as they approached the corner of Eight and Chesnut, "you seem to have a pretty good idea of life in general."

"Life!" echoed the magnificent Gus, in that tone of enthusiasm peculiar to the convivialist when recovering from the first excitement of the bottle. "Life! What is it? As brilliant and as brief as a champagne bubble. To-day a jolly carouse in an oyster cellar, to-morrow a nice little pic-nic party in a grave-yard. One moment you gather the apple, the next it is ashes. Everything fleeting, and nothing stable, everything shifting and changing, and nothing substantial. A bundle of hopes and fears, deceits and confidences, joys and miseries, strapped to a fellow's back like pedlar's wares."

"Huzza! Bravo, the reverend Gus Lorrimer preache. And what moral does your reverence deduce from all this?"

"One word, my fellow, ENJOY! Enjoy till the last nerve loses its delicacy of sense; enjoy till the last sinew is unstrung; enjoy till the eye flings out its last glance. till the voice cracks and the blood stagnates; enjoy, always enjoy, and at last ——"

"Aye, aye, that terrible *at last* ——"

"At last, when you can enjoy no longer, creep into a nice cozy house some eight feet deep, by six long and two wide, wrap yourself up in a comfortable quilt of white, and tell the worms, those jolly gleaners of the scraps of the feast of life, that that may fall to and be d——d to 'em."

"Ha, ha, Lorrimer! Who would have thought this of you?"

"Tell me, my fellow, what business do you follow?"

"Rather an abrupt question. However, I'm the junior partner in the importing house of Livingston, Harvey, & Co., along Front-street."

"And I," replied Gustavus, slowly and with deliberation, "And I am junior and senior partner in a snug little wholesale business of my own. The firm is Lorrimer & Co., the place of business is everywhere about town, and the business itself is enjoyment, nothing but enjoyment; wine and women for ever! And as for the capital, I've an unassuming sum of one hundred thousand dollars, am independent of all relations, and bid fair to live at least a score of years longer. Now, my fellow, you know me; come, spice us up a few of your own secrets. Have you no interesting little amour for my private ear?"

'By Heaven, I'd forgot all about it!" cried Byrnewood, starting aside from his companion as they stood in the full glare of the gas-lamp at the corner of Eighth and Chesnut-streets, "I'd forgotten all about the letter!"

"The letter? What letter?"

"Why, just before Petriken hailed me in Chesnut-street this evening, or rather last evening, a letter was placed in my hands, which I neglected to read. I know the hand-writing on the direction, however. It's from a dear little love of a girl, who, some six months ago, was a servant in my father's house. A sweet girl, Lorrimer, and—you know how these things work, she was lovely, innocent, and too confiding, and I was but a man."

"Rather a low walk of business for you, my boy! However, let's read the letter by lamplight."

"Here it is—'Dear Byrnewood—I would like very much to see you to-night. I am in great distress. Meet me at the corner of Fourth and Chesnut-streets at nine o'clock or you will regret it to the day of your death. Oh, for God's sake, do meet me. ANNIE.' What a pretty hand she writes, eh! Lorrimer! That 'for

God's sake' is rather cramped, and, egad! there's the stain of a tear."

"These things are quite customary. These letters and these tears. The dear little women can only use these arguments when they yield too much to our persuasions."

"And yet, d——n the thing, how unfortunate for the girl my acquaintance has proved! She had to leave my father's house on account of the circumstance becoming too apparent, and her parents are very poor. I should have liked to have seen her to-night. However, it will do in the morning. And now, Lorrimer, which way?"

"To the 'queer old house' down town. By-the-bye, there goes the state house, one o'clock, by Jupiter! We've two good hours yet to decide the wager. Let's spend half an hour in a visit to a certain friend of mine. Here, Byrnewood, let me instruct you in the mysteries of the 'lark.'"

And, leaning aside, the magnificent Gus whispered in the ear of his friend, with as great an appearance of mystery as the most profound secret might be supposed to demand.

"Do you take, my fellow?"

"Capital, capital," replied Byrnewood, crushing the letter into his pocket, "we shall crowd this night with adventures, that's certain!"

The dawn of daylight, it is true, closed the accounts of a night somewhat crowded with incidents. Did these merry gentlemen who stood laughing so cheerily at the corner of Eighth and Chesnut-streets, at the hour of one, their faces glowing in the light of the midnight moon, did they guess the nature of the incidents which five o'clock in the morning could disclose? God of heaven! might no angel of mercy drop from the skies and warn them back in their career

No warning came, no omen scared them back. Passing down Eighth-street, they turned up Walnut, which they left at Thirteenth. Turning down Thirteenth they presently stood before a small old-fashioned two storied building, with a green door and a bulk window, that occupied nearly the entire width of the front, protruding in the light. A tin sign, placed between the door and window, bore the inscription,

"*. *****, ASTROLOGER."

"Wonder if the old cove's in bed," exclaimed Lorrimer, and as he spoke the green door opened, as if in answer to his question, and the figure of a man, muffled up in the thick folds of a cloak, with his hat drawn over his eyes, glided out of the astrologer's house, and hurried down Thirteenth-street.

"Ha, ha, devilish cunning, but not so cunning as he thinks!" laughed Byrnewood; "I saw his face it's old Grab-and-Snatch, the president of the —— Bank, which everybody says is on the eve of a grand blow-up!"

"The respectable old gentleman has been consulting the stars with regard to the prospects of his bank, ha, ha? However, my boy, the door is open, let's enter!" let's enter! And Lorrimer had placed one foot upon the door step as he uttered these words, but as suddenly withdrew it, as a tall female form caught his eye, evidently waiting until he should unbar the narrow doorway.

The figure was closely veiled, but by the flickering ligh of the adjoining lamp, Lorrimer half thought that he discerned the features of Emily Walravern. He gazed for a moment in uncertainty, but as if reconciling the improbability of Emily being in such a locality with a sudden recollection, he exclaimed:

'Now Brynewood, let's enter, Let's consult this familiar of the Fates, this intimate acquaintance of the future!"

CHAPTER IV

THE ASTROLOGER.

The building which Lorrimer and Brynewood entered was of that peculiar style of architecture which characterised some of the earliest fanciful erections of the settlers, vestiges of which may yet be seen, fast crumbling into oblivion. Half mansion, half cottage in its appearance, with its gable-fronts, leaden windows, and sharp-pointed roof, terminating in battlements resembling two opposing flights of stairs, starting at the eaves on each side and terminating in a little flat turret, ornamented with a weathercock or vane, the building appeared a fit residence for a singular man in the practice of a yet more singular mystery.

It consisted of two stories, the ascent to the second floor being by a spiral staircase directly in front of the door which was ornamented with a cumbrous brass knocker curiously wrought in the device of some nondescript, and which appeared to be kept burnished with zealous industry.

In a small room, remarkable for the air of comfort imparted by the combined effects of the neatly panelled walls, and a roaring wood fire, sat a man of some forty-five winters, bending over the table in the corner, covered with strange-looking books and loose manuscripts.

The light of the iron lamp which stood in the centre of the table, resting on a copy of Cornelius Agrippa, fell full and strongly over the face and form of the Astrologer, disclosing every line of his countenance, and illumining the corner where he sat, while the more distant parts of the room were comparatively dim and shadowy.

But had the walls and recesses of the apartment been examined with a close scrutiny, or the master knowledge of the initiated had exhibited the closer peculiarities of its dark and dimly shadowed boundaries, it is questionable whether admiration for the skill of the workman employed in producing such minute and elaborate finish, or wonderment at the ingenuity of the inventor of such secret panels, and revolving walls, would have been uppermost in his contemplation. Uncase the walls, and long dark cavities or passages, communicating with other habitations might have been discerned, leading far, far away, like a vein of mineral poison through gold, and communicating with the mysterious and subterranean vaults of Monk-hall.

The features of the occupant of this small chamber did not appear those of an individual whose prior existence had been such as to render the precaution of secret avenues necessary. His bearing had none of that restlessness, that constant half-watching, which betokens guilt; and his pale furrowed countenance seemed more the result of worldly struggling, and studiousness than aught else that might enter the conception of a suspicious observer. And, indeed, such an idea would have been injustice, for, however intimate the denizens of Monk-hall might have been with these means of ingress and egress, certain is it that they were unknown to the astrologer, who had for some length of time occupied his present habitation. A casual discovery would have been of little effect, and an adventuresome search would most probably only have entangled the fearless one in a labyrinth of dark mazy passages, an easy victim to the lurking assassin, or a lingering sufferer in the horrors of starvation.

The astrologer knew not of the connection his simple room had with the brothel and the gaming-house; and at the period of our history the passages we have alluded to had fallen into disuse, those acquainted with their existence having passed away to the regions of death.

As he sat in the large old-fashioned arm-chair, bending down earnestly over a massive manuscript, covered with strange characters and crossed by intricate lines, the lamp beams disclosed a face, which, somewhat plain and unmeaning in repose, was now agitated by an expression of the deepest interest. The brow, neither very high nor very low, shaded by tangled locks of thin brown hair, was corrugated with deep furrows, the eyebrows were firmly set together, the nostrils dilated, and the lips slightly compressed, while the full grey eye staring vacantly on the manuscript, indicated by the glassy film spread over each pupil, that the mind of the Astrologer, instead of being occupied with outward objects, was buried within itself, in the contemplation of some intricate subject of thought.

The eye might continue to perform its functions as an optical instrument, but the figures which it displayed on the retina excited no corresponding interest in the brain. The body was there, indeed, but the soul appeared to be absent on one of those flights which the disciples of Mesmer tell us are the privilege of the perfect clairvoyante. But into the fresh "fields and pastures new" to which the spirit might have winged its way, it is not our province to follow.

There was nothing in the dress of the man, or in the appearance of his room, that might realize the ideas commonly attached to the Astrologer and his den. Here were no melo-dramatic curtains swinging solemnly to and fro, brilliant and terrible with the emblazoned death's-head and cross-bones. Here were no blue lights imparting a lurid radiance to a row of grinning skeletons ; here were no ghostly forms standing pale and erect, their glassy eyes freezing the spectator's blood with horror ; here was neither goblin, devil, nor mischievous ape, which, as every romance reader knows, have been the companions of the astrologer from time immemorial ; here was nothing but a plain man, seated in an old-fashioned arm-chair, within the walls of a comfortable room, warmed by a roaring little stove.

No cap of sable relieved the astrologer's brow, no gown of black velvet, tricked out with mysterious emblems in gold and precious stones, fell in sweeping fold around the outlines of his spare figure. A plain white over-coat, much worn and out at the elbows, a striped vest not remarkable for its shape or fashion, a cross-barred neckerchief, and a simple linen shirt collar, completed the attic of the astrologer who sat reading at the table.

The walls of the room were hung with the horoscopes of illustrious men, Washington, Byron, and Napoleon, delineated on large sheets of paper, and surrounded by plain frames of black wood ; the table was piled with the works of Silby, Lilly, Cornelius Agrippa, and other masters in the mystic art ; while at the feet of the astrologer nestled a fine black cat, whose large whiskers and glossy fur, would seem to afford no arguments in favour of the supposition entertained by the neighbours, that she was a devil in disguise, a sort of familiar spirit on leave of absence from the infernal regions.

"I'm but a poor man," said the astrologer, turning one of the leaves of the massive volume in manuscript which he held in his hand. "I'm but a poor man, and the lawyer, and the doctor, and the parson all despise me, and yet," his lip wreathed with a sneering smile, "this little room has seen them all within its walls, begging from the humble man some knowledge of the future. Here they come—one and all—the fools, pretending to despise my science, and yet willing to place themselves in my power, while they affect to doubt. Ha, ha, here are their nativities, one and all ! That," he continued, turning over a leaf, "is the horoscope of a clergyman — holy man of God ! He wanted to know whether he could ruin an innocent girl in his congregation without discovery. And that is the horoscope of a lawyer, who takes fees from both sides. His desire is to know, whether he can perjure himself in a case now in court without detection. Noble counsellor ! This doctor," and he turned over another leaf, "told me that he had a delicate case in hand. A pretty girl has been ruined and so on — the seducer wants to destroy the fruit of his crime, and desires the doctor to undertake the job. Doctor wants to know what moment will be auspicious—ha, ha !"

And thus turning from page to page, he disclosed the remarkable fact, that the great, the good, and the wise of the Quaker City, who met the mere name of astrology, when uttered in public, with a most withering sneer, still under the cover of night, were happy to steal to the astrologer's room, and obtain some glimpses of their future destiny through the oracle of the stars.

"A black-eyed woman—lusty and amorous—wants to know whether she can present her husband with a pair of horns on a certain night ? I warned her not to proceed in her course of guilt. She does proceed, and will be exposed to her husband's hate and public scorn."

And thus murmuring, the astrologer turned to another leaf.

"The horoscope of a puppy-faced editor ! A spaniel, a snake, and an ape ; he is a combination of the three. Wants to know when he can run off with a lady of the ballet at the theatre, without being caught by his creditors ? Also, whether next Thursday is an auspicious day for a little piece of roguery he has in view ? The penitentiary looms darkly in the distance ; let the editor of the 'DAILY BLACK MAIL beware."

Another leaf inscribed with a distinguishable name, arrested the astrologer's attention.

"Ha ha ! This fellow is a man of fashion, a buck of Chesnut-street, and a colonel ! He lives, I know how ; the fashionables who follow in his wake don't dream of his means of livelihood. He has committed a crime—an astounding crime ; wants to know whether his associate will betray him ? I told him he would. The colonel laughed at me, although he paid for the knowledge. In a week the fine, sweet, perfumed gentleman will be lodged at public expense."

The astrologer laid down the volume, and in a moment seemed to have fallen into the same train of thought, marked by the corrugated brow and glassy eye, that occupied his mind at the commencement of this scene. His lips moved tremulously, and his hands ever and anon were pressed against his wrinkled brow. Every moment his eye grew more glassy, and his mouth more fixedly compressed, and at last, leaning his elbows on the table, with his hands nervously clasped, his gaze was fixed on the blank wall, opposite, in a wild and vacant stare that betrayed the painful abstraction of his mind from all visible objects.

And as he sat there enrapt in thought, a footstep, inaudible to his ear, creaked on the stairway that ascended into the astrologer's chamber from the room below, and in a moment, silent and unperceived, Gus Lorrimer stood behind his chair, looking over his head, his very breath hushed and his hands upraised.

"In all my history I remember nothing half so strange. All is full of light except one point of the future, and that is dark as death !" Thus ran the murmured soliloquy of the astrologer—"and yet they will be here to-night—here—both of them, or there's no truth in the stars. Lorrimer must beware———"

"Ha, ha, ha," laughed a bold and manly

voice, " an old stage trick, that. You didn't hear my footsteps on the stairs did you? Oh no, oh no. Of course you didn't. Come, come, my old boy, that clap-trap mention of my name is rather too stale, even for a three-fipenny-bit melo-drama———"

The sudden start which the astrologer gave, the unaffected look of surprise which flashed over his features at the sight of the gentleman of pleasure, convined Lorrimer that he had done him rank injustice.

" Sit down sir, I have much to say to you," said the astrologer, in a voice strikingly contrasted with his usual tone, it was so deep, and so calmly deliberate, "last Thursday morning at this hour you gave me the day and hour of your birth. You wished me to cast your horoscope. You wished to know whether you would be successful in an enterprise which you meditated. Am I correct in this?"

" You are, my old humbug; that is, my friend," replied Lorrimer, flinging himself into a seat.

" Humbug!" cried the other with a quiet sneer; "you may alter your opinion after a while, my young friend. Since last Thursday morning I have given the most careful attention to your horoscope. It is one of the most startling ever I beheld. You were born under one of the most favourable aspects of the heavens, born, it would seem, but to succeed in all your wishes; and yet your future fate is wrapt in some terrible mystery———"

" Like a kitten in a wet blanket, for instance!" said Lorrimer, in the vain endeavour to shake off a strange feeling of awe, produced by the manner of the astrologer.

" This night I was occupied with your horoscope when a strange circumstance attracted my attention. Even while I was examining book after book, in the effort to see more into your future, I discovered that you were making some new acquaintance at some festival, some wine-drinking or other affair of the kind. This new acquaintance is a man with a pale face, long dark hair, and dark eyes. So the stars tell me. Your fate and the fate of this young man are linked together till death. So the heavens tell me, and the heavens never lie."

" Yes, yes, my friend, very good," replied Gustavus with a smile, "very good, my dear sir. Your conclusions are perfect; your prophetic gift without reproach. But you forget one slight circumstance; I have made no new acquaintance to-night! I have been at no wine-drinking! I have seen no interesting young man with a pale face and long dark hair———"

" Then my science is a lie!" exclaimed the astrologer, with a puzzled look. " The stars declare that this very night you first came in contact with the man, whose fate henceforth is linked with your own. The future has a doom in store for one of ye. The stars do not tell me which shall feel the terror of the doom, but that it will be inflicted by one of ye upon the other is certain."

" Well, let us suppose, for the sake of argument, that I did meet this mysterious young man with long black hair. What follows?"

" Three days ago, a young man, whose appearance corresponds with the indication given by the stars of the new acquaintance you were to make this very night, came to me and desired me to cast his horoscope. The future of this young man is as like yours as night is to night. He too, is threatened with a doom either to be suffered or inflicted. This doom will lower over his head within three days. At the hour of sunset on next Saturday, Christmas eve, a terrible calamtty will overtake him. At the same hour, and in the same manner, a terrible calamity will blacken your life for ever. The same doubt prevails in both cases; whether you will endure this calamity in your own person, or be the means of inflicting its horrors on some other man, doomed and fated by the stars———"

" What connection has this young man with the 'new acquaintance' which you say I have formed to-night?"

" I suspect that this young man and your new acquaintance are one. If so, I warn you, by your soul, beware of him, this stranger to you!"

" And why beware of me?" said a calm and quie voice at the shoulder of the astrologer.

A though a shell had burst in the centre of that quiet room, he started, he trembled, and arose to his feet. Byrnewood, the young merchant, calm and silent, stood beside him.

" I warn ye," he shrieked in a tone of wild excitement, with his grey eyes dilating and flashing beneath the woven eyebrows, " I warn ye both beware of each other! Let this meeting at my house be the last on earth, and ye are saved! Meet again, or pursue any adventure together, and ye are lost, and lost for ever! I tell ye, scornful men that ye are, that ask my science to aid you, and then mock its lessons, I tell you, by the living God who writes his will in letters of fire on the wide scroll of the firmament, that in the hand of the future is a goblet steeped in the bitterness of death, and that goblet one or the other must drink, within three little days!"

And striding wildly along the room, while Byrnewood stood awed, and even the check of Lorrimer grew pale, he gave free impulse to one of those wild deliriums of excitement peculiar to his long habits of abstraction and thought. The full truth, the terrible truth, seemed crowding on his brain, arrayed in various images of horror, and he shrieked forth his interpretation of the future, in wild and broken sentences.

" Young man, three days ago you sought to know the future. You had never spoken to the man who sits in yonder chair. I cast your horoscope; I found your destiny like the destiny of this man who affects to sneer at my science. My art availed me no further. I could not identify you with the man who first met Lorrimer this night, amid revelry and wine. Now I can supply the broken chain. You and his new-formed acquaintance are one. And now the light of the stars breaks more plainly on me—within three days, one of you will die by the other's hand——"

Lorrimer slowly arose to his feet, as though the effort gave him pain. His cheek was pale, and beaded drops of sweat stood on his brow. His parted lips, his upraised hands, and flashing eyes attested his interest in the astrologer's words. Meanwhile, starting suddenly aside, Byrnewood veiled his face in his hands, as his breast swelled and quivered with sudden emotion.

Stern and erect, in his plain white overcoat, untricked with gold or gems, stood the astrologer, his tangled brown hair flung back from his brow, while, with his outstretched hand and flashing eye, he spoke forth the fierce images of his brain.

"Three days from this, as the sun goes down, on Christmas eve, one of you will die by the other's hand. As sure as there is a God in heaven, his stars have spoken, and it will be so!"

"What will be the manner of the death?" exclaimed Lorrimer, in a low-toned voice, as he endeavoured to subdue the sudden agitation inspired by the astrologer's words, while Byrnewood raised his head and awaited the answer with evident interest.

"There is the cloud and the mystery," exclaimed the astrologer, fixing his eye on vacancy, while his outstretched hand trembled like a leaf in the wind. "The death will overtake the doomed man on a river, and yet it will not be by water; it will kill him by means of fire, and yet he will not perish in the midst of flames."

There was a dead pause for a single instant. There stood the astrologer, his features working as with a convulsive spasm, the light falling boldly over his slight figure and homely attire, and there at his side, gazing in his face, stood Byrnewood, the young merchant, as if a spell had fallen on him, while on the other side, Gustavus Lorrimer, half-recoiling, his brow woven in a frown, and his dark eyes flashing with a strange glance, seemed making a fearful effort to command his emotion, and dispel the gloom which the weird prophecy had flung over his soul.

"Pah! What fools we are! To stand here listening to the ravings of a madman or a knave," cried Byrnewood, with a forced laugh, as he shook off the spell that seemed to bind him. "What does he know of the future—more than we? Eh, Lorrimer? Perhaps, sir, since you are so familiar with fate, destiny, and all that, you can tell us the nature of the adventure on which Lorrimer is bound to-night?"

The astrologer turned and looked upon him. There was something so calmly scornful in his glance, that Byrnewood averted his eyes.

"The adventure is connected with the honour of an innocent woman," said the astrologer. "More than this I know not, save that a foul outrage will be done this very night. And, hark ye, sir, either the heavens are false, or your future destiny hangs upon this adventure. Give up the adventure at once, go back in your course, part from one another, part this moment never to meet again, and you will be saved. Advance, and you are lost!"

Lorrimer stood silent, thoughtful, and pale as death. It becomes me not to look beyond the veil that hangs between the visible and invisible, but it may be, that in the silent pause of thought which the libertine's face manifested, his soul received some indications of the future from the very throne of God. Men call these sudden shadows, presentiments; to the eyes of angels they may be, but messages of warning spoken to the soul, in the spirit-tongues of those awful beings whose habitation is beyond the threshold of time. What did Lorrimer behold that he stood so silent, so pale, so thoughtful? Did Christmas eve, and the river, and the death, come terrible and shadow-like to his soul?

"Pshaw! Lorrimer, you are not frightened by the preachings of this fortune-teller?" cried Byrnewood with a laugh and a sneer. "You will not give up the girl? Ha! ha! scared by an owl! Ha! ha! What would Petriken say? Imagine the rich laugh of Mutchins. Ha! ha! Gus Lorrimer scared by an owl!"

"Give up the girl!" cried Lorrimer, with a blasphemous oath, that profaned the name of the Saviour. "Give up the girl! Never! She shall repose in my arms before daylight. Heaven nor hell shall scare me back! There's your money, Mister Fortune-teller; your croaking deserves the silver, the d——l knows. Come on, Byrnewood—let us away."

"Wait till I pay the gentleman for our coffins," laughed Byrnewood, flinging some silver on the table. "See that they're ready by Saturday night, old boy. D'ye mind? You are hand-in-glove with some respectable undertaker, no doubt, and can give him our measure. Good-bye, old fellow; good-bye. Now, Lorrimer, away."

"Away, away to Monk-hall!"

And in a moment they had disappeared down the stairway, and were passing through the lower room towards the street.

"On Christmas eve, at the hour of sunset—" shrieked the Astrologer, his features convulsed with anger, and his voice wild and piercing in its tones—"One of you will die by the other's hand! The winding sheet is woven, and the coffin made—you are rushing madly on your doom!"

CHAPTER V.

DORA LIVINGSTON

It was a nice cozy place, that old counting-house room, with its smoky walls, its cheerful coal-fire burning in the rusty grate, and its stained and blackened floor. A snug little room, illuminated by a gas-light, subdued to a shadowy and sleepy brilliancy, with the Merchant's Almanac and four or five old pictures scattered along the walls, an old-oaken desk with immense legs, all carved and curled into a thousand shapes, standing in one corner, and a massive door, whose glass window opened a mysterious view into the regions of the warehouse, where casks of old cogniac lay, side by side, in lengthened rows, like jolly old fellows at a party, as they whisper quietly to one another on the leading questions of the day.

Seated in front of the coal fire, his legs elevated above his head, resting on the mantel-piece, a gentleman, of some twenty-five years, with his arms crossed and a pipe in his mouth, seemed engaged in an earnest endeavour to wrap himself up in a cloak of tobacco smoke, in order to prepare for a journey into the land of Nod, while the tumbler of punch standing on the table at his elbow, showed that he was by no means opposed to that orthodox principle which recognises the triple marriage of brandy, lemon, and sugar, as a highly necessary addition to the creature comforts of the human being, in no way to be despised or neglected by thinking men.

You would not have called this gentleman well-proportioned, and yet his figure was long and slender; you could not have styled his dress eminently fashionable, and yet his frock-coat was shaped of the finest black cloth; you would not have looked upon his face as the most handsome in the world, and yet it was a finely-marked countenance, with a decided, if not highly intellectual, expression. If the truth must be told, his coat, though fashioned of the finest cloth, was made a little too full in one place, a little too scant in another, and buttoned up somewhat too high in the throat, for a gentleman whose ambition it was to flourish on the southern side of Chesnut-street, amid the animated cloths and silks of a fashionable promenade. And then the large black stock, encircling his neck, with the crumpled, though snow-white, shirt collar, gave a harsh relief to his countenance, while the carelessly-disposed wristbands, crushed back over the upturned cuffs of his coat, designated the man who went in for comfort, and flung fashion to the haberdashers and dry goods' clerks.

As for his face, whenever the curtain of tobacco smoke rolled aside, you beheld, as I have said, a finely-marked countenance, with rather lank cheeks, a sharp aquiline nose, thin lips, biting and sarcastic in expression, a full square chin, and eyes of the peculiar class, intensely dark and piercing in their glance, that remind you of a flame without heat, cold, glittering and snake-like. His forehead was high and bold, with long and lanky black hair falling back from its outlines, and resting, without love-lock or curl, in straight masses behind each ear.

"Queer world this!" began our comfortable friend, falling into one of those broken soliloquies, generated by the pipe and the bowl, in which the stops are supplied by puffs of smoke, and the paragraph terminated by a sip of the punch—"Don't know much about other worlds, but it strikes me that if a prize were offered somewhere by somebody, for the queerest world a-going, this world of ours might be rigged up nice, and sent in like a bit of show beef, as the premium queer world. No man smokes a cigar that ever tried a pipe, but an ass. I was a small boy once—ragged little devil *that* Luke Harvey, who used to run about old Livingstone's importing warehouse. Indelicate little fellow: wore his ruffles out behind. Kicked and cuffed because he was poor—served him right—damn 'im. Old Liv. died—young Albert took the store—capital, cool one hundred thousand. Luke Harvey rose to a clerkship. Began to be a fine fellow—well-dressed, and of course virtuous. D——d queer fellow, Luke. Last year taken into partnership along with a young fellow whose daddy's worth at least one hundred thousand. Firm now—Livingstone, Harvey, and Co. Clever punch, that. Little too much lemon—d—— it, the sugar's out.

"Queer thing, that! Some weeks ago a respectable old gentleman in white cravat and hump-back, came to counting house. Old fellow hailed from Charleston. Had rather a Jewish twang on his tongue. Presented Livingstone a letter of credit drawn by a Charleston house on our firm. Letter from Grayson, Ballenger, & Co., for a cool hundred thousand. Old white cravat got it. D——n that rat in the partition—why can't he eat his victuals in quiet? Two weeks since, news came that G. B. & Co, never gave such a letter—a forgery, a complete swindle. Comfortable, that. Hot coals on one's bare skull quite pleasant in comparison. Livingstone in New York been trying for a week to track up the villain. Must get new pipe to-morrow. Mem. get one with Judas Iscariot painted on the bowl. Honest rogue, that. Went and hanged himself after he sold his master. Wonder how full the town would be if all who have sold their God for gold would hang themselves? Hooks in market house would rise. Bear queer fruit—eh? D——d good tobacco. By-the-bye must go home. Another sip of the punch and I'm off. Ha—ha—good idea that of the handsome colonel! Great buck, man of fashion and long-haired Apollo. Called here this evening to see me—smelt like a civet cat. Must flourish his pocket-book before my eyes by way of a genteel brag. Dropped a letter from a bundle of notes. Valuable letter that. Wouldn't part with it for a cool thousand—rather think it will raise the devil—let me see—"

And laying down his pipe, Mr. Luke Harvey drew a neatly folded billet-doux from an inside pocket of his coat, and holding it in the glare of the light perused its direction, which was written in a fair and delicate woman's hand.

"'Col. Fitz-Cowles—United States Hotel,'" he murmured, "good idea, colonel, to drop such a letter out of your pocket-book. Won't trouble you none? 'Spose not—ha, ha, ha, d——d good idea!"

The idea appeared to tickle him immensely, for he chuckled in a deep, self-satisfied tone, as he drew on his bearskin overcoat, and even while he extinguished the gas-light, and covered up the fire, his chuckle grew into a laugh, which deepened into a hearty guffaw, as striding through the dark warehouse, he gained the front door, and looked out into the deserted street.

"Ha, ha, ha—to drop such a dear creature's letter!" he laughed, locking the door of the warehouse. "Wonder if it won't raise h—l? I loved a woman. Luke, you were a d——d fool that time. Jilted—yes jilted; that's the word I believe? Maybe I won't have my revenge? Perhaps not—very likely not."

With this momentous letter, so carelessly dropped by the insinuating millionaire, Colonel Fitz-Cowles, resting on his mind, and stirring his features with frequent spasmodic attacks of laughter, our friend, Mr. Harvey, pursued his way along Front-street, and turning up Chesnut-street, arrived at the corner of Third, where he halted a few moments in order to ascertain the difference in the time, between his gold-repeater and the State House clock, which had just struck one.

While thus engaged, intently perusing the face of his watch by the light of the moon, a stout middle-aged gentleman, wrapped up in a thick over-coat, with a carpet bag in his hand, came striding rapidly across the street, and for a moment stood silent and unperceived at his shoulder.

"Well, Luke, is the repeater right and the State House wrong?" said a hearty cheerful voice, and the middle-aged gentleman laid his hand on Mr. Harvey's shoulder.

"Ah, ha! Mr. Livingstone, is that you?" cried Luke, suddenly wheeling round, and gazing into the frank and manly countenance of the new-comer. "When did you get back from New York?"

"Just this moment arrived. I did not expect to return within a week from this time, and therefore come upon you by a little surprise. I wrote to Mrs. L. yesterday, telling her I would not be in town till the Christmas holidays were over. She'll be rather surprised to see me, I suppose?"

"Rather," echoed Luke drily.

"Come, Luke, take my arm, and let's walk up towards my house. I have much to say to you. In the first place have you anything new?"

While Mr. Harvey is imparting his budget of news to the senior partner of the firm of Livingstone, Harvey and Co., as they stroll slowly along Chesnut-street, we will make some few notes of his present appearance.

Stout, muscular, and large-boned, with a figure slightly inclining towards corpulence, Mr. Livingstone strode along the pavement with a firm and measured step, that attested all the matured strength and vigour peculiar to robust middle age. He was six feet high, with broad shoulders and muscular chest. His face was full, bold, and massive, rather bronzed in hue, and bearing some slight traces of the ravages of small-pox. Once or twice as he walked along, he lifted his hat from his face, and his forehead,

rendered more conspicuous by some slight baldness, was exposed to view. It was high, and wide, and massive, bulging outward prominently in the region of the reflective organs, and faintly relieved by his short brown hair. His eyes, bold and large, of a calm clear blue, were rendered strangely expressive by the contrast of the jet-black eyebrows. His nose was firm and Roman in contour, his mouth marked by full and determined lips, his chin square and prominent, while the lengthened outline of the lower jaw, from the chin to the ear, gave his countenance an expression of inflexible resolution. In short, it was the face of a man, whose mind, great in resources, had only found room for the display of its tamest powers, in enlarged mercantile operations, while its dark and desperate elements, from the want of adversity revenge or hate to rouse them into action, had lain still and dormant for some twenty long years of active life. He never dreamed himself that he carried a hidden hell within his soul.

Had this man been born poor, it is probable that in his attempt to rise, the grim hand of want would have dragged from their lurking-places, these dark and fearful elements of his being. But wealth had lapped him at his birth, smiled on him in his youth, walked by him through life, and the moment for the trial of all his powers had never happened. He was a fine man, a noble merchant, and a good citizen—we but repeat the stereotyped phrases of the town —and yet, quiet and close, near the heart of this cheerful-faced man, lay a sleeping devil, who had been dozing away there all his life, and only waiting the call of destiny to spring into terrible action, and rend that manly bosom with his fangs.

"Have you heard any news of the—forger?" asked Luke Harvey, when he had delivered his budget of news—"any intelligence of the respectable gentleman in the white cravat and hump-back?"

"He played the same game in New York that he played in our city. Wherever I went, I heard nothing but 'Mr. Ellis Mortimer, of Charleston, bought goods to a large amount here, on the strength of a letter of credit, drawn on your house by Grayson, Ballenger, and Co.,' or that 'Mr. Mortimer bought goods to a large amount in such-and-such a store, backed by the same letter of credit—' no less than twelve wholesale houses gave him credit to an almost unlimited extent. In all cases the goods were despatched to the various auctions and sold at half-cost, while Mr. Ellis Mortimer pocketed the cash——"

"And you have no traces of this prince of swindlers?"

"None! all the police in New York have been raising heaven and earth to catch him for this week past, but without success. At last I have come to the conclusion that he is lurking about this city, with the respectable sum of two hundred thousand dollars in his possession. I am half inclined to believe that he is not alone in this business, there may be a combination of scoundrels concerned in the affair. To-morrow the police shall ransack every hiding-hole and cranny in the city. My friend, Col. Fitz-Cowles gave me some valuable suggestions before I left for New York; I will ask his advice, in regard to the matter, the first thing in the morning."

"Very fine man, that Col. Fitz-Cowles," observed Luke, as they turned down Fourth-street. "Splendid fellow. Dresses well—gives capital terrapin suppers at the United States—inoculates all the bucks about town with his style of hat. Capital fellow—son of an English earl—aint he, Mr. Livingstone?"

"So I have understood," replied Mr. Livingstone, not exactly liking the quiet sneer which lurked under the innocent manner of his partner. "at least so it is rumoured."

"Got lots of money—a millionaire—no end to his wealth. By-the-bye, where the d——l did he come from? Isn't he a southern planter with acres of niggers and prairies of cotton?"

"Luke, that's a very strange question to ask me. You just now asked me, whether he was the son of an English earl—didn't you?"

"Believe I did. To tell the truth, I've heard both stories about him, and some dozen more. An heir-apparent to an English earldom, a rich planter from the south, the son of a Boston *magnifique*, the only child of a rich Mexican—these things, you will see, don't mix well. Who the devil is our long-haired friend, any how!"

"Tut-tut, Luke, this is all folly. You know that Col. Fitz-Cowles is received in the best society, mingles with the *ton* of the Quaker City, is 'squired about by our judges and lawyers, and can always find scores of friends to help him spend his fortune."

"Fine man, that Col. Fitz-Cowles. Very," said the other in his dry and biting tone.

"Do you know, Luke, that I think the married men are the happiest in the world?" said Livingstone, drawing the arm of his partner closely within his own. "Now look at my case for instance. A year ago I was a miserable bachelor. The loss of one hundred thousand dollars then would have driven me frantic. Now I have a sweet young wife to cheer me, her smile welcomes me home; the first tone of her voice, and my loss is forgotten!"

The merchant paused. His eye glistened with a tear, and he felt his heart grow warm in his bosom, as the vision of his sweet young wife, now so calmly sleeping on her solitary bed, rose before him. He imagined her smile of welcome as she beheld him suddenly appear by her bed-side; he felt her arms so full and round twining fondly round his neck, and he tried to fancy—but the attempt was vain—the luxury of a kiss from her red ripe lips.

"You may think me uxorious, Luke," he resumed in his deep manly voice. "But I do think that God never made a nobler woman than my Dora! Look at the sacrifice she made for my sake! Young, blooming, and but twenty summers old she forgot the disparity of my

years, and consented to share my bachelor's-home."

"She *is* a noble woman," observed Luke, and then he looked at the moon and whistled an air from the very select operatic spectacle of 'Bone Squash.'"

"Noble in heart and soul!" exclaimed Livingstone, "confess, Luke, that we married men live more in an hour that dull bachelors in a year."

"Oh—yes—certainly! You may well talk when you have such a handsome wife! Egad if I wasn't afraid it would make you jealous, I would say that Mrs. Livingstone has the most splendid form I have ever beheld."

There was a slight contortion of Mr. Harvey's upper lip as he spoke, which looked very much like a sneer.

"And then her heart, Luke, her heart! So noble, so good, so affectionate! I wish you could have seen her, where I first beheld her, in a small and meanly furnished apartment, at the bed-side of a dying mother! They were in reduced circumstances, for her father had died insolvent. He had been my father's friend, and I thought it my duty to visit the widowed mother and the orphan daughter. By-the-bye, Luke, I now remember that I saw you at their house in Wood street once, did you know the family?"

"Miss Dora's father had been kind to me," said Luke in a quiet tone. There was a strange light in his dark eye as he spoke, and a remarkable tremor on his lip.

"Well, well, Luke, here's my house," exclaimed Mr. Livingstone, as they arrived in front of a lofty four storied mansion, situated in the aristocratic square, as it is called, along south Fourth street. "It is lucky I have my dead-latch key. I can enter without disturbing the servants. Come up stairs, into the front parlour with me, Luke; I want to have a few more words with you about the forgery."

They entered the door of the mansion, passed along a wide and roomy entry, ascended a richly carpeted staircase, and, traversing the entry in the second story, in a moment stood in the centre of the spacious parlour, fronting the street on the second floor. In another moment, Mr. Livingstone, by the aid of some lucifer matches which he found on the mantle, lighted a small bed-lamp, standing among the glittering volumes that were piled on the centre table. The dim light of the lamp flickering around the room, revealed the various characteristics of an apartment furnished in a style of lavish magnificence. Above the mantle flashed an enormous mirror; on one side of the parlour was an inviting sofa, on the other a piano; two splendid ottomans stood in front of the fireless hearth, and curtains of splendid silk hung drooping heavily along the three lofty windows that looked into the street. In fine, the parlour was all that the upholsterer and cabinet maker combined could make it, a depository of luxurious appointments and costly furniture.

"Draw your seat near the centre table, Luke," cried Mr Livingstone, as he flung himself into a comfortable rocking chair, and gazed around the room with an expression of quiet satisfaction. " Don't speak too loud, Luke, for Dora is sleeping in the next room. You know I want to take her a little by surprise, eh, Luke? She doesn't expect me from New York for a week yet, I am the last person in the world she thinks to see to-night. Clearly so, ha! ha!"

And the merchant chuckled gaily, rubbed his hands together, glanced at the folding doors that opened into the bed-chamber, where slept his blooming wife, and then turning round, looked in the face of Luke Harvey with a smile, that seemed to say—" I can't help it if you bachelors are miserable—pity you, but can't help it."

"It would be a pity to awaken Mrs. Livingstone," said Luke, fixing his brilliant dark eye on the face of the senior partner, with a look so meaning and yet so mysterious, that Mr. Livingstone involuntarily averted his gaze; "a very great pity. By-the-bye, with regard to the forgery———"

"Let me recapitulate the facts. Some weeks ago we received a letter from the respectable house of Grayson, Ballenger, & Co., Charleston, stating that they had made a large purchase in cotton from a rich planter—Mr. Ellis Mortimer, who, in a week or so, would visit Philadelphia, with a letter of credit on our house for one hundred thousand dollars. They gave us this intimation in order that we might be prepared to cash the letter of credit at sight. Well, in a week a gentleman of respectable exterior appeared, stated that he was Mr. Ellis Mortimer, presented his letter of credit; it was cashed, and we wrote to Grayson, Ballenger, & Co., announcing the fact.

"They returned the agreeable answer that Mr. Ellis Mortimer had not yet left Charleston for Philadelphia, but had altered his intention, and was about to sail for London. That the gentleman in the white cravat and hump-back was an impostor, and the letter of credit a— forgery. There was considerable mystery in the affair; for instance, how did the impostor gain all the necessary information with regard to Mr. Mortimer's visit, how did he acquire a knowledge of the signature of the Charleston house?"

"Listen and I will tell you. Last week, in New York, I received a letter from the Charleston house announcing these additional facts. It appears that in the beginning of fall they received a letter from a Mr. Albert Hazelton Munroe, representing himself as a rich planter in Wainbridge, South Carolina. He had a large amount of cotton to sell, and would like to procure advances on it from the Charleston house. They wrote him an answer to his letter, asking the quality of the cotton, and so forth, and soliciting an interview with Mr. Munroe when he visited Charleston. In the beginning of November Mr. Munroe, a dark-complexioned man, dressed like a careless country squire, entered their store for the first time, and commenced a series of negotiations about his cotton, which had resulted in nothing, when another

planter, Mr. Ellis Mortimer, appeared in the scene, sold his cotton, and received the letter of credit on our house. Mr. Munroe was in the store every day—was a jolly unpretending fellow—familiar with all the clerks—and on intimate terms with Messrs. Grayson, Ballenger, & Co. The letter written to our house, intimating the intended visit of Mr. Mortimer to this city, had been very carelessly left open for a few moments on the counting-house desk, and Mr. Munroe was observed glancing over its contents by one of the clerks. The Charleston house suspected him of the whole forgery in all its details—"

"Very likely. He saw the letter on the counter—forged the letter of credit—and despatched his accomplice to Philadelphia without delay."

"Now for the consequences of this forgery. On Monday morning next we have an engagement of one hundred thousand dollars to meet, which, under present circumstances, may plunge our house into the vortex of bankruptcy. Unless this impostor is discovered, unless his connection with this Munroe is clearly ascertained before next Monday, I must look forward to that day as one of the greatest danger to our house. You see our position, Luke?"

"Yes, yes," answered Luke, as he arose, and advancing, gazed fixedly into the face of Mr. Livingstone, "I see our position, and I see your position in more respects than one———"

"Confound the thing, man, how you stare in my face. Do you see anything peculiar about my countenance, that you peruse it so attentively?"

"Ha, ha," cried Luke, with a hysterical laugh, "ha, ha! Nothing but horns. Horns, sir, I say, horns. A fine branching pair! Ha, ha! Why, d—n it, Livingstone, you won't be able to enter the church door, next Sunday, without stooping—those horns are so d———d large!"

Livingstone looked at him with a face of blank wonder. He evidently supposed that Luke had been seized with sudden madness. To see a man who is your familiar friend and partner, abruptly break off a conversation on matters of the utmost importance, and stare vacantly in your face as he compliments you on some fancied resemblance you bear to a full-grown stag, is, it must be confessed, a spectacle somewhat unfrequent in this world of ours, and rather adapted to excite a feeling of astonishment whenever it happens.

"Mr. Harvey, are you mad?" asked Livingstone, in a calm, deliberate tone.

Harvey slowly leaned forward and brought his face so near Livingstone's that the latter could feel his breath on his cheek. He applied his mouth to the ear of the senior partner, and whispered a single word.

When a soldier, in battle, receives a bullet directly in the heart, he springs into the air with one convulsive spasm, flings his arms aloft, and utters a groan that thrills the man who hears it with a horror never to be forgotten. With that same convulsive movement—with that same deep groan of horror and anguish, Livingstone, the merchant sprang to his feet, and confronted the utterer of that single word.

"Harvey," he said, in a low tone, and with white and trembling lips, while his calm blue eye flashed with that deep glance of excitement, terrible when visible in a calm blue eye. "Harvey, you had better never been born, than utter that word again. To trifle with a thing of this kind is worse than death. Harvey, I advise you to leave me—I am losing all command of myself—there is a voice within me tempting to murder you—for God's sake quit my sight."

Harvey looked in his face, fearless and undaunted, though his snake-like eye blazed like a coal of fire, and his thin lips quivered as with the death spasm.

"Cuckold!" he shrieked in a hissing voice, with a wild hysterical laugh.

"TAKE YOUR HAND FROM MY THOAT OR I'LL DO YOU A MISCHIEF."—SEE PAGE 18.

Livingstone started back aghast. The purple veins stood out like cords on his bronzed forehead, and his right hand trembled like a leaf as it was thrust within the breast of his coat. His blue eye—great God! how glassy it had grown—was fixed upon the form of Luke Harvey as if meditating where to strike.

"To the bedchamber," shrieked Luke. "If she is there, I am a liar and a dog, and deserve to die. Cuckold—I say, and will prove it—to the bedchamber.

And to the bedchamber with an even stride, though his massive form quivered like an oak shaken by a hurricane, strode the merchant. The folding door slid back—he had disappeared into the bedchamber.

There was silence for a single instant, like the silence of the graveyard, between the last word of the prayer, and the first rattling of the clods upon the coffin.

In a moment Livingstone again strode into the parlour. His face was the hue of ashes. You could see that the struggle at work within his heart was like the agony of the strong man wrestling with death. This struggle was ten-fold more terrible than death—death in its vilest form. It forced the big beaded drops of sweat out from the corded veins on his brow, it drove the blood from his face, leaving a black disco-loured streak beneath each eye.

"She is not there," he said, taking Luke by the hand, which he wrung with an iron grasp, and murmured again. "She is not there."

"False to her husband's bed and honour," exclaimed Luke, the agitation which had con-vulsed his face, subsiding into a look of heart-wrung compasion, as he looked upon the terrible results of his disclosure. "False as hell, and vile as false!"

An object on the centre table, half concealed by the bed-lamp, arrested the husband's attention. He thrust aside the lamp and beheld a note, ad-dressed to himself, in Mrs. Livingstone's hand.

With a trembling hand the merchant tore the note open, and while Luke stood fixedly regard-ing him, perused its contents.

And as he read, the blood came back to his checks, the glance to his eyes, and his brow red-dened over with one burning flash of indigna-tion.

"Liar and dog!" he shouted, in tones hoarse with rage, as he grasped Luke Harvey by the throat with a sudden movement. "Your lie was well coined, but look here! Ha, ha," and he shook Luke to and fro like a broken reed. "Here is my wife's letter. Here, sir, look at it, and I'll force you to eat your own foul words. Here, expecting that I might suddenly return from New York, my wife has written down that she would be from home to-night. A sick friend, a school-day companion, now reduced to widow-hood and penury, solicited her company by her dying bed, and my wife could not refuse. Read, sir, oh read!"

"Take your hand from my throat or I'll do you a mischief," murmured Luke, in a choaking voice, as he grew black in the face. "I will, by God."

"Read, sir, oh read!" shouted Livingston, as he forced Luke into a chair and thrust the letter into his hands. "Read, sir, and then crawl from this room like a vile dog as you are. To-morrow I will settle with you."

Luke sank in the chair, took the letter, and with a pale face, varied by a crimson spot on each cheek, he began to read, while Livingstone, towering and erect, stood regarding him with a look of incarnate scorn.

It was observable that while Luke perused the letter, his head dropped slowly down as though endeavouring to see more clearly, and his unoccupied hand was suddenly thrust within the breast of his overcoat.

"That is a very good letter. Well written, and she minds her stops," exclaimed Luke, calmly, as he handed the letter back to Mr. Livingstone. "Quite an effort of composition. I didn't think Dora had so much tact."

The merchant was thunderstruck at the com-posure exhibited by the slanderer and the liar. He glanced over Luke's features with a quick nervous glance, and then looked at the letter which he held in his hand."

"Ha! This is not the same letter!" he shouted, in tones of mingled rage and wonder. "This letter is addressed to 'Col. Fitz-Cowles.'"

"It was dropped in the counting house by the colonel this evening," said Luke, with the air of a man who was prepared for any hazard. "The colonel is a very fine man. A favourite with the fair sex. Read it—oh read."

With a look of wonder Mr. Livingstone opened the letter. There was a quivering start in his whole frame, when he first observed the hand-writing.

But as he went on, drinking in word after word, his countenance, so full of meaning and expression, was like a mirror, in which different faces are seen, one after another, by sudden transition. At first his face grew crimson, then it was pale as death in an instant. Then his lips dropped apart, and his eyes were covered with a glassy film. Then a deep wrinkle shot upward between his brows, and then, black and ghastly, the circles of discoloured flesh were visi-ble beneath each eye. The quivering nostrils—the trembling hands—the heaving chest—did man ever die with a struggle terrible as this?

He sank heavily into a chair, and crushing the letter between his fingers, buried his face in his hands.

"Oh my God," he groaned—"Oh my God—and I loved her so!"

And then between the very fingers convul-sively clutching the fatal letter, there fell large and scalding tears, drop by drop, pouring heavily, like the first tokens of a coming thunder-bolt, on a summer day.

Luke Harvey arose, and strode hurriedly along the floor. The sight was too much for him to bear. And yet as he turned away he heard the groans of the strong man in his agony, and the heart-wrung words came, like the voice of the dying, to his ear—

"Oh my God, oh my God, and I loved her so!"

When Luke again turned and gazed upon the betrayed husband, he beheld a sight that filled him with unutterable horror.

There, as he sat, his face buried in his hands, his head bowed on his breast, his brow was per-fectly exposed to the glare of the lamp-beams, and all around that brow, amid the locks of his dark brown hair, were streaks of hoary white. The hair of the merchant had withered at the root. The blow was so sudden, so blighting, and so terrible, that even his strong mind reeled, his brain tottered, and in the effort to command his reason, his hair grew white.

"Would to God I had not told him," mur-mured Luke. "I knew not that he loved her so—I knew not—and yet—ha, ha, I loved her once."

"Luke, my friend," said Livingstone in a tremulous voice as he raised his face—"Know you anything of the place named in the letter?"

"I do, and will lead you there;" answered Luke, his face resuming its original expression of agitation. "Come!" he cried, in a husky voice, as olden-time memories seemed striving at his heart—"Come!"

"Can you gain me access to the house, to the —the room?"

"Did I not track them thither last night? Come!"

The merchant slowly rose and took a pair of pistols from his carpet bag. They were small and convenient travelling pistols, mounted in silver, with those noiseless "patent" triggers that emit no clicking sound by way of warning. He inspected the percussion caps, and sounded each pistol barrel.

"Silent and sure," muttered Luke. "They are each loaded with a single ball."

"Which way do you lead? To the southern part of the city?"

"To Southwark," answered Luke, leading the way from the parlour. "To the rookery, to the den, to the pest-house!"

In a moment they stood upon the door step of the merchant's princely mansion, the vivid light of the December moon, imparting a ghastly hue to Livingstone's face, with the glassy eyes, rendered more fearful by the discoloured circles of flesh beneath, the furrowed brow, and the white lips, all fixed in an expression stern and resolute as death.

Luke flung his hand to the south, and his dark impenetrable eyes shone with meaning. The merchant placed his partner's arm within his own, and they hurried down Fourth-street with a single word from Luke—

"To Monk-hall!"

CHAPTER VI.

MONK-HALL.

THE mansion, known as Monk-hall, but rarely seen by intrusive eyes, had been originally erected by a wealthy foreigner, sometime previous to the Revolution. Who this foreigner was, his name or his history, has not been recorded by tradition. But tradition stated that the wealthy proprietor, not satisfied with building a fine house with three stories above ground, had also constructed three stories of spacious chambers below the level of the earth. The neatly-constructed stable at the end of the garden was said to be connected with the house, some hundred yards distant, by a subterranean passage. In short the seclusion of the mansion, its singular structure, its wall of brick and its grove of impenetrable trees, gave rise to all sorts of stories, and the proprietor has come

down to our time with a decidedly bad character, although it is more than likely that he was nothing but a wealthy Englishman, whimsical and eccentric, the boon-companion and friend of Governor Evans, the rollicking Chief-Magistrate of the Province.

The southern front of the house—alas how changed—alone is now visible. The shutters on one side of the hall door are nailed up and hermetically closed, while, on the other, shutters within the glasses bar out the light of day. The stable one hundred yards distant from Monk-hall is still in existence, standing amidst the edifices of a busy street, its walls old and tottering, its ancient stable-floor turned into a bulk window, surmounted by the golden balls of a pawnbroker, while within its precincts, rooms furnished for household use supply the place of the stalls of the olden-time. Does the subterranean passage still exist? Future passages of our story may possibly answer the question.

Monk-hall, although its exterior was so desolate, had its outside-door of green blinds and varied by a big brass plate, which bore the respectable and saintly name of "ABIJAH K. JONES," in immense letters, half indistinct with dirt and rust, but who this Abijah K. Jones was, no one knew.

To return to our story. The moon was shining brightly over the old mansion, while the opposite side of the alley lay in dim and heavy shadow. The numerous chimneys with their fantastic shapes rose grimly in the moonlight, like a strange band of goblin sentinels, perched on the roof to watch the mansion. The general effect was that of an ancient structure falling to decay, deserted by all inhabitants save the rats that gnawed the wainscot along the thick old walls.

Dim and indistinct, like the booming of a distant cannon, the sound of the state-house bell, thrilled along the intricate maze of streets and alleys. It struck the hour of two. The murmur of the last stroke of the bell, so dim and indistinct, was mingled with the echo of approaching footsteps, and in a moment two figures turned the corner of an alley that wound among the tangled labyrinth of avenues, and came hastening on toward the lonely mansion; lonely even amid tenements and houses, gathered as thickly together as the cells in a bee-hive.

"I say, Gus, what a devil of a way you've led me!" cried one of the strangers, with a thick cloak wrapped round his limbs, "up one alley and down another, around one street and through another, backwards and forwards, round this way and round that, damme if I can tell which is north or south except by the moon!"

"Hist! my fellow, don't mention names; cardinal doctrine that in an affair of this kind," answered the tall figure, whose towering form was enveloped in a frogged overcoat. "Remember you pass in as my friend. Wait a moment—we'll see whether old Devil-Bug is awake."

Ascending the granite steps of the mansion, he gave three distinct raps with his gold-headed cane, on the surface of the brass-plate. In a moment the rattling of a heavy chain, and the sound of a bolt, slowly withdrawn, were heard within, and the door of the mansion, beyond the outside door of green blinds, receded about the width of an inch.

"Who's there, a disturbin' honest folks this hour of the night," said a voice, that came grumbling through the blinds of the green door, like the sound of a grindstone that hasn' been oiled for some years. "What the devil do you want? Go about your business—or I'll call the watch."

"I say, Devil-Bug, what hour of the night is it?" exclaimed Lorrimer in a whispered tone.

"'Dinner time,'" replied the grindstone voice slightly oiled. "Come in, sir. Didn't know 'twas you. How the devil should I? Come in."

As the voice grunted the invitation, Lorrimer seized Byrnewood by the arm, and glided through the opened door.

Byrnewood looked around in wonder, as he discovered that the front door opened into a small closet or room, some ten feet square, the floor bare and uncarpeted, the ceiling darkened by smoke, while a large coal fire, burning in a rusty grate, afforded both light and heat to the apartment.

The heat was close and stifling, while the light, but dim and flickering, disclosed the form of the door-keeper of Monk-hall, as he stood directly in front of the grate, surrounded by the details of his den.

"This is *my friend*," said Lorrimer in a meaning tone. "You understand me, Devil-Bug?"

"Yes," grunted the grindstone voice. "I understand. O'course. But my name is 'Bijah K. Jones, if you please, my pertikler friend. I never know'd sich a individooal as Devil-Bug."

It requires no great stretch of fancy to imagine that his Satanic Majesty, once on a time, in a merry mood, created a huge insect, in order to test his inventive powers. Certainly that insect —which it was quite natural to designate by the name of Devil-Bug—stood in the full light of the grate, gazing steadfastly in Byrnewood's face. It was a strange thickset specimen of flesh and blood, with a short body, marked by immensly broad shoulders, long arms and thin distorted legs. The head of the creature was ludicrously large in proportion to the body. Long masses of stiff black hair fell tangled and matted over a forehead, protuberant to deformity. A flat nose with wide nostrils, shooting out into each cheek like the smaller wings of an insect, an immense mouth whose heavy lips disclosed two long rows of bristling teeth, a pointed chin, blackened by a heavy beard, and massive eyebrows meeting over the nose, all furnished the details of a countenance, not exactly calculated to inspire the most pleasant feelings in the world. One eye, small, black, and shapen like a bead, stared steadily in Byrnewood's face, while the other socket was empty, shrivelled and orbless. The eyelids of the vacant socket were joined together like the opposing edges of a curtain,

while the other eye gained additional brilliancy and effect from the loss of its fellow member.

The shoulders of the Devil-Bug protruding in unsightly knobs, the wide chest, and the long arms, with talon-like fingers, so vividly contrasted with the thin and distorted legs, all attested that the remarkable strength of the man was located in the upper part of his body.

"Well, Abijah, are you satisfied?" asked Lorrimer, as he preceived Byrnewood shrink back with disgust from the door-keeper's gaze— "This gentleman, I say, is my friend?"

"So I s'pose," grunted Abijah— "Here, Musquito, mark this man—here, Glow-worm, mark him, I say. This is Monk Gusty's friend. Can't you move quicker, you ugly devils?"

From either side of the fire-place, as he spoke, emerged a tall herculean negro, with a form of strength and sinews of iron. Moving slowly along the floor, from the darkness which had enshrouded their massive outlines, they stood silent and motionless, gazing with looks of stolid indifference upon the face of the new-comer. Byrnewood had started aside in disgust from the Devil-Bug, as he was styled in the slang of Monk-hall, but certainly these additional insects nestling in the den of the other, were rather singular specimens of the glow-worm and musquito. Their attire was plain and simple. Each negro was dressed in coarse corduroy trowsers, and a flaring red flannel shirt. The face of the Glow-worm was marked by a hideous flat nose, a receding forehead, and a wide mouth with immense lips, that buried all traces of a chin, and disclosed two rows of teeth protruding like the tusks of a wild boar. Musquito had the same flat nose, the same receding forehead, but his thick lips, tightly compressed, were drawn down on either side towards his jaw, presenting an outline something like the two sides of a triangle, while his sharp and pointed chin was in direct contrast to the long chinless jaw of the other. Their eyes, large, rolling and vacant, stared from bulging eyelids, that protruded beyond the outline of the brows. Altogether, each negro presented as hideous a picture of mere brute strength, linked with a form scarcely human, as the imagination of man might well conceive.

"This is Monk Gusty's friend—"muttered Abijah, or Devil-Bug, as the reader likes— "Mark him, Musquito—mark him, Glow-worm, I say. Mind ye now—this man don't leave the house except with Gusty? D'ye hear, ye black devils?"

Each negro growled assent.

"Queer specimens of musquito and glow-worm, I say—" laughed Byrnewood in the effort to smother his disgust—"Eh? Lorrimer?"

"This way, my fellow—"answered the magnificent Gus, gently leading his friend through a small door, which led from the doorkeeper's closet—"This way. Now for the club—and then for the wager!"

Looking round in wonder, Byrnewood discovered that they had passed into the hall of an old-time mansion, with the beams of the moon falling from a skylight in the roof far above, thrown over the windings of a massive staircase.

"This is rather a strange place—ch? Gus?" whispered Byrnewood, as he gazed around the hall, and marked the ancient look of the place—"why the d—l don't they have a light—those insects—ha ha—whom we have just left?"

"Secrecy—my fellow—secrecy! Those are the 'police' of Monk Hall, certain to be at hand in case of a row. You see, the entire arrangements of this place may be explained in one word—it is easy enough for a stranger—that's you, my boy—to find his way in, but it would puzzle him like the devil to find his way out,—That is, without assistance. Take my arm Byrnewood—we must descend to the club room——"

"Descend!"

"Yes, my fellow. Descend, for we hold our meetings one story under ground. It's likely all the fellows, or monks, to speak in the slang of the club, are now most royally drunk, so I can slide you in among them without much notice. You can remain there while I go and prepare the bride, ha, ha, ha! the bride, for your visit."

Meanwhile, grasping Byrnewood by the arm, he had led the way along the hall, beyond the staircase, into the thick darkness which rested upon this part of the place, unillumined by a ray of light.

"Hold my arm as tight as you can," he whispered; "There is a staircase somewhere here. Softly, softly, now I have it. Tread with care, Byrnewood. In a moment we will be in the midst of the monks of Monk Hall."

And as they descended the subterranean stairway, surrounded by the darkness of midnight, Byrnewood found it difficult to subdue a feeling of awe which began to spread like a shadow over his soul. This feeling it was not easy to analyze. It may have been a combination of feelings; the consideration of the darkness and loneliness of the place, his almost entire ignorance of the handsome libertine who was now leading him he knew not where, or perhaps, the earnest words of the astrologer, fraught with doom and death, came home to his soul like a vivid presentiment, in that moment of uncertainty and gloom.

"Don't you hear their shouts, my boy," whispered Lorrimer; "faith, they must be drunk as judges, every man of them. Why Byrnewood, you're as still as death."

"To tell you the truth, Lorrimer, this place looks like the den of some wizard—it's so d——d gloomy."

"Here we are at the door, now mark me, Byrnewood, you must walk in the club-room, or monk's room as they call it, directly at my back. While I salute the monks of Monk-hall, you will slide into a vacant seat at the table, and mingle in the revelry of the place until I return."

Stooping through a narrow door, whose receding panels flung a blaze of light along the darkness of the passage, Lorrimer, with Byrne-

wood at his back, descended three wooden steps that led from the door-sill to the floor, and in a moment, stood amid the revellers of Monkhall.

In a long, narrow room, lighted by the blaze of a large chandelier, with a low ceiling and a wide floor, covered with a double range of carpets, around a table spread with the relics of their feast, were grouped the Monks of Monkhall.

They hailed Lorrimer with a shout, and as they rose to greet him, Byrnewood glided into a vacant arm-chair near the head of the table, and in a moment his companion had disappeared.

"I'll be with you in a moment, Monks of Monk-hall," he shouted as he glided through the narrow door—"A little affair to settle up stairs—you know me—nice little girl—ha, ha, ha!"

"Ha, ha, ha!" echoed the band of revellers, raising their glasses merrily on high.

Byrnewood glanced hurriedly around. The room, long and spacious as it was, the floor covered with the most gorgeous carpeting, and the low ceiling, embellished with a faded painting in fresco, still wore an antiquated, not to say, dark and gloomy appearance. The walls were concealed by huge panels of wainscot, intricate with uncouth sculpturings of fawns and satyrs, and other hideous creations of classic mythology. At one end of the room, reaching from floor to ceiling, glared an immense mirror, framed in massive walnut, its glittering surface, reflecting the long festal board, with its encircling band of revellers. Inserted in the corresponding panels of the wainscot, on either side of the small door, at the opposite end of the room, two large pictures, evidently the work of a master hand, indicated the mingled worship of the devotees of Monk-hall. In the picture on the right of the door, Bacchus, the jolly god of mirth and wine, was represented rising from a festal-board, his brow wreathed in clustering grapes, while his hand swung aloft a goblet filled with the purple blood of the grape. In the other painting, along a couch as dark as night, with a softened radiance falling over her uncovered form, lay a sleeping Venus, her full arms, twining above her head, while her lips were dropped apart, as though she murmured in her slumber. Straight and erect, behind the chair of the President or Abbot of the board, arose the effigy of a monk, whose long black robes fell drooping to the floor, while his cowl hung heavily over his brow, and his right hand raised on high a goblet of gold. From beneath the shadow of the falling cowl, glared a fleshless skeleton head, with the orbless eye-sockets, the cavity of the nose, and the long rows of grinning teeth, turned to a faint and ghastly crimson by the lamp beams. The hand that held the goblet on high, was a grisly skeleton hand; the long and thin fingers of bone, twining firmly around the glittering bowl.

And over this scene, over the paintings and the mirror, over the gloomy wainscot along the walls, and over the faces of the revellers with the Skeleton-Monk, grinning derision at their scene of bestial enjoyment, shone the red beams of the massive chandelier, the body and limbs of which were fashioned into the form of a grim Satyr, with a light flaring from his skull, a flame emerging from each eye, while his extended hands flung streams of fire on either side, and his knees were huddled up against his breast. The design was like a nightmare dream, so grotesque and terrible, and it completed the strange and ghostly appearance of the room.

Around the long and narrow board, strewn with the relics of the feast, which had evidently been some hours in progress, sate the Monks of Monk-hall, some thirty in number, flinging their glasses on high, while the room echoed with their oaths and drunken shouts. Some lay with their heads thrown helplessly on the table, others were gazing round in sleepy drunkenness, others had fallen to the floor in a state of unconscious intoxication, while a few there were who still kept up the spirit of the feast, although their incoherent words and heavy eyes proclaimed that they too were fast advancing to that state of brutal inebriety, when strange-looking stars shine in the place of the lamps, when the bottles dance and even tables perform the cracovienne, while all sorts of beehives create a buzzing murmur in the air.

There was another person who regarded this scene of brutal mirth with the same cool glance as Byrnewood. He was a young man with a massive face, and a deep piercing brown eye. His figure was somewhat stout, his attire careless, and his entire appearance disclosed the young Philadelphia lawyer. Changing his seat to Byrnewood's vicinity, he entered into conversation with the young merchant, and after making some pointed remarks in regard to the various members of the company, he stated that he had been lured thither by Mutchins, who fancied he might cheat him out of a snug sum at the roulette table, or the faro-bank in the course of the night.

"Roulette - table — faro - bank ?" muttered Byrnewood, incredulously.

"Why, my friend," cried the young lawyer, who gave his name as Boyd Merivale, "don't you know that this is one of the vilest rookeries in the world? It unites in all its details the house-of-ill-fame, the clubhouse, and the gambling hell. Egad! I well remember the first time I set my foot within its doors! What I beheld then, I can never forget."

"You have been here before, then ?"

"Yes have I! As I perceive you are unacquainted with the place, I will tell you my experience of

A NIGHT IN MONK-HALL.

Six years ago, in 1836, on a foggy night in spring, at the hour of one o'clock, I found myself reposing in one of the chambers of this mansion, on an old-fashioned bed, side by side with a girl, who, before her seduction, had resided in my native village. It was one o'clock when I was aroused by a hushed sound, like the noise of a distant struggle. I awoke, started up in bed, and looked round. The room was entirely without light, save from the fire-place, where a few pieces of half-burned wood, emitted a dim and uncertain flame. Now it flashed up brightly, giving a strange lustre to the old furniture of the room, the high-backed mahogany chairs, the antiquated bureau, and the low ceiling, with heavy cornices, around the walls. Again the flame died away and all was darkness. I listened intently. I could hear no sound, save the breathing of the girl who slept by my side. And as I listened, a sudden awe came over me. True, I heard no noise, but that my sleep had been broken by a most appalling sound, I could not doubt. And the stories I had heard of Monk-hall came over me. Years before, in my native village, a wild rollicking fellow, Paul Western, cashier of the County Bank, had indulged my fancy with strange stories of a brothel, situated in the outskirts of Philadelphia. Paul was a wild fellow, rather good looking, and went often to the city on business. He spoke of Monk-hall as a place hard to find, abounding in mysteries, and darkened by hideous crimes committed within its walls. It had three stories of chambers beneath the earth, as well as above. Each of these chambers was supplied with trap-doors, through which the unsuspecting man might be flung by his murderer, without a moment's warning. There was but one range of rooms above the ground, where these trap-doors existed. From the garret to the first story, all in the same line, like the hatchways in a storehouse, sank this range of trap-doors, all carefully concealed by the manner in which the carpets were fixed. A secret spring in the wall of any one of these chambers, communicated with the spring hidden beneath the carpet The spring in the wall might be so arranged, that a single footstep pressed on the spring, under the carpet, would open the trap-door, and plunge the victim headlong through the aperture. In such cases no man could stride across the floor without peril of his life. Beneath the ground another range of trap-doors were placed in the same manner, in the floors of three stories of the subterranean chambers. They plunged the victim—God knows where! With such arrangements for murder above and beneath the earth, might there not exist hideous pits or deep wells, far below the third story under ground, where the body of the victim would rot in darkness for ever? As I remembered these details, the connection between Paul Western, the cheerful bachelor, and Emily Walraven, the woman who was sleeping at my side, flashed over my mind. The child of one of the first men of B———, educated without any regard to expense by the doating father, with a mind singularly masculine, and a tall queenly form, a face distinguished for its beauty, and a manner remarkable for its ladylike elegance, poor Emily had been seduced some three years before, and soon after disappeared from the town. Her seducer no one knew, though from some hints dropped casually by friend Paul, I judged that he at least could tell. Rumours came to the place, from time to time, in relation to the beautiful but fallen girl. One rumour stated that she was now living as the mistress of a wealthy planter, who made his residence at times in Philadelphia. Another declared that she had become a common creature of the town, and this—great God, how terrible! killed her poor father. The rumour flew round the village to-day—next Sunday old Walraven was dead and buried. They say that in his dying hour he charged Paul Western with his daughter's shame, and shrieked a father's curse upon his head. He left no property, for his troubles had preyed on his mind until he neglected his affairs, and he died insolvent.

Well two years passed on, and no one heard a word more of poor Emily. Suddenly in the spring of 1836, when this town as well as the whole Union was convulsed with the fever of speculation, Paul Western, after a visit to Philadelphia, with some funds of the bank, amounting to nearly thirty thousand dollars, in his possession, suddenly disappeared, no one knew whither. My father was largely interested in the bank. He despatched me to town, in order that I might make a desperate effort to track up the footsteps of Western. Some items in the papers stated that the cashier had fled to Texas, others that he had been drowned by accident, others that he had been spirited away. I alone possessed a clue to the place of his concealment—thus ran my thoughts at all events—and that clue was locked in the bosom of Emily Walraven, the betrayed and deeply-injured girl. Sometime before his disappearance, and after the death of old Walraven, Paul disclosed to me, under a solemn pledge of secresy, the fact that Emily was living in Philadelphia, under his protection, supported by his money. He stated that he had furnished rooms at the brothel called Monk-hall. With this fact resting on my mind, I had hurried to Philadelphia. For days my search for Emily Walraven was in vain. One night, when about giving up the chase as hopeless, I strolled to the Chesnut-street theatre. Forrest was playing Richelieu—there was a row in the third tier—a bully had offered violence to one of the ladies of the town. Attracted by the noise, I joined the throng rushing up stairs, and beheld the girl who had been stricken, standing pale and erect, a small poignard in her upraised hand, while her eyes flashed with rage as she dared the drunken 'buffer' to strike her again. I stood thunderstruck as I recognized Emily Walraven in the degraded yet beautiful woman who stood before me. Springing forward, with one blow I felled the bully to the floor, and in another moment seizing Emily by the arm, I hurried down stairs, evaded the constables, who were about to arrest her, and gained the street. It was yet early in the evening—there were no cabs in the street—so I had to walk home with her.

All this I remembered well, as I sat listening in the lonely room.

I remembered the big tears that started from her eyes when she recognised me, her wild exclamations when I spoke of her course of life.

"Don't talk to me," she had almost shrieked as we hurried along the street, "it's too late for me to change now. For God's sake let me be happy in my degradation."

I remembered the warm flush of indignation that reddened over her face, as pointing carelessly to a figure which I observed through the fog, some distance ahead, I exclaimed,—

"Is not that Paul Western yonder?"

Her voice was very deep and not at all natural in its tone as she replied, with assumed unconcern,—

"I know nothing about the man."

At last, after threading a labyrinth of streets, compared to which the puzzling-garden was a mere frolic, we had gained Monk-hall, the place celebrated by the wonderful stories of my friend Western. Egad! as we neared the door I could have sworn that I beheld Western himself disappear in the door, but this doubtless, I reasoned, had been a mere fancy.

Silence still prevailed in the room, still I heard but the sound of Emily breathing in her sleep, and yet my mind grew more and more heavy, with some unknown feeling of awe. I remembered with painful distinctness the hang-dog aspect of the door-keeper who had let us in, and the cut-throat visages of his two attendants seemed staring me visibly in the face. I grew quite nervous. Dark ideas of murder, and the devil knows what, began to chill my very soul. I bitterly remembered that I had no arms. The only thing I carried with me was a slight cane, which had been lent me by the landlord of the —— Hotel. It was a mere switch of a thing.

As these strange things came stealing over me, the strange connexion between the fate of Western and that of the beautiful woman who lay beside me, the sudden disappearance of the former, the mysterious character of Monk-hall, the startling sounds which had aroused me, the lonely appearance of the room, fitfully lighted by the glare on the hearth, all combined, deepened the impression of awe, which had gradually gained possession of my faculties. I feared to stir. You may have felt this feeling—this strange and incomprehensible feeling—but if you have not, just imagine a man seized with the night-mare when wide awake.

I was sitting upright in bed, chilled to the very heart, afraid to move an inch, almost afraid to breathe, when, far, far down through the chambers of the old mansion, I heard a faint hushed sound, like a man endeavouring to cry out when attacked by night-mare, and then—great God how distinct!—I heard the cry of "Murder, murder, murder!" far, far, far below me.

The cry aroused Emily from her sleep. She started up in the bed and whispered, in a voice without tremor—"What is the matter Boyd?"

"Listen," I cried with chattering teeth, and again, up from the depths of the mansion welled that awful sound, "Murder! murder! murder!" growing louder every time. Then far, far, far down I could hear a gurgling sound. It grew fainter every moment. Fainter, fainter, fainter. All was still as death.

"What does this mean?" I whispered almost fiercely, turning to Emily by my side—"What does this mean?" And a dark suspicion flashed over my mind.

The flame shot upward in the fire-place, and revealed every line of her intellectual countenance.

Her dark eyes looked firmly in my face as she answered, "In God's name I know not!"

The manner of the answer satisfied me as to her firmness, if it did not convince me of her innocence. I sat silent snd sullen, conjecturing over the incidents of the night.

"Come Boyd," she cried, as she arose from the bed—"You must leave the house. I never entertain visitors after this hour. It is my custom. I thank you for your protection at the theatre, but you must go home."

Her manner was calm and self-possessed. I turned to her in perfect amazement.

"I will not leave the house," I said, as a dim vision of being attacked by assassins on the stairway, arose to my mind.

"There is Devil-Bug and his cut-throat negroes," thought I—"nothing so easy as to give me a 'cliff' with a knife from some dark corner; nothing so secret as my burial-place in some dark hole in the cellar."

"I won't go home," said I, aloud.

Emily looked at me in perfect wonder. It may have been affected, and it may have been real.

"Well then, I must go down stairs to get something to eat," she said, in the most natural manner in the world—"I usually eat something about this hour."

'You may eat old Devil-Bug and his niggers, if you like," I replied, laughing—"But out of this house my father's son don't stir till broad day light."

With a careless laugh, she wound her nightgown round her, opened the door, and disappeared in the dark. Down, down, down, I could hear her go, her footsteps echoing along the stairway of the old mansion, down, down, down. In a few moments all was still.

Here I was, in a pretty "fix." In a lonely room at midnight, ignorant of the passages of the wizard's den, without arms, and with the pleasant prospect of the young lady coming back with Devil-Bug and his niggers to despatch me. I had heard the cry of "Murder"—so ran my reasoning—they, that is the murderers, would suspect that I was a witness to their guilt, and, of course, would send me down some trap-door on an especial message to the devil.

This was decidedly a bad case. I began to look around the room for some chance of escape, some arms to defend myself, or perhaps from a motive of laudable curiosity, to know something more about the place where my death was to happen.

One moment, regular as the ticking of a clock, the room would be illuminated by a flash of red lighted from the fire-place, the next it would be dark as a grave. Seizing the opportunity afforded by the flash, I observed some of the details of the room. On the right side of the fire-place there was a closet : the door fastened to the post by a very singular button, shaped like a diamond; about as long as your little finger and twice as thick. On the other side of the fire-place, near the ceiling, was a small oblong window, about as large as two half sheets of writing paper, pasted together at the ends. Here let me explain the use of this window. The back part of Monk-hall is utterly destitute of windows. Light, faint and dim you may be sure, is admitted from the front by small windows, placed in the wall of each room. How many rooms there are on a floor, I know not, but be they five or ten, or twenty, they are all lighted in this way.

Well, as I looked at this window, I perceived one corner of the curtain on the other side was turned up. This gave me very unpleasant ideas. I almost fancied I beheld a human face pressed against the glass, looking at me. Then the flash on the hearth died away, and all was dark. I heard a faint creaking noise—the light from the hearth again lighted the place—could I believe my eyes—the button on the closet-door turned slowly round !

Slowly—slowly—slowly it turned, making a slight grating noise. This circumstance, slight as it may appear to you, filled me with horror. What could turn the button, but a human hand? Slowly, slowly it turned, and the door sprung open with a whizzing sound. All was dark again. The cold sweat stood out on my forehead. Was my armed murderer waiting to spring at my throat ? I passed a moment of intense horror. At last, springing hastily forward, I swung the door shut, and fastened the button. I can swear that I fastened it as tight as ever button was fastened. Regaining the bed I silently awaited the result. Another flash of light—Great God! —I could swear there was a face pressed against the oblong window ! Another moment and it is darkness—creak, creak, creak—is that the sound of the button again ? It was light again, and there, before my very eyes, the button moved slowly round ! Slowly, slowly, slowly !

The door flew open again. I sat still as a statue. I felt it difficult to breathe. Was my enemy playing with me, like the cat ere she destroys her game !

I absently extended my hand. It touched the small black stick given me by the landlord of the —— Hotel, in the beginning of the evening. I drew it to me, like a friend. Grasping it with both hands, I calculated the amount of service it might do me. And as I grasped it, the top seemed parting from the lower portion of the cane. Great God! It was a sword cane! Ha, ha! I could at least strike one blow! My murderers should not dispatch me without an effort of resistance. You see my arm is none of the puniest in the world ; I may say that there are worse men than Boyd Merivale for a fight.

Clutching the sword-cane, I rushed forward, and standing on the threshold of the opened door, I made a lunge with all my strength through the darkness of the recess. Though I extended my arm to its full length, and the sword was not less than eighteen inches long, yet to my utter astonishment, I struck but the empty air! Another lunge and the same result!

Things began to grow rather queer. I was decidedly beat out, as they say. I shut the closet door again, retreated to the bed, sword in hand, and awaited the result. I heard a sound, but it was the footstep of poor Emily, who that moment returned with a bed-lamp in one hand, and a small waiter, supplied with a boiled chicken and bottle of wine, in the other. There was nothing remarkable in her look, her face was calm, and her boiled chicken and bottle of wine, decidedly common place.

"I STEPPED UPON THE STRING—THE TRAP-DOOR SUNK BELOW ME."—SEE PAGE 26.

"Great God!" she cried as she gazed in my countenance; "What is the matter with you? Your face is quite livid, and your eyes are fairly starting from their sockets."

"Good reason," said I, as I felt that my lips were clammy and white. "That button has been going round ever since you left, and that door has been springing open every time that it was shut."

"Ha, ha, ha," she laughed. "Would it have sprung open if you had not shut it?"

This was a very clear question and easy to answer; but,—

"Mark you, my lady," said I, "Here am I in a lonely house, under peculiar circumstances. I am waked up by the cry of 'murder,' a door springs open without a hand being visible, a face peers at me through a window. As a matter of course I suspect there has been foul work done here to-night. And through every room of this house, Emily, you must lead the way, while I follow, this good sword in hand. If the light goes out, or if you blow it out, you are to be pitied, for in either case, I swear by the Living God, I will run you through with this sword,"

"Ha, ha, ha," she fairly screamed with laughter as she sprung to the closet door. "Behold the mystery ?"——

And with her fair fingers she pointed to the socket of the button, and to the centre of the door. The door had been 'sprung,' as it is termed, by the weather. That is, the centre bulged inward, leaving the edge toward the door-post to press the contrary direction. The socket of the button, by continual wear, had been increased to twice its original size. Whenever the door was first buttoned, the head of the screw pressed against one of the edges of the socket. In a moment the pressure of the edge of the door, which you will remember was directed outward, dislodged the head of the screw, and it sank well nigh half an inch, into the worn socket of the button. Then the button removed farther from the door than at first, would slowly turn and the door spring open. All this was plain enough, and I smiled at my recent fright.

"Very good, Emily," I laughed. "But the mystery of this sword, what of that? I made a lunge in the closet and it touched nothing."

"You are suspicious, Boyd," she answered with a laugh; "But the fact is, the closet is rather a deep one."

"Rather," said I, "and so are you my dear."

There may have been something very meaning in my manner, that certainly, although her full black eyes looked fixedly on me, yet I thought her face grew a shade paler as I spoke.

"And my dear," I continued. "What do you make of the face peeping through the window ?"

"All fancy—all fancy," she replied, but as she spoke I saw her eye glance hurriedly toward the very window. Did she too fear that she might behold the face ?

"We will search the closet," I remarked, throwing open the door. "What have we here? Nothing but an old cloak hanging to a hook—let's try it with my sword!"

Again I made a lunge with my sword; again I thrust at the empty air.

"Emily, there is a room beyond this cloak—you will enter first if you please."

"Oh, now that I remember, this closet does open into the next room;" she said gaily, although her cheek—so it struck me—grew a little paler and her lip trembled slightly. "I had quite forgotten the circumstance."

"Enter Emily, and don't forget the light."

She flung the door aside, and passed on with the light in her hand. I followed her. We stood in a small room, lighted like the other by an oblong window. There was no other window, no door, no outlet of any sort. Even a chimney-

place was wanting. In one corner stood a massive bed—the quilt was unruffled. Two or three old fashioned chairs were scattered round the room, and from the spot where I stood looking over the foot of the bed, I could see the top of another chair, and nothing more, between the bed and the wall.

A trifling fact in Emily's behaviour may be remarked. The moment the light of the lamp which she held in her hand flashed round the room, she turned to me with a smile, and leading the way round the corner of the foot of the bed, asked me in a pleasant voice,—

"Did I see anything remarkable there ?"

She shaded her eyes from the lamp as she spoke, and toyed me playfully under the chin. You will bear in mind that at this moment, I had turned my face toward the closet by which we had entered. My back was therefore toward the part of the room most remote from the closet. It was a trifling fact, but I may as well tell you, that the manner in which Emily held the light, threw that portion of the room, between the foot of the bed and the wall in complete shadow, while the rest of the chamber was bright as day.

Smilingly, Emily toyed me under the chin, and at that moment I thought she looked extremely beautiful.

By Jove! I wish you could have seen her eyes shine, and her cheek—Lord bless you—a full blown rose wasn't a circumstance to it. She looked so beautiful, in fact, as she came sideling up to me, that I stepped backward, in order to have a full view of her before I pressed a kiss on her pouting lips. I did step back, and did kiss her. It wasn't singular, perhaps, but her lips were hot as coal. Again she advanced to me, again chuckled me under the chin. Again I stepped back to look at her, again I wished to taste her lips so pouting, but rather warm, when ——

To tell you the truth, stranger, even at this late day the remembrance makes my blood run cold!

—— When I heard a sound like the sweeping of a tree limb against a closed shutter, it was so faint and distant, and a stream of cold air came rushing up my back.

I turned round carelessly to ascertain the cause. I took but a single glance, and then I sprung at least ten feet from the place. There, at my very back, between the bed and the wall, opposite its foot, I beheld a carpeted space some three feet square, sinking slowly down, and separating itself from the floor. I had stepped my foot upon the spring—made ready for me, to be sure—and the trap-door sank below me.

You may suppose my feelings were somewhat excited. In truth, my heart, for a moment, felt as though it was turning to a ball of ice. First I looked at the trap door and then at Emily. Her face was pale as ashes, and she leaned, trembling, against the bedpost. Advancing, sword in hand, I gazed down the trap-door. Great God! how dark and gloomy the pit looked! From room to room, from floor to floor, a succession of traps had fallen—far below—it looked like a mile, although that was but an exaggeration natural to a highly excited mind—far, far below gleamed a light, and a buzzing murmur came up this hatchway of death.

Stooping slowly down, sword in hand, my eye on the alert for Miss Emily, I disengaged a piece of linen from a nail, near the edge of the trap-door. Where the linen—it was a shirt wristband—had been fastened, the carpet was slightly torn, as though a man in falling had grasped it with his finger ends.

The wristband was, in more correct language, a ruffle for the wrist. It came to my mind, in this moment, that I had often ridiculed Paul Western for his queer old bachelor ways. Among other odd notions, he had worn ruffles at his wrist. As I gathered this little piece of linen in my grasp, the trap-door slowly rose. I turned to look for Miss Emily, she had changed her position, and stood pressing her hand against the opposite wall.

"Now, Miss Emily, my dear," I cried, advancing toward her, "give me a plain answer to a plain question, and tell me, what the devil do you think of yourself?"

Perfectly white in the face, she glided across the room and stood at the foot of the bed, in her former position, leaning against the post for support. You will observe that her form concealed the chair, whose top I had only seen across the bed.

"Step aside, Miss Emily, my dear," I said, in as quiet a tone as I could command, "or you see, my lady, I'll have to use a little necessary force."

Instead of stepping aside, as a peaceable woman would have done, she sits right down in the chair, fixing those full black eyes of her's on my face, with a glance that looked very much like madness.

Extending my hand, I raised her from the seat. She rested like a dead weight in my arms. She had fainted. Wrapped in her night-gown I laid her on the bed, and then examined the chair in the corner. Something about this chair attracted my attention. A coat hung over the round—a blue coat with metal buttons. A buff vest hung under this coat; and a high stock, with a shirt collar.

I knew these things at once. They belonged to my friend, Paul Western.

"And so, my lady," I cried, forgetting that she had fainted; "Mr. Western came home from the theatre to his rooms, arrived just before us, took off his coat and vest, and stock and collar—maybe was just about to take off his boots—when he stepped on the spring, and in a moment was in ———."

Taking the light in one hand, I dragged or carried her into the other room, and laid her on the bed. After half an hour or so, she came to her senses.

"You see—you see," were her first words, uttered with her eyes flashing, like live coals, and her lips white as marble. "You see, I could not help it, for my father's curse was upon him!"

She laughed wildly, and lay in my arms a maniac.

Stranger, I'll make a short story of the thing now. How I watched her all night till broad day, how I escaped from the house—for Mr. Devil-Bug, it seems, didn't suspect that I knew anything—how I returned home without any news of Paul Western, are matters as easy to conceive as to tell.

Why didn't I institute a search? Fiddle, fiddle! Blazon my name to the world as a visiter to a bagnio? Sensible thing, that! And then, although I was secure in my own soul, that the clothes which I had discovered belonged to Paul Western, it would have been most difficult to establish this fact in court. One word more and I have done

Never since that night has Paul Western been heard of by living man. Never since that night has Emily Walraven been seen in this breathing world. You start. Let me whisper a word in your ear. Suppose Emily joined in Western's murder from motives of revenge, what then were Devil-Bug's? (He of course was the real murderer.) Why the money to be sure. Why be troubled with Emily as a witness of his guilt, or a sharer of his money? This is rather a—a dark house, and it's my opinion, stranger, that he murdered her too!

"Ha, ha—why here's all the room to ourselves! All the club have either disappeared, or lie drunk on the floor! I saw Fitz-Chowles—I know him—sneak off a few moments since, I could tell by his eye that he is after some devil's trick. And so, wishing you good night, stranger, I'll vanish! Beware of the Monks of Monk-hall!"

Byrnewood was alone.

His head was depressed, his arms were folded, and his eye, gazing vacantly on the table, shone and glistened with the internal agitation of his brain. He sate there, silent, motionless, awed to the very soul. The story of the stranger had thrilled him to the heart, had aroused a strange train of thought, and now rested like an oppressive weight upon his brain.

Byrnewood gazed around. With a sudden effort he shook off the spell of absence, which, mingled with an incomprehensible feeling of awe, had enchained his faculties. He looked around the room. He was, indeed, alone. Above him, the hideous Satyr chandelier still flared its red light over the table, o'er the mirror, and along the gloomy wainscot of the walls. Around the table, grouped in various attitudes of unconscious drunkenness, lay the members of the drinking party, the merry Monks of Monk-hall. There lay the poet, with his sanguine face shining redly in the light, while his hand rested on the bare scalp of the wigless editor, there snored some dozen merchants, all doubled up together, like the slain in battle, and there, a solitary doctor who had fallen asleep on his knees, was dozing away with one eye wide open, while his righ hand brushed away a solitary fly from his pimpled nose.

The scene was not calculated to produce the most serious feelings in the world. There was inebriety—as the refined phrase it—in every shape, inebriety on its face, inebriety with its mouth wide open, inebriety on its knees brushing a fly from its nose, inebriety groaning, grunting, or snorting, inebriety doubled up—mingled in a mass of limbs, heads and bodies, woven together—or flat inebriety simply straightened out on its back with its nose performing a select overture of snores. To be brief, there, scattered over the floor, lay drunkenness—as the vulgar will style it—in every shape, modeled after various patterns, and taken by that ingenious artist, the bottle, fresh from real life.

Raising his eyes from the prostrate members of the club, Byrnewood started with involuntary surprise as he beheld, standing at the table's head, the black-robed figure of the Skeleton-Monk, with his hand of bone flinging aloft the goblet, while his fleshless brow glared in the light, from the shadow of the falling cowl. As the light flickered to and fro, it gave the grinning teeth of the skeleton the appearance of life and animation for a single moment. Byrnewood thought he beheld the teeth move in a ghastly smile; he even fancied that the orbless sockets, gleaming beneath the white brow, flashed with the glance of life, and gazed sneeringly in his face.

He started with involuntary horror, and then sate silent as before. And as you can feel cold or heat steal over you by slow degrees, so he felt that same strange feeling of awe, which he had known that night for the first time in his life, come slowly over him, moving like a shadow over his soul, and stealing like a paralysis through his every limb. He sate like a man suddenly frozen.

"My God!" he murmured—and the sound of his voice frightened him—"How strange I feel! Can this be the first attack of some terrible disease—or—is it, but the effect of the horrible story related by the stranger? I have read in books that a feeling like this steals over a man, just before some terrible calamity breaks over his head—this is fearful as death itself!"

He was silent again, and then the exclamation broke from his lips,—

"Lorrimer—why does he not return? He has been absent full an hour—what does it mean? Can the words of that—pshaw! that fortune-teller have any truth in them? How can Lorrimer injure me—how can I injure him? Three days hence—Christmas—ha, ha—I believe I'm going mad—there's cold sweat on my forehead."

As he spoke he raised his left hand to his brow, and in the action, the gleam of a plain ring on his finger met his eye. He kissed it suddenly, and kissed it again and again? Was it the gift of his ladye-love?

"God bless her—God bless her! Woe to the man who shall do *her* wrong—and yet poor Annie."

He rose suddenly from his seat and strode towards the door.

"I know not why it is, but I feel as though an invisible hand was urging me onward through the rooms of this house! And onward I will go, until I discover Lorrimer, or solve the mystery of this den. God knows, I feel—pshaw! I'm only nervous—as though I was walking to my death."

Passing through the narrow door-way, he cautiously ascended the dark staircase, and in a moment stood on the first floor. The moon was still shining through the distant skylight, down over the windings of the massive stairway. All was silent as death within the mansion. Not a sound, not even the murmur of a voice or the hushed tread of a footstep could be heard. Winding his cloak tightly around his limbs, Byrnewood rushed up the staircase, traversing two steps at a time, and treading softly for fear of discovery. He reached the second floor. Still the place was silent and dismal, still the column of moonlight pouring through the skylight over the windings of the staircase, only rendered the surrounding darkness more gloomy and indistinct. Up the winding staircase he resumed his way, and in a moment stood upon the landing or hall of the third floor. This was an oblong space, with the doors of many rooms fashioned in its walls. Another stairway led upward from the floor, but the attention of Byrnewood was arrested by a single ray of light, that for a moment flickered along the thick darkness of the southern end of the hall. Stepping forward hastily, Byrnewood found all progress arrested by the opposing front of a solid wall. He gazed toward his left—it was so dark that he could not see his hand before his eyes. Turning his glance to the right, as his vision became more accustomed to the darkness, he beheld the dim walls of a long corridor, at whose entrance he stood, and whose farther extreme was illumined by a light, that to all appearance, flashed from an open door. Without a minute's thought he strode along the thickly carpeted passage of the corridor; he stood in the full glow of the light flashing from the open door.

Looking through the doorway, he beheld a large chamber furnished in a style of lavish magnificence, and lighted by a splendid chandelier. It was silent and deserted. From the ceiling to the floor, along the wall opposite the doorway, hung a curtain of damask silk, trailing in heavy folds along the gorgeous carpet. Impelled by the strange impulse that had urged him thus far, Byrnewood entered the chamber and without pausing to admire its gorgeous appointments, strode forward to the damask curtain.

He swung one of its hangings aside, expecting to behold the extreme wall of the chamber. To his entire wonder, another chamber, as spacious as the one in which he stood, lay open to his gaze. The walls were all one gorgeous picture evidently painted by a master-hand. Blue skies, deep green forests, dashing waterfalls and a cool calm lake, in which fair women were laving their limbs, broke on the eyes of the intruder, as he turned his gaze from wall to wall. A curtain of azure, sprinkled with a border of golden leaves, hung along the farther extremity of the room. In one corner stood a massive bed, whose snow-white counterpane, fell smoothly and unruffled to the very floor, mingling with the long curtains, which, pure and stainless as the counterpane, hung around the couch in graceful festoons, like the wings of a bird guarding its resting place.

"The bridal-bed," murmured Byrnewood, as he flung the curtains of gold and azure hurriedly aside.

A murmur of surprise, mingled with admiration, escaped from his lips, as he beheld the small closet, for it could scarcely be called a room, which the undrawn curtaining threw open to his gaze.

It was indeed a small and elegant room, lined along its four sides with drooping curtains of faint-hued crimson silk. The ceiling itself was but a continuation of these curtains, or hangings, for they were gathered in the centre by a single star of gold. The carpet on the floor was of the same faint crimson colour, and the large sofa, placed along one side of the apartment, was covered with velvet, that harmonized in hue, with both carpet and hangings. On the snow-white cloth of a small table placed in the centre of the room, stood a large wax candle, burning in a candlestick of silver, and flinging a subdued and mellow light around the place. There was a neat little couch, standing in the corner, with a toilette at its foot. The quilt of the couch was ruffled, as though some one had lately risen from it, and the equipage of the toilette looked as though it had been recently used.

The faint light falling over the hangings, whose hue resembled the first flush of day, the luxurious sofa, the neat diminutive couch, the small table in the centre, the carpet whose colours were in elegant harmony with the hue of the curtains, all combined, gave the place an air of splendid comfort—if we may join these incongruous words—that indicated the sleeping chamber of a lovely woman.

"This has been the resting place of the bride," murmured Byrnewood, gazing in admiration around the room. "It looks elegant it is true, but if she is the innocent thing Lorrimer would have me believe, then better for her to have slept in the foulest gutter of the streets, than to have lain for an instant in this woman-trap."

There was a woman's dress—a frock of plain black silk—flung over one of the rounds of the sofa. Anxious to gather some idea of the form of the bride—oh, foul prostitution of the name!—from the shape of the dress, Byrnewood raised the frock and examined its details. As he did this, the sound of voices came hushed and murmuring to his ear from a room opposite the chamber which he had but a moment left. Half

occupied in listening to these voices, Byrnewood glanced at the dress which he held in his hand, and as he took in its various details of style and shape, the pupil of his full black eye dilated, and his cheek became colourless as death.

Then the room seemed to swim around him, and he pressed his hand forcibly against his brow, as if to assure himself that he was not entangled in the mazes of some hideous dream.

Then letting his own cloak and the black silk dress fall on the floor at once, he walked with a measured step toward that side of the room opposite the painted chamber.

The voices grew louder in the next room. Byrnewood listened in silence. His face was even paler than before, and you could see how desperate was the effort which he made to suppress an involuntary cry of horror, that came rising to his lips. Extending his hand, he pushed the curtain slightly aside, and looked into the next room.

The extended hand fell like a dead weight to his side.

Over his entire countenance flashed a mingled expression of surprise and horror, and woe, that convulsed every feature with a spasmodic movement, and forced his large black eyes from their very sockets. For a moment he looked as if about to fall lifeless on the floor, and then it was evident that he exerted all his energies to control his most fearful agitation. He pressed both hands nervously against his forehead, as though his brain was tortured by internal flame. Then he reared his form proudly erect, and stood apparently firm and self-possessed, although his countenance looked more like the face of a corpse than the face of a living man.

And as he stood there, silent and firm, although his very reason tottered to its ruin, there glided to his back, like an omen of death, pursuing the footsteps of life, the distorted form of the door-keeper of Monk-hall, his huge bony arms upraised, his hideous face convulsed in a loathsome grin, while his solitary eye glared out from its sunken socket, like a flame lighted in a skull, grotesque yet terrible.

In vain was the momentary firmness which Byrnewood had aroused to his aid! In vain was the effort that suppressed his breath, that clenched his hands, that forced the clammy sweat from his brow! He felt the awful agony that convulsed his soul rising to his lips—he would have given the world to stifle it—but in vain, in vain were all his superhuman efforts.

One terrific howl, like the yell of a man flung suddenly over a cataract, broke from his lips. He thrust aside the curtain, and strode madly through its folds into the next room.

CHAPTER VIII.

MOTHER NANCY AND LONG-HAIRED BESS.

"So ye have lured the pretty dove into the cage, at last," said the old lady, with a pleasant smile. You're a reg'lar keen one, I must say!"

"Spankin' cold night, I tell ye, Mother Nancy," exclaimed the young lady in black, as she flung herself into a chair, and tossed her bonnet on the old sofa, "precious time I've had with that little chit of a thing! Up one street and down another, I've been racing for this blessed hour! And the regular white and black 'uns I've been forced to tell! Oh crickey, don't mention 'em, I beg."

"Sit down, Bess, sit down, Bessie, that's a dove," said the delighted old lady, "and tell us all about it from the first! These things are quite refreshin' to us old stagers."

"What a perfect old d—l," muttered Bessie, as she drew her seat near the supper table, "these oysters are quite delightful—stewed to a turn, I do declare," she continued, aloud, "got a little drop o' the 'lively' eh, mother?"

"Yes, dovey: here's the key of the closet. Get the bottle, my dear. A leetle, jist a leetle, don't go ugly with one's tea——"

While the tall and queenly Bessie is securing a drop of the lively, we will take a passing glance at Mother Perkins, the respectable Lady Abbess of Monk-hall.

As she sat in that formal arm-chair, straight and erect, her portly form clad in sombre black, with a plain white collar around her neck and a bunch of keys at her girdle, Mother Nancy looked, for all the world, like a quiet old body, whose only delight was to scatter blessings around her, give alms to the poor, and bestow unlimited amounts of tracts among the vicious. A good, dear, old body, was Mother Nancy, although her face was not decidedly prepossessing. A low forehead, surmounted by a perfect Tower-of-Babel of a cap, a little sharp nose looking out from two cheeks disposed in immense collops of yellowish flesh, two small grey eyes encircled by a wilderness of wrinkles, a deep indentation where a mouth should have been, and a sharp chin, ornamented with a slight 'imperial' of stiff grey beard; such were the details of a countenance, on which seventy years had showered their sins, and cares, and crimes, without making the dear old lady, for a moment, pause in her career.

And such a career! God of Heaven! did womanhood, which in its dawn or bloom, or full maturity, is so beautiful, which even in its decline is lovely, which in trembling old age is venerable, did womanhood ever sink so low as this? How many of the graves in an hundred churchyards, graves of the fair and beautiful, had been dug by the gouty hands of the vile old hag, who sat chuckling in her quiet arm chair? How many of the betrayed maidens, found rotting on the river's waves, dangling from the garret rafter, starving in the streets, or resting, vile and loathsome, in the deadhouse, how many of these will, at the last day, when the accounts of this lovely earth shall be closed for ever, rise up and curse the old hag with their ruin, with their shame, with their unwept death?

The details of the old lady's room by no means indicated her disposition, or the course of her life. It was a fine old room, with walls neatly papered, all full of nooks and corners, and warmed by a cheerful wood fire blazing on the spacious hearth. One whole side of the room seemed to have been attacked with some strange eruptive disease, and broken out into an erysipelas of cupboards and closets. An old desk that might have told a world of wonders of Noah's Ark from its own personal experience, could it have spoken, stood in one corner, and a large side-board, on whose top a fat fellow of a decanter seemed drilling some raw recruits of bottles and glasses into military order, occupied one entire side of the room, or cell, of the Lady Abbess.

There are few persons in the world who have not a favourite of some kind, either a baby, or a parrot, or a canary, or a cat, or, in desperate cases, a pig. Mother Nancy had her favourite as well as less reputable people. A huge bull dog, with sore eyes and a ragged tail—that seemed to have been purchased at a second-hand store during the bad times—lay nestling at the old lady's feet, looking very much like the candidate whom all the old and surly dogs would choose for alderman, in case the canine race had the privilege of electing an officer of that honourable class, among themselves. This dog, so old-bachelor-like and aldermanic in appearance, the old lady was wont to call by the name of 'Dolph,' being the short for 'Dolphin,' of which remarkable fish the animal was supposed to be a decided copy.

"Here's the 'lively,' Mother Nancy," observed Miss Bessie, as she resumed her seat at the supper table. "It's the real hot stuff and no mistake. The oysters, if you please—a little o' that pepper. Any mustard there? Now then, Mother, let's be comfortable."

"But," observed the old lady, pouring a glass of the 'lively' from a decanter labelled 'Brandy,' "but Bessie my love, I'm a-waiting' to hear all about this little dove whom you trapped to-night."

It may be as well to remark that Bessie was a tall queenly girl of some twenty-five, with a form that had once been beautiful beyond description, and even now in its ruin, was lovely to look upon, while her faded face, marked by a high brow and raven-black hair, was still enlivened by the glance of two large dark eyes, that were susceptible of any expression, love or hate, revenge or jealousy; anything but fear. Her complexion was a very faint brown with a deep rose-tint on each cheek. She was still beautiful, although a long career of dissipation had given a faded look to the outlines of her face, indenting a small wrinkle between her arching brows, and slightly discolouring the flesh beneath each eye.

"This here 'lively' is first-rate, after the tramp I've had," said Bessie as her eyes grew brighter with the 'lively' effects of the bottle, "You know, Mother Nancy, it's three weeks since Gus mentioned the *thing* to me.'"

"What thing, my dear?"

"Why that he'd like to have a little dove for

himself—something above the common run. Something from the aristocracy of the Quaker City, you know?"

"Yes my dear. Here Dolph—here Dolph-ee—here's a nice bit for Dolph."

"Gus agreed to give me something handsome if I could manage it for him, so I undertook the thing. The bread if you please, mother. You know I'm rather expert in such matters?"

"There ain't your beat my dear. Be quiet Dolph—that's a nice Dolph-ee."

"For a week all my efforts were in vain. I couldn't discover anything that was likely to suit the taste of Gus. At last he puts me on the right track himself."

"He did, did he? Ah deary my, but Gus is a regular lark. You can't produce his ekle."

"One day strolling up Third-street, Gus was attracted by the sight of a pretty girl, sitting at the window of a wealthy merchant, who has just retired from business. You've heard of old Arlington? Try the 'lively' mother. Gus made some inquiries; found that the young lady had just returned, from the Moravian boarding school at Bethlem. She was innocent, inexperienced, and all that. Suited Lorrimer's taste. He swore he'd have her."

"So you undertook to catch her, did ye?"

"That did I. The way I managed it was a caution. Dressing myself in solemn black, I strolled along Third-street, one mild winter evening, some two weeks since. Mary—that's her name—was standing at the front door, gazing carelessly down the street. I tripped up the steps and asked in my most winning tone—"

"You can act the lady when you like, Bess. That's a fact."

"Whether Mr. Elmwood lived there? Of course she answered 'No.' But in making an apology for my intrusion, I managed to state that Mr. Elmwood was my uncle, that I had just come to the city on a visit, and had left my aunt's in Spruce-street, but a few moments ago, thinking to pay a nice little call on my dear old relative."

"Just like you, Bessie! So you scraped acquaintance with her?"

"Fresh from boarding school, as ignorant of the world as the babe unborn, the girl was interested in me, I suppose, and swallowed the white'uns I told her, without a single suspicion. The next day about noon, I met her as she was hurrying to see an old aunt, who lived two or three squares below her father's house. She was all in a glow, for she had been hurrying along rather fast, anxious to reach her aunt's house, as soon as possible. I spoke to her—proposed a walk—she assented with a smile of pleasure. I told her a long story of my sorrows; how I had been engaged to be married, how my lover had died of consumption about a month ago; that he was sich a nice young man, with curly hair, and hazel eyes, and that I was in black for his death. I put peach fur over her eyes, by whole hands full I tell you. The girl was interested, and like all young girls, she was delighted to become the *confidante* of an amiable

young lady, who had a little love-romance of real life, to disclose. Oysters, Mother Nancy."

"The long and short of it was, that you wormed yourself into her confidence? That's it my dear? Keep still Dolph, or Dolph's mammy would drop little bit of hot tea on Dolph's head."

"We walked out together for three days, just toward dark in the evening. You can fancy, mother, how I wound myself into the heart of this young girl. Closer and closer every day I tightened the cords that bound us, and on the third evening I believe she would have died for me."

"Well, well, child, when did Gusty first speak to her? A little more of the 'gunpowder' my dear."

"One evening I persuaded her to take a stroll along Chesnut-street with me. Gus was at our heels you may be sure. He passed on a little-a-head determined to speak to her, at all hazzards. She saved him the trouble. Lord love you, Mother Nancy, she spoke to him first."

"Be still Dolph—be still Dolph-ee! Now, Bessie, that's a little too strong! Not the tea, but the story. She so innocent and baby-like speak first to a strange man! Ask me to believe in tea made out of turnip tops will ye?"

"She mistook him for a Mr. Belmont whom she had seen at Bethlehem. He did not undeceive her; until she was completely in his power. He walked by her side that evening up and down Chesnutstreet, for nearly an hour. I saw at once, thather girlish fancy was caught by his smooth tongue, and handsome form. The next night he met us again, and the next, and the next—Lordpity her—the poor child was now entirely at his mercy."

"Ha! ha, Gusty is sich a devil. Put the kettle on the fire, my dear. Let's try a little of the 'Lively.' And how did she—this baby-faced doll—keep these walks secret from the eyes or her folks? Eh? Bessie?"

"Easy as that," replied Bessie, gracefully snapping her fingers. "Every time she went out she told 'father and mother' that she went to see her old aunt. I hinted at first, that our friendship would be more romantic, if concealed from all intrusive eyes. The girl took the hint. Lorrimer with his smooth tongue, told her a long story about his eccentric uncle who had sworn he should not marry, for years to come; and therefore he was obliged to keep his attentions to her. hidden from both of their families. Gusty was dependent on this old uncle, you know? Once married, the old uncle would relent as he beheld the beauty and innocence of the young—*wife!* So Gusty made her believe. You can imagine the whole trap. We had her in our power. Last night she consented to leave her home for Lorrimer's *family* mansion. He was to marry her, the approval of his uncle—that imaginary old gentleman—was to be obtained, and on Christmas Eve, Mr. and—ha, ha, ha—*Mistress* Lorrimer, were to rush into old

Middleton's house, fall on their knees, invoke the old man's blessing; be forgiven and be happy! Hand us the toast Mother Nancy."

"And to-night the girl *did* leave the old folks' house? Entered the door of Monk-hall, thinking it was Lorrimer's *family* mansion, and to-morrow morning at three o'clock will be married—eh? Bess?"

"Married, pshaw! *Over the left.* Lorrimer said he would get that fellow Petriken to personate the parson—Mutchins the gambler, acts the old uncle; you, Mother Nancy must dress up for the kind and amiable grand-ma——suit you to a T? Lorrimer pays high for his rooms you know?"

"'Spose it must be done. It's now after ten o'clock. You left the baby-face sleeping, eh? At half-past two you'll have to rouse her to dress. Be quiet Dolph or I'll scald its head—that's a dear. Now Bessie tell me the truth, did you never regret that you had undertaken the job? The girl you say is so innocent?"

"Regret?" cried Bess with a flashing eye. "Why should I regret? Have I not as good a right to the comforts of a home, to the smile of a father, the love of a mother, as she? Have I not been robbed of all these? Of all that is most sacred to woman? Is this innocent Mary, a whit better than I was when the devil in human shape first dragged me from my home? I feel happy—aye happy—when I can drag another woman into the same foul pit, where I am doomed to lie and rot."

"Yet this thing was so innocent," cried the good old lady, patting Dolph on the head; "I confess I laugh at all qualms—all petty scruples, but you were so different when first I knew you—you Emily, you!"

"Emily," shrieked the other as she sprung suddenly to her feet. "You hag of the devil—call me by that name again, and as God will judge at the last day, I'll throttle you!" She shook her clenched hand across the table, and her eyes were bloodshot with sudden rage. "'Emily!' Your mother called you by that name when a little child," she cried with a burst of feeling, most fearful to behold in one so fallen; "Your father blessed you by that name, the night before you fled from his roof! 'Emily!' Aye, he, the foul betrayer, whispered that name with a smile as he entered the chamber, from which he never came forth again. You remember it old hell-cat, do ye?"

"Not so loud. Good G—d, not so loud," cried the astonished Mother Nancy; "Abuse me Bessie dear, but not so loud; down Dolph don't mind the girl, she's mad—not so loud, I say."

"I can see him now!" cried the fallen girl, as with her tall form raised to its full height, she fixed her flashing eyes on vacancy—"He enters the room—that room with the—the trap-door you know? 'Good night Emily,' he said, and smiled—'Emily,' and—my father had cursed him! I laid me down and rested by another man's side. He thought I slept. Slept! ha, ha! When, with my entire soul, I listened to the footstep in the next room—ha, ha—when I heard the creaking sound of the falling trap, when I drank in the cry of agony, when I heard that name 'Emily, oh Emily,' come shrieking up the pit of death! My father had cursed him, and he died! 'Emily'—oh my God," and she wrung her hands in very agony; "roll back the years of my life, blot out the foul record of my sins, let me, oh God—you are all powerful and can do it—let me be a child again, a little child, and though I crawl through life in the rags of a beggar, I will never cease to bless—oh God—to bless your name."

She fell heavily to her seat, and, covering her face with her hands, wept the scalding tears of guilt and shame.

"'Gal's been a-takin' opium," said the old lady, calmly, "and the fit's come on her. 'Sarves her right. 'Told her never to mix her brandy with opium."

"Did I regret having undertaken the ruin of the girl," said Bess, in a whisper, that made even the old lady start with surprise. "Regret? I tell ye, old hell-dame as ye are, that my very heart strings seemed breaking within me to-night, as I led her from her home."

"What the d——l did you do it for, then? Here's a nice Dolph—eat a piece o' buttered toast—that's a good Dolph-ee."

"When the seducer first assailed me," continued Bess, in an absent tone, "he assailed a woman with a mind stored with knowledge of the world's ways, a soul full as crafty as his own, a wit sharp and keen as ever dropped poison or sweetness from a woman's tongue! But this girl, so child-like, so unsuspecting, so innocent! my God! how it wrung my heart, when I first discovered that she loved Lorrimer, loved him without one shade of gross feeling, loved him without a doubt, warmly, devotedly, with all the trustfulness of an angel soul fresh from the hands of God! Never a bird fell more helplessly into the yawning-jaws of the snake that had charmed it to ruin, than poor Mary fell into the accursed wiles of Lorrimer! And yet I, *I* aided him."

"So you did. The more shame for you to harm sich a dove. Go up stairs, my dear, and let her loose. We'll consent, won't we? Ha, ha! Why Bess, I thought you had more sense than to go on this way. What will become of you?"

"I suppose that I will die in the same ditch where the souls of so many of my vile sisterhood have crept forth from their leprous bodies? Eh, Mother Nance? Die in a ditch? 'Emily' die in a ditch? And then in the next world—ha, ha, ha—I see a big lake of fire, on which souls are dancing like moths in a candle—ha, ha, ha!"

"Reely, gal, you must leave off that opium. Gus promised you some five or six hundred if you caught this gal, and you can't go back now."

"Yes, yes I know it! I know it! Forward's the word if the next step plunges me in hell."

And the girl buried her face in her hands, and was silent again. Let not the reader wonder at the mass of contradictions heaped together in the character of this miserable wreck of a woman. One moment conversing in the slang of a brothel, like a thing lapped from her birth in pollution; the next, whispering forth her ravings in language indicative of the educated woman of her purer days; one instant glorying in her shame, the next recoiling in horror as she viewed the dark path which she had trodden, the dark path she was treading, and the still darker path which she had yet to tread. These paradoxes are things of every day occurrence, only to be explained when the

LORRIMER AND MARY ARLINGTON IN THE ROSECHAMBER.

mass of good and evil found in every human heart, is divided into distinct parts, no more to mingle in one, no more to occasion an eternal contest in the self-warring heart of man.

"Well, well, Bessie, go to bed and sleep a little, that's dear," said the old lady with a pleasing smile. "Opium isn't good for you, and you know it. A leetle nap 'ill do you good Sleep a bit, and then you'll be right fresh for the wedding. Three o'clock you know. Come along, Dolph, mommy must go 'tend to some leetle things about the house, Come along Dolphee. Sleep a leetle, Bessie, that's a dear!"

CHAPTER IX.

A CHAPTER IN WHICH EVERY WOMAN MAY FIND SOME LEAVES OF HER OWN HEART, READ WITH THE EYES OF A HIGH AND HOLY LOVE.

"MARY!"

Oh sweetest name of woman! name by which some of us may hail a wife, or a sister in heaven; name so soft, and rippling, and musical, name of the mother of Jesus, made holy by poetry and religion!—how foully were you profaned by the lips that whispered your sound of gentleness in the sleeper's ear!

"Mary!"

The fair girl stirred in her sleep, and her lips dropped gently apart as she whispered a single word—

"Lorraine!"

"The assumed name of Lorrimer," exclaimed the woman who stood by the bedside. "Gus has some taste, even in his vilest loves! But, with this girl—this child—good Heaven! how refined! He shrunk at the very idea of her voice whispering the name which had been shouted by his devil-mates at a drinking bout! So he told the girl to call him—not Gusty, no no, but something musical—Lorraine!"

And stooping over the couch, the queenly woman, with her proud form arrayed in a dress of snow-white silk, and her raven-black hair gathered in thick tresses along her neck, so full and round, applied her lips to the ear of the sleeper, and whispered in a softened tone—

"Mary! Awake—it is your wedding night!"

The room was still as death. Not a sound save the faint breathing of the sleeper; all hushed and still. The light of the wax candle standing on the table in the centre of the rose chamber—as it was called—fell mild and softened over the hangings of faint crimson, with the effect of evening twilight.

The maiden—pure and without stain—lay sleeping on the small couch that occupied one corner of the closet. Her fair limbs were enshrouded in the light folds of a night-robe, and she lay in an attitude of perfect repose, one glowing cheek resting upon her uncovered arm, while over the other, waved the loosened curls of her glossy hair. The parting lips disclosed her teeth, white as ivory, while her youthful bosom came heaving up from the folds of her night-robe, like a billow that trembles for a moment in the moonlight, and then is suddenly lost to view. She lay there in all the ripening beauty of maidenhood, the light falling gently over her young limbs, their outlines marked by the easy folds of her robe, resembling in their roundness and richness of proportion, the swelling fulness of the rose-bud that needs but another beam of light, to open it into its perfect bloom.

The arching eyebrows, the closed lids, with the long lashes resting on the cheek, the parted lips, and the round chin, with its smiling dimple, all these were beautiful, but oh how fair and beautiful the maiden's dreams! Rosier than her cheek, sweeter than her breath, lovelier than her kiss—lovely as her own stainless soul, on whose leaves was written but one motto of simple meaning—"*Love in life, in death, and for ever.*"

And in all her dreams she beheld but one form, heard the whisper of but one voice, shared the sympathies of but one heart! *He* was her dream, her life, her *God*—him had she trusted with her all, in earth or heaven, him did she love with the uncalculating abandonment of self, that marks the first passion of an innocent woman!

And was there aught of *earth* in his love? Did the fever of sensual passion throb in the pulses of her virgin blood? Did she love Lorrimer because his eye was bright, his form magnificent, his countenance full of healthy manliness? No, no, no! Shame on the fools of either sex, who read the first love of a stainless woman, with the eyes of sense. She loved Lorrimer for a something which he did not possess, which vile worldings of his class never will possess. For the magic with which her fancy had enshrouded his face and form, she loved him for the wierd fascination which *her own soul* had flung around his very existence, for a dream of which *he* was the idol, for a waking trance in which *he* walked as her good angel, for imagination, for fancy, for anything but *sense*, she loved him.

It was her first love.

She knew not that this fluttering fascination, which bound her to his slightest look or tone, like the charmed bird to the lulling music which the snake is said to murmur, as he ensnares his prey, she knew not that this fluttering fascination, was but the blind admiration of the moth, as it floats in the light of the flame, which will at last consume it.

She knew not that in her own organization, were hidden the sympathies of an animal as well as of an intellectual nature, that the blood in her veins only waited an opportunity to betray her, that in the very atmosphere of the holiest love of woman, crouched a sleeping fiend, who at the first whisperings of her wronger, would arise with hot breath and blood-shot eyes, to wreak eternal ruin on her woman's honour.

For this is the doctrine we deem it right to hold in regard to woman. Like man she is a combination of an animal, with an intellectual nature. Unlike man her animal is a *passive* thing, that must be roused ere it will develope itself in action. Let the intellectual nature of woman be the only object of man's influence, and woman will love him most holily. But let him play with her animal nature as you would toy with the machinery of a watch, let him rouse the treacherous blood, let him fan the pulse into quick, feverish throbbings, let him warm the heart with convulsive beatings, and the woman becomes, like himself, but a mere animal. *Sense* rises like a vapour, and utterly darkens *Soul*.

And shall we heap shame on woman, because man, neglecting her holiest nature, may devote all the energies which God has given him, to rouse her gross and earthy powers into action? On whose head is the shame, or whose the wrong? Oh, would man but learn the solemn truth, that no angel around God's throne is purer than woman when her intellectual nature alone is stirred into development, that no devil crouching in the flames of hell is fouler than woman, when her animal nature alone is roused into action. Would man but learn and revere this fearful truth, would woman but treasure it in her inmost soul, then would never a shriek arise to heaven, heaping curses on the betrayer's head, then would never a wrong done to maiden virtue, give the suicide's grave its victim, then in truth, would woman walk the earth, the spirit of light that the holiest lover ever deemed her!

And the maiden lay dreaming of her lover, while the form of the tall and stately woman, stood by the bed-side, like an evil angel, as with a mingled smile and sneer, she bade the girl arise, for it was her wedding night. *Her wedding night!*

"Mary! Awake, it is your wedding night!"

Mary murmured in her sleep, and then opened her large blue eyes, and arose in the couch.

"Has—*he* come?" were the first words she murmured in her musical tones, that came low and softened to listener's ear, "Has *he* come?"

"Not yet, not yet, my dear," said long-haired Bess, assisting the young maiden to rise from the couch, with all imaginable tenderness of manner. "You see Mary love, it's half-past two o'clock and over, and of course, high time for you to dress. Throw back your night-gown my love, and let me arrange your hair. How soft and silky; it needs but little aid from my hands, to render each tress a perfect charm."

"Is it not very strange Bessie," said Mary opening her large blue eyes with a bewildered glance as she spoke.

"What is strange? I see nothing strange except the remarkable beauty of these curls—"

"That I should first meet him, in such a singular manner, that he should love me, that for his sake I should fly to his uncle's mansion, and that you Bessie, my dear good friend, should consent from mere friendship to leave your home and bear me company. All this is very strange, how like the stories we read in a book! And his stern old uncle you say has relented?"

"Perfectly resigned to the match my dear. That's the way with all these relations,—is not that curl perfect?—when they've made all the mischief they can, and find it amounts to nothing, at the last moment they roll up their eyes, and declare with a sigh, that they're *resigned* to the match. And his dear old grandma, she lives here you know? There that is right, your curls should fall in a shower over your snow-white neck. The dear old lady is in a perfect fever to see you! She helped me to get everything ready for the wedding."

"Oh Bessie. Is it not most sad?" said Mary, as her blue eyes shone with a glance of deep feeling, "to think that Albert and you should love one another, so fondly, and after all, that

he should die, leaving you alone in this cheerless world! How terrible! *If* Lorraine should die."

A deep shade of feeling passed over Mary's face, and her lip trembled. Bessie held her head down, for a moment, as her fair fingers, ran twining among the tresses of the bride. Was it to conceal a tear, or a smile?

"Alas! *He* is in his grave! Yet it is the *memory* of his love, that makes me take such a warm interest in your union with Lorraine. This plain fillet of silver, with its diamond star, how well it becomes your brow! You never found a woman, who knew what it was to love, that would not fight for two true hearted lovers, against the world! Do you think, Mary dear, that I could have sanctioned your flight to this house, if my very soul had not been interested in your happiness? Not I! not I! Now slip off your night-gown my dear. Have you seen the wedding-dress?"

"It seems to me," said Mary, whose thoughts dwelt solely on her love for Lorrimer, "that there is something deeply touching in a wedding that is held at this hour of the night! Everything is calm and tranquil; the earth lies sleeping, while Heaven itself watches over the union of two hearts that are all in all to each other."

The words look plain and simple, but the tone in which she spoke was one of the deepest feeling. Her very soul was in her words. Her blue eyes dilated with a sudden enthusiasm, and the colour went and came along her glowing cheek, until it resembled a fair flower, one moment resting in the shade, the next bathing in the sunlight.

"Let me assist you to put on this wedding dress. Is it not beautiful? That boddice of white silk was Lorrimer's taste. To be sure I gave the dress-maker a few hints. Is it not perfect? How gently the folds of the skirt rest on your figure! Why, Mary, you are too beautiful? Well, well, handsome as he is, Lorrimer ought to be half crazy with vanity, when such a bride is hanging on his arm."

A few moments sufficed to array the maiden for the bridal.

Mary stood erect on the floor, blush after blush coursing over her cheek, as she surveyed the folds of her gorgeous wedding dress.

It was in truth a dress most worthy of her face and form. From the shoulders to the waist her figure was enveloped in a boddice of snow-white satin, that gathered over her swelling bosom, with such gracefulness of shape, that every beauty of her form,—the width of the shoulders, and the gradual falling off of the outline of the waist, was clearly perceptible.

Fitting closely around the bust, it gave to view her fair round neck, half-concealed by the drooping curls of glossy hair, and a glimpse of each shoulder, swelling away into the fulness of the virgin bosom, that rose heaving above the border of lace. From the waist downward, in many a fold, but with perfect adaptation to her form, the gorgeous skirt of satin fell sweeping to the floor, leaving one small and tiny foot, enclosed in a neat slipper, that clung to it as though it had grown there, exposed to the eye.

The soft light falling over the rose-hued hangings of the room, threw the figure of the maiden out from the dim back-ground, in gentle and effective prominence. Her brown tresses showering down over each cheek, and falling along her neck and shoulders, waved gently to and fro, and caught a glossy richness from the light. Her fair shoulders, her full bosom, her long but not too slender waist, the downward proportions of her figure, swelling with the full outlines of ripening maidenhood; all arrayed in the graceful dress of snow-white satin, stood out in the dim light, relieved most effectively by the rose-hued hangings, in the back-ground.

As yet her arms, unhidden by sleeve or robe, gave their clear, transparent skin, their fulness of outline, their perfect loveliness of shape, all freely to the light.

"Is it not a gorgeous dress?" said long-haired Bess, as she gazed with unfeigned admiration upon the face and form of the beautiful maiden. "As gorgeous, dear Mary, as you are beautiful!"

"Oh it will be such a happy time!" cried Mary, in a tone that scarcely rose above a whisper, while her blue eyes flashed with a glance of deep emotion; "there will sit my father and there my mother, in the cheerful parlour on Christmas Eve! My father's grey hairs and my mother's kindly face, will be lighted up by the same glow of light. And their eyes will be heavy with tears—with weeping for me, Bessie, their 'lost child,' as they will call me. When behold! the door opens, Lorraine enters with me, his wife, yes, yes, his wife by his side. We fling ourselves at the feet of our father and mother, for they will be ours, then! We crave their forgiveness! Lorraine calls me his wife; we beg their forgiveness and their blessing in the same breath! Oh it will be such a happy time! And my brother he will be there too—he will like Lorraine, for he has a noble heart! Don't you see the picture, Bessie? I see it as plainly as though it was this moment before me, and my father, oh how he will weep when again he clasps his daughter in his arms!"

There she stood, her fair hands clasped trembling together, her eyes flashing in ecstacy, while her heart throbbing and throbbing like some wild bird endeavouring to burst the bars of its cage, sent her bosom heaving into view.

Bessie made no reply. True she attempted some common-place phrase, but the words died in her throat. She turned her head away, and —thank God, she was not yet fallen to the lowest deep of woman's degradation—a tear, big and scalding, came rolling down her cheek.

And while Mary stood with her eyes gazing on the vacant air, with the manner of one entranced, while Bess, poor and fallen woman, turned away her face to hide the falling tear, the curtains that concealed the entrance to the painted chamber were suddenly thrust aside, and the figure of a man came stealing along with a noiseless footstep.

Gus Lorrimer, silent and unperceived, in all the splendour of his manly beauty, stood gazing upon the form of his victim, with a glance of deep and soul-felt admiration.

His tall form was shown to the utmost advantage by a plain suit of black cloth. A dress coat of the most exquisite shape, black pantaloons that fitted neatly around his well-formed limbs, a vest of plain white Marseilles, gathering across the outlines of his massive chest, a snow-white shirt front, and a falling collar, confined by a simple black cravat: such were the brief details of his neat but effective costume. His manly face was all in a glow with health and excitement. Clustering curls of dark brown hair fell carelessly along his open brow His clear, dark hazel eye, gave forth a flashing glance, that failed to reveal anything but the frank and manly qualities of a generous heart. You did not read the villain in his glance. The aquiline nose, the rounded chin, the curving lip, darkened by a graceful moustache, the arching eyebrows, which gave additional effect to the dark eyes; all formed the details of a countenance that ever struck the beholder with its beaming expression of health, soul, and manliness combined.

And as Gus Lorrimer stood gazing in silent admiration upon his victim, few of his boon companions would have recognised, in his thoughtful countenance, the careless though handsome face of the reveller, who gave life and spirit to their drinking scenes.

The truth is, there were two Lorrimers in one. There was a careless, dashing, handsome fellow, who could kill a basket of champagne with any body, drive the neatest 'turn out' in the way of horse flesh that the town ever saw, carry a 'frolic' so far that the watchman would feel bound to take it up and carry it a little farther.—This was the magnificent Gus Lorrimer.

And then there was a tall, handsome man, with a thoughtful countenance, and a deep, dark hazel eye, who would sit down by the side of an innocent woman, and whisper in her ear, in a low-toned voice for hours together, with an earnestness of manner and an intensity of gaze, that failed in its effect, not one in a hundred times. Without any remarkable knowledge derived from education, this man knew every leaf of woman's many-leaved heart, and knew how to apply the revealings, which the fair book opened to his gaze. His gaze, in some cases, in itself was fascination; his low-toned voice, in too many instances, whispered its sentences of passion to ears that heard it to their eternal sorrow. This man threw his whole soul in his every passion. He pleaded with a woman, like a man under the sentence of death pleading for his life. Is it a wonder that he was but rarely unsuccessful? This man, so deeply read in woman's heart, was the 'inner man' of the handsome fellow with the dashing exterior. Assum ing a name, never spoken to his ear, save in the soft whispers of one of his many victims, he styled himself Lorraine Lorrimer.

"Oh, Bessie, is not this love a strange mystery?" exclaimed Mary, as though communing with her own heart. "Before I loved, my soul was calm and quiet. I had no thought beyond my school books; no deeper mystery than my embroidery-frame. Now—the very air is changed. The atmosphere in which I breathe is no longer the same. Wherever I move his face is before me. Whatever may be my thoughts, the thought of him is never absent for a moment. In my dreams I see him smile. When awake, his eyes, so deep, so burning in their gaze—even when he is absent—seem for ever looking into mine. Oh, Bessie—tell me, tell me—is it given to man to adore his God? Is it not also given to woman to adore the one she loves? Woman's *religion* is her *love!*"

And as the beautiful enthusiast, whose mind had been developed in utter seclusion from the world, gave forth the revelations of her heart, in broken and abrupt sentences, Lorrimer drew a step nearer, and gazed upon her with a look in which passion rose predominant, even above admiration.

"Oh, Bessie, can it be that his love will ever grow cold? Will his voice ever lose its tones of gentleness, will his gaze ever cease to bind me to him, as it enchains me now?"

"Mary!" whispered a strange voice in a low and softened murmur.

She turned hastily round, she beheld the arms outspread to receive her, she saw the manly face of him she loved all a-glow with rapture, her fair blue eyes returned his gaze.

"Lorraine," she murmured, in a faint whisper, and then her head rested upon his bosom, while her form trembled in his embrace. "Oh, Lorraine," she again murmured, as, with one fair hand resting upon each arm of her lover, she gazed upward in his face, while her blue eyes shone with all the feeling of her inmost soul. "Oh, Lorraine, will you love me ever?"

"Mary," he answered, gazing down upon her blushing face, as he uttered her name in a prolonged whisper, that gave all its melody of sound to her ear, "Mary, can you doubt me?"

And as there he stood gazing upon that youthful face, now flushed over with an expression of all-trusting love, as he drank in the glance of her large blue eyes, and felt her trembling form resting gently in his arms, the foul purpose of his heart was, for a moment forgotten, for a moment his heart rose swelling within him, and the thought flashed over his soul, that, for the fair creature who hung fascinated on his very look, his life he could willingly lay down.

"Ha, ha," muttered Bess, who stood regarding the pair with a glance of doubtful meaning, "I really believe that Lorrimer is quite as much in love as the poor child! Good idea, that! A man whose heart has been the highway of a thousand loves—a man like this, to fall in love with a mere baby-face! Mary, dear," she continued aloud, too happy to break the reverie which enchained the seducer and his victim. "Mary, dear, hadn't I better help you to put on your wedding robe?"

Lorrimer turned and looked at her with a sudden scowl of anger. In a moment his face resumed its smile.

"Mary," he cried, laughingly, "let me be your costumer, for once. My hands must help you on with your wedding robe. Nay, nay, you must not deny me. Hand me the dress, Bessie."

It was a splendid robe, of the same satin as the other part of her dress. Gathering tightly around her form, it was designed to remain open in front, while the skirt fell trailing along the floor. Falling aside from the bust, whose outlines were so gracefully developed by the tight-fitting boddice of white satin, its opposite sides were connected by interlacing threads of silver cord, crossed and recrossed over the heaving bosom. Long and drooping sleeves, edged with silver lace, were designed to give bewitching glimpses of the maiden's full and rounded arms. In fine, the whole dress was in the style of some sixty years since, such as our grand-dames designated by the euphonious name of "a gown and curricle."

"How well the dress becomes you, Mary!" exclaimed Lorrimer, with a smile as he flung the robe over her shoulders. "How elegant the fall of that sleeve! Ha, ha, Mary, you must allow me to lace these silver cords in front. I'm afraid I would make but an awkward lady's maid. What say you, Bessie? Mary, your arms seem to love the light embrace of these drooping sleeves. You must forgive me, Mary, but I thought the style of the dress would please you, so I asked our good friend Bessie here to have it made. By my soul, you give additional beauty to the wedding dress. Is she not beautiful, Bessie?"

"Most beautiful," exclaimed Bess, as, for the moment, her gaze of unfeigned admiration was fixed upon the bride, arrayed in the full splendour of her wedding robes—"Most beautiful!"

"Mary, your hand," whispered Lorrimer to the fair girl, who stood blushing at his side.

With a heaving bosom, and a flashing eye, Mary slowly reached forth her fair and delicate right hand. Lorrimer grasped the trembling fingers within his own, and winding his unoccupied arm around her waist he suffered her head, with all its shower of glossy tresses, to fall gently on his shoulders. A blush, warm and sudden, came over her face. He impressed one long and lingering kiss upon her lips. They returned the pressure, and clung to his lips as though they had grown there.

"Mary, my own sweet love," he murmured in a low tone, that thrilled to her very heart— "Now I kiss you as the dearest thing to me in the wide world. Another moment, and from those same lips will I snatch the first kiss of my lovely bride! To the wedding room my love!"

Fair and blushing as the dawn, stainless as

the new-fallen snow, loving as one of God's own cherubim, he led her gently from the place, motioning onward with his hand, as again and again he whispered, "To the wedding room my love, to the wedding room!"

"To the wedding room," echoed Bess, who followed in her bridesmaid robes. "To the wedding room—ha, ha, ha, say rather to h—ll!"

There was something most solemn, not to say thoughtful and melancholy, in the appearance of that lonely room. It was wide and spacious, and warmed by invisible means, with heated air. Huge panels of wainscotting covered the lofty walls, and even the ceiling was concealed by massive slabs of dark walnut. The floor was all one polished surface of mahogany, destitute of carpet or covering of any kind. A few high-backed mahogany chairs, standing along the walls, were the only furniture of the place. The entrance to the rose chamber, was concealed by a dark curtain, and in the western and northern walls, were fashioned two massive doors, formed like the wainscotting, of dark and gloomy walnut.

In the centre of the glittering mahogany floor, arose a small table or altar, covered with a drooping cloth, white and stainless as the driven snow. Two massive wax candles, placed in candlesticks of silver, stood on the white cloth of the altar, imparting a dim and dusky light to the room. In that dim light the sombre panelling of the walls and the ceiling, the burnished floor of mahogany, as dark as the walnut-wood that concealed the ceiling and the walls, looked heavy and gloomy, as though the place were a vault of death, instead of a cheerful wedding room.

As yet the place was silent and solitary. The light flickered dimly along the walls, and over the mahogany floor, which shone like a rippling lake in the moonlight. As you gazed upon the desolate appearance of that place, with the solitary wax lights burning like two watching souls, in the centre, you would have given the world to have seen the room tenanted by living beings; in its present stillness and solitude, it looked so much like one of those chambers in olden story, where the ghosts of a departed family were wont to assemble once a year, in order to revive the memories of their lives on earth.

It might have been three o'clock, or even half an hour later, when the western door swung slowly open, and the clergyman, who was to solemnize this marriage, came striding somewhat unsteadily along the floor. Clad in robes of flowing white—he had borrowed them from the theatre—with a prayer book in his hand, Petriken as he glanced uneasily around the room, did not look at all unlike a minister of a particular class. His long, square, lugubrious face, slightly varied by red streaks around each eye, was tortured into an expression of the deepest solemnity. He took his position in silence, near the altar.

Then came the relenting uncle, striding heavily at the parson's heels. He was clad in a light blue coat with metal buttons, a buff vest, striped trowsers, and an enormous scarf, whose mingled colours of blue and gold, gathered closely around his short fat neck. His full-moon face, looking very much like the face of a relenting uncle, who is willing to bestow mercy upon a wild young dog of a nephew, to almost any extent, afforded a pleasant relief to his pear-shaped nose, which stood in the light, like a piece of carved work from a crimson wall. Silently the relenting uncle took his position beside the venerable clergyman.

Then, dressed in solemn black, the respected grandma of the bridegroom, who was in *such* a fever to see the bride, came stepping mincingly along the floor, glancing from side to side with an amiable look that ruffled the yellowish flesh of her colloped cheeks.

The "imperial" on her chin had been softened down, and with the aid of a glossy dress of black silk, and a Tower of Babel cap, she looked quite venerable. Had it not been for a certain twinkle in her eyes, you could have fallen in her arms and kissed her; she looked so much like one of those dear old souls, who make mischief in families and distribute tracts and cold victuals to the poor. The grandma took her position on the left of the clergyman.

And in this position, gathered around the altar, they stood for some five minutes, silently awaiting the appearance of the bridegroom and the bride.

CHAPTER X.

THE BRIDAL.

"I say Mutchy, my boy," said Petriken, in a tone that indicated some lingering effects of his late debauch. "How *do* I do it? Clever hey? D'ye like this face? Good is it? If my magazine fails, I think I'll enter the ministry for good. Why not start a church of my own? When a man's fit for nothin' else, he can always find fools enough to build him a church, and glorify him into a saint—"

"Do you think I do the uncle well?" whispered Mutchins, drawing his shirt collar up from the depths of his scarf, into which it had fallen; "Devilish lucky you gave me the hint in time. 'Been the devil to pay if we'd a-disappointed Gus. What am I to say, Silly. 'Is she not beautiful!' in a sort of an aside tone, and then fall on her neck and kiss her? Eh, Silly?"

"That'll be coming it too strong," said Petriken, smoothing his two-coloured hair. "You're merely to take her by the finger-tips, and start as if her beauty overcame you, then exclaim 'God bless you my love, God bless you—' as though your feelings were too strong for utterance."

"'God bless you, my love,'" echoed Mutchins, "'God bless you,' that will do, hey

Silly! I feel quite an interest in her, already. Now, aunty, my dear and kind-hearted old relative, what in the d—l are you to do?'

"Maybe I'll get up a convulsion or two," said the dear old lady, as her colloped cheeks waggled heavily with a smile—her enemies would have called it a hideous grin. "Maybe I'll do a hysteric or so. Maybe I won't? Dear me, I'm in such a fever to see my little pet of a grand-daughter! Ain't I?"

"Hist!" whispered Petriken. "There they are in the next room. I think I heard a kiss. Hush! Here they come—d—n it, I can't find the marriage ceremony."

No sooner had the words passed his lips, than Lorrimer appeared in the small doorway opening into the rose chamber, and stepped softly along the floor of the walnut room. Mary in all her beauty hung on his arm. Her robe of satin wound round her limbs, and trailed along the floor as she walked. At her side came Long-haired Bess, glancing in the faces of the wedding guests with a meaning smile.

"Nephew, I forgive you. God bless you, my dear—I approve my nephew's choice—God bless you, my dear."

And, as though his feelings overcame him, Mutchins veiled his face in a large red handkerchief, beneath whose capacious shelter he covertly supplied his mouth with a fresh morsel of tobacco.

"And is this 'my grandchild?' Is this the dear pet? How I shall love her? Shan't I, grandson? Oh my precious, how do you do?"

The clergyman saluted the bride with a low bow.

A deep blush came mantling over Mary's face as she received these words of affection and tokens of kindness from the minister and the relatives of her husband, while a slight, yet meaning expression of disgust flashed over Lorrimer's features, as he observed the manner in which his minions and panders performed their parts.

With a glance of fire, Lorrimer motioned the clergyman to proceed with the ceremony.

This was the manner of the marriage.

Hand joined in hand, Lorrimer and Mary stood before the altar. The bridesmaid stood near the trembling bride, whispering slight sentences of consolation in her ear. On the right hand of the clergyman, stood Mutchins, his red round face subdued into an expression of the deepest solemnity; on the other side the vile hag of Monk Hall, with folded arms, and grinning lips, calmly surveyed the face of the young bride.

In a deep-toned voice, Petriken began the sublime marriage ceremony of the Protestant Episcopal Church. There was no hope for the bride now. Trapped, decoyed, betrayed, she was about to be offered up, a terrible sacrifice, on that unhallowed altar. Her trembling tones, joined with the deep voice of Lorrimer in every response, and the marriage ceremony drew near its completion.

"There is no hope for her now," muttered Bess, as her face shone with a glance of momentary compassion. "She is sold into the arms of shame!"

And at that moment, as the bride stood in all her beauty before the altar, her eyes downcast, her long hair showering down over her shoulders, her face warming with blush after blush, while her voice in low tones murmured each trembling response of the fatal ceremony, at the very moment when Lorrimer gazing upon her face with a look of the deepest satisfaction, fancied the fulfilment of the maiden's dishonour, there shrieked from the next chamber, a yell of such superhuman agony and horror, that the wedding guests were frozen with a sudden awe, and transfixed like figures of marble to the floor.

The book fell from Petriken's trembling hands; Mutchins turned pale, and the old hag started backward with sudden horror, while Bess stood as though stricken with the touch of death. Mary, poor Mary, grew white as the grave-cloth, in the face; her hand dropped stiffly to her side, and she felt her heart grow icy within her bosom.

Lorrimer alone, fearless and undaunted, turned in the direction from whence that fearful yell had shrieked, and as he turned he started back with evident surprise, mingled with some feelings of horror and alarm.

There, striding along the floor, came the figure of a young man, whose footsteps trembled as he walked, whose face was livid as the face of a corpse, whose long black hair waved wild and tangled, back from his pale forehead. His eye—Great God! it shone as with a gleam from the flames of perdition.

He moved his trembling lips, as he came striding on—for a moment the word, he essayed to speak, stuck in his throat.

At last with a wild movement of his arms, he shouted in a voice whose tones of horror, mingled with heart-rending pathos, no man would like to hear twice in a life time, he shouted a single word,—

"Mary!"

The bride turned slowly round. Her face was pale as death, and her blue eyes grew glassy as she turned. She beheld the form of the intruder. One glance was enough.

"My brother!" she shrieked, and started forward as though about to spring in the stranger's arms; but suddenly recoiling she fell heavily upon the breast of Lorrimer.

There was a moment of silence—all was hushed as the grave.

The stranger stood silent and motionless, regarding the awe-stricken bridal party, with one settled and burning gaze. One and all, they shrank back as if blasted by his look. Even Lorrimer turned his head aside and held his breath, for very awe.

The stranger advanced another step, and stood gazing in Lorrimer's face.

"*My Sister!*" he cried in a husky voice, and then as if all further words died in his throat, his face was convulsed by a spasmodic movement, and he shook his clenched hand madly in the seducer's face.

"Your name," cried Lorrimer, as he laid the fainting form of the bride in the arms of long-haired Bess, "your name is Byrnewood. This lady is named Mary Arlington. There is some mistake here. The lady is no sister of yours."

"My name," said the other, with a ghastly smile; "ask this pale-faced craven what is my name! He introduced me to you this night by my full name. You at once forgot all but my first name. My name, sir, is Byrnewood Arlington; a name, sir, you will have cause to remember in this world, and—devil that you are—in the next, if you harm the slightest hair on the head of this innocent girl."

Lorrimer started back aghast. The full horror of his mistake rushed upon him—and in that moment, while the fainting girl lay insensible in Bessie's arms; while Petriken, and Mutchins, and the haggard old abbess of the den, stood stricken dumb with astonishment, quailing beneath the glance of the stranger, a long and bony arm was thrust from behind the back of Byrnewood Arlington, the grim face of Devil-bug shone for a moment in the light, and then a massive hand, fell like a weight upon the the wick of each candle, and the room was wrapt in midnight blackness.

Then there was a trampling of feet to and fro, a gleam of light flashed for a moment through the passage, opening into the rose chamber, and then all was dark again.

"They are bearing my sister away," was the thought that flashed over the mind of the brother, as he rushed towards the passage of the rose chamber, "I will rescue her from their grasp at the peril of my life!"

He rushed along, in the darkness, towards the curtain that concealed the entrance into the rose chamber. He attempted to pass beyond the curtain, but he was received in the embrace of two muscular arms, that raised him from his feet as though he had been a mere child, and then dashed him to the floor, with the impulse of a giant's strength.

"Ha, ha, ha !" laughed a hoarse voice, "you don't pass here, mister. Not while 'Bijah's about! No you don't my feller—ha, ha, ha !"

"A light, Devil-bug," exclaimed a voice, that sounded from the centre of the darkened room.

In a moment a light, grasped in the talon fingers of the door-keeper of Monk Hall, flashed around the place. Silent and alone Gus Lorrimer stood in the centre of the room, his arms folded across his breast, while the dark frown on his brow was the only outward manifestation of the violence of the struggle that had convulsed his very soul, during that solitary moment of utter darkness. Calling all the resources of his mind to his aid, he had resolved upon his course of action.

"It is a fearful remedy, but a sure one," he muttered as he again faced Brynewood, who had just risen from the floor, where he had

been thrown by Mr. Abijah K. Jones. "Begone Devil-bug," he continued, aloud, "but wait without and see that Glow-worm and Musquito are at hand," he added, in a meaning whisper. "Now, sir, I have a word to say to *you*," and as he spoke he confronted the brother of the girl whose ruin he had contrived, with the ingenuity of an accomplished libertine, mingled with all the craft of an incarnate fiend.

Aching in every limb from his recent fall, Byrnewood stood pale and silent, regarding the libertine with a settled gaze. In the effort to command his feelings, he pressed his teeth against his lower lip, until a thin line of blood trickled down to his chin.

"You will allow that this is a most peculiar case," exclaimed Gus, with a calm gaze, as he confronted Byrnewood; "one in fact, that demands some painful thought. Will you favour me with ten minutes private conversation ?"

"You are very polite," exclaimed Byrnewood, with a withering sneer. "Here is a man, who commits a wrong, for which h—— itself has no name, and then—instead of shrinking from the sight of the man he has injured, beyond the power of words to tell—he coolly demands ten minutes private conversation."

"It is your interest to grant my request," replied Lorrimer, with a manner as collected as though he had merely said "Pass the bottle, Byrnewood !"

"I presume I must submit," replied Byrnewood; "but after the ten minutes are past, remember, that there is not a fiend in h—ll whom I would not sooner hug to my bosom, than grant one moment's conversation to—a—a—man—ha, ha—a man like you. My sister's honour may be in your power; but remember, that as surely as you wrong her, so surely you will pay for that wrong with your life."

"You, then, grant me ten minutes conversation ? You give me your word that during this period, you will keep your seat, and listen patiently to all that I may have to say ? You nod assent. Follow me, then. A footstep or so this way, will lead us to a pleasant room, the last of this range, where we can talk the matter over."

He flung open the western door of the walnut room, and led the way along a narrow entry, up a stairway with some five steps, and in a moment stood before a small doorway, closing the passage at the head of the stairs. At every footstep of the way, he held the light extended at arm's length, and regarded Byrnewood with the cautious glance of a man who is not certain at what moment a concealed enemy may strike him in the back.

"My library, sir," exclaimed Lorrimer, as pushing open the door, he entered a small oblong room, some twenty feet in length and about half that extent in width. "A quiet little place where I sometimes amuse myself with a book. There is a chair, sir, please be seated."

Seating himself upon a small stool, that stood

near the wall of the room, furthest from the door, Byrnewood with a single glance, took in all the details of the place. It was a smal unpretending room, oblong in form, with rows of shelves along it longest walls, facing each other, supplied with books of all classes, and of every description from the ponderous history to the trashy novel. The other walls at either end were concealed by plain and neat paper. of a modern pattern, which by no means harmonized with the ancient style of the carpet, whose half faded colours glowed dimly in the light, Along the wall of the chamber opposite Byrnewood, extended an old fashioned sofa, wide and roomy as a small sleeping couce ; and from the centre of the place, arose a massive table, fashioned like a chest, with substantial sides of carved oak supplying the place of legs, To all appearance it was fixed, and jointed nto the floor of the room.

BYRNEWOOD DELIVERED TO THE CUSTODY OF THE NEGROES AY LORRIMER.

Altogether the entire room, as its details were dimly revealed by the beams of the flickering lam, wore a cheerless and desolate look, increased by the absence of windows from the walls, and the ancient and worn-out appearance which chacterized the stool, the sofa and the table, the only furniture of the place, There was no visible hearth, and no sign of fire, while the air cold and chilling had a musty and unwholesome taint, as though the room had not been visited or opened for years.

Placing the lamp on the solitary table, Lorrimer, flung himself carelessly on the sofa, and motioned Byrnewood, to draw his seat nearer to the light. As Byrnewood seated himself beside the chest-like table, with his cheeks resting on his hand, the full detals of his countenance, so pale, so colourless, so corpse-like, were disclosed to the keen gaze of Lorrimer. The face of the brother, was perfectly calm, although the large black eyes, dilated with a glance that revealed the soul, turning madly on itself and gnawing its own life, in very madness of thought while from the lips tightly compressed, there still trickled down the same thin line of blood, rendered even more crimson and distinct, by the extreme pallor of the countenance.

"You will at least admit, I have won the wager," said Lorrimer, in a meaning tone, as he fixed his gaze upon the death-like countenance of Byrnewood Arlington.

Byrnewood started, raised his hands suddenly as if about to grasp the libertine by the throat, and then folding his arms tightly over his chest, he exclaimed in a voice marked by unnatural calmness.

"For ten minutes, sir, I have promised to listen to all—all you may have to say. Go on, sir. But do not, I beseech you, tempt me too far."

"Exactly half-past three by my repeater," coolly replied Lorrimer, looking at his watch, "at twenty minutes to four, our conversation ends. Very good. Now, sir, listen to my proposition. Give me your word of honour, and your oath, that when you leave this house, you will preserve the most positive secrecy with regard to—to—everything—you may have witnessed within its walls; promise me this, under your word of honour and your solemn oath, and I will give you my word of honour, my oath, that, in one hour from daybreak, your sister shall be taken to her home, pure and stainless, as when first she left her father's threshold. Do you agree to this?"

"Do you see this hand," answered Byrnewood, with a nervous tremor of his lips, that imparted an almost savage sneer to his countenance. "Do you see this flame? Sooner than agree to leave these walls, without—my—my—without Mary, pure and stainless, mark ye, I would hold this good right hand in the blaze of this lamp, until the flesh fell blackened and festering from the very bone. Are you answered?"

"Excuse me, sir, I was not speaking of any anatomical experiments, however interesting such little efforts in the surgical line, may be to you. I wished to make a compromise———"

"A *compromise*," echoed Byrnewood.

"Yes, a compromise. That melodramatic sneer becomes you well, but it would suit the pantomimist at the Walnut-street Theatre much better. What have I done with the girl, that you or any other young blood about town, would not do, under similar circumstances. Who was it, that entered so heartily into the joke of the sham marriage, when it was named in the oyster cellar? Who was it called the astrologer a knave—a fortune-teller—a catch-penny cheat, when he—simple man!—advised me to give up the girl? I perceive, sir, you are touched. I am glad to observe, that you appreciate the graphic truth of my remarks. You will not sneer at the word 'compromise' again, will you?"

"Oh, Mary! oh, Mary!"—whispered Byrnewood, drawing his arms yet more closely over his breast, as though in the effort to command his agitation, "Mary! Was I placing your honour in the dice-box, when I made the wager with yonder—man? Was it your ruin the astrologer foretold, when he urged this devil to turn back in his career? Was it my voice that cheered him onward in his work of infamy? Oh Mary, was it for *this*, for *this*, that I loved you as brother never loved sister? Was it for this, that I wound you close to my inmost heart, since first I could think or feel? Was it for this, that in the holiest of all my memories, all my hopes, your name was enshrined? Was it for this, that I pictured, again and again, every hour in the day, every moment of the night, the unclouded prospects of your future life? Oh Mary, oh Mary, I may be wrong, I may be vile, I may be sunken as low as the man before me, yet my love for you, has been without spot, and without limit! And now Mary—oh now."

He paused. There was a husky sound in his throat, and the blood trickled faster from his tortured lip.

Lorrimer looked at him silently for a moment and then, taking a small pen-knife from his pocket, began to pare his nails, with a quiet and absent air, as though he did'nt exactly know what to do with himself. He wore the careless and easy look of a gentleman, who, having just dined, is wondering where in the deuce he shall spend the afternoon.

"I say, Byrnie my boy," he cried suddenly, with his eyes fixed on the operations of the knife, "odd, ain't it? That little affair of yours, with Annie? Wonder if she has any brother? Keen cut that."

Had Mr. Lorrimer intended the allusion, about the keenness of the "cut," for Byrnewood instead of his nail-paring knife, the remark would, perhaps, have been equally applicable. Byrnewood shivered at the name of Annie, as though an ague-fit had passed suddenly over him. The "cut" was rather keen, and somewhat deep. This careless kind of intellectual surgery, sometimes makes ghastly wounds in the soul, which it so pleasantly dissects.

"May I ask what will be your course, in case you leave this place, without the lady? You are silent. I suppose there will be a suit instituted for abduction and a thousand legal et ceteras? This place will be ransacked for the girl, and your humble servant will be threatened with the Penitentiary? A pleasant prospect, truly. Why do you look so earnestly at that hand?"

"You have your pleasant prospects, I have mine," exclaimed Byrnewood with a convulsive smile. "You see that right hand, do you? I was just thinking, how long it might be, ere that hand would be reddened with your heart's blood—"

"Poh! poh! Such talk is boyish. D'ye agree to my proposition? Yes or no?"

"You have had my answer."

"In case I surrender the girl to you, will you then promise unbroken secrecy, with regard to the events of this night?"

"I will make no terms whatever with a scoundrel and a coward!" hissed Byrnewood, between his clenched teeth.

"Pshaw! It is high time this mask should be cast aside," exclaimed Lorrimer, as his eye flashed with an expression of triumph, mingled with anger and scorn. "And do you suppose that on any condition, or for any consideration, I would let this fair prize slip from my grasp? Why, innocent that you are, you might have piled oath on oath, until your very breath grew husky in the effort, and still—still despite of all your oaths, the girl would remain mine!'

"Know me as I am! Not the mere man-about-town, not the wine-drinking companion, not the fashionable addle-head you think me, but the *Man of Pleasure!* You will please observe, how much lies concealed in that title. You have talents, these talents have been from childhood, devoted to books, or mercantile pursuits. I have some talent, I flatter myself, and that talent, aided and strengthened in all its efforts by wealth, from very boyhood, has been devoted to pleasure, which, in plain English, means woman.

"Woman, the means of securing her affection, of compassing her ruin, of enjoying her beauty, has been my book, my study, my science, nay my profession from boyhood. And am I to be foiled in one of the most intricate of all my adventures by such a child—a mere boy like you? are you to frighten me, to scare me back in the path I have chosen, to wrest this flower, to obtain which I have perilled so much, are you to wrest this flower from my grasp? You are so strong, so mighty, you talk of reddening your hand in my heart's blood, and all such silly vapouring, that would be hissed by the pit-boys, if they but heard it spouted forth by a fifth-rate hero of the green-room—and yet with all this, *you are my prisoner.*"

"*Your prisoner?*" echoed Byrnewood, slowly rising to his feet.

"Keep cool, sir," cried Lorrimer, with a glance of scorn. "Two minutes of the ten yet remain. I have your word of honour, you will remember. Yes, *my prisoner!* Why, do you suppose for a moment that I would let you go forth from this house, when you have it in your power to raise the whole city on my head? You know that I have placed myself under the ban of the laws by this adventure. You know that the penitentiary would open its doors to enclose me, in case I was to be tried for this affair. You know that popular indignation, poverty and disgrace, stare me in the very eyes, the moment this adventure is published to the world, and yet—ha, ha, ha!—you still think me the egregious ass to open the doors of Monk-hall to you, and pleasantly bid you go forth and ruin me for ever! Sir, you are my prisoner."

"Ha! ha! ha! I will be even with you," laughed Byrnewood. "You may murder me, in the act, but I still have the power to arouse the neighbourhood. I can shriek for help. I can yell out the cry of murder from this foul den, until your doors are flung open by the police, and the secrets of your rookery laid bare to the public gaze."

"Scream, yell, cry out, until your throat cracks! Who will hear you? Do you know how many feet you are standing above the level of the earth? Do you know the thickness of these walls? Do you know that you stand in the tower-room of Monk-hall? Try your voice, by all means, I should like to hear you cry murder or fire, or even hurra for some political candidate, if the humour takes you."

Byrnewood sank slowly into his seat, and rested his cheek upon his hand. His face was even paler than before, the consciousness that he was in the power of this libertine, for life or death, or any act of outrage, came stealing round his heart, like the probings of a surgeon's knife.

"Go on sir," he muttered, biting his nether lip, until the blood once more came trickling down to his chin. "The hour is yours. *Mine will come.*"

"At my bidding, not a moment sooner," laughed Lorrimer, rising to his feet. "Why, man, death surrounds you in a thousand forms, and you know it not. You may walk on death, you may breathe it, you may drink it, you may draw it to you with a finger's-touch, and yet be as unconscious of its presence as a blind man is of a shadow in the night."

Byrnewood slowly from his seat. He clasped his hands nervously together, and his lips muttered an incoherent sound as he endeavoured to speak.

"Do what you will with me;" he cried, in a husky voice, "but oh, for the sake of God, do not wrong my sister!"

"She is in my power," whispered Lorrimer, with a smile, as he gazed upon the agitated countenance of the brother—"She is in my power!"

"Then by the eternal God, you are in mine?" shrieked Byrnewood, as with one wild bound he sprang at the tall form of Lorrimer, and fixed both hands around his throat, with a grasp like that of the tigress when she fights for her young. "You are in my power! You cannot unloose my grasp! Ha—ha—you grow black in the face! Struggle!—struggle! With all your strength you cannot tear my hands from your throat—you shall die like a felon, by the eternal God!"

Lorrimer was taken by complete surprise. The wild bound of Byrnewood had been so sudden, the grasp of his hands was so much like the terrific grasp with which the drowning man makes a last struggle for life, that the handsome Gus Lorrimer reeled to and fro like a drunken man, while his manly features darkened over with a hue of livid blackness as ghastly as it was instantaneous. The struggle lasted but a single moment. With the convulsive grasp tightening around his throat, Lorrimer sank suddenly on one knee, dragging his antagonist with him, and as he sank, extending his arm with an effort as desperate as that which fixed the clenched fingers around his throat, he struck Byrnewood a violent blow with his fist, directly behind the ear. Byrnewood sank senseless to the floor, his fingers unclosing their grasp of Lorrimer's throat, as slowly and stiffly as though they were seized with a sudden cramp.

"Pretty devilish and d——d hasty!" muttered Lorrimer, arranging his cravat and vest; "left the marks of his fingers on my throat, I'll be bound! Hallo—Musquito! Hallo, Glow-worm —here's work for you!"

The door of the room swung suddenly open, and the herculean negroes stood in the doorway, their sable faces agitated by the same hideous grin, while the sleeves of the red flannel shirts, which formed their common costume, rolled up to the shoulders, disclosed the iron sinews of their jet black arms.

"Mark this man, I say——"

"Yes—massa—I doo-es," chuckled Musquito, as his loathsome lips, inclining suddenly downward toward the jaw, on either side of his face, were convulsed by a brutal grin. "Dis nigger nebber mark a man yet, but dat *somefin'* cum ob it."

"Massa Gusty no want de critter to go out ob dis 'ere door?" exclaimed Glow-worm, as the long rows of his teeth, bristling from his thick lips, shone in the light like the fangs of some strange beast, "'spose he go out ob dat door? 'Spose de nigger no mask him head, bad? Ain't Glow-worm, got fist? Hah-hah! 'Sketo, did you ebber see dis chile (child) knock an ox down. Hah-hah!"

"You are to watch outside the door all night," exclaimed Lorrimer, as he stood upon the threshold, "let him not leave the room on the peril of your lives. D'ye mark me, fellows?"

And as he spoke, motioning the negroes from the room, he closed the door, and disappeared.

He had not gone a moment, when Byrnewood, recovering from the stunning effect of the blow which had saved Lorrimer's life, slowly staggered to his feet, and gazed around with a bewildered glance.

"'*On Christmas Eve,*'" he murmured, wildly, as though repeating words whispered to his ear in a dream, "'*On Christmas Eve at the hour of sundown, one of ye will die by the other's hand—the winding sheet is woven and the coffin made!*'"

CHAPTER XI

DEVIL-BUG.

"It don't skeer me, I tell ye! For six long years day and night, it has laid by my side, with its jaw broke, and its tongue stickin' out, and yet I aint a bit skeered! There it is now —on the left side, ye mind—in the light of the fire. Aint it an ugly corpse? Hey? A reel

nasty christian, I tell ye! Jist look at the knees drawed up to the chin, jist look at the eyes, hanging out on the cheeks, jist look at the jaw, all smashed and broke—look at the big, black tongue, stickin' from between the teeth—say it aint an ugly corpse, will ye?

"Sometimes I can hear him groan—only sometimes! I've always noticed when anything bad is a goin' to come across me, that critter groans and groans! Jist as I struck him down, he lays before me now. Whiz—wh-i-z he came down the hatchway—three stories, every bit of it! Curse it, why hadn't I the last trapdoor open? He fell upon the floor, pretty much mashed up, but—but he wasn't dead——

"He riz on his feet. Just as he lays on the floor—in his shirt sleeves, with his jaw broke and his tongue out—he riz on his feet. Didn't he groan? I put him down, I tell ye! Down —down! Ha, what was a sledge-hammer to this fist, in that pertikler minnit? Crack, crack went the spring of the last trap-door— and the body fell—the devil knows where— I don't. I put it out o' my sight, and yet it came back to me, and crouched down at my side, the next minnit. It's been there ever since. If I sleep, or if I'm wide awake, it's there—there—always on my left side, where I hain't got no eye to see it, and yet I do—I do see it. What a cussed fool I was arter all! To kill him, and he not got a cent in his pockets! Bah! Whenever I think of it, I grow feverish. And there he is now, with his ugly jaw. How he lolls his tongue out—and his eyes! Ugh! But I aint a bit skeered. No. Not me. I can bear wuss things than that 'ar."

The light from the blazing coal-fire streamed around the door-keeper's den. Seated close by the grate, in a crouching attitude, his feet drawn together, his big hands grasping each knee with a convulsive clutch, his head lowered on his breast, and his face warmed to a crimson red by the glare of the flame, moistened with thick drops of perspiration, Devil-bug turned the orbless eye-socket to the floor at his left side, as though it was gifted with full powers of sight, while his solitary eye, grew larger and more burning in its fixed gaze, until at last, it seemed to stand out from his overhanging brow, like a separate flame.

The agitation of the man was at once singular and fearful. Oozing from his swarthy brow, the thick drops of sweat fell trickling over his hideous face, moistening his matted hair, until it hung, damp and heavy over his eyebrows. The lips of his wide mouth receding to his flat nose and pointed chin, disclosed the long rows of bristling teeth, fixed as closely together, as though the man, had been suddenly seized with lock-jaw. His face was all one loathsome grimace, as with his blazing eye, fixed upon the fire, he seemed gazing upon the floor at his left with the shrunken and eyeless socket of the other side of his face.

This creature, who sat crouching in the light of the fire, muttering words of strange meaning to himself, presented a fearful study for the christian and philanthropist. His soul was like his body, a mass of hideous and distorted energy.

Born in a brothel, the offspring of foulest sin and pollution. he had grown from very childhood in full and continual sight of scenes of vice, wretchedness and squalor.

From his very birth, he had breathed an atmosphere of infamy.

To him, there was no such thing as good in the world.

His world—his place of birth—his home in infancy—childhood and manhood, his only theatre of action, had been the common house of ill-fame. No mother had ever spoken words of kindness to him; no father had ever held him in his arms. Sister, brother, friends, he had none of these. He had come into the world without a name; his present one, being the standing designation of the successive door-keepers of Monk hall, which he in vain endeavoured to assume, leaving the slang title bestowed on him in childhood, to die in forgetfulness.

Abijah K. Jones he might call himself, but he was Devil-bug still.

His loathsome look, his distorted form, and hideous soul, all seemed to crowd on his memory at the same moment, when the word 'Devil-bug' rang on his ear. That word uttered, and he stood apart from the human race; that word spoken, and he seemed to feel, that he was something distinct from the mass of men, a wild beast, a snake, a reptile, or a devil incarnate—anything but a man.

The same instinctive pleasure that other men may feel in acts of benevolence, of compassion or love, warmed the breast of Devil-bug, when employed in any deed marked by especial cruelty. This word will scarcely express the instinctive impulse of his soul, he loved not so much to kill, as to observe the blood of his victim, fall drop by drop, as to note the convulsive look of death, as to hear the last throattling rattle in the throat of the dying.

For years and years, the instinctive impulse had worked in his own bosom without vent. The murder which had dyed his hands with human blood for the first time, some six years ago, opened wide to his soul, the pathway of crime, which it was his doom and his delight to tread. Ever since the night of the murder, his victim, hideous and repulsive, had lain beside him, crushed and mangled, as he fell through the death trap. The corpse was never absent from his fancy which in this instance had assumed the place of eyesight. Did he sit—it was at his left side. Did he walk—crushed and mangled as it was, it glided with. him. Did he sleep—it still was at his side, ever present with him, always staring him in the face, with all its loathsome details of horror and bloodshed.

Since the night of the murder, a longing desire had grown up, within this creature, to lay another corpse beside his solitary victim. Where there he thought, two corses, ever at his side, the terrible details of the mangled form and crushed countenance of the first, would loose half their horror, all their distinctness. He longed to surround himself with the phantoms of new victims. In the *number* of his crimes he even anticipated pleasure.

It was this man, this deplorable moral monstrosity, who knew no God, who feared no devil, whose existence was one instinctive impulse of cruelty and bloodshed, it was this outlaw of heaven and earth and hell, who held the life of Byrnewood Arlington in his grasp.

"It's near about mornin' and that ere boy ought to have somethin' to eat. A leetle to drink—per'aps? Now sup-pose, I should take him up, a biled chicken and a bottle o' wine. He sits down by the table o' course to eat—I fix his plate on a pertikler side. As he planks down into the cheer, his foot touches a spring. What is the consequence? He git's a fall three stories down the hatchway—reether an ugly tumble and hurts hisself. Sup-pose he drinks the wine? He git's crazy, and won't know nothin' for days. Very pecooliar wine—got it from the doctor who used to come here—dont kill a man, only makes him mad-like. The man with th' poker isn't nothin' to this stuff—Hallo! Who's there?"

"Only me, 'Bijah," cried a woman's voice, and the queenly form of long-haired Bess, with a dark shawl thrown over her bridesmaid's dress, advanced towards the light, "I've just left Lorrimer. He's with the girl, you know; he sent me down here to tell you to keep close watch on that young fellow."

"Jist as if I could'nt do it meself," grunted Abijah in his grindstone voice, "always a orderin' a feller about—that's his way. Spose you cant make yourself useful? Kin you? Then take some biled chicken and a bottle o' wine up to the young chap. Guess he's most starved."

"Shall *I* get the chicken and the wine?" asked Bess, gazing steadily in Abijah's face.

"What the thunder you look in my face that way fur? No you shan't git 'em. Git 'em meself. Wait here till I come back. Don't let any one in without the pass word, 'What hour of the night?' and the answer 'Dinner time,' you know."

And as Devil-bug strode heavily from the den, and was heard going down into the cellars of the mansion, Bess stood silent and erect before the fire, her face, shadowed by an expression of painful thought, while her dark eyes shot a wild glance from beneath her aching brows, suddenly compressed in a frown.

"Some mischief at work, I suppose," she whispered in a hissing voice. "I've sold myself to shame, but not to murder."

A low knock resounded from the front door.

Suddenly undrawing the bolt and flinging the chain aside, Bess gazed through a crevice of the opened door, upon the new comers, who stood beyond the outside door of green blinds.

"Who's there?" she said in a low voice.

"Ha—ha," laughed one of the strangers;

'It's bonny Bess. 'What hour of the night,' is it, my dear?"

"'Dinner time,' you fool," replied the young lady, opening the outside door. "Come in Luke! Ha! There is a stranger with you! Your friend, Luke?"

"Aye, aye, Bessie my love," answered Luke, as he entered the den, with the stranger at his side. "Did ye hear the Devil-bug say whether there was fire in my room? All right, hey? And cards you know, Bess, cards? This gentleman and I want to amuse ourselves with a little game. By-the-bye, where's Fitz Cowles? I should like him to join us. Seen him to-night, my dear?"

"Upstairs you know, Luke," answered Bess, with a meaning smile; "'Veiled figure,' Luke, you know? That's a game above your fancy I should suppose?"

And as she said this with an expressive glance of her dark eye, Bess observed that the stranger who accompanied Luke, was a very tall, stout man, wrapped up in a thick over-coat, whose upraised collar concealed his face to the very eyes. His eyes were visible for a single moment, however, as half-hidden by the shadow of Luke's figure, the stranger strode swiftly across the floor of the den. Bess started with a feeling of terror, akin to the awe one experiences in the presence of a madman, as those eyes, so calm, and yet so burning in their fixed gaze, flashed for a moment in the red light.

"Luke, I am ready," said the stranger, in a smothered voice. "To *the room*, Luke—to *the room!*"

Without a word, Luke led the way from the den, and in a moment Bess heard the half-hushed sound of their footsteps, as they ascended the staircase of the mansion.

"That's a strange eye for a man who's only a-goin to play cards," muttered Bess, as she stood by the fire-place. "Now it's more like the eye of a man who's been playin' all night, and lost his very soul in a game with the d——l! Lord! But that's a wicked eye for a dark night!"

"Here's the biled chicken and the wine," grated the harsh voice of Devil-bug, who approached the fire with a large waiter in his arms.

"Take it up to the feller, Bess. He's hungry p'raps? And d'ye mind gal, set his plate on the side of the table furthest from the door?"

"Any particular reason for that, 'Bijah?"

"Cuss it gal, can't you do it without axing questions! It's only a whim o' mine. That bottle is worth its weight in red goold. Don't taste such Madeery every day, I tell you. Poor fellow, guess he's a-most starved."

"Well, well, I'll take him the chicken and the wine," exclaimed Bess, pleasantly, as she took possession of the waiter with its cold chicken and luscious wine. "Hang it though, when I come to think o'it, why could'nt you have taken it up yourself! 'Bijah, you're growin' lazy."

"Mind gal," grunted Devil-bug as the girl disappeared through the door. "Set his plate on the side of the table furthest from the door.

D'ye hear! It's a whim o'mine, furthest from the door, d'ye hear."

"Furthest from the door," echoed Bess, and in a moment her footsteps resounded with a low pattering noise along the massive staircase.

"The *spring* and the *bottle*," muttered Devil-bug as he resumed his seat beside the fire. "It seems to me, I should like to creep up stairs, and listen at his door, to see how them things work. The niggers is there; but no matter. May be he'll howl, or groan, or do all sorts of ravin's? Gusty did not exactly tell me to do all this, but I guess he'll grin as wide as anybody, when the thing *is* done. It seems to me I should like to see how them things works; It 'ud be nice to listen a bit at his door. Wonder if that gal suspicions anything?"

He rubbed his hands earnestly together, as a man is wont to do under the influence of some pleasing idea, and his solitary eye dilated and sparkled with a glance of the most remarkable satisfaction. A slight chuckle shook his distorted frame, and his lips performed a succession of vivid spasms, which an ignorant observer might have confounded under the general name of laughter.

"Poor feller, guess he's cold without a fire," said the complacent Devil-bug, as he rubbed his hands cheerfully together. "I might build him a little fire. I might—I might—ha! ha! ha!" He arose slowly to his feet, and laughed so loud, that the echoes of his voice resounded from the den, along the hall, and up the staircase of the mansion. "I might try *that*," he cried with a hideous glow of exultation. "Wonder *how that* would *work?*"

Opening the door of a closet on one side of the fire-place, he drew from its depths a small furnace of iron, such as house-wives use for domestic purposes. He placed the furnace in the full light of the fire, surveyed it closely, rubbed his hands pleasantly together yet once more, while a deep chuckle shook his form from head to foot. His face wore an expression of extreme good humour—the visage of a drunken idler, as he flings a penny to a ragged sweep, was nothing in comparison.

"A leetle kindlin' wood," he muttered, drawing to the fire an old sack that had lain concealed in the darkness. "And a leetle charcoal makes a *rougeing* hot fire! Fat pine and charcoal—ha, ha, ha! Rather guess the poor fellow's cold! Now for a light! Cuss it, how the fat pine blazes!"

He waited but a single moment for the wood and charcoal to ignite. It flared up at first in a smoky blaze, and then subsided into a clear and brilliant flame. Seizing the iron handle of the furnace, Devil-bug suddenly raised it from the floor, and rushed from the den, and up the staircase of the mansion, as though his very life hung on his speed. And as he ascended the stairway, the light of the furnace, gradually increasing to a vivid flame, was thrown upward over his hideous face, turning the beetling brow, the flat nose, and the wide mouth with its bristling teeth, to a hue of dusky red. One moment, a he swung the furnace from side to side, you beheld his face and form in a glow of blood-red light, and the next it was suddenly lost to view, while the vessel of iron, with its burning coals, seemed gliding up the stairway, impelled by a single swarthy hand, with fingers like talons, and sinews starting out from the skin like knotted cords.

"Halloo! I didn't know Monk Luke was in his room," he muttered, as he paused for a moment before a massive door, opening into the hall, which extended along the mansion, above the first staircase. "There's a streak of light from the keyhole of his door! And voices inside his room—no matter! The charcoal's a-burnin'—and—wonder how that 'ill work?"

And up the staircase of the mansion he pursued his way, flinging the blazing furnace from side to side, while his face, grew like the visage of a very devil, as again the words rose to his lips,—

"The charcoal's a-burnin'—wonder how that i'll work?"

The light still flickered through the keyhole of the massive door.

Within the sombre panels, it shone over the rich furniture of an apartment, long and wide, with high ceiling and wainscotted walls. There was a gorgeous carpet on the floor, a thickly curtained bed in one corner, a comfortable fire burning in the grate, and a large table standing near the centre of the room, on which a plain lamp, darkened by a heavy shade, was burning. The shade flung the light of the lamp down over the table—it was covered with books, cards, and wine glasses—and around the carpet, for the space of a yard or more, while the other portions of the apartment were enveloped in a faint twilight.

And in that dim light, near the fire, stood two men, steadfastly regarding each other in the face. The snakelike eye of the tall and slender man, was fixed in keen gaze upon the bronzed face of his companion, whose stout and imposing form seemed yet more large and commanding in its proportions, as occasional flashes from the fire-place lighted up the dim twilight. It was a strange thing, to see those large blue eyes, gleaming from the bronzed face, with such a calm and yet burning lustre.

"Luke—to the—the—room," whispered a voice, husky with suppressed agitation.

"He is calm," muttered Luke to himself. "I led him a d—l of a way in order to give him time to command his feelings. He is calm now—and—it's too late to go back."

Extending his hand he reached a small dark lanthorn from the mantelpiece, and walked softly across the floor. Opening the door of a wide closet, he motioned Livingstone to approach.

"You see, this is rather a spacious closet," Luke whispered, as silently drawing Livingstone within the recess, he closed the door, leaving them enveloped in thick darkness. "The back wall of the closet, is nothing less than a portion of the wainscotting of the next room. Give me your hand—it is firm, by G—d. Do you feel

that bolt? It's a little one, but once withdrawn, the panelling swings away from the closet like a door, and—egad!—the next room lays before you!"

While Livingstone stood in the thick darkness of the closet, silent as death, Luke slowly drew the bolt. Another touch, and the door would swing open into the next room. Luke could hear the hard breathing of the merchant, and the hand which he touched suddenly became cold as ice.

As though by mere accident, in that moment of suspense, when their joined fingers touched the bolt, Harvey allowed the door of the dark lanthorn to spring suddenly open. The face of Livingstone, every line and feature, was disclosed in the light, with appalling distinctness. Luke was prepared for a sight of some interest, but no sooner did the light fall on the merchant's face, than he gave a start of involuntary horror. It was as though the face of a corpse, suddenly recalled to life, had risen before him. White and livid, and ghastly, with the discoloured circles of flesh deepening beneath each eye, and with the large blue eyes steadily glaring from the dark eyebrows, it was a countenance to strike the very heart with fear and horror. The firm lip wore a blueish hue, as though the man had been dead for days, and corruption was eating its way through his vitals. Around his high and massive brow, hung his hair, in slight masses; fearful streaks of white resting like scattered ashes, among the locks of dark brown.

"Well, Luke—you—see—I am calm," whispered Livingstone, smiling, with his lips compressed. "I—am—calm."

Luke slowly withdrew the bolt, and closed the door of the lanthorn. The secret door of the wainscotting swung open with a faint noise.

"Listen!" he whispered to Livingstone, as the dark room lay before them. "Listen!"

And with his very breath hushed, Livingstone silently listened. A low sound like a woman breathing in her sleep, came faintly to his ear. Luke felt the merchant start as though he was reeling beneath a sudden blow.

"Give me the dark lanthorn," whispered Livingstone. "The pistols I have!" he continued, hissing the words through his clinched teeth. "The room is dark, but I can discern the outlines of the bed."

He pressed Luke by the hand with a firm grasp, took the lanthorn, carefully closing its door, and strode with a noiseless footstep, into the dark room.

Luke remained in the closet, listening with hushed breath.

There was a pause for a moment, it seemed an age to the listener. Not a sound, not a footstep, not even the rustling of the bed-curtains. All was silent as the grave-vault, which has not been disturbed for years.

Luke listened. He leaned from the closet and gazed into the dark room. It was indeed dark. Not the outline of a chair, or a sofa, or the slightest piece of furniture could he discern

True, near the centre of the place, arose a towering object, whose outlines seemed a shade lighter than the rest of the room. This might be the bed, thought Luke, and again, holding his breath, he listened for the slightest sound.

All was dark and still.

Presently Luke heard a low gurgling noise, like the sound produced by a drowning man. Then all was silent as before.

In a moment the gurgling noise was heard again and a sudden blaze of light streamed around the room.

CHAPTER XII.

THE TOWER ROOM

"MY sister is in his power, for any act of wrong, for any deed of outrage! And I cannot strike a blow in her defence! A solitary wall may separate us—in one room the sister pleads with the villain for mercy—in the other, trapped and imprisoned, the brother hears her cry of agony, and cannot—cannot raise a finger in her behalf! Ha! The door is fast—I hear the hushed breathing of negroes on the other side. I have read many legends of a place of torment in the other world, but what devil could contrive a hell like this?"

He flung himself on the sofa, and covered his face with his hands. The lamp burning dimly on the solitary table, flung a faint and dusky light around the walls of the tower room.

Byrnewood lay in dim shadow, with his limbs thrown carelessly along the sofa, his outspread hands covering his face, while the long curls of his raven-black hair, fell wild and tangled over his forehead. As he lay there, with his dress disordered and his form resting on the sofa, in an attitude which, careless as it was, resembled the crouching position of one who suffered from the cold chill succeeding fever, you might have taken him for an inanimate effigy, instead of a living and breathing man.

No heaving of the chest, no quick and gasping respiration, no convulsive movements of the fingers, indicated the agitation which shook his soul to its centre. He lay quiet and motionless his white hands, concealing his livid face, while a single glimpse of his forehead was visible between the tangled locks of his raven hair.

The silence of the room was broken by the creaking of the door, as it swung slowly open.

Bess silently entered the room, holding the waiter with the cold chicken and bottle of Madeira in her hands. She hurriedly closed the door and advanced to the solitary table. Her face was very pale, and her long dark hair, hung in disordered tresses around her full voluptuous neck. The dark shawl which she had thrown over her bridesmaid's dress, had fallen from her shoulders and hung loosely from her arms as she walked. Her entire appearance betrayed agitation and haste.

"He sleeps!" she murmured, arranging the refreshments—provided by Devil-bug—along the surface of the chest-like table—"Fix his plate on the side of the table furthest from the door"—what could the monster mean? Ha! There may be a secret spring on that side of the table, which the foot of the victim is designed to touch. I'll warn him of his danger—and then, the *bottle*."

She said she would warn Byrnewood of his danger, and yet she lingered about the small table, her confused and hurried manner betraying her irresolution and changeability of purpose. Byrnewood still lay silent and motionless on the sofa. As far from slumber as the victim writhing on the rack, he was still unconscious of the presence of long-haired Bess. His mind was utterly absorbed in the harrowing details of the mental struggle that shook his soul to its foundations.

At first, arranging the knife and plate on one side of the table, and then on the other, now placing the bottle in one position and again in another, it was evident that long-haired Bess was absent, confused and deeply agitated. The side-long glance, which every other instant, she threw over her shoulder at the reclining form of Byrnewood, was fraught with deep and painful meaning. At last, with a hurried footstep, she approached the sofa, and glancing cautiously at the door, which hung slightly ajar, she laid her hand lightly on Byrnewood's shoulder.

"I come to warn you of your danger," she whispered in his ear.

Byrnewood looked up in wonder and then an expression of intolerable disgust impressed every line of his countenance.

"Your touch is pollution," he said, shaking her hand from his shoulder. "You were one of the minions of the villain. You plotted my sister's dishonour."

"I come to warn you of your danger!" whispered Bess, with a flashing eye. "You behold refreshments spread for you on yonder table. You see the bottle of wine. On peril of your life don't drink anything—"

"But rale good brandy," grated a harsh voice at her shoulder. "Liqu-ood hell-fire for ever! That's the stuff, my feller! Ha! ha! ha!"

With the same start of surprise, Byrnewood sprang to his feet, and Bess turned hurriedly around, while their eyes were fixed upon the face of the new-comer.

Devil-bug. hideous and grinning, with the furnace of burning coals in his hand, stood before them. His solitary eye rested upon the face long-haired Bess with a meaning look, and his visage passed through the series of spasmodic contortions peculiar to his expressive features, as he stood swinging the furnace from side to side.

"You can go, Bessie, my duck," he said, with a pleasant way of speaking, original with himself. "This 'ere party don't want you no more. You see, my feller citizen," he continued, turning to Byrnewood, "yer humble servant thought you might be hungry, so he sent you suffin' to eat. Thought you might be cold; so he brung you some coals to warm yesself. You can retire, Bessie!"

He gently led her to the door, fixing his eye upon her face, with a look, as full of venom as a spider's sting.

"You'd a-spilt it all—would yo'?" he hissed the whisper in her ears as he pushed her from the room, "good night, my dear," he continued aloud, "You better go home. Your mammy' a waitin' tea for you. Now I'll make you a little bit o' fire, mister, if you please,"

"Fire?" echoed Byrnewood, "I see no fireplace."

"That's all you know about it,," answered Devil-bug, swinging the furnace from side to side "You think them 'are's books do you? **Look** a little closer, next time. The walls are only

LORRIMER CAPTIVATES MARY ARLINGTON'S IMAGINATION.—*Page* 54.

painted like books and shelves—false book-cases you see. And then there's glass doors, just like real book-cases. They did it in the old times—them queer old chaps as used to keep house here, all alone to themselves. Nice fireplace, aint it?"

He opened two folding leaves of the false book-case near the centre of the wall opposite the door, and a small fire-place neatly white-washed and free from ashes or the remains of any former fire, became visible. Stooping on his knees, Devil-bug proceeded to arrange the furnace in the hearth, while the half-closed folding leaves of the book-case, well nigh concealed him from view.

"A false bookcase on either side of the room! Ha! Books of all classes, painted on the panels within the sashes, with inimitable skill! They deceived me in the dim light of yonder lamp. What can this mean? By my life, I shrewdly suspect that these bookcases, conceal secret passages leading from this den."

Byrnewood flung himself on the sofa, and again covered his face with his hands.

"Blazes up quite comfortable," muttered Devil-bug, as half concealed by the folding doors of the central part of the bookcase, he stooped over the furnace of blazing coal, warming his hands in the flame. "A nice fire, and a nice fire-place. But I'll have to discharge my bricklayer for one thing; got him to fix up this hearth not long ago—scoundrel walled up the chimbley. Did ye ever hear of sich rascality? Konsekence is, this young genelman will be rather uncomfortable a'cause the charcoal smoke wont find no vent. If I should happen to shut the door right tight he might die. He might so. Things jist as bad have happened afore now. He might die. Ha—ha—ha," he chuckled as ne retired from the fire-place, screening the blazing furnace with the half-closed doors of the book-case.—"Wonder how that'll work."

He approached the side of Byrnewood, with that same hideous grin distorting his features, but had not advanced two steps, when he started backward with a movement of involuntary horror.

"Look here, you sir," he whispered, grasping Byrnewood by the arm. "Jist look here a minnit. You see the floor at my left side, do you? Now tell us the truth, aint there a dead man layin' there? His jaw broke and his tongue out? Not that I'm afeered, but I wants to satisfy my mind. Jist take a good look while I hold still."

"I see nothing but the carpet," answered Byrnewood with a look of loathing, as he observed this strange being, standing before him, motionless as a statue, while his left hand pointed to the floor, "I see nothing but the carpet."

"Don't see a dead man, with his knees drawed up to his breast, and his tongue stickin' out? Well that's queer. I'd take my book oath, that the feller was a lyin' there, nasty as a snake. Hows'ever refresh yourself, young man. There's plenty to eat and drink and—" he pointed to the hearth as he spoke. "There's a nice comfortable fire. Good charcoal—and—I wonder how that'll work."

Closing the door, he stood in the small recess at the head of the stairs, leading to the tower-room. The huge forms of the negroes, Musquito and Glow-worm, were flung along the floor, while their hard breathing indicated that they slumbered on their watch. Listening intently for a single moment, at the door of the tower-room, Devil-bug slowly turned the key in the lock, and then withdrawing it from the keyhole placed it in his pocket. He stepped carefully over the forms of the sleeping negroes, and passed his hands slowly along the panelling of the recess, opposite the door.

"The spring—ha, ha—I've found it," he muttered in the darkness. "The bookcases

don't conceal no passage between the walls of this 'ere tower, and the room itself, do they? O'course they do not. Quiet little places where a feller can say his prayers and eat ground nuts. Ha, ha, ha! I must see how that 'ill work."

The panelling slid back as he touched the spring and Devil-bug disappeared into the secret recess or passage, between the false bookcases and the massive walls of the tower, as the solitary chamber, rising from the western wing of Monk-hall, was termed in the legends of the place.

Meanwhile, within the tower-room, Byrnewood Arlington paced slowly up and down the floor, his arms folded, and his face impressed with a fixed expression that forced his lips tightly together, darkened his brow in a settled frown, and drove the blood from his entire visage, until it wore the livid hues of death.

"My sister in his power! Last night she was pure and stainless—to-morrow morning dawns and she will be a thing stained with pollution—dishonoured by a hideous crime! No lapse of time—no prayers to Heaven—no bitter tears of repentance can ever wash out the foul stains of her dishonour. And I am a prisoner, while she shrieks for help and shrieks in vain."

As Byrnewood spoke, striding rapidly along the floor, a grateful warmth began to steal rapidly around the room, dispelling the chill and damp which seemed to infect the very air with an unwholesome taint.

"And we have been children together! I nave held her in these arms when she was but a babe—a smiling babe, with golden hair and laughing cheeks! And then when she left home for school how it wrung my soul to part with her! So young—so light-hearted—so innocent! Three years pass—she returns grown up into a lovely girl—whose pure soul, a very devil would not dare to tarnish, she returns to bless the sight of her father and her mother with her laughing face, and she is—dishonoured! I never knew the meaning of the word till now—dishonoured by a villain."

He flung himself on the sofa, and covered his face with his hands.

"And yet I—I wronged an innocent girl, because she was my father's servant! Great God; can she have a brother to feel for her ruin? My punishment is just, but Mary, oh! whom did she ever harm, whom could she ever wrong?"

He was silent again. And while his brain was tortured by the fierce struggles of thought, while the memories of earlier days came thronging over his soul—the image of his sister, present in every thought, and shining brightest in each old time, he could feel the grateful heat which pervaded the atmosphere of the room, restoring warmth and comfort to his limbs, while the blood flowed more freely in his veins.

There was a long pause in which his very soul was absorbed in a delirium of thought. It may have been the effect of internal agitation, or the result of his half-crazed intellect acting on his physical system, but after the lapse of a few minutes, he was aroused from his reverie by a painful throbbing around his temples, which, for a single moment, destroyed all consciousness, and just as suddenly restored him to a keen and terrible sense of his appalling situation. Now his brain seemed to swim in a wild delirium, and in a single instant, as the throbbing around his temples grew more violent, his mental vision, seemed clearer and more vigorous than ever.

"I can scarcely breathe!" he muttered, as he fell back on the sofa, after a vain attempt to rise. "There is a hand grasping me by the throat, I feel the fingers clutching the veins with the grasp of a demon. My heart, ah! it is turning to ice—to ice, and now it is fire! My heart is a ball of flame—the blood boils in my veins."

He sprung to his feet with a wild bound, and his hands clutched madly at his throat, as though he would free the veins from the grasp of the invisible fingers which were pressing through the very skin.

He staggered to and fro along the floor, with his arms flung overhead, as if to ward off the attacks of some invisible foe.

His face was ghastly pale one moment, the next it flushed with the hues of a crimson flame. His large black eyes dilated in their glance, and stood out from the lids as though they were about to fall from their sockets. His mouth distended with a convulsive grimace, while his teeth were firmly clenched together. One instant his brain would be perfectly conscious in all its operations, the next his senses would swim in a fearful delirium.

"My God—my God!" he shouted in one of those momentary intervals of consciousness, as he staggered wildly along the floor; "I am dying—I am dying! My breath comes thick and graspingly—my veins are chilled. Ha, ha, they are turned to fire again."

Even in his delirium he was conscious of a singular circumstance. A portion of the panneling of the false bookcase, along the wall opposite the fire, receded suddenly within the sash of the central glass-door, leaving a space of black and vacant darkness. The aperture was in the top of the book case, near the ceiling of the room.

Turning towards the hearth, Byrnewood endeavoured to regain the sofa, but the room seemed swimming around him, and with a wild movement he again staggered toward the bookcase opposite the fire.

He started backward as a new horror met his gaze.

A hideous face glared upon him from the aperture of the book-case, like some picture of a fiend's visage, suddenly thrust against the glass-door of the book-case.

A hideous face, with a single burning eye, with a wide mouth distending in a loathsome grin, with long rows of fang-like teeth, and a protuberent brow, overhung by thick masses of matted hair. This face alone was visible, surrounded by the darkness which marked the outline of the aperture. It was, indeed, like a hideous picture framed in ebony, although you could see the muscles of the face in motion, while the flat nose was pressed against the glass of the bookcase, and the thick lips were now tightly closed, and again distending in hideous grin.

"Ho! ho! ho!" a laugh like the shout of a devil came echoing through the glass, faint and subdued, yet wild and terrible to hear. "The charcoal—the charcoal! wonder how *that'll work!*"

Byrnewood stood silent and erect, while the throbbing of his temples, the gasping of his breath, and the deadening sensation around his heart subsided for a single moment.

The full horror of his situation rushed upon him. He was dying by the gas escaping from charcoal, in a room rendered impervious to the air, closed and sealed for the purpose of this horrible death.

A brilliant idea flashed across his brain.

"I will overturn the furnace," he muttered, rushing towards the earth, "I will extinguish the flame!"

With a sudden bound he sprang forward, but in the very action he fell to the floor like a drunken man.

His breath came in thick convulsive gasps, his heart grew like a mass of fire, while his brain was tortured by one intense and agonizing throb of pain, as though some invisible han had wound a red hot wire round his forehead. He lay on the floor, with his outspread hands grasping the air in the effort to rise.

"It works—it works!" shouted the voice of Devil-bug, as his loathsome countenance was pressed against the glass-door of the book-case. "Ha! ha! ha! he is on the floor—he cannot rise—he is in the clutch of death. How the poor feller kicks and scuffles!"

A wild—wild shriek echoing from a distant room came faintly to Byrnewoods ear. That sound of a woman's voice, shrieking for help in an emphasis of despair, aroused the dying man from the spell which began to deaden his senses.

"It is my sister's voice!" he exclaimed, springing to his feet with a last effort of strength, "she is in the hands of the villain, I will save her—I will save her."

"The sister outraged! The brother murdered!" shouted Devil-bug, through the glass door —"I wonder how *that'll work!*"

Byrnewood rushed towards the door, it was locked and secured. All hope was vain. Die, whilst his sister's shriek for aid rang on his ears —die, with the loathsome face of his murderer pressed against the glass—while his blazing eye feasted on his last convulsive agonies—die, with youth on his brow, with health in his heart! die, with all purposed vengeance for his sister's wrongs unfulfilled; die, by no sudden blow, by no dagger thrust—by no pistol shot, but by the most loathsome of all deaths—by suffocation.

"Ha, ha!" the thought flashed over his brain—"the hangman's rope were a priceless luxury to me in this dread hour."

Staggering slowly along the floor, with footsteps as heavy as though he had leaden weights attached to his feet, he approached the chest-like table, and with a faint effort to recover his balance, sunk down on the floor in a crouching position, while his outspread hands clutched faintly at the air.

In a moment he rolled slowly from side to side, and lay on his back, with his face to the ceiling and his arms extended on either side. His eyes were suddenly covered with a glassy film, his lower jaw separated from the upper, leaving his mouth wide open, while the room grew warmer—the air more dense and suffocating.

"Help—help!" murmured Byrnewood, in a smothered voice, like the sound produced by a man throttled by nightmare. "Help—help!"

"By-a-baby, go to sleep, that's a good feller;" the voice of Devil-bug came like a faint echo through the glass; "a drop from the bottle 'ud do you good, and, jist reach your right hand a leetle bit further. There ain't no spring there, I suppose? ain't there? Ho-ho-ho."

And Brynewood could feel a delicious languor stealing over his frame as he lay there on the floor, helpless and motionless, while the voice of Devil-bug rang in his ears. The throbbing of his temples had subsided, he no more experienced the quick gasping struggle for breath, his heart no more passed through the quick transitions from cold to heat, from ice to fire, his veins no more felt like streams of molten lead. He was sinking quietly in a soft and pleasing slumber. The film grew more glassy in each eye, his jaws hung further apart, and the heaving of his chest subsided, until a faint and tremulous motion was the only indication that life had not yet fled from his frame. His outspread arms seemed to grow stiffened and dead as he rested on the floor, while the joints of the fingers moved faintly to and fro, with a fluttering motion that afforded a strange contrast to the complete repose of his body and limbs. His feet were pointed upward, like the feet of a corpse arrayed for burial.

The dim light burning on the chest-like table afforded a faint light to the ghastly scene. There were the untouched refreshments, the cold chicken and the bottle of wine, giving the place the air of a quiet supper-room, there were the false book-cases, indicating a resort for meditation and study, there was the cheerful furnace, its glowing flame flashing through the half-closed doors, speaking a pleasant tale of fireside joys and comforts, and there, along the carpet, stiffening and ghastly lay the form of Byrnewood Arlington, slowly and quietly yielding to the slumber of death, while a hideous face peered through the glass-door, all distorted by a sickening grimace, and a solitary eye, that gleamed like a live coal, drank in the tremulous agonies of the dying man.

"Reach his hand a leetle bit further—that's a good feller. Won't have no tumble down three stories, nor nothin' if his fingers touch the spring? Ho-ho! Jist look how his fingers tremble—He, he, he! Hallo! He's on his feet agin'!"

With the last involuntary struggle of a strong man wrestling for his life, Byrnewood Arlington sprang to his feet, and reaching forth his hand with the same mechanical impulse that had raised him from the floor, he seized the bottle of wine; he raised it to his lips, and the wine poured gurgling down his throat.

"Hain't got no opium in, I suppose? Not the least mossel. Cuss it, how he staggers! Believe on my soul he's comin' to life agin'."

Byrnewood glanced around with a look of momentary consciousness. The drugged wine for a single moment created a violent re-action in his system, and he became fully sensible of the awful death that awaited him. He could feel the hot air warming his cheek, he could see the visage of Devil-bug peering at him through the glass-door, and the danger which menaced his sister came home like some horrible phantom to his soul. He felt in his very soul that but a single moment more of consciousness would be permitted him for action. That moment past, and the death by charcoal would be quietly and surely accomplished.

"Keep me, oh Heaven!" he whispered as his mind ran over various expedients for escape. "Aid me, in this, my last effort, that I may live to avenge my sister's dishonour."

It was his design to make one sudden and desperate spring toward the glass-door, through which the hideous visage of Devil-bug glared in his face and as he madly dashed his hands through the glass, the room would be filled with a current of fresh air.

This was his resolve, but it came too late. As he turned to make this desperate spring, his heel pressed against an object resembling a nail or spike, which has not been driven to the head, in the planking of a floor, but suffered to remain half-exposed and open to the view.

And yet the very moment Byrnewood's heel pressed against the trifling object, the floor on which he stood gave way beneath him, with a low rustling sound; half of the chamber was changed into one black and yawning chasm, and the lamp standing on the table suddenly disappeared, leaving the place wrapped in thick darkness.

Another moment passed, and while Byrnewood reeled in the darkness, on the verge of the sunken trap-door, a hushed and distant sound echoed far below, as from the depths of some deep and dismal well. The lamp had fallen in the chasm, and the faint sound heard far, far below, was the only indication that it had reached the bottom of the gloomy void, sinking down like a well into the cellars of Monk-hall.

Byrnewood tottered on the verge of the chasm, while a current of cold air came sweeping upward from its depths. The foul atmosphere of the tower-room lost half its deadly qualities in a single moment as the cool air, came rushing from the chasm.

Byrnewood felt the effects of the charcoal rapidly passing from his system, and his mind regained its full consciousness as his hot brow received the freshening blast of winter air, pouring over the parched and heated skin.

But the current of pure air came too late for his salvation. Tottering in the darkness, on the very verge of the sunken trap-door, he made one desperate struggle to preserve his balance, but in vain; for a moment his form swung to and fro, and then his feet slid from under him, and then with a maddening shriek, he fell.

"God save poor Mary!"

How that last cry of the doomed man shrieked around the paneled walls of the tower-room.

"Wonder how *that'll work!*" the hoarse voice of Devil-bug shrieked through the darkness. "Down—down—down, ha! ha! Three stories down—down—down! I wonders how that'ill work!"

Separated from the tower room by the glass-door, Devil-bug pressed his ear against the glass, and listened for the death groans of the doomed man.

A low moaning sound, like the groan of a man who trembles under the operations of a surgeon's knife came faintly on his ear. In a moment Devil-bug thought he heard a sound like a door suddenly opened, and then the murmur of voices whispering some quick hurried words, resounded along the tower-room. Then there was a subdued noise like a man struggling on the brink of the chasm, and then a hushed sound, that might have been taken for the tread of a footstep mingled with the closing of a door, came faintly through the glass of the book-case.

Gliding silently from the secret recess behind the panneling of the tower-room, Devil-bug stepped over the forms of the slumbering negroes and descended the stairway leading to the walnut-room. The scene of the wedding was wrapt in midnight darkness. Passing softly along the floor, Devil-bug reached the entrance to the rose chamber, and flung the hangings aside with a cautious movement of his talon-like fingers.

"I merely wanted a light," exclaimed Devil-bug, as he stood gazing into the rose chamber; "but here's a candle, and a purty sight into the bargain."

He disappeared through the doorway, and after the lapse of a few moments again emerged into the walnut-room, holding a lighted candle in his hand.

"Amazin' circumstance that," he chuckled, as he strode across the glittering floor. "The brother *fell* in that 'are room, and the sister *fell* in that, about the same time. They *fell* in different ways though. Strange world this;

let's see what become of the brother—charcoal and opium, ho! ho! ho!"

Before another moment had elapsed, he stood before the door of the tower-room. Musquito and Glow-worm still slumbered on their watch, their huge forms and hideous faces dimly developed in the beams of the light which the doorkeeper carried in his hand. Devil-bug listened intently for a single moment, but not the slightest sound disturbed the silence of the tower-room.

He opened the door, he strode along the carpet, he sood on the verge of the chasm produced by the falling of the death-trap.

"Down—down! three stories, and the pit below; ah! let me hold the light a leetle nearer. Every trap-door is open—he is safe enough. Think I see suffin' white a flutterin' away down there! Hollered pretty loud as he fell—devilish ugly tumble—guess it'ill work quite nice for Lorrimer!"

Stooping on his knees with the light extended in his right hand, he again gazed down the hatchway, his solitary eye flashing with excitement as he endeavoured to pierce the gloom of the dark void beneath.

"He's gone to see his friends below! Sartin sure. No sound—no groan—not even a holler!"

Arising from his kneeling position, Devil-bug approached the recess of the fire-place. On either side, a plain panel of oak concealed the secret nook behind the false book-case. Placing his hand cautiously along the panel to the right, Devil-bug examined the details of the carving in each corner, and along its side, with a careful eye.

"Hasn't been opened to-night," he murmured. "Leads to the walnut-room, by a round-about way. Convenient little passage, if that fool had only knowed on it!"

In an instant he stood outside of the tower-room door, holding the key in one hand, and the candlestick in the other.

"Git up, you lazy d——ls!" he shouted, bestowing a few pointed kicks upon the carcasses of the sleeping negroes. "Git up, and mind your eyes, or else I'll pick 'em out o' your heads to play marbles with."

Glow-worm arose slowly from the floor, and Musquito, opening his eyes with a sleepy yawn, stared vacantly in the doorkeeper's face.

"D'ye hear me? Watch this feller, and see that he don't escape. He's a sleepin' now, but there's no knowin'—Watch! I say, watch!"

He shuffled slowly along the narrow passage, looking over his shoulder at the grinning negroes as he passed along, while his face wore its usual pleasant smile, as he again muttered in his hoarse tones,—

"Watch him, ye dogs! I say, watch him!"

Another moment, and he stood before the entrance of the rose-chamber, holding the curtaining aside, while his eyes blazed up with an expression of malignant joy. He raised the light on high, and stood silently gazing through the doorway, as though his eyes beheld a spectacle of strange and peculiar interest.

And while he stood there chuckling pleasantly to himself, with the full light of the candle flashing over his loathsome face, two figures stood crouching in the darkness, along the opposite side of the room, and the eastern door hung slightly ajar, as though they had entered the place but a moment before.

Once or twice Devil-bug turned as though the sound of suppressed breathing struck his ear, but every time the shadow of the candle fell along the opposite side of the room, the crouching figures were concealed from view.

"Quite a pictur," chuckled Devil-bug, as he again gazed through the doorway of the rose-chamber; "a nice little gal and a handsome feller! Ha, ha, ha."

He disappeared through the curtaining while his pleasant chuckle came echoing through the doorway with a sound of continued glee, as though the gentleman was highly amused by the spectacle that broke on his gaze.

The silence of the rose-chamber was broken by the tread of a footstep, and the figure of a man came stealing through the darkness with the form of a queenly woman by his side.

"Advance and save your sister's honour," the deep-toned whisper broke thrillingly on the air.

The man advanced with a hurried step, flung the curtain hastily aside and gazed within the rose-chamber.

The horror of that silent gaze would be ill-repied by an eternity of joy.

CHAPTER XIII.

THE CRIME WITHOUT A NAME.

"My brother consents? · Oh, joy, Lorraine—he consents!"

"Your brother consents to our wedding, my love."

"How did he first discover that the wedding was to take place to-night?"

"It seems that for several days he has noticed you walking out with Bess. You see, Mary, this excited his suspicions; he watched you with all a brother's care, and to-night tracked Bess and you, to the doors of this mansion. He was not certain, however, that it was you whom he saw enter my uncle's house."

"And so he watched all night around the building? Oh, Lorraine, he is a noble brother!"

"At last grown feverish with his suspicions, he rung the bell, aroused the servant, and when the door was opened rushed madly up stairs, and reached the wedding room. You know the rest. After the matter was explained to him, he consented to keep our marriage secret until Christmas eve; he has left the house satisfied that you are in the care of those who love you. To-morrow, Mary, when you have recovered from the effects of the surprise—which your brother's sudden entrance occasioned—to-morrow we will be married!"

"And on Christmas eve, hand linked in hand, we will kneel before our father and ask his blessing."

"One kiss, Mary, love—one kiss, and I will leave you for the night."

And leaning fondly over the fair girl, who was seated on the sofa, her form enveloped in a flowing night-robe, Lorrimer wound his right arm gently around her neck, bending her head slowly backward in the action, and suffering her rich curls to fall showering on her shoulders, while her upturned face, all radiant with affection lay open to his burning gaze, and her ripe lips dropped slightly apart, disclosing the ivory teeth, seemed to woo and invite the pressure of his kiss.

One kiss silent and long, and the lover and the fair girl seemed to have grown to each other's lips.

The wax light standing on the small table of the rose-chamber, fell mild and dimly over this living picture of youth and passion.

The tall form of Lorrimer clad in solemn black, contrasting forcibly with the snow-white robes of the maiden, his arms flung gently around her neck, her upturned face half hidden by the falling locks of his dark brown hair, their lips joined and their eyes mingling in the same deep glance of passion, while her bosom rose heaving against his breast, and her arms half upraised seemed about to entwine his form in their embrace—it was a moment of pure and hallowed love on the part of the fair girl, and even the libertine for an instant forgot the vileness of his purpose, in that long and silent kiss of stainless passion.

"Mary!" cried Lorrimer, his handsome face flushing over with transport, as silently gliding from his standing position he assumed his seat at her side; "oh, that you were mine! We would flee togethe. rom the heartless world—in some silent and shadowy valley, we would forget all but the love which made us one."

"We would seek a home, quiet and peaceful as that which this book describes," whispered Mary, laying her hand on Bulwer's play of the Lady of Lyons. "I found the volume on the table, and was reading it when you came in. Oh, it is all beauty and feeling. You have read it Lorraine?"

"Again and again, and have seen it played a hundred times; 'The home, to which could love fulfil its prayer, this hand would lead thee,'" he murmured, repeating the first lines of the celebrated description of the Lake of Como, "and yet Mary this is mere romance—a creation of the poet's brain—a fiction as beautiful as a ray of light, and as fleeting. I might tell you a story of a real valley and a real lake—which I beheld last summer, where love might dwell for ever, and dwell in eternal youth and freshness."

"Oh, tell me—tell me," cried Mary, gazing in his face with a look of interest.

"Beyond the fair valley of Wyoming, of which so much has been said and sung, there is a high and extensive range of mountains, covered with thick and gloomy forests. One day last September, when the summer was yet in its freshness and bloom, towards the hour of sunset, I found myself wandering through a thick wood that covered the summit of one of the highest of these mountains. I had been engaged in a deer hunt all day—had strayed from my comrades—and now as night was coming on, was wandering along a winding path, that led to the top of the mountain."

Lorrimer paused for a single instant, and gazed intently in Mary's face. Every feature was animated with sudden interest, and a warm flush hung freshly on each cheek.

And as Lorrimer gazed upon the animated face of the innocent girl, marking its rounded outlines, its hues of youth and loveliness, its large blue eyes beaming so gladly upon his countenance, the settled purpose of his soul, came home to him like a sudden shadow darkening over a landscape, after a single gleam of sunlight.

It was the purpose of this libertine to dishonour the stainless girl before he left her presence.

Before day-break she would be a polluted thing, whose name, and virtue, and soul, would be blasted for ever.

In that silent gaze, which drank in the beauty of the maiden's face, Lorrimer arranged his plan of action. The book which he had left upon the table, the story which he was about to tell, were the first intimations of his atrocious design. While enchanting the mind of the maiden with a story full of romance, it was his intention to awake her animal nature into full action. When her veins were all alive with fiery pulsations, when her heart grew animate with sensual life, when her eyes swam in the humid moisture of passion, then she would sink helplessly into his arms, and like the bird to the snake, flutter to her ruin.

"'Force'—'violence!' These are but the tools of grown-up children, who know nothing of the mystery of woman's heart,' the thought flashed over Lorrimer's brain, as his lip wore a very slight but meaning smile. "I have deeper means than these! I employ neither force nor threats, nor violence! My victim is the instrument of her own ruin—without one rude grasp from my hand, without one threatening word, she swims willingly to my arms!"

He took the hand of the fair girl within his own, and looking her steadfastly in the eye, with a deep gaze which every instant grew more vivid and burning, he went on with his story—and his design.

"The wood grew very dark. Around me were massive trees with thick branches, and gnarled trunks, bearing witness of the storms of an hundred years. My way led over a path covered with soft forest-moss, and now and then red gleams of sunlight shot like arrows of gold, between the overhanging leaves. Darker and darker, the twilight sank down upon the forest. At last, missing the path, I knew not which way to tread. All was dark and indistinct. Now falling over a crumbling limb, which had been thrown down by a storm long before, now entangled by the wild vines, that overspread portions of the ground, and now missing my foothold in some hidden crevice of the earth, I wandered wearily on. At last climbing up a sudden elevation of the mountain, I stood upon a vast rock, that hung over the depths below, like an immense platform. On all sides but one, this rock was encircled by a waving wall of forest leaves. Green shrubs swept circling around, enclosing it like a fairy bower, while the eastern side lay open to the beams of the moon, which now rose grandly in the vast horizon. Far over wood, far over mountain, far over ravine and dell, this platform-rock, commanded a distant view of the valley of Wyoming.

"The moon was in the sky, Mary, the sky was one vast sheet of blue, undimmed by a single cloud; and beneath the moonbeams lay a sea of forest-leaves, while in the dim distance, like the shore of this leafy ocean, arose the roofs and steeples of a quiet town, with a broad river rolling along the dark valley like a banner of silver, flung over a sable pall."

"How beautiful!"

And as the murmur escaped Mary's lips, the hand of Lorrimer grew closer in its pressure, while his left arm wound gently around her waist.

"I stood entranced by the sight. A cool breeze came up the mountain side, imparting a grateful freshness to my cheek. The view was indeed beautiful, but I suddenly remembered that I was without resting-place or shelter. Ignorant of the mountain paths, afar from any farm-house or village, I had still a faint hope of discovering the temporary habitation of some hunter who encamped in these forest-wilds.

"I turned from the magnificent prospect—I brushed aside the wall of leaves, I looked to the western sky. I shall never forget the view—which, like a dream of fairy-land, burst on my sight, as pushing the shrubbery aside, I gazed from the western limits of the platform-rock.

"There, below me, imbedded in the very summit of the mountain, lay a calm lake, whose crystal waters, gave back the reflection of forest and sky, like an immense mirror. It was but a mile in length, and half that distance in width. On all sides, sudden and steep, arose the encircling wall of forest trees. Like wine in a goblet, that calm sheet of water lay in the embrace of the surrounding wall of foliage. The waters were clear, so tranquil, that I could see, down, down, far, far beneath, as if another world was hidden in their depths. And then from the heights, the luxuriant foliage as yet untouched by autumn, sank in waves of verdure to the very brink of the lake, the trembling leaves dipping into the clear cold waters with a gentle motion. It was very beautiful, Mary, and——"

"Oh, most beautiful!"

The left hand of Lorrimer gently stealing round her form, rested with a faint pressure upon the folds of the night-robe, over her bosom, which now came heaving tremulously into light.

"I looked upon this lovely lake with a keen delight; I gazed upon the tranquil waters, upon the steeps crowned with forest trees—one side in heavy shadow, the other gleaming in the advancing moonbeams. I seemed to inhale the quietness, the solitude of the place, as a holy influence, mingling with the very air I breathed, and a wild transport aroused my soul into an outburst of enthusiasm.

"Here," I cried, "is the home for love! Love pure and stainless, flying from the crowded city, here can repose beneath the shadow of quiet rocks, beside the gleam of tranquil waters, within the solitudes of endless forests. Yon sky so clear, so cloudless, has never beheld a sight of human misery or woe. Yon lake, sweeping beneath me like another sky, has never been crimsoned by human blood. This quiet valley hidden from the world now, as it has been hidden since the creation, is but another world where two hearts that love, that mingle in one, that throb for each other's joy can dwell for ever in the calm silence of unalloyed affection."

"A home for love such as angels feel."

Closer and more close the hand of Lorrimer pressed against the heaving bosom, with but the slight folds of the night-robe between.

"Here, beside this calm lake, whenever the love of a true woman shall be mine, here, afar from the cares and realities of life, will I dwell! Here, with the means which the accident of fortune has bestowed, will I build, not a temple, not a mansion, not a palace! But a cottage, a quiet home, whose roof shall arise, like a dear hope in the wilderness, from amid the green leaves of embowering trees."

"You spake thus, Lorraine? Do I not love you as a true woman should love? Is not your love calm and stainless as the waters of the mountain lake? We will dwell there, Lorraine! Oh, how like romance will be the plain reality of our life!"

"Oh! Mary, my own true love, in that moment as I stood gazing upon the world-hidden lake, my heart all throbbing with strange impulses, my very soul steeped in a holy calm, your form seemed to glide between my eyes and the moonlight! The thought rushed like a prophecy over my soul, that one day, amid the barren wilderness of hearts, which crowd the world, I should find one, one heart whose impulses should be stainless, whose affection should be undying, whose love should be mine! Oh! Mary, in that moment, I felt that my life would, one day, be illumined by your love."

"And then you knew me not? Oh, Lorraine, is there not a strange mystery in this affection, which makes the heart long for the love which it shall one day experience, even before the eye has seen the beloved one?"

Brighter grew the glow on her cheek, closer pressed the hand on her bosom, warmer and higher arose that bosom in the light.

"And there, Mary, in that quiet mountain valley, we will seek a home, when we are married. As soon as summer comes, when the trees are green, and the flowers burst from among the moss along the wood-path, we will hasten to the mountain lake, and dwell within the walls of our quiet home. For a home shall be reared for us, Mary, on a green glade that slopes down to the water's brink, with the tall trees sweeping away on either side.

"A quiet little cottage, Mary, with a sloping roof and small windows, all fragrant with wild flowers and forest vines! A garden before the door, Mary, where in the calm summer morning, you can inhale the sweetness of the flowers, as they breath forth in untamed luxuriance. And then, anchored by the shore, Mary, a light sail-boat will be ready for us ever; to bear us over the clear lake in the early dawn, when the mist winds up in fleecy columns to the sky, or in the twilight, when the red sun flings his last ray over the waters, or in the silent night, when the moon is up, and the stars look kindly on us from the cloudless sky."

"Alas! Lorraine! Clouds may come, and storms, and winter."

"What care we for winter, when eternal spring is in our hearts! Let winter come with its chill, and its ice, and its snows! Beside our cheerful fire, Mary, with our hands clasping some book, whose theme is the trials of two hearts that loved on through difficulty, and danger or death, we will sit silently, our hearts throbbing with one delight, while the long hours of the winter evening glide quietly on. Do you see the fire, Mary? How cheerily its beams light our faces as we sit in its kindly light! My arm is round your waist, my cheek is laid next to yours, our hands are locked together and your heart, Mary, oh, how softly its throbbings fall on my ear!"

"Oh, Lorraine! Why is there any care in the world, when two hearts can make such a heaven on earth, with the holy lesson of an all-trusting love."

"Or it may be, Mary," and his gaze grew deeper, while his voice sank to a low and thrilling whisper. "Or it may be, Mary, that while we sit beside our winter fire, a fair babe, do not blush, my wife, a fair babe will rest smileing on your bosom."

"Oh, Lorraine," she murmured, and hid her face upon his breast, the long brown tresses, covering her neck and shoulders like a veil, while Lorraine wound his arms closely round her form, and looked around with a glance full of meaning.

There was triumph in that glance. The libertine felt her heart throbbing against his breast as he held her in his arms, he felt her bosom panting and heaving, and quivering with a quick

fluttering pulsation; and as he swept the clustering curls aside from her half-hidden face, he saw
that her cheek glowed like a new-lighted flame.

"She is mine!" he thought, and a smile of
triumph gave a dark aspect to his handsome
face. In a moment Mary raised her glowing
countenance from his breast. She gazed around,
with a timid, frightened look. Her breath came
thick and gaspingly. Her cheeks were all a-
glow, her blue eyes swam in a hazy dimness.
She felt as though she was about to fall swoon-
ing on the floor. For a moment all consciousness seemed to have failed her, while a delirious
languor came stealing over her senses. Lorrimer's form seemed to swim in the air before
her, and the dim light of the room gave place to
a flood of radiance, which seemed all at once to
pour on her eyesight from some invisible source.

LIVINGSTONE ABOUT TO INFLICT VENGEANCE ON THE ADULTERESS.

Soft murmurs like voices heard in a pleasant
dream, fell gently on her ears, the languor came
deeper and more mellow over her limbs; her
bosom rose no longer quick an gaspingly, but in
long pulsations, that urged the full globes in
all their virgin beauty, softly and slowly into
view. Like billows they rose above the folds
of the night robe, while the flush grew warmer
on her cheek, and her parted lips deepened into
a rich vermillion tint.

"She is mine!" and the same dark smile
flushed over Lorrimer's face. Silent and
motionless he sat, regarding his victim with a
steadfast glance.

"Oh, Lorraine," she cried in a faint tone, as
she read a nameless something in his eye, and a
sudden light seemed to break upon her,—"do
not harm me!"

Pure, stainless, innocent, her heart a heaven
of love, her mind child-like in its knowledge of

the world, she knew not what she feared. She did not fear the shame which the good world would heap upon her, she did not fear the dishonour, because it would be followed by such pollution that no man in honour might call her wife—no child of innocence might whisper her name as mother—she did not fear the foul wrong, as society with its million tongues and eyes, fears it, and holds it in abhorence, ever visiting the guilt of the man upon the head of his trembling victim.

Mary feared the dishonour, because her soul, with some strange consciousness of approaching evil, deemed it a foul spirit, who had arisen not so much to visit her with wrong as to destroy the love she felt for Lorrimer. Not for herself, but for his sake, she feared that nameless crime, which already glared upon her from the blood-shot eyes of her lover. Her *lover*!

"Oh, Lorraine, you will not harm me! For the sake of God, save me—save me!"

She clasped his hand with a closer grasp and gathered it tremblingly to her bosom, while her eyes dilating with a glance of terror, were fixed upon his face.

"Mary—this is madness—nothing but madness," he said in a voice grown hoarse with passion, and rudely tore his hand from her grasp.

Another instant, and stooping suddenly, he caught her form in his arms, and raised her struggling from her very feet.

"Mary you are mine!" he hissed the whisper in her ear, and gathered her quivering form more closely to his heart.

There was a low-toned hideous laugh, muttering or growling through the air as he spokes and the form of Devil-bug stole with a hushed footstep from the entrance of the walnut chamber, and seizing the light in his talon-fingers, glided from the room, with the same hyena laugh which had announced his appearance.

"The trap—the bottle—the fire, for the brother," he muttered as his solitary eye glanced upon the libertine and his struggling victim, neither of whom had marked his entrance. "For the sister, ha! ha! ha! The 'handsome' Monk Gusty, 'tends to her! t'Bijah did'nt listen for nothin'—ha, ha! this beats the charcoal quite hollow."

He disappeared, and the rose chamber was wrapt in midnight darkness.

Darkness! There was a struggle, and a shriek, and a prayer. Darkness! There was an oath and a groan, mingling in chorus. Darkness! A wild cry for mercy, a name madly shrieked, and a fierce execration. Darkness! Another struggle, a low moaning sound, and a stillness like that of the grave. Now darkness and silence mingle together and all is still.

In some old book of mysticism and superstition, I have read this wild legend, which mingling as it does the terrible with the grotesque, has still its meaning and its moral:

In the sky, far, far above the earth—so the legend runs—there hangs an awful bell, invisible to mortal eye, which angel hands alone may toll, which is never tolled save when the unpardonable sin is committed on earth, and then its judgment peal rings out like the blast of the archangel's trumpet, breaking on the ear of the criminal, and on his ear alone, with a sound that freezes his blood with horror. The peal of the bell, hung in the azure depths of space announces to the guilty one that he is an outcast from God's mercy for ever, that his crime can never be pardoned, while the throne of the eternal endures; that in the hour of death his soul will be darkened by the hopeless prospect of an eternity of wo; wo without limit, despair without hope; the torture of the never-dying worm, and the unquenchable flame, for ever and for ever.

Reader! Did the sound of the judgment bell, pealing with one awful toll from the invisible air break over the soul of the libertine, as in darkness and in silence, he stood shuddering over the victim of his crime?

If in the books of the last day there shall be found written down, but one unpardonable crime, that crime will be known as the foul wrong accomplished in the gaudy rose chamber of Monk Hall, by the wretch who now stood trembling in the darkness of the place, while his victim lay senseless at his feet.

There was darkness and silence for a few brief moments, and then a stream of light flashed around the rose chamber.

Like a fiend, returned to witness some appalling scene of guilt which he had but a moment left, Devil-bug stood in the doorway of the walnut chamber. He grimly smiled as he surveyed the scene.

And then with a hurried gesture, a pallid face, and blood-shot eyes, as though some phantom tracked his footsteps, Lorrimer rushed madly by him, and disappeared into the painted chamber. At the very moment of his disappearance Devil-bug raised the light on high, and started backward with a sudden impulse of surprise.

"Dead — dead and come to life!" he shrieked, and then the gaze of his solitary eye was fixed upon the entrance of the walnut room. With a mechanical gesture he placed the light upon the table and fled madly from the chamber, while the curtains opening into the walnut room rustled to and fro for a single instant, and then a ghastly face, with livid cheeks and burning eyes appeared between the crimson folds gazing silently around the place, with a glance that no living man would choose to encounter for his weight in gold—it was so like the look of one arisen from the dead.

CHAPTER XIV.

THE GUILTY WIFE.

THE light of the dark-lantern streamed around the spot where the merchant stood.

Behind him all was darkness, while the

lantern, held extended in his left hand, flung a ruddy blaze of light over the outlines of the massive bed. Long silk curtains of rich azure fell drooping in voluminous folds to the very floor, concealing the bed from view; while from within the gorgeous curtaining, that low softened sound like a woman breathing in her sleep, came faintly to the merchant's ear.

Livingstone advanced. The manner in which he held the lantern flung his face in shadow, but you could see that his form quivered with a tremulous motion, and in the attempt to smother a groan which arose to his lips, a thick gurgling sound, like the death-rattle, was heard in his throat.

Gazing from the shadow that enveloped his face, Livingstone, with an involuntary glance took in the details of the gorgeous couch—the rich curtaining of light azure satin, closely drawn around the bed; the canopy overhead surmounting by a circle of glittering stars, arranged like a coronet; and the voluptuous shapes, assumed by the folds, as they fell drooping to the floor, all burst like a picture on his eye.

Beside the bed stood a small table—resembling a lady's work-stand, covered with a plain white cloth. The silver sheath of a large bowie knife, resting on the white cloth, shone glittering in the light, and attracted the merchant's attention.

He laid the pistol which he held at his right side upon the table, and raised the bowie knife to the light. The sheath was of massive silver, and the blade of the keenest steel. The handle fashioned like the sheath, of massive silver, bore a single name engraved in large letters near the hilt, Algernon Fitz-Cowles, and on the blade of polished steel, amid a wreath of flowers glittered the motto, in the expressive slang of southern braggarts, "Stranger avoid a snag."

Silently Livingstone examined the blade of the murderous weapon. It was sharp as a razor, with the glittering point inclining from the edge, like a Turkish dagger. The merchant grasped the handle of this knife in his right hand, and holding the lantern on high, advanced to the bedside.

"His own knife," muttered Livingstone, "shall find its way to his cankered heart."

With the point of the knife, he silently parted the hangings of the bed, and the red glare of the lantern flashed within the azure folds, revealing a small portion of the sleeping couch.

A moment passed, and Livingstone seemed afraid to gaze within the hangings, for he turned his head aside more than once, and the thick gurgling noise again was heard in his throat. At last, raising the lantern gently overhead, so that its beams would fall along a small space of the couch, while the rest was left in darkness, and grasping the knife with a firmer hold, he gazed upon the spectacle disclosed to his view.

Her head deep sunken in a downy pillow, a beautiful woman lay wrapt in slumber. By the manner in which the folds of the coverlid were disposed, you might see that her form was full,

large and voluptuous. Thick masses of jet-black hair fell, glossy and luxuriant, over her round neck and along her uncovered bosom, which swelling with the full ripeness of womanhood, rose gently in the light. She lay on her side, with her head resting easily on one large, round arm, half hidden by the masses of black hair, streaming over the snow-white pillow, while the other arm was flung carelessly along her form; the light falling softly over the clear transparent skin, the full roundness of its shape, and the small and delicate hand, resting gently on the coverlid.

Her face appearing amid the tresses of her jet-black hair, like a fair picture half-hidden in sable drapery, was marked by a perfect regularity of feature, a high forehead, arching eye-brows, and long dark lashes, resting on the velvet skin of each glowing cheek. Her mouth was opened slightly as she slept, the ivory whiteness of her teeth, gleaming through the rich vermillion of her parted lips.

She lay on that gorgeous couch in an attitude of voluptuous ease; a perfect incarnation of the sensual woman, who combines the beauty of a mere animal with an intellect strong and resolute in its every purpose.

And over that full bosom, which rose and fell with the gentle impulse of slumber, over that womanly bosom, which should have been the home of pure thoughts and wifely affections, was laid a small and swarthy hand, whose fingers, heavy with rings, pressed against the ivory skin, all streaked with veins of delicate azure, and clung twiningly among the dark tresses that hung drooping over the breast as its globes rose heaving into view, like worlds of purity and womanhood.

It was a strange sight for a man to see, whose only joy in earth or heaven was locked within that snowy bosom; and yet Livingstone, the husband, stood firm and silent, as he gazed upon that strange hand, half hidden by the drooping curls.

It required but a slight motion of his hand, and the glare of the light flashed over the other side of the couch. The flash of the lantern, among the shadows of the bed, was but for a moment, and yet Livingstone beheld the face of a dark-hued man, whose long dark hair mingled its heavy curls with the glossy tresses of his wife, while his hand reaching over her shoulder, rested, like a thing of foul pollution upon her bosom.

They slumbered together, slumbered in their guilt, and the avenger stood gazing upon their faces while their hearts were as unconscious of his glance, as they were of the death which glittered over them in the upraised knife.

"Wife of mine—your slumber shall be deep and long."

And as the whisper hissed from between the clenched teeth of the husband, he raised the dagger suddenly aloft, and then brought it slowly down, until its point quivered within a finger's width of the heaving bosom, while the light of the lantern held above his head, streamed over his livid face, and over the blooming countenance of his fair young wife.

The dagger glittered over her bosom; lower and lower it sank, until, a deeper respiration, a single heart-drawn sigh might have forced the silken skin upon the glittering point, when the guilty woman murmured in her sleep.

"Algernon—a coronet—wealth and power," were the broken words that escaped from her lips.

Again the husband raised the knife, but it was with the hand clenched, and the sinews stiffened for the work of death.

"Seek your Algernon in the grave," he whispered, with a convulsive smile, as his blue eyes, all alive with a glance, like a madman's gaze, surveyed the guilty wife. "Let the coronet be hung around your fleshless skull—let your wealth be a coffin, and—ha! ha! your power—corruption and decay."

It may have been that some feeling of the olden-time, when the image of that fair young wife dwelt in the holiest temple of his heart, came suddenly to the mind of the avenger, in that moment of fearful suspense, for his hand trembled for an instant and he turned his gaze aside, while a single scalding tear rolled down his livid cheek.

"Algernon," murmured the wife. "We will seek a home.—"

"In the grave!"

And the dagger rose, and gleamed like a stream of flame overhead, and then sank down with a whirring sound.

Is the bosom red with the stain of blood?

Has the keen knife severed the veins and pierced the heart?

The blow of a strong arm, stricken over Livingstone's shoulder, dashed his hand suddenly aside, and the knife sank to the very hilt in the pillow, within a hair's breadth of Dora's face. The knife touched the side of her cheek, and a long and glossy curl, severed from her head by the blow, lay resting on the pillow.

Livingstone turned suddenly round, with a deep muttered oath, while his massive form rose towering to its full height. Luke Harvey stood before him, his cold and glittering eye fixed upon his face with an expression of the deepest agitation.

"Stand back, sir," muttered Livingstone with a quivering lip. "This spot is sacred to me! I want no witness to my wrong, nor to my vengeance!"

"Ha, ha!" sneered Luke, bending forward until his eyes glared fixedly in the face of the husband. "Is this a vengeance for a man like you?"

"Luke, again I warn you, leave me to my shame and its punishment."

"'Shame' 'punishment!' ha, ha! You have been wronged in secret, slowly and quietly wronged, and yet would punish that wrong, by a blow that brings but a single pang!"

"Luke, you are right," whispered Livingstone, his agitated manner subsiding into a look of calm and fearful determination. "The wrong has been secret, long in progress, horrible in result. So let the punishment be. She shall see the death," and his eyes flashed with a maniac wildness. "She shall see the death as it slowly approaches, she shall feel it as it winds its very fangs into her heart, she shall know that all hope is in vain, while my voice will whisper in her ear, 'Dora, it is by my will that you die. Shriek, Dora, shriek for aid! Death is cold and icy—I can save you! I your husband! I can save you, but will not! Die, adultress, die.'"

"Algernon," murmured Dora, half awakened from her sleep. "There is a cold hand laid against my cheek."

"She wakes!" whispered Luke, "the dagger—the lantern."

It required but a single moment for Livingstone to draw the knife from the pillow, where it rested against the blooming cheek of the wife, while Luke, with a sudden movement grasped the lantern and closed its door, leaving the chamber wrapt in midnight darkness.

The husband stood motionless as a stone, and Luke held his very breath, as the voice of Dora broke on their ears, in tones of alarm and terror.

"Algernon," she whispered, as she started from her slumber. "Awake. Do you not hear the sound of voices by the bedside? Hist! Could it have been a dream? Algernon."

"Deuced uncomfortable to be waked up this way," murmured a sleepy voice. "What's the matter, Dora? What about a dream?"

"I was awakened just now from my sleep by the sound of voices. I thought a blaze of light flashed round the room, while my hus—that is, Livingstone stood at the bedstead. And then I felt a cold hand laid against my cheek."

"Ha, ha! Rather good that! D'ye know, Dora, that I had a dream too? I dreamt that I was in the front parlour, second story you know, in your house in Fourth-street, when the old fellow came in and read your note on the table. Ha, ha! and then, are you listening? I thought the old gentleman while he was reading, turned to a bright pea-green in the face, and—"

"Hist! Do you not hear some one breathing in the room?"

"Pshaw! Dora, you're nervous! Go to sleep, my love. Don't lose your rest for all the dreams in the world. Good night, Dora!"

"A little touch of farce with our tragedy," half muttered Luke, as a quiet chuckle shook his frame. "Egad! If they talk in this strain much longer, I'll have to guffaw! It's rather too much for my risibles, this is! A husband standing in the dark by the bedside, while his wife and her paramour are telling their pleasant dreams, in which he figures as the hero."

Whether a smile passed over Livingstone's face, or a frown, Luke could not tell, for the room was dark as a starless night, yet the quick gasping sound of a man struggling for breath, heard through the darkness, seemed to indicate anything but the pleasant laugh or the jovial chuckle.

"They sleep again!" muttered Luke. "She has sunken into slumber while death watches at the bedside. Curse it, how the fellow snores!"

There was a long pause of darkness and silence. No word escaped the husband's lips, no groan convulsed his chest, no half-muttered cry of agony, indicated the struggle that was silently rending his soul, as with a viper's fangs.

"Livingstone," whispered Luke, after a long pause. "Where are you? Confound it man, I can't hear you breathe. I'm afraid to uncover the light, it may awaken them again. I say, Livingstone, hadn't we better leave these quarters?"

"I could have borne expressions of remorse from her lips—I could have listened to sudden outpourings of horror wrung from her soul by the very blackness of her guilt, but this grovelling familiarity with vice!"

"Matter-of-fact pollution, as you might observe," whispered Luke.

"Luke, I tell you, the cup is full to overflowing—but I will drain it to the dregs!"

"Now's your time," whispered Luke, as swing the curtain aside, he suffered the light of the lantern to fall over the bed· "Dora looks quite pretty, Fitz-Cowles decidedly interesting."

"And on that bosom have I slept!" exclaimed Livingstone, in a voice of agony, as he gazed on his slumbering wife. "Those arms have clung round my neck—and *now!* Ha! Luke, you may think me mad, but I tell ye man, that there is a spirit of a slow and silent revenge creeping through my veins. *She* has *dishonoured* me! Do you read anything like *forgiveness* in my face?"

"Not much on't I assure you. But come, Livingstone—let's be going. This is not the time nor place for your revenge. Let's travel."

Livingstone laid down the bowie knife, and with a smile of bitter mockery, seized a small pair of scissors from the work-basket which stood on the table.

"You smile Luke?" he whispered, as leaning over the bedside, he laid his hand upon the jet-black hair of the slumbering Fitz-Cowles; "Ha! ha! I will leave the place, but d'ye see, Luke, I must take some slight keepsake, to remind me of the gallant colonel. A lock of his hair, you know, Luke."

"Egad! Livingstone, I believe you're going mad! A lock of his hair! Phsaw! You'll want a straight jacket soon."

"And a lock of my Dora's hair," whispered Livingstone, as his blue eyes flashed from beneath his dark eyebrows, while his lips wore that same mocking smile. "But you see the knife saved me all trouble. Here is a glossy tress severed by the colonel's dagger. Now let me wind them together, Luke, let me lay them next to my heart, Luke—yes, smile my fellow—Ha! ha! ha!"

"Hist! Your wife stirs in her sleep—you will awaken them again."

"D'ye know, Luke," cried Livingstone, drawing his partner close to his side, and looking in his face with a vacant glance, that indicated a temporary derangement of intellect, "d'ye know, Luke, that I didn't do that o' my own will? Hist! Luke—closer—closer—I'll tell you. The devil was at the bedside, Luke; he whispered it in my ear, he bade me take these keepsakes—ha! ha! ha! what a jolly set of fellows we are! And then, Luke," his voice sank to a thrilling whisper, "he pointed with his iron hand to *the last scene,* in which my vengeance shall be complete. She shall beg for mercy, Luke; aye, on her knees, but—ha! ha! ha!—*kill—kill—kill!* is written in letters of blood before my eyes, everywhere, Luke, everywhere. Don't you see it?"

He pointed vacantly at the air as he spoke, and seized Luke by the shoulder, as though he would command his attention to the blood-red letters.

Luke was conscious that he stood in the presence of a madman.

Inflexible as he was in his own secret purpose of revenge upon the woman who had trampled on his very heart, Luke still regarded the merchant with a feeling akin to brotherhood. As the fearful fact impressed itself on his soul that Livingstone stood before him, deprived of reason, an expression of the deepest feeling shadowed the countenance of Luke, and his voice was broken in its tones as he endeavoured to persuade the madman to leave the scene of his dishonour and shame.

"Come! Livingstone! let us go," said Luke, taking his partner by the arm, and leading him gently towards the closet.

"But I've got the keepsakes safe, Luke," whispered Livingstone, as the light flashed from his large blue eyes. "d'ye see the words in the air, Luke? Now they change to her name—Dora, Dora, Dora! All in blood-red letters. I say, Luke, let's have a quiet whist party—there's four of us—Dora and I, you and Fitz-Cowles."

"I'm willing," exclaimed Luke, as with a quick movement he seized the pistol—left by Livingstone on the table, and concealed it within the breast of his great coat. "Suppose we step into the next room and get everything ready for the party."

"You're keen, Luke, keen, but I'm even with you," whispered Livingstone as his livid face lighted up with a sudden gleam of intelligence; "here we stand on the threshhold of this closet—we are about to leave my wife's bed-room. You think I'm mad. Do I look like a madman? I know there is no whist-party to be held this night, I know that—hist! Luke, don't you see it all pictured forth in the air? The scene of my vengeance! In colours of blood, painted by the devil's hand? Yonder, Luke—yonder! How red it grows—and then in letters of fire, everywhere, everywhere is written—Dora, Dora, Dora!"

"It was a fearful spectacle to see that strong man, with his imposing figure raised to its full stature, and his thoughtful brow lit up with an expression of idiotic wonder, as standing on the verge of the secret door, he pointed wildly at the blood-red picture his fancy had drawn in the vacant air, while his blue eyes dilated with a maniac glance, and his face grew yet more livid and ghastly.

"Come, Livingstone," cried Luke, gently leading him through the closet, "you had better leave this place."

"And yet Dora is sleeping here? My young wife? The mother of my children? D'ye think, Luke, that I'd have believed you last Thursday morning, if you had then told me this? 'Livingstone, this day-week, you will leave a chamber in a brothel, and leave your young wife, sleeping in another man's arms.' But never mind, Luke—it will be all right. For I tell ye, it is there, there before me in co-lours of blood! That last scene of my venge-ance! And there—there—in letters of flame—Dora! Dora! Dora!

And while the fair young wife slept quietly in the bed of guilt and shame, Luke led the merchant from the room, and from the house.

CHAPTER XV.

THE DISHONOUR.

ALL was silent within the rose chamber. For a single moment that pale visage glared from the crimson hangings, concealing the en-trance to the walnut room, and then with a measured footstep Brynewood Arlington ad-vanced along the floor, his countenance ghastly as the face of Lazarus, at the very instant, when in obedience to the words of the Incarnate, life struggled with corruption and death, over his cheek and brow.

Bring home to your mind the scene when Lazarus lay prostrate in the grave, a stiffened corpse, his face all clammy with corruption, the closed eyes surrounded by loathsome circles of decay, the cheeks sunken, and the lips fallen in; let the words of Jesus ring in your ears, "Lazarus come forth!" And then as the blue eyelids slowly unclose, as the gleam of life shoots forth from the glassy eye, as the flush of health struggles with the yellowish hue of decay along each cheek, as life and death mingling in that face for a single moment, maintain a fearful combat for the mastery; then I pray you gaze upon the visage of Byrnewood Arlington, and mark how like it is to the face of one risen from the dead; a ghastly face, on whose fixed outline the finger-traces of corrup-tion are yet visible, from whose eyes the film of the grave is not yet passed away.

The gaze of Brynewood, as he strode from the entrance of the walnut chamber, was rivetted to the floor. Had the eyes of the rattle-snake gleamed from the carpet, slowly drawing its victim to his ruin, Brynewood could not have fixed his gaze upon the object in the centre of the floor with a more fearful and absorbing intensity.

There, thrown prostrate on the gaudy carpet, insensible and motionless, the form of Mary Arlington lay at the brother's feet.

He sank silently on his knees.

He took her small white hand, now cold as marble, within his own—he swept the un-bound tresses back from her pallid brow—her eyes were closed as in death, her lips hung apart, the lower one trembling with a scarcely perceptible movement, her cheeks were pale as ashes, with a deep red tint in the centre.

Byrnewood uttered no sound, nor shrieked forth any wild exclamation of revenge, or woe, or despair. He silently drew the folds of the night-robe round her form, and veiled her bosom—but a moment agone warmed into a glow by the heart's fires, now paled by the fingers of the ravisher—he veiled her fair young bosom from the light.

It was a sad sight to look upon. That face, so fair and blooming but a moment passed, now pale as death, with a spot of burning red on the centre of each cheek; that bosom, a moment since heaving with passion, now still and motionless; those delicate hands with tiny fingers, which had bravely fought for honour, for virtue, for purity, an instant ago, now resting cold and stiffened by her side.

Thick tresses of dark brown hair hung round her neck. With that same careful movement of his hand, Brynewood swept them aside. Along the smooth surface of that fair neck, like some noisome reptile trailing over a lovely flower, a large vein, black and distorted, shot upward, darkening the glossy skin, while it told the story of the maiden's dishonour and shame.

"My sister!" was the solitary exclamation that broke from Brynewood's lips as he gazed upon the form of the unconscious girl, and his large dark eye, dilating as he spoke, glanced around with an expression of strange meaning.

He raised her form in his arms, and kissed her cold lips again and again. No tear trickled from his eyelids; no sigh heaved his bosom; no deep muttered execration manifested the agitation of his soul.

"My sister!" he again whispered, and gathered her more close to his heart.

A slight flush deepening over her cheek, even while he spoke, gave signs of returning consciousness.

Mary slowly uncovered her eyes, and gazed with a wandering glance around the room. An instant passed ere she discovered that she lay in Brynewood's arms.

"Oh, brother," she exclaimed, not with a wild shriek, but in a low-toned voice, whose slightest accent quivered with an emphasis of despair. "Oh, brother! Leave me—leave me. I am not worthy of your touch. I am vile, brother, oh, most vile! Leave me—leave me, for I am lost!"

"Mary!" whispered Brynewood, resisting her attempt to unwind his arms from her form, while the blood, filling the veins of his throat, produced an effect like strangulation—"Mary! Do not—do not speak thus—I—I——"

He could say no more, but his face dropped on her cold bosom, and the tears which he had silently prayed for came at last.

He wept, while that low choking noise, sounding in his throat, that involuntary heaving of the chest, that nervous quivering of the lip, all betokened the strong man wrestling with his agony.

"Do not weep for me, brother," she said, in the same low toned voice, "I am polluted, brother, and am not worthy of the slightest tear you shed for me. Unwind your arms, brother, do not resist me, for the strength of despair is in these hands, unwind your arms, and let me no longer pollute you by my touch.

There was something fearful in the expression of her face as she spoke. She was no longer the trembling child, whose young face marked the inexperience of her stainless heart. A new world had broken upon her soul, not a world of green trees, silver streams, and pleasant flowers, but a chaos of ashes, and mouldering flame; a lurid sky above, a blasted soil below, and one immense horizon of leaden clouds, hemming in the universe of desolation.

She had sprung from the maiden into the woman, but a blight was on her soul for ever. The crime had not only stained her person with dishonour, but, like the sickening warmth of the hot-house, it had forced the flower of her soul, into sudden and unnatural maturity. It was the maturity of precocious experience. In her inmost soul, she felt that she was a dishonoured thing, whose very touch was pollution, whose presence, among the pure and stainless, would be a bitter mockery and foul reproach. The guilt was not hers, but the ruin blasted her purity for ever.

"Unwind your arms, my brother," she exclaimed, tearing herself from his embrace with all a maniac's strength, "I am polluted. You are pure. Oh do not touch me, do not touch me. Leave me to my shame—oh leave me."

She unwound her form from his embrace, and sank crouching into a corner of the rose-chamber, extending her hands with a frightful gesture, as though she feared his slightest touch.

"Mary," shrieked Brynewood, flinging his arms on high with a movement of sudden agitation, "Oh, do not look upon me thus! Come to me, oh Mary—come to me for I am your brother."

The words, the look, and the trembling movement of his outspread arms, all combined, acted like a spell upon the intellect of the ruined girl. She rose wildly to her feet, as though impelled by some invisible influence, and fell tremblingly into her brother's arms.

While one dark and horrible thought was working its way through the avenues of his soul, he gathered her to his breast again and again.

And in that moment of silence and unutterable thought, the curtains leading into the painted chamber were slowly thrust aside, and Lorrimer again appeared upon the scene. Stricken with remorse, he had fled with a madman's haste from the scene of his crime, and while his bosom was torn by a thousand opposing thoughts, he had endeavoured to drown the voice within him, and crush the memory of the nameless wrong. It was all in vain. Impelled by an irresistable desire, to look again upon the victim of his crime, he re-entered the rose-chamber. It was a strange sight, to see the brother kneeling on the floor, as he gathered his sister's form in his arms, and yet the seducer gave no sign nor indication of surprise.

A fearful agitation was passing over the libertine's soul, as unobserved by the brother or sister, he stood gazing upon them with a wandering glance. His face, so lately flushed with passion, in its vilest hues, was now palest and livid. His white lips, trembled with a nervous movement, and his hands, extended on either side, clutched vacantly at the air, as though he wrestled with an unseen foe.

While the thought of horror was slowly darkening over Brynewood's soul, a thought as dark and horrible gathered like a phantom over the mind of Lorrimer.

A single word of explanation, will make the subsequent scene clear and intelligible to the reader.

From generation to generation the family of the Lorrimer's had been subject to an aberration of intellect, as sudden as it was terrible; always resulting from any peculiar agitation of mind, which might convulse the soul with an emotion remarkable for its power or energy. It was an hallucination, a temporary madness, a sudden derangement of intellect. It always succeeded an uncontrolable outburst of anger, or grief, or joy. From father to son, since the family had first come over to Pennsylvania, with the proprietor and peace-maker William Penn, this temporary derangement of intellect had descended as a fearful heritage.

Lorrimer had been subject to this madness but once in his life, when his father's corse lay stiffened before his eyes. And now, as he stood gazing upon the form of the brother and sister, Lorrimer felt this temporary madness stealing over his soul, in the form of a strange hallucination, while he became conscious, that in a single moment the horror which shook his frame, would rise to his lips in words of agony and fear.

"Raise your hands with mine, to Heaven, Mary," exclaimed Brynewood as the thought which had been working over his soul, manifested its intensity in words. "Raise your hands with mine, and curse the author of your ruin! Lift your voice with mine, up to the God who beheld the wrong—who will visit the wronger with a doom meet for his crime—lift your voice with mine, and curse him."

"Oh Byrnewood, do not, do not curse *him.* The wrong has been done, but do not, I beseech you, visit his head with a curse."

"Hear me, oh God, before whom I now raise my hands, in the vow of justice! In life I will be to this wretch as a fate, a doom, a curse!"

"I am vile—oh God—steeped in the same vices which blacken the heart of this man, cankered by the same corruption. But the office, which I now take on myself, raising this right hand to thee, in witness of my fixed purpose, would sanctify the darkest fiend in hell! I am the avenger of my sister's wrong! She was innocent, she was pure, she trusted and was betrayed! I will avenge her! Before thee, I swear to visit her wrong, upon the head of her betrayer, with a doom never to be forgotten in the memory of man. This right hand I dedicate to his solemn purpose—come what will come what may, let danger threaten or death, stand in my path, through sickness and health, through riches or poverty, I now swear to hold my steady pathway onward, my only object in life—the avengement of my sister's wrong! He shall die by this hand—oh God—I swear it by thy name—I swear it by my soul—I swear it by the fiend who impelled the villain to this deed of crime."

As he whispered forth his oath, in a voice which speaking from the depths of his chest, had a hollow and sepulchral sound, the fair girl flung herself on his breast, and with a wild shriek essayed to delay the utterance of the curse by gathering his face to her bosom.

For a moment her efforts were successful. Lorrimer had stood silent and pale, while the deep-toned voice of Byrnewood Arlington, breaking in accents of doom upon his ear, had aided and strengthened the strange hallucination which was slowly gathering over his brain like a mighty spell.

"There is a wide river before me, its broad waves tinged with the last red rays of a winter sunset," such were the words he murmured, extending his hand, as though pointing to the scene, which dawned upon his soul. "A wide river with its waves surging against the wharves of a mighty city. Afar I behold steeples and roofs and towers, all glowing in the beams of the setting sun; and as I gaze, the waves turn to blood, red and ghastly blood—and now the sky is a flame, and the clouds sweep slowly past, bathed in the same crimson hue All his blood—the river rushes before me, and the sky and the city—all pictured in colours of blood.

"An invisible hand is leading me to my doom. There is death for me, in yonder river, and I know it, yet down, down to the rivers banks, down, down into the red waters, I must go. Ha! ha! 'Tis a merry death! The blood-red waves rise above me—higher, higher, higher! Yonder is the city, yonder the last rays of the setting sun, glitter on the roof and steeple, yonder is the blood-red sky—and ah! I tell ye I will not die—you shall not sink me beneath these gory waves! Devil! Is not your vengeance satisfied—must you feast your eyes with the sight of my closing agonies—must your hand grasp me by the throat, and your foot trample me beneath the waves? I tell you I will not, will not die."

"Ha—ha—ha! Here's purty going's on," laughed the hoarse voice of Devil-bug, as the hideous form appeared in the doorway of the walnut-chamber, with his attendant negroes at his back, "Seems the gal helped him off. There he sits—the ornery feller, with his sister in his arms—while Gusty is a doin' some ravins on his own indivdooal hook. Come here Glowworm—here Musquito—come here my pets, and 'tend to this leetle family party."

In another instant the rose-chamber became the scene of a strange picture.

Byrnewood had arisen to his feet, while Lorrimer stood spell bound by the hallucination which possessed his brain. The handsome libertine stood in the centre of the room, his face the hue of ashes, while with his hazel eyes, glaring on vacancy, he clutched wildly at the air, starting backward at the same moment, as though some invisible hand was silently impelling him to the brink of the blood-red river, which rolled tumultuously at his feet, which slowly gathered around him, and began to heave upward to his very lips.

On one side, in a half-kneeling position, crouched Mary Arlington, her large blue eyes starting from her pallid face, as with her upraised hands crossed over her bosom, she gazed upon the agitated countenance of the seducer, with a glance of mingled awe and wonder; while, on the other side, stern and erect, Byrnewood, with his pale visage darkening in a settled frown, with one foot advanced, and his hand upraised, seemed about to strike the libertine to the floor.

In the background, rendered yet more hideous by the dimness of the scene, Devil-bug stood grinning in derisive triumph as he motioned his attendants, the herculean negroes to advance and secure their prey.

There was silence for a single moment. Lorrimer still stood clutching at the vacant air, Mary still gazed upon his face in awe, Byrnewood yet paused in his mediated blow, while Devil-bug, with Musquito and Glowworm at his back, seemed quietly enjoying the entire scene, as he glanced from side to side with his solitary eye.

"Unhand me—I will not die," shrieked Lorrimer, as he fancied that a phantom hand, gathered tightly round his throat, while the red waters swept surging to his very lips, "I will not die—I defy—ah! ah! You strangle me."

"The hour of your death has come! You have said it—and it shall be so!" whispered Byrnewood, advancing a single step, as his dark eyes were fixed upon the face of Lorrimer, "while your own guilty heart spreads a blood-red river before your eyes, this hand—no phantom hand—shall work your death!"

He sprang forward, while a shriek arose from Mary's lips, he sprang forward with his eyes blazing with excitement, his outspread hand ready for the work of vengeance, but as he sprang, the laugh of Devil-bug echoed at his back, and the sinewy arms of the negroes gathered round his form, and flung him as suddenly to the floor.

"Here's fine goin's on," exclaimed Devil-bug as he glanced from face to face. "A feller who's been a leetle too kind to a gal, stands a-makin' speeches at nothin.' The gal kneels on the carpet as though she were a gettin' up a leetle prayer on her own account; and this 'ere ornery feller—git a good grip o' him you bull-dogs—sets up a small shop o' cussin' and sells his cusses for nothin'! Here's a tea party for ye."

"What does all this mean, Devil-bug," exclaimed Lorrimer, in his usual voice, as the hal-

DEVIL-BUG AND HIS NEGROS SEPARATE BYRNEWOOD AND LORRIMER.

lucination passed from him like a dream, leaving him utterly unconscious of the strange vision which had a moment since absorbed his very soul, "what does all this mean? Ha! Byrnewood and Mary—I remember? You are her brother are you not?"

"I am her avenger," said Byrnewood, with a ghastly smile, as he endeavoured to free himself from the grasp of the negroes, "and your exe-

cutioner! Within three days you shall die by this hand."

"Ha—ha—ha!" laughed Devil-bug, "there's more than one gentleman as has got a say in that leetle matter! How d'ye feel, young man? Did you ever take opium afore! You won't go to sleep nor nothin'? We cant do what we like with you? Kin we? Ho-ho-ho! *I wonders how that 'ill work.*

PART II.

THE DAY AFTER THE NIGHT.—THE FORGER.

CHAPTER I.

FITZ-COWLES AT-HOME.

THE scene changes to a chamber in the fourth story of the TON HOTEL, which arises along Chestnut street, a monster-building, with some hundred windows varying its red-brick face, in the way of eyes, covered with green-blind shutters, looking very much like so many goggles intended to preserve the sight of the visual organs aforesaid; while the verandah, on the ground floor, affording an entrance to the bar-room, might be likened to the mouth of the grand edifice, always wide open and ready to swallow a customer.

The sunshine of a cold, clear winter morning was streaming dimly between the half-closed inside shutters of the small chamber on the fourth story. The faint light, pouring between the shutters of the two windows looking to the south, served to reveal certain peculiar characteristics of the place.

There was a dressing bureau, surmounted by a hanging mirror, standing between the two windows of the chamber. Along the marble top of the bureau were disposed various bottles of perfumes, whose strong scent impregnated the atmosphere with remarkable reminiscences of musk, and orange, and lemon, and *patchoully ;* a pair of well-used kid gloves, which had been white yesterday; and a rumpled black scarf; a play-bill figured off with intoxicated letters, displaying the entertainment at the Walnut-street theatre the night before; and a glittering bowie knife, side by side with its silver sheath.

All over the carpet were scattered Windsor chairs, either grouped in circles, as though they were talking about the various gentry who had reposed on their well-cushioned seats, or fixed in strange positions along the walls, like waiters at a party, overburdened with coats and vests and stocks, and other articles of apparel, thrown carelessly over their rounds; or yet again flung down on the floor, with their heels in the air, as though they had taken a drop too much, and didn't know how to get up again.

There was a large sofa on one side of the room, a coal fire blazing in the grate opposite; while in the dim distance, you might perceive the dim outlines of a bed, and hear the deep bass of a heavy snore, which held a concert of its own, within the closely drawn curtains.

Altogether, that entire room, located in the fourth story of the Ton House, said as plainly as a room can say, that somebody had come home very late last night, or very early this morning, most probably in liquor; and called up as witnesses to this interesting assertion, the chairs thrown disorderly about the floor, the gloves and bowie knife on the dressing bureau, the hat on the sofa, and the heavy snore within the bed.

Sitting in the blaze of light streaming between the aperture of the half-closed shutters, was a small creole boy, whose slight yet perfectly proportioned form was perched on the edge of a Windsor chair, as with his legs crossed and his hair flung back from his tawney face, the young gentleman was briskly engaged in elaborating a fashionable boot into the requisite degree of polish.

The boy was eminently handsome. His face was a light brown in hue, yet perfectly regular in every feature; his complexion clear as a ripe Leckel pear, his lips red as May cherries, his eyebrows pencilled and arching, and his eyes full large, and black, brilliant as diamonds, and glittering as icicles. Long curling hair, marked by that peculiar jet black, tinged with a shade of deep blue, which designates the child of white and African parents, fell waving around his neck and face, in stiffened locks, resembling in their texture, the mane of a horse. His form, light springy and agile, was the ideal of a creole cupid. Not an outline too large or too small, not the slightest disproportion visible in a single limb, with small feet and delicate hands, a waist as lithe as a willow, and a hollow in the back like a bow gently bent; the creole was altogether one of the most beautiful things ever fashioned by the hand of Nature.

He was a pretty child, and yet his large black eyes had something in their glance which spoke of a precocious intimacy with the vices and intrigues of manhood.

"Massa tole Dim to polish dat boot until he see his face in de morroccor," muttered the young gentleman, brushing away at the glittering leather, "Dim can see his nose, and his two eyes in de boot, but the mouth aint not perfect. Stop a minnit, I bring dat feature out—ha, ha, ha !"

It was a pleasure to hear the little fellow talk, there was such a delicate accent lingering on his words; and his laugh, not at all similar to the usual African guffaw, was a quiet chuckle, which rolled lusciously in his mouth like a delicious morsel, whose sweetness he wished to enjoy at leisure.

"'Tink I shall hab to discharge massa. Debbil of a flare-up 'tween me and him some day when I tells him; "I don't want you any more, you sah !—you kin take dem wages and go !" Kep Dim up till broke ob day. Say dat morroccor don't shine? Break de lookin'-glass's heart

I tells you. Till broke ob day kep Dim a waitin' and den tumbles into bed, widout so much as giving de chile a-quataw! oh—de High-Golly."

This appeal to Master Endymion's favourite saint, the High-Golly, supposed to be some imaginary deity, created by the fertile fancy of the young Creole, was occasioned by a sudden mishap with the boot, which, resenting a vigorous push of the brush, slipped out of his hands, and went spinning across the room.

"Wonder if the debbil aint in that morroccor? I jis does. Nebber see sich a boot in all my born days. I lay a bran new brass dollar, dat if I was to set dat boot at de head of the stair, and no watch him, he'd streak it right off to de bar room, and call for a mint-julap, an' pull out his quartair to pay for it. I jis try him some day. Ha! ha! ha!"

"I say, Dim!"

"Yes, massa. I'se about ——"

"I say, Dim," continued the voice, which resounded from the interior of the bed-curtains, in the dark corner of the room, where the snore had been heard; "I say, Dim, what kind of a day is it?"

"Bran new day, massa. Got it's new coat and trowses on."

"I say, Dim, what have we got to do to-day?"

"Last night de curnel gib dis chile a kick, in order to mem'randum dese tings on Dim's memory. Dis mornin' you got to pay all your creditors. Dey comes in about an hour. High-Golly! aint dere a lot ob 'em? Den you got to see de lady who libs in Fourth-street. Den you got to go down town, to see if ole Devil-bug keeps dat dere feller safe. You knows who I means? Den you got to give Dim a quataw, and not to gib him no kick, by no means."

"Dressing-gown, Dim!"

"Yes, massa."

"Got any hot water ready for me, Dim?"

'Biles like a steam ingine."

"Light up the room, Dim!"

And in obedience to this request, Endymion flung back the shutters, and the full glare of the sunlight poured into the room. The owner of the voice and snore heard from within the curtains, sprung from the bed, and assuming the dressing-gown, advanced toward the windows.

Colonel Fitz-Cowles—the handsome Colonel Fitz-Cowles—stood revealed in the light, his dark-hued face looking somewhat worn and haggard around the eyes, while his slender form, attired in the rainbow morning-gown and close fitting drawers, though well proportioned and graceful in its outlines, by no means displayed that perfection of symmetry which distinguished the person of the millionaire in broad daylight, along Chestnut-street. For instance, the colonel was thicker around the waist, thinner about the hips, smaller in the region of the calves than was usual with him, when arrayed in full dress. His face was very pale, and his cheeks lacked that deep vermillion tint which gave such life to his dusky countenance at the evening party, or the afternoon parade.

"Dim, you d——l!" exclaimed the colonel, bestowing a gentle hint upon the gentleman of colour with the toe of his slipper. "Go down and get my breakfast. Tell the cook to butter my toast, and broil my steak directly. Vanish!"

Dim vanished through the door at the extreme end of the apartment. Arranging his shaving materials on the marble top of the dressing bureau, Fitz-Cowles commenced the solemn ceremonies of the toilette.

"Good razor that! Keen! Bad soap this—must kick the barber who sold it to me. Just think of my ticklish position! In debt up to the ears; forced to leave the United States Hotel only a day since, in order to avoid my creditors; perched in the fourth story of the Ton House; and why?—because I can't use the solid stuff locked up in that old hair trunk. Can't use it; somebody might find out something if I did. Curse the thing, but I think the old trunk's laughing at me!"

Razor in hand, Fitz-Cowles stooped to the floor, and drew from beneath the sofa an old hair trunk, which looked as if it had been through all Napoleon's campaigns, and suffered in the battle of Waterloo; it was so battered, and scarred, and weather-beaten, with great wounds of uncovered leather visible among the worn-out hair of its exterior.

"A hundred thousand locked up in that old ruffian of a trunk!" muttered Fitz-Cowles, gazing upon the object with an angry scowl; "half in sovereigns, half in notes! The d——l throttle the fool, why couldn't he get it all in American gold?"

"De toast is buttered, and de steak is briled," and as he spoke, Endymion entered the room, carrying the breakfast of his master in his hands. "Muss discharge dat cook. She gits quite sassy."

"Dim," cried Fitz-Cowles, making a hideous face in the glass in the effort to shave his chin; "set my breakfast down by the fire, and come here. Now, Dim, answer me one question, Who are we?"

"Massa take de chile for a phillysofer! Dat berry cute question. Sometime we are a plantaw from the souf; sometime we are a son of Mexican prince; oder time we come from Englan', and our fader is a lord. De High-Golly! we are so many tings, that de debbil hisself couldn't count 'em."

"Where were we this time last month?"

"Charleston, massa."

"The month before?"

"New Orleans, massa."

"Month afore that—eh, Dim?"

"Bos'on, massa."

"How long since we first fixed our quarters in this city?"

"Six month ago, and been a travellin' about eber since. Led dis chile a debbil of a life."

"What were we travelling about for—eh?"

"Axe de ole hair trunk. He tell you plain as pie-crust."

"I'll tell you what it is, Dim," exclaimed Fitz-Cowles, laying down the razor, and turning to the handsome creole boy. "If you ever whisper a word to anybody about anything you may have seen or heard while you travelled about with me these last six months, I'll just take this knife, and skin you, you black scoundrel; skin you—d'ye hear?"

Dim looked up into the scowling face of his master, with a glance of perfect calmness. The brow of Fitz-Cowles was disfigured by a hideous frown, and his entire countenance, wore an expression, characteristic of a low bully, who has been accustomed to the vilest haunts, in the most corrupt cities of the south. Dim was used to these sudden outbursts of passion, when his master, dropping his gentlemanly repose of manner, was wont to stand before him with his bowie knife in hand, while with a threatening tongue and sullen brow, he bade him reveal the things he had seen and the words he had heard, if he dared.

"You black scoundrel, d'ye hear?"

"De High-Golly! Dim aint black, and Dim aint no scoundrel. Yes Massa, I hears."

"If you ever whisper a word, mind, a word, I'd just take this bowie knife, and cut your head from your body! I'd do't I tell you."

"What make you do dat for? Dim could'nt draw bref den."

"Pshaw! You know better than to whisper a word. Here—help me to dress Dim. My corsets, Dim."

"Here they are Massa," cried Dim, throwing open one of the drawers of the dressing bureau. "New pair Massa?"

"Lay that morning gown on the chair. Now lace me. Tighter I say, that'll do. That's about the waist we want, isn't it, Dim?"

"Yes Massa. Dat's de wasp complete!"

"Hips, Dim."

"Which hip you want, Massa? Big hip or little hip?" cried Endymion, rummaging in the open drawer. "Dis pair do?"

"More subdued, Dim, more subdued. Just large enough to make my frock coat set out in the skirt. That's the idea."

With a careful movement, Endymion strapped certain detached portions of padding around his master's form below the waist, and in a moment this part of the ceremony was finished, giving quite a voluptuous swell to the outline of the colonel's figure.

"Calves, Dim."

"Which boots Massa wear to-day? Hab dis big calf or de toder one?"

"We want a good calf to-day, Dim. A large fat calf. That pair will do. Tie it round the leg—there, there. Draw the stocking over it, gently—gently! That's about the outline, eh?"

"Dicky, or a shirt, to-day, eh Dim?"

"Shirt, Massa, as you are goin' to hold your lebee!"

"Ha! ha! Wont there be a lot 'o 'em, the creditors? Black scarf, Dim?"

"Dar it is, Massa. Turn de collar down and tie up de scarf wid dis gole pin, dat's de ticket!"

"Now, Dim, my slippers. She worked them for me, you know, Dim? How many ladies are engaged to be married to us, if we will have them?"

"Dare's the soap biler's daughter, who spends her fader's fortin in perfumery. Dare's de rich grocery man's daughter, and de hardware merchant's daughter, and de wool merchant's only chile, and dare's——"

"Oh, d—— them; the set is cursed low. Black pants, Dim? Which is our principal ticket in the female line, eh, Dim?"

"Ha, ha, ha! down fourth street, Massa. De old genelman in New York, and de lady at home by herself! De High-Golly!"

"Vest, Dim. The new black vest, which, last night came home from the tailor. What hour will the creditors be here?"

"Dey come in that ar door," observed Endymion, pointing to the door on the right of the western window. "And accordin' to your directions, dey is shown into dat door, which conducts 'em into de large saloon, where dare's fire to warm their hands, and cheers to rest their bodies."

"Hallo, Dim, there's a tap at the door," exclaimed Fitz-Cowles, as arrayed in the full morning costume, with a gaudy silk wrapper, all broken out into spots of green, blue, and red, thrown round his limbs, he resumed his seat in the easy chair, beside the breakfast table. "I know the knock, it is Count Common Sewer, show him in."

Opening the door near the western window, Dim made a profound bow, as he ushered the visitor into the presence of Col. Fitz-Cowles.

"De editaw ob de Daily Black Mail, Mistaw Poodle, sah—Buzby Poodle, s-a-h!"

"Ha, ha! Curnel, *Bon jour*, as we say in French. Seen the 'Black Mail' this morning. Capital on dit about your gold mines—quite the thing—*ensemble de chose*, as we say in domestic French."

As he spoke, Buzby Poodle, Esq., stood bowing and scraping in the centre of the vacant space of carpet, extending before the breakfast table. Buzby Poodle wasn't handsome. Not precisely. He was a little thickset man, with a short heavy body, shaped something like a pine-knot, and irregular legs, fashioned like a pair of inverted parentheses, or like a pair of sickles with their backs placed together. It must be confessed that his legs were deplorably knock-kneed nearly acquainted with each other at the knees, and quite distant in their intercourse at the feet. Buzby's feet were not small; Douzzle the bootmaker has been heard to say, with evident pain, that he would just as soon make slippers for a young hippopotamus, as boots for Buzby. You could not positively say that Buzby's hands were small, or delicate, or decently aristocratic. Very short in the fingers, and very thick across the palm and back, Buzby's hands reminded you of a terrapin's fin ; they were such peculiar hands.

Buzby's face wasn't handsome. It may have been expressive, or intellectual, but it was not handsome. Looking upon his countenance, you were aware of the presence of a saffron lum of flesh, with a small projection in the centre for a nose, a delicate gash below this projection for a mouth, and two faint stripes of whity-brown hair, in the way of eyebrows. His eyes, looking from beneath the brows, without the intervention of anything you might call an eyelid, had a deplorable half-cooked appearance, very much like the visual organs of a salt mackerel roasting on the griddle. A delicate strand of forehead, about half an inch in width, was agreeably relieved by a dense thicket of curly brown hair. There were mysterious rumours about town with regard to this luxuriant hair. Several of Buzby's intimates had been observed to smile, when the ladies complimented him on his delightful curls; Pettito's the wig maker, always grew mysterious when Poodle's head of hair, was called in question, and once—but that was on a drinking party, when Pettitoes, intellects were muddled, he had said, with a melo-dramatic scowl, that "there was some people in this 'ere world as stuck 'emselves up mighty high, and yet wore dead people's—hum—he wouldn't say what they wore—but they wore dead people's—hum—he could tell what."

The general contour of his face was so singular, and—to use a word which he delighted to repeat on every occasion—so *unique*, that Coddle St. Giles, the celebrated miniature painter, who, having been honoured with the patronage of Queen Victoria, had painted the whole royal family from Her Majesty down to the lap-dog, said with a painful grimace, that he had never experienced such extraordinary feelings as came over him, when pourtraying Buzby on costly ivory, but once before in his life, and that—to use Coddle's delicious cockney dialect—"wos when the Royal Menageries had visited my native town, and I'ad the extr'onery honour to depict the lineaments of the female hourang-houtang."

Altogether, Buzby Poodle, Esq., was an extraordinary man; something out of the common run of men; a specimen of that high pressure style of editorial genius which the Quaker City admires and loves, to the bottom of its universal heart.

"Like that hint about your gold mines,—eh, curnel?" observed Buzby, flinging his cloak on a chair, and seating himself beside the breakfast table, " Nice steak for breakfast. Quite *recherche*—as we say in French. Don't care if I do take a pull with you. Get me a plate, Dim—"

" Why Buzby, this will *do*; yes certainly," observed Fitz-Cowles, stirring his spoon in the coffee, while he glanced over the pages of the " Daily Black Mail "—" But what a bad smell your paper has! Quite an odour. The *patch-*

cully, Dim. Now, get a plate for Count Common Sewer—"

" You are so jocular," exclaimed Buzby with a pleasant laugh—" You have such a quantity of fun about you! "Count Common Sewer!" ha, ha,, good! You like that *on dit,* then ?"

" Yes, Buzby, but you must touch 'em up tomorrow about the mysterious stranger at the Ton House; supposed to be the son of an English Earl; *perhaps* a Prince. You know, my boy?"

" Don't I!" exclaimed Buzby taking up Fitz-Cowles's toast between his fingers—" It takes me—*Il pris moi,* as we say in domestic French."

" Now Buzby," exclaimed Fitz-Cowles, fixing his dark eyes on the unmeaning face of the editor, with a look, that made the little fellow tremble in his shoes, " You know I pay you well, for these little advertisements. As a matter of course, you have some knowledge of my affairs; little knowledge, very little, but you might use it some day to my injury. What security have I that you will not do so ?"

" What security! Good Heaven's, curnel!" cried Buzby rising from his chair—" Can you suspect me ? This is *too* much" and Poodle's voice grew quite pathetic, " Why, curnel, to show what are my feelings towards you, I will now place myself completely in your power."

" As how ?"

Buzby made no reply, but striding with a cautious step to every door in the room, he assured himself that they were fast locked and secured; and then with an air of the deepest mystery approached Fitz-Cowles, and gazed steadily in his face.

" What the devil do you mean ?" exclaimed Fitz-Cowles, as he observed the boiled eyes fixed upon his countenance.

" There, there, I'm in your power. The secret's out. Nobody knows it but myself and wife. Now you know it too. You can ruin me if you like."

" What the devil do you mean ?"

" Why, why," exclaimed Buzby, fingering away at his curly hair—" *I wear a wig !*"

" Ha ! ha ! ha !" roared Fitz-Cowles, as Poodle stood before him, holding his head of hair in his hand—" Ha ! ha ! ha ! Count Common Sewer, you do look like old Jocko, the wonderful ape—whom they exhibited some time ago at the Masonic Hall ! Oh, Jupiter, I shall die ! Ha ! ha ! ha ! *That* head—*that* head !"

It was not the most solemn sight in the world. There stood Buzby, calm and solemn, his luxuriant head of hair extended in his right hand, while the outline of his *real* head, clothed with a short, wiry stubble of *real* hair, became painfully distinct in the light of the morning sun,

" And how is this to place you in my power?" asked Fitz-Cowles, after his laughter had subsided to a quiet chuckle—" Oh, Jupiter! *that* head! Buzby, do put on your wig, or you'll drive me into convulsions."

" How is this to place me in your power ?"

exclaimed Poodle in a half-offended tone, as he resumed his curly head of hair. "Would I figure so largely behind the scenes of the theatre, if the *ballet* girls knew I wore a wig? Curse it, the very *supes* would laugh at me, and the scene-shifters would not hesitate to jeer me! Fitz-Cowles, it may seem foolish to you, who have no such feelings of a tender nature, but—but—my whole existence is wound up in that head o' hair."

"The deuce it is! Why, Poodle, you did'nt know that it was thrown into my plate last night, at Monk-hall, did you?"

"Was it, though? Then I must have been drunk," exclaimed Buzby, with a look of the deepest mortification. "That accounts for the peculiar "sticky" state of my hair this morning —think any of the fellows noticed it?"

"Too drunk for that, Busby! By-the-bye, you must have had a great many 'tender adventures' in your time! Eh, Poodle."

"Hallo, Massa, open dis here door," the voice of Endymion, who had been down stairs in search of a plate for Buzby, was heard in the entry, "I hab got de plate for 'common sewer.'"

In a moment the door was opened, and Dim entered with a plate and some additional refreshments; which having been placed upon the table, Fitz-Cowles and Buzby resumed their breakfast.

"'Tender adventures?'" cried Poodle, masticating a piece of toast as he dropped his knife and fork. "D'ye see that?"

He drew a small pocket bible from his bosom as he spoke, and displayed it complacently before the eyes of the astonished Fitz-Cowles. It was corpulent with letters, inserted between the leaves, like so many anchovies, between various thin slices of bread and butter.

"This rather goes a-head of the wig! What may it mean, Buzby?"

"Don't you see, I keep all my love letters in the Bible? Ah, me! If I wasn't married! Well, well, it can't be helped! But these letters might tell a strange tale."

"Let them tell it by all means," observed Fitz-Cowles; and Buzby pushing his chair back from the table, and displaying his legs very wide apart, laid the pocket-bible on one knee, and commenced a soliloquy something after the following fashion.

"That's from a delightful creature, curnel," he observed, turning over one of the leaves of the bible, and extracting a letter. "She loves me. Of course, I had to be complaisant. Faint heart never won fair lady—*Le cœur ennuyé ne jamais pas engagé belle blanche*—as we say in French. That's from a vocalist, that from an actress, and that, ah, curnel, there's a mystery about it!"

"How so?"

"It's from an unknown lady. I've tried to find out her name through the clerks of the Post-office, but in vain. She's a southern planter's daughter, curnel. Rich, beautiful, just seventeen. Offers me her hand—don't know I'm hooked. Ah me! it would make the tears come into your eyes if I was to read this letter; there, curnel, is a lock of her hair."

And Buzby, with a look of subdued melancholy, slowly unfolded the letter, and held up in the sunlight a lock of reddish, brownish hair, which, long and slender, looked amazingly like a patent whip lash.

Fitz-Cowles preserved the gravity of his face with considerable difficulty, while the creole, Endymion, who stood at Poodle's shoulder, placed his hands alternately to his mouth, and the pit of his stomach, as though he was suffering under intermitting attacks of the cholera and toothache.

Buzby sat in the full light of the morning sun, holding the lock of hair, extended in his right hand, while his other hand absently grasped the pocket bible.

"You see she is a noble girl," he exclaimed, gazing fixedly upon the lock of hair, with a glance of painful melancholy. "Loves me. Spoke of my early struggles in her letter. Asked me if the world hadn't been hard with me? If the iron grasp of persecution hadn't been on my shoulder ever since the days of slips and pap-spoons? If it didn't gall me considerably to think my genius wasn't appreciated? If——"

Buzby paused, and with a look of tender melancholy, jerked the pinkish lock of hair up and down, as a carter cracks his whip.

The action was too much for Fitz-Cowles. He burst into a roar of laughter, while Dim, the creole, went rolling over the floor, holding his hands to his side, as though he was labouring under an epileptic fit.

"Curse me if I see any reason for laughing in this manner," exclaimed Buzby, rising angrily from his seat. "That's a very singular boy of yours, curnel. D—n him, he lays there wriggling like a snake."

"Ha! ha! ha! This is too good," roared Fitz-Cowles. "Of course I had no hand in writing that letter," he muttered to himself. "Get up, Dim, and behave yourself!"

"Massa, dis quite convulses us—it does— he! he! he!" exclaimed Dim, rising to his feet, "massa didn't send me to the barber, nor nothing to buy dat hair?" he chuckled, in a whisper inaudible to Buzby's ears, "Dim didn't take de letter to de pos' offis? De High-Golly!"

"This is quite a tender affair, *Il est une affaire tendre*, as we say in domestic French," exclaimed Buzby, resuming his seat, with this sentiment in his peculiarly detestable French. "'Pon honour, Curnel—it's a fact. The girl— the unknown—loves me devotedly. I should suppose that she read my—paper. How d'ye feel after the bruise last night?"

"Capital. I intend to have some fun this morning. You see my governor hasn't sent me my usual quarterly remittance. My creditors have been hunting me down for the last fortnight. I have been attacked in the street, assaulted in the theatre, besieged in my hotel.

As a last resort, I appointed a day for each of them to call and see me; and even named the hour. Of course each creditor is ignorant of the fact, that I have made the same appointment, with every one of his fellow blood-suckers. It happens to-day at ten o'clock, in the next room—this glorious family party!"

"Ha! ha! ha!" laughed Buzby Poodle. This beats some insolent schedules quite hollow! I say some, because I e had a little business in that line myself. Out of curiosity—mind ye, only from curiosity, I have looked over some of the schedules in the court, devoted to such interesting affairs."

"And you discovered something rich, I s'pose?"

"The old proverb says, 'a man is known by the company he keeps'—*comprenez-vous un homme par ses campagnons du voyage*—as we say in domestic French. Now I'm of the opinion that a man is known by his schedule. There's a schedule filed at the proper court, under the delicate nose of their honours, which says queer things for the character of its signer. One day he went round town, the jolly dog, getting seven coats, on credit, mind ye, from seven tailors; rings from this jeweller, and breast-pins from that; boots by quantity, and hats by the half-dozen; in short, there was scarcely a store in Chesnut-street that he didn't do; not a credulous merchant—ha, ha, ha! but was diddled by him, on this remarkable day."

"Well, well, what was the result?"

"One day, like a clock, he went exclusively on tick—the next day the clock stopped going. It was wound up to a considerable extent. The creditors looked blue. Their friends and pitcher took the Bankrupt Law!"

"De High-Golly! By de way dat chap tells de story, one 'ud think he did all dat his ownself! Ha, ha!"

"Buzby, your paper must make you some considerable amount of *l'argent*. How d'ye manage the "Daily Black Mail?""

This question appealed to the noblest sympathies of Poodle's heart. He rose slowly from his seat, he glanced round with an expression of condescending pride, and his face became radiant with a sudden enthusiasm.

"How do I manage the 'Daily Black Mail?'" he exclaimed, extending his right fin, in the manner of a stump-orator, who wishes to enrapture a mass meeting, consisting of a few dirty boys, one loafer, and two small dogs. "I do it a little in the footpad line. A big motto at the papers head, *Fiat justitia*, you know the rest. Do I want the cash? I stick in an article charging some well-known citizen with theft, or seduction, or some more delightful crime. Citizen comes down in a rage, wants the article contradicted in next day's paper. He pays for the contradiction, of course. I have known a mere *on dit* that so-and-so, had committed a hideous crime, to bring me in as much as a cool hundred at a lick."

"How do you manage to acquire so much favour with the sex?"

"Take the theatre, for instance. A new actress appears. Suppose her virtuous, or silly. I make advances. She foolishly repels me—very likely calls me a puppy. Next day an *on dit* appears in 'Black Mail,' headed, 'Licentiousness of the stage,' and embracing some compassionate allusion to the lady aforesaid. You understand? I damage her reputation by a paragraphical slur."

"And she capitulates?"

"Sometimes; and sometimes she don't. But I keep up this delightful fire of genteel insinuations, delicate allusions, and spicy *on dits*. If the girl's character is ruined, it isn't my fault, I'm sure."

"It's quite refreshing to hear you talk in this way. Are not times pretty dull with you now?"

"Oh, Lord, yes! Hasn't been a suicide for a week. Not even a murder about town, nor a nigger baby killed. I do wish something lively would spring up for Christmas—now an 'abduction case' with the proper trimmings. would go it with a rush! *Allez avec une furie* as we say in domestic French.

"How d'ye stand with the other papers?"

"Guess, when I tell you one slight circumstance. They regard my paper as a sort of literary galley, in which ever aspirant for fame must serve his time. An author, who has once been connected with my sheet, is regarded as a convict all his life by the rest of the world newspaporial. Good phrase that!"

"D'ye edit your paper, by yourself?"

"Bless you no! I know a trick worth two o'that—*Je comprend un artifice double-la*, as we say in domestic French. Whenever I find an author in extreme distress, rather out of pocket, you know? I take him into my office; give him a dog's salary, and make him do a dog's work."

"Dog's work, indeed! If he assists in getting up your paper!" was the murmured remark of Fitz-Cowles.

"Should he leave me—and they always do leave me after a month or so, I libel him on every occassion, and talk about ingratitude, ha, ha, ha! But the poor devil can never get rid of the crime of having been connected with my paper! That sticks to him like 'original sin' to a Puritan!"

"Well, Buzby, you have given me some fresh ideas about newspapers," observed Fitz-Cowles, "I thought I knew them like a book. You have given me a new wrinkle!"

He said this and gazed silently into the saffron face of Buzby Poodle.

Oh, glorious liberty of the press, let us take the opportunity by this quiet moment, and chaunt a psalm in your praise. Oh, glorious press, what a comfort it must be to you, to think and feel in your inmost heart, that Buzby Poodle who sits smiling in yonder chair, is no reality, no fact, but a mere fictitious impersonation of all the evils which spring around your life and darken your existence.

Oh, magnificent Quaker City, with your warehouses, and your churches, your theatres, and your brothels your banks and your insane hospitals, your loan companies and your alms houses, how delightful to all your denizens, must be the reflection that Buzby Poodle is no living nuisance, but an airy though loathsome creation of the author's brain.

Nursed from his very infancy in the purlieus of the dance house; an associate of the ruffian and the courtezan, from his earliest childhood; crawling from the pages of his foul journal, over the fairest reputations in the community; sneering at the character of this man's virtuous wife, blasting with his leprous pen, that man's stainless child; in his person and soul, one hideous blot and breathing deformity, an ulcer cankering over the bosom of society, a bravo who stabs for his dollar, a hireling who without character, without reputation, without even a name, prowls abroad, selling his sheet, to any man that will buy it, for any purpose under heaven, a tolerated infamy, an uncaged jail-bird, an unconvicted felon—oh, glorious, Qnaker City, does it not make your moral heart grow warm, when you remember that a creature, despicable as this, had no existence in fact, but is only a fancy of the author, a fiction of his brain.

Other cities may have their abominations in the shape of a licentious press, with marketable editors, who have in their time, pursued every honest occupation, from body-snatching up to newspaper publishing, but the Quaker City, like the ideal town of some far-off El Dorado, is so pure, so spotless, that an author in search of a cut-throat editor, by the portraiture of whose character he means to throw a dark relief around the brighter portions of his pages, must set his wits to work, and *invent, a Buzby Poodle* !

Oh, rare invention—Buzby Poodle—long may it be, ere a thing like you, shall start into tangible existence, and all be wigged and sickle-legged, walk visibly along Chesnut-street; a diminutive incarnation of a most nauseous emetic.

"Go to [the door, Dim ! There's the first of the creditors ! Be quiet, Poodle, and enjoy the fun."

"Yes Massa, I opens the door," cried Endymion, as the hoarse voice of creditor one was heard in the next room.

"Tell Colonel Fitz-Cowles that Mr. Bluffly Bulk want's to see him."

And as the hoarse voice echoed through the aperture, Mr. Bluffly Bulk appeared in the doorway, driving an immense paunch before him, as he walked along. His small head overlooked his immense corporation, like a pea observing the circumference of a pumpkin.

"Well, Fitz-Cowles," said Mr. Bulk, "I've called according to appointment. You owe me a fee in the case of 'Commonwealth vs. Fitz-Cowles,—charge, lathering a watchman. The fee is 'fifty.' Pay it, and let me go."

"Do me the kindness to step this way," exclaimed Fitz-Cowles with one of his best bows, as he motioned creditor one toward the small door opposite. "In a moment I'll see you; and settle this little matter."

Bluffly Bulk Esq. disappeared within the eastern door, muttering strange curses as he walked along.

"Dar goes ten o'cloc' Massa," exclaimed Dim, listening at the key-hole of the western door. "De High-Golly! I hear more of 'em in the nex' room."

"Show 'em in Dim ! One at a time ! ha ! Whom have we here ! My friend Smith he upholsterer."

A little thin man, with a narrow face, a starved nose, and a green overcoat, advanced and seized Fitz-Cowles earnestly by the hand.

"Note to pay to-day, sir," he said in a thrilling whisper. "Bill for the curtains you got of me when you was at the United States Hotel. Six hundred and fifty-two dollars, twelve-and-a-half cents. Tight times, sir. Money very scarce, shall I give you a receipt, sir ?"

"In the next room if you please," observed Fitz-Cowles, with a pleasant smile. "You see, my old fellow, we'll fix that matter in a minute."

"Bless your eyes, massa, dey are a-growlin' like cat-an' dog in toder room !" observed Dim, holding the door slightly open. "I hear's 'em a-comin' up de stairs; and I hears de sarvant a-showin' 'em into the next room."

"This grows quite refreshing ! Almost equal to a schedule at the Insolvent Court !"

"Is Misther Fitz-Cow-howles, in the house himself, jest ? Be aisy there, ye nager, and let me come in. Dhrop a word into his private ear, that Michael O'Flannagan, French boot maker from Paris, is a wantin' to get the taste ov a sight of him."

And a large-boned man, attired in a shabby white great coat, with an old fur cap drawn over his eyes, came rushing into the room. He stood full six feet in his stockings; and his red face, seen through the apertures of his hair and whiskers, all of the same burning red, looked very much like the countenance of a man who won't stand upon trifles; or occupy his time in breaking the hind legs of a flea.

"Oh, the blases ! But them sixteen pair of stairs give me a pain in the side; the top o' th' marning' to ye, curnel, its yerself that's looking' like a canary-bird the-day. Shall we finger the pewther, curnel ? Cinshider the seventeen pair o' boots, all done and complated by Michael O'Flannagan, French boot maker, from the city o' Pari-i-s, in the old counthry."

"He's got the real Parisian accent !" exclaimed Buzby Poodle. "Talks like a native. Quite *au fait* !"

"The accshent ? And who the devil should have the accshent, but me ? Wasn't I brot up all my life, a giniwine Frenchman, and didn't my father fight with ould Boney, in the scrimmage of Waterloo ?"

"You speak it like a native, Mikey. This

way; I'll talk to you in a minute. Show 'em in Dim"

"Mistaw Douzzle, de toder boot maker from Paris!"

A mouldy looking man, of short stature, and a heavy face, invested by a dampish beard of some indefinable colour was now shown into the room, with his arms hanging straight by his sides, like pendulums to some walking clock.

"Curnel, I ish in want fery mosh ov da[t] small bill for de French boots. Times is hard; mine wife is sick, and von child has got de measles. Eight pair of fine French boots, seven dollars a-pair, seven eight ish fordy-eight."

"Next room Douzzle. See you in a minute. Keep on showin' 'em in, Dim."

"I 'ave the honour to present my small bill,

THE CREDITORS OF COLONEL FITZ COWLES ENGAGE IN A GENERAL COMBAT.

exclaimed a little man in a cockney face, and brown sack coat. "To one portrait of Col. Fitz-Cowles, fifty dollars. Very much in want of money, to-day, sir. Obliged to you for a little. Never since I 'ad the extron'ery honour to paint Her Royal Majesty Victoria and Prince Halbert, with the 'ouses o' Parliament and the lap-dog in the background, never since that ere

blessed moment have I taken so much pains with a mini'ture as with yours! Out of wood, sir, out of coal, out of ivory, sir."

"Not out of brass I hope? Ha! ha! ha! There I had you St. Giles! Walk into the next room if you please! Pass 'em this way, Dim"

And Dim did pass them that way to some

considerable extent. It should be borne in mind that Col. Fitz-Cowles had been living for some time past in a style of princely splendor, kept up and supported by a numerous retinue of credulous tradesmen. The results of this princely style, now manifested themselves in the shape of some four-and-thirty creditors, who came pouring from the ante-room, one after another, in quick succession, with their bills in hand, and their demands ringing loudly on the air, like a delightful chorus to the grand drama of the Bankrupt law.

"A small bill for horse hire. To a chaise and four," began a little thick-set man, with brown whiskers, and a short bang up, smelling strongly of the race-course. "To a chaise and four, seventeen times."

"My little bill for ten coats, fifteen pair of pants, fourteen vests and a dickey," interrupted a solemn looking personage, pressing hurriedly forward. "Firm of Flunk, Checkley and Co. Five hundred and fifty dol—"

"I ave furnish you with parfumerie, to dis amount."

"Seventy one pair of gloves, White kid. Hoskin's."

"To the use of my cab, Gineral Washington won-hunter' and fafty times."

"To, the 'gentleman's universal wardrobe, an' furnishin' store,' Col. Fitz-Cowle's debtor, sixteen fine shirts, and——"

"My bill for dry goods, sir," said a pompous man, with a snub nose and immense ragged whiskers, "M'Whiley Mumshell, sir. Two hundred and six——"

"'Pothecary's bill for med'cine. Seven bottles Swain's Panacea."

"Ha, ha! This beats the insolvent court! What a scene for the next 'Black Mail!'"

"De High-Golly! Dey come wid a parfac looseness dis time!"

"Gentlemen, gentle-men," exclaimed Fitz-Cowles, looking from face to face with a pleasant smile. "You are really too impatient. To see you rushing forward in this style, one would think I had the wealth of Girard in my pockets. Step into the next room, gentlemen. All your demands shall be satisfied."

A murmur of satisfaction burst from the contrasted throng, and in an instant they had all disappeared into the next room.

"Now, Buzby, let's wait a few minutes until they begin to grow feverish. When I think they've worked themselves up into proper humour, we'll step in, and take a look at them. I'll show you how to bluff off a creditor."

"I thought I was rather *au fait* at that business myself. However, *onter noos*, as we say in domestic French."

CHAPTER II.

FITZ-COWLES AND HIS CREDITORS.

IN a large saloon, furnished in a style of magnificence, popularly known as the gingerbread styles, with immense red silk curtain along the windows, scattered patches of gilt glittering around the cornices, and a collossal mirror above the mantle, sate the four-and thirty creditors, waiting for the appearance of the *millionaire*.

The softened light which came through the drawn curtains, gave a mild and shadowy effect to the figures of the patient band, while it was quite delightful to witness the animated expression of their countenances, as gazing into each others eyes, they seemed to wonder why in the deuce they were all penned up there together, like various kinds of cattle at an agricultural fair.

Bluffly Bulk, Esq., the fat lawyer sat glaring upon the little bootmaker, Douzzle, as though he was wondering what kind of a fry the fellow would make for his breakfast; Michael O'Flannagan, the Parisian bootmaker, was engaged in polishing his shoes on the handsome hearth-rug; Coddle St. Giles, gazed vacantly around with the look of a man who has been feloniously decoyed into a den of thieves, while the rest of the four-and-thirty creditors were occupied in examining their various bills, which they raised frequently in the light, and crushed between their fingers, as though the action was productive of great peace of mind and tranquility of spirit.

A buz-buz of satisfaction responded through the saloon.

Col. Fitz-Cowles appeared in the doorway with Buzby Poodle, and Endymion at his back.

"Gentlemen," said the colonel, placing one hand between his back and his flashy morning-robe, while he waved the other gently up and down, "I owe you money."

"That you do," muttered Bluffly Bulk, Esq., stamping his cane on the floor; and a buz-buz from the four-and-thirty creditors, confirmed the truth of the sentiment. It was quite pleasing to see how much unanimity of feeling existed on this point. Had there been only half the concurrence of opinion visible in the doings of most of our religious conventions, synods and conferences, the world would have been christianized long ago.

"I owe you money, and I mean to pay it."

"He means to pay it! Hurrah! Three times, hurrah!"

"I mean to make your fortunes. I should suppose you all want money rather bad?"

"Deuced bad." "Cursed bad." "Och, do'nt I?" "Wife and children, one sick with the measles." "Starvation." "Go to jail." "Out of wood, out of coal, out of ivory."

"If I don't pay you this morning I suppose it will ruin you all?"

"Totally." "Have to leave the city." "Cant think on't." "Horrible." "Och whillaloo!" "Ruin me, root and branch!"

"Well, then, gentlemen, I will make your fortunes. You have a pleasing countenance, my friend Bluffly Bulk, a respectable person. You shall oversee the hands. Yes, yes, that'll ust suit you. Master Flannagan, imagine yourself perched on the edge of a well, some hundred fathoms deep, telling the labourers below to mind their eyes and be d—d to 'em. 'Hoist away my hearties,' d'ye take? Coddle St. Giles, your remarkable talents will here be called into requisition. You can take drawings of the mines, publish 'em when we all get back, splendid volume—letter press by Silvester J. Petriken, of the Western Hem. Flunk, my dear friend Flunk, of the firm of Flunk, Checkley and Co., merchant tailors, you can make up a lot of clothes for the miners. 'Gad gents, I like the plan altogether; it will suit our ivarious talents. It will make our fortunes."

" Gintlemen, me name is Mikey O'Flannagan, bootmaker, from Paris, and me father fought with ould Boney, and so ye see there's some larnin' in our family, but may the devil fly away wid me, if I can make out what the curnel manes. By Julius Caysar, but we're all a listenin' to a gintleman from the insane hozpittal !"

" What in the d—l do you mean ?" exclaimed Bluffly Bulk, growing like a turkey-cock in the face as he fixed his eyes upon Fitz-Cowles, who stood in the centre of the saloon, in an attitude of deep abstraction. " Be so kind as to explain yourself !"

" Yes, the plan is feasible," exclaimed Colonel Fitz-Cowles, elevating his eyebrows with an absent stare. " But there's a rough desert to pass through before we reach the mines. Plenty of Mexicans and Texans—not to mention the Indians and wild beasts. Still the mines are productive : on my father's estate you know ? I'm *incog.* just now, but when the company is in full operation, under the combined patronage of Santa Anna, the Mexican government, and Sam Houston, I'll make known the old man's name."

" Sir," cried Bluffly Bulk, in a voice of thunder, " Will you tell us what you mean ?"

" Arrah, man, and be quick at it !"

" Oblige us with some slight knowledge."

" Guess he wants a straight-jacket."

" Tell you what I mean ?" exclaimed Fitz-Cowles, starting from his reverie. " With pleasure. You see gentlemen, I propose to make your fortunes, by allowing you to enter your names, as stockholders of 'the Grand Montezuma Gold-Mining Company of the gold mines of Huancatepapetel, district of Tolpcaptl, South Mexico—Algernon Fitz-Cowles, *President*, Bluffly Bulk, *Secretary*, Board of Directors as follows—' you can fill up the blank at your leisure you know ? I will allow you, each to take ten shares of the capital stock at £100 per share ; and we will say nothing about the small sums I owe you. Mere trifles you know, Bluffly, in consideration of the post of secretary being tendered you, one hundred shares will be the smallest number you can be permitted to take."

Fitz-Cowles paused, and looked around to note the effects of his important proposition. There was a dead silence in the saloon. You might have heard a pin drop. The four and thirty creditors looked into one another's faces, but said nothing. Buzby Poodle and Dim the creole, concealed themselves among the window-curtains, which quivered and shook as with a sudden convulsion.

" Gentlemen, d'ye like my proposition ?" said Fitz-Cowles, blandly. " Is it feasible ? We can all go to Huancatapepetel together ; times are so hard in this city. Those that are married can take their families with them ; those that are single will get families soon enough on their arrival at the mines. You are silent, it is with surprise I suppose ? Or d'ye want to advance some small amount on your shares ? No, gentlemen, I can't think of that ! The trifles I owe you one and all, will more than pay for your shares."

" Well, may I be rammed into a shot gun, and fired off at a nigger riot, if this isn't the coolest thing I've heard of for some time !" and as he spoke the fat laywer started from his feet, and confronted Fitz-Cowles, " Zounds, sir, what do you take me for ?"

" A fine fat old gentleman," replied Fitz-Cowles, bowing, " who would make a capital superintendent of the mines. By Jupiter ! Bluffly, that person of yours carries respectability in its every outline. It is worth at least a thousand shares to the company."

The storm long gathering and silent in its growth, burst suddenly over the head of Fitz-Cowles. One and all the four and thirty creditors rose, one and all they poured forth their anger in broken words and bitter curses.

" J—s the villain !" " The scoundrel." " Swindler." " This is wot I gits for his mini'-tur !" " I'm paid for the fifteen coats and —" " Here's the cash for my gloves !" " Tish is damdt pat, my wife sick, and de shildren got de measles." " Hurrah ! Let's whack into 'im !"

" This beats an insolvent schedule all hollow !" laughed Buzby Poodle, peering out from behind the curtains. " Gad ! what a scene for the Black Mail ! Four and thirty creditors, of all shapes, sizes and patterns, surrounding Fitz-Cowles, who greets 'em with a commiserating smile ! Ha, ha ! Capital."

" De High-Golly !" shouted Dim, thrusting his head from the other curtain, " dey look as dey eat massa up widout any pepper or salt ;"

" Gentlemen—will you hear me !" shouted Fitz-Cowles in a voice of thunder, as he gazed upon the four-and-thirty threatening faces. " Will you or will you not ? Am I to be insulted in my own house ? Dim—go and call the servants, and have these fellows trundled down stairs."

" Well, sir, what do you propose ?" cried Bluffly Bulk, his voice rising above the tumult, " No more humbug, sir."

" You then reject my offer, made with the best feelings in the world, to combine you, one and all into the Grand Montezuma Gold-Mining Company of the Huancatepapetel."

" ' Huancatty-kettle-polly' be d——d !'

shouted Flunk the tailor, pressing forward, as he shook his clenched hand in the air.

"Pitch 'Gwan-goett-polly' to the divil!" screamed O'Flannagan the boot maker.

"Just as you like, gentlemen. Pitch Huancatepapetel to the devil, by all means. But I was about to observe that the various sums, which I owe you separately, taken in a lump, amount to something over three thousand dollars. You are interested. Well now, my fellows, here's the difficulyt. I've but a thousand dollars cash in my possession. You can divide it among you, if you like."

"Now you *talk*," observed Bluffly Bulk, with a pleasing smile, as though the previous remarks of Fitz-Cowles had not risen even to the dignity of talk. "Of course my little fee of fifty dollars, will be satisfied out of this sum, in precedence to all other claims."

"Av course me little bill of thirty sivin dollars, sixty cents," observed Mr. Flannagan, stepping briskly forward, as he thrust his hands deep into the vacuum of his great coat pockets, "Will take the presidence of your thrifling claims."

"Of course, curnel, my bill of two hundred and fifty, for dry goods," mildly exclaimed Mr. Whiley Mumshell, pulling his ragged whiskers, with a hand, all glittering with costly rings. "My little bill will be considered, first of all."

"And is it the likes of ye, to stand afore me? The devil dhrag me under a narrow, but ould rat-face, you've a dale of imperdence in them same whiskers."

"Curnel, don't forgit the min'itur'—" "Nor the horse-hire—" "Remember the gloves—" "Isn't I to be paidt for my poots?" "De parfumerie Monsieur Viz-Cowle—" "Jist stand back there, will ye—" "Devil take your impudence—I'm as good as you—" "Say that again—" "Youre another—" "My bill, curnel—" "Mine I say—" "Wife and five children, won sick wid de measles—"

"Gentlemen—do be calm—" cried Fitz Cowles as he viewed the gathering storm —"Remember gentlemen, that you are gentlemen Be calm Flannagan—Quiet yourself Bluffly —Sooth your excited feelings Mumshell —"

"Will you settle my bill"—shrieked Bluffly Bulk, red in the face with anger—"Yes or no!"

"Botherashin! Stand back ould porpoise—and let me give him a receipt—or is it a row ye're a-wantin'—"

"D—d Irishman, grated Bluffly between his teeth.

"D—d Irishman," am I? And me a Paryshian barn? For the sake of my ould man, who was an Irishman, and who fit wid Boney at Watherloo—take that."

And with his clenched hand he aimed a blow, full at the immense corporation of the fat lawyer. The blow brushed Mumshell's whiskers and took effect on the person of the lawyer. The effect was terrific. In an instant the four and thirty creditors, their bills in hand, were all mingled through each other, every man striking the man who stood next to him, without regard to consequences, while Bluffly and Flannagan went at it, tooth and nail, exchanging fisticuffs with remarkable good will.

The scene was peculiar. A forest of fists, rising up and down, a mass of angry faces, all mingled together, some four and thirty bodies of all sizes and descriptions, twisting and winding about with so much rapidity, that they all looked like the different limbs of some strange monster, undergoing a violent epileptic fit.

"Gentlemen, do be calm."

"Go your death—*Allez-vous votre mort!* as we say in domestic French. Hit 'em again! *frappez duex fois!* That's it!—Give him another! *donnez lui un autre!*"

"You scoundrel—I'll prosecute you for damages."

"Damages, you ould porpoise, then by my father's soul, I'll damage you a thrifle more!"

"This is shameful! Show me the man who struck me in the eye."

"Bi Gott! I vill murder somebodys tirectly."

"Let me up! It wasn't me that struck you!"

"I'll take the wo'th of my gloves out o' somebody."

"Oh, my h-eye! 'Ere's a purty minature for you!"

"Oh, whililoo! Any one here that'll say I wasn't a Paryshian born? Fight it out, boys—lather it into one another; Whoop! Say that black mark under yer eye isn't a bit o' patchwork, will ye? Jest say it! Come on six ov ye—I ain't pertikler which! Hurrah! There goes the lookin'-glass! Crack—smash—bang! Thry it agin, ould porpoise! This bates Watherloo, hurray, hurray!"

CHAPTER III.

THE mirror which hung above the dressing bureau, reflected the handsome form of Col. Fitz-Cowles. It must be confessed that the colonel looked decidedly interesting, as standing before the mirror, in the glare of the morning sun, he surveyed his form for the last time, ere he sallied forth on Chesnut-street. His figure, with its broad chest and tapering waist, was enveloped in a close-fitting overcoat of dark cloth, which, falling open along the breast, disclosed his black scarf, gathered over his shirt front with a plain gold pin, and tastefully disposed within the collar of his glossy coat and satin vest, whose jet black hues were in harmony with the other portions of his attire.

The dark visage of the colonel, relieved by long curling locks of jet-black hair, was surmounted by an elegant hat, remarkable for its conical crown and width of brim. This was the much admired and very aristocratic "Fitz-Cowles' hat," worn by all the distinguished bloods of the Quaker City. Introduced by the gallant colonel, it soon became the rage, and was at the time of which we write, the standing test of fashion and elegance among the exquisites of Chestnut-street.

"Dim," said the colonel, gently waving the gold-headed cane, which he held within the white kid glove of his right hand, "Are they all gone?"

"All turned out, massa. De sarvants tumble 'em down stairs more an half hour ago."

"Dim," continued the colonel, impregnating his snow white handkerchief with an additional scent of patchoully. "What's the damage!"

"De looking-glass 'bove de mantel broke in a tousan' pieces—one ob de winder curtains torn down. De berry debbell kicked up all ober de room—"

"Buzby—" resumed the colonel, passing a comb lightly through the locks of his jet-black hair, "How did you like it?"

"Quite *recherche*. But won't they sue you for their various debts?"

"Let them sue and be hanged! The amount I owe them, applied in the proper way, would command a great influence in court. Why man, I've got the price of seven judges, ten juries, and some score of lawyers, in my pocket. These things are all for sale—"

"Ha! ha! This is libellous! Hello!—There's a knock at the door—"

"See who it is Dim—"

"Dim opened the door at the extreme end of the bed-chamber. He gazed for an instant through the aperture, and then closing the door with a sudden movement, he came running to his master's side, his eyes dilating with surprise, and his tawny face pale as Fitz-Cowles's white kid gloves.

"What in the deuce is the matter, Dim?"

"Oh, Golly Massa! Oh Lor! Oh de debbil!" cried the creole, dancing about the room.

"Shall I knock you down with the chair you scoundrel? Or would you like to be held out of a fourth-story window, by the heels, again?"

Dim approached his master's side, and whispered in his ear.

The colonel's face grew suddenly pale, and a blasphemous oath escaped from his lips.

"Buzby, go into the next room," he cried harshly, with the same tone he would use in getting rid of a troublesome dog; "be quick, I have a visitor, whom I must see alone. Why do you stand there, staring in my face like an idiot? Begone I say, I must be alone."

Buzby Poodle, disappeared through the saloon door, with a look of malignant anger, that boded no good to his friend, Colonel Fitz-Cowles.

"Open the door. D'ye hear Dim?" shouted the colonel, as his face grew paler, and his dark eye, emitted a clear flashing glance, that betokened powerful though suppressed emotion. "Show our visitor in."

Dim opened the door at the end of the bed-chamber, farthest from the windows, and the visitor entered. It must be confessed that the

suprise which the mere utterance of his name occasioned, might be easily explained, when the singular appearance of the new-comer, was taken into consideration.

A short, thickset, little man, dressed in a suit of glossy black cloth, advanced from the open door. His face, which from its remarkable length, gave you the idea of a horse's head, affixed to the remnant of a human body, seemed to lay upon his heart, while his shoulders arose on either side, as high as his ears, and his back protruding in a shapeless lump, was visible above the outline of his head.

His face, it is true, from its extreme length, and the peculiar manner in which it seemed to lay on his breast might have appeared distorted and deformed, yet were the features perfectly regular, the nose was a decided aquiline, the mouth well-proportioned and indicative of firmness, the chin, full and round, while the high forehead with the dark eyebrows, overarched two large and brilliant eyes whose intense lustre beaming from a face, marked by a clear healthy complexion, gave the beholder the idea, that he beheld a supernatural, rather than a human being.

Should the latter portion of this description, appear overstrained, the reader will remember, that the diminutive stature of the strange visitor, the hump on his back, and the manner in which his face seemed to rest on his chest, all gave additional effect to the expression of his face and eyes. "Jew," was written on his face as clearly and distinctly as though he had fallen asleep at the building of the Temple at Jerusalem, in the days of Solomon, the rake and moralist and after a nap of three thousand years, had waked up in the Quaker City, in a state of perfect and Hebraic preservation.

"You are here, are you?" whispered Fitz-Cowles in a tone of ungovernable rage, "Why, is this? Why have you left your hiding place in broad daylight?"

"I've comsh bekos I vanted to comsh," said the Jew calmly, as he folded his hands across his breast.

"You have, have you?" whispered Fitz-Cowles as the gleam of rage brightened in his dark eyes. "Do you know, you dog, you miserable dog, that I've a great notion to give you a taste of this."

And as he spoke, quick as thought, he flung open the breast of his over-coat, and drawing the bowie knife from a secret pocket, he brandished it above the head of the Jew, with a look of ungovernable hatred.

"Puts away te carving-knife—Puts away te carving-knives," said the humpback, with a bitter, though scarcely perceptable sneer. "You vill not hurts noboty."

"Perhaps you will tell me why you have left your hiding place! In broad day, with all the police at your heels? Ha, ha, this is delightful! Curse that Devil-bug," he muttered as he strode to the window. "How could he have let this dog escape?"

"I tells you vy I 'ave left dat nashty plashe,'

said the Hebrew in the coolest manner imaginable; "bekos it vos a nashty plashe! Bekos dese little hands do all te vorks—and may be after all, you reaps te profit. I mosh hide in dat hole, viles you valksh Chestnut-streets? Vos dat de kontraksh? You keep your pargain vill yous?"

"And what was that bargain?" exclaimed Fitz-Cowles again facing the Jew.

"Ven te tings vos done, yov vos to gif me ten thousand tollars in goldt. I vos to sail for Europes. Vot have you done? Left me to rots among roppers and tiefs, viles you walksh Cheshtnut-streets! Got-tam!"

The Jew sate down, or rather fixed himself on the sofa, and looked up calmly into the flushed countenance of Fitz-Cowles.

"Well, well, Von Gelt, lets shake hands, and talk the matter over."

"We may talksh as mosh as we pleashes, but we tont shake handts."

"Just as you like. Well, Judas, is that your first name Von Gelt?"

"Supposh it vos my naturs!" Vonder how long afore the handsome curnels would be—Father Moses—I know veres."

"So you threathen, me, do you Gabriel? Ha! ha! This is amusing. May I ask what you propose to do?"

"To morrow mornings I vill take te carsh for New Yorksh. Nex tay I vill sail for Europes. To tay, you will gif me, ten tousandt tollars."

"But Judas—that is Gabriel—Judas for short, you know? you must remember that I have not ten thousand dollars in my possession."

"Veres is te ole hair trunksh?"

"But Gabriel," exclaimed Fitz-Cowles in a conciliating tone, as he seated himself, beside the table opposite the Jew. "But Gabriel you know that it is impossible for us to have this money, for months to come. The sovereigns and the notes, might be recognized at once. It is better to wait a little while and make sure of the whole sum beyond a chance of detection. Pen and ink, Dim."

"Meaviles te poleesh ranshack Monk-halls, andt fint me, hit avay among tiefs and roppers. No, no! I vill bear tish no longers. Tish tay I mosh have ten tousandt tollars, or—or—,"

"Or—or—" echoed Fitz-Cowles as he scrawled a few words on a sheet of gilt-edged paper. "Or—or—You was about to observe."

"May be I can git ten tousandt tollars, someveres else," said the Jew with a meaning look.

"Ah, ah! You grow humourous, Gabriel," observed Fitz-Cowles with a smile. "Please deliver this little note to Devil-bug if you should chance to see him again, before you start for Europe. Will you Gabby?"

"Ha! vot is tish!" exclaimed the hump-backed Jew, as is eye glanced over the note, which read as follows:—

"DEVIL-BUG—Our friend leaves us to-morrow. It is all right. Aid him as far as you can, in anything that concerns his departure.

THE ABBOT."

"Den you conshents?" exclaimed Gabriel, with a smile of triumph. "You vil gif me te monish?"

"Of course, of course. You know I would never refuse you anything, Gabriel. You must be careful though, Gabriel, with the money. Mighty careful."

"Vot a fool I vos, ever to part mit it!" muttered Gabriel. "I hadt it all in mine own handts won time."

"Excuse me one moment, Gabriel, while I write a note to my jeweller," said Fitz-Cowles, with a pleasant smile. "Here, Dim, take this ring and this note down to Melchior the jeweller, in Fourth-street near Chestnut. Hurry back, d'ye hear?"

As he seized the note and folded it, Fitz-Cowles gazed smilingly in the face of the Hebrew. But when he took the diamond ring from his finger, and handed it to Dim, with one quick flashing glance of his dark eyes, the smile deepened into an agreeable laugh, and Fitz-Cowles looked, for all the world, like a man whose mind is unburdened by a single care. And this, while his life and fortune hung upon the note which he handed to the creole!

"Dim, you understand? This ring and note are for the jeweller in Fourth-street below Chestnut."

"Yes, Massa," answered Dim, with a stolid and imperturable expression of countenance. "I'll be back d'rectly."

That note was the death warrant of the Jew.

Thus it read:—

"DEVIL-BUG—When the Jew comes back to Monk-hall he will have about his person ten thousand dollars. You can pay yourself for the care and trouble you have had with him. The ring will tell you what I mean.

THE ABBOT."

"Now, Gabby," exclaimed Fitz-Cowles, as Dim hastened from the room. "You can amuse yourself by looking out of the window, while I get you the money."

As the handsome Algernon, stooping to the floor, drew the hair trunk from beneath the sofa, Gabriel, the Jew, rose from his seat and advanced toward the window.

"Dere's noting like improvin' vous times," he muttered, as he seized an object, which lay exposed on the top of the dressing bureau. "Father Moses! He vill svear ven he misshes dis ting."

"Ten notes of a thousand dollars each," murmured Fitz-Cowles, locking the trunk again. "Much good will they do him! Devil-Bug is such an amiable man!"

"Now I vill pegone!" exclaimed Gabriel, hastily concealing the notes within the breast of his overcoat. "Dish countries is too hot to holdt me."

He strode to the door, and looked back at Fitz-Cowles, as he uttered this pleasant good-bye.

"Farewells! Ven ve meetsh agin may ve pe in betterish spiritsh. Goot byesh!"

He disappeared, and in a moment was heard passing hurriedly along the entry without the bedchamber.

"Go!" shrieked Fitz-Cowles, the moment he had disappeared. "Go, and to your death!"

He paced hurriedly along the room, his brow darkening over with a heavy frown, and his eye blazing with excitement.

"Ha! The door leading into the saloon is ajar, could any one have listened to our conversation?" he pushed the door open and glanced around the spacious apartment, as he spoke. "Ha, ha! There is no one in this room! What a fool I am to fancy a listener near. And yet that fellow, Buzby—but he's too cowardly to betray a man. He might muster courage to betray a lame nigger woman, or a sick rag-picker, but a man—never!"

He closed the door leading into the saloon, as he spoke.

And as the door closed, the form of a man stole softly from the folds of the silken window curtains, and Buzby Poodle stood disclosed in the light. His face was very pale, and his hands trembled like pendulums very much out of order.

"Here's a secret worth a fortune," he exclaimed, as he passed through the saloon door, into the winding entry of the fourth story. "Betray a rag-picker, indeed! Ho! ho! What if I betray a forger?"

Meanwhile Fitz-Cowles strode swiftly along the floor of his bedchamber, his face and manner betraying the wild excitement which possessed his soul.

"If I manage my cards right I am safe! Ha! ha! That Jew got up some very neat letters from my father, the Earl of Lyneswold, Lincolnshire, England! To give the d—l his due, the Jew managed these letters with a masterly hand. The English post-marks and all! I showed them to Dora, together with a parchment, containing our pedigree—the Lyndeswolds of Lyndeswold! I have used the Jew, and now—egad! he must retire from the scene! By next Monday morning I can arrange everything! And then, as from the decks of a steamer bound for England, I gaze upon the receding shores of America, with Dora's smiles in my face, and the cash rattles in my pocket, then—ha, ha, ha! how I shall laugh at these fools of the Quaker City!"

CHAPTER IV.

DORA LIVINGSTONE AT HOME.

THE *boudoir* was lighted by two long and narrow windows looking to the south. The morning sunshine shone mildly round the place, through the folds of the thick curtains of light silk, which hung drooping along the windows.

In shape, the room was sexagonal, with pedestals of dark marble, standing along four of the six walls. On the top of one pedestal stood an alabaster vase, containing flowers of the choicest hues and fragrance, gathered from the conservatory, which was visible through the small door; on the summit of the second, was placed a statue of Venus de Medici, sculptured by a master hand, in snow-white marble; the third supported another vase, also filled with flowers, while the top of the fourth was occupied by an image of the Virgin Mary, her eyes raised upwards to Heaven, and her hands clasped over the crucifix, resting upon her bosom.

The small door leading into the adjoining conservatory, located in the second story of the western wing of Livingstone's princely mansion, hung slightly ajar. A delightful fragrance, the breath and sweetness of many flowers, pervaded the atmosphere. The perfume of the full-blown rose, the penetrating scent of the heliotrope, the delightful odour of the arbor vitæ, mingling with the fragrance of a thousand other plants and flowers, created an air of delicious and intoxicating sweetness.

The appointments of the *boudoir*—or, perhaps, closet would be the more correct designation, were neat and classic. Four handsome gothic chairs, with worked-cloth seats, disposed along the walls, an elegant sofa, placed between two of the pedestals, a severely-classic table of snow-white marble standing opposite, all burdened with books in costly binding, strewn over its surface; and a gorgeous Turkey carpet, whose deep rich colours were in effective contrast to the light and delicate papering of the walls; all combined produced an effect of elegance and taste, heightened and refined by the vases of flowers, and the marble statues presenting beauty in the contrasted forms of religion and love.

The heat of the conservatory, mingling with the sweetness of its flowers, imparted a fragrant warmth to the *boudoir*. No stove, nor grate, with glaring coal or crackling wood, was therefore needed to render the place comfortable.

Altogether the entire room was embued with an air of spiritual repose, of dreamy languor, which would have been very etherial indeed, if it had not been for the presence of the small breakfast table, which stood in the centre of the carpet, like a plain and stubborn earthly fact, with its silver coffee-pot, porcelain cup, and buttered toast, disposed along the surface of a snow-white cloth. However, the coffee was cold, and the toast untasted. This was something in favour of the spirituality of the *boudoir*.

Through the dim light which imparted a twilight effect to the room, you might discern the outlines of a woman's form, as she lay reclining on the sofa. Her form, full, large, and voluptuous, was enveloped in the folds of a snow-white morning gown, which gathering lightly around her queenly figure, displayed the symmetry of her rounded arms, the fulness of her bust, and the swelling outlines of her person, in the richest varieties of light and shade. A single red gleam of sunlight, escaping through the folds of the window-curtain, streamed over the whiteness of her snowy neck.

Her head resting on the sofa cushion, with the dark hair falling carelessly around, her eyes were half-closed in dreamy reverie, and the brightness of her glance, subdued to a hazy dimness, which attested the absence of her thoughts from all outward things, stole mildly from the shadow of the long and trembling lashes.

Her entire attitude was that of a person absorbed in some delightful reverie. Her hands were gently clasped in front of her form, her limbs, as you might see by the folds of her dress, were carelessly crossed, one over the other, while one small and delicate foot, with the slender ancle, encased in the snow-white stocking, was visible, as she lay with her voluptuous person thrown lightly along the sofa.

She was indeed a beautiful and voluptuous woman. The deep vermillion of her lips, the burning flush crimsoning each cheek, the blackness of her eye-lashes and pencilled brows, the long dark hair, which when all unbound, fell in thick and glossy tresses, below her waist, the fullness of her bosom, the swelling roundness of her limbs, the smallness of her feet, and the delicacy of her hands, with long and tapering fingers, all attested her loveliness and beauty; while the swimming glance of her large eyes, indicated the innate voluptuousness of her nature.

Her eyes, were of that deep and well-like brightness, which seems to throw open to the vision of the gazer, not only their mellowed glance and dazzling radiance, but the entire prospect of the hidden soul. You gazed not upon, but into, those eyes, and felt that you were in the presence of a mighty intellect and a sensual organization.

As she lay reclining on the sofa, a low murmur of delight escaped from her lips, and a flush like the sunny-side of a ripening peach, lightened over her face and neck. Her eye-lids slowly unclosing, revealed her large dark eyes, animate with an expression of sudden delight, and beaming with a swimming brightness that finds no parallel, save in the glance of a lovely and voluptuous woman.

Dora rose slowly to her feet, and stood erect upon the floor.

"That were a boon, worth the peril of a soul to win!" she whispered in a low and softened tone, as her hands absently toyed with the rose, which rested upon her bosom— "A coronet, yes, yes, a coronet! This is a fair brow they tell me—how well the glittering circlet of diamonds would become its beauty! A coronet! But one short year ago, a poor girl, clad in the threadbare costume, which seems to belong by right, to poverty-stricken gentility, watched by the bedside of a dying mother, in a meanly-furnished apartment, faintly illumined by the beams of a flickering lamp. Now that poor girl is the wife of one of the merchant-princes of the city, rolls in wealth,

almost without limit, and of course moves among the first circles of the aristocracy of this good city! Such aristocracy, ha, ha! Like a specimen of paste-board statuary, giving but a grotesque outline of the reality, which it is intended to represent! Another year! Ha! ha! My brain grows wild! Another year and this same poor girl, may, no, no, will stand among the glittering circles of a royal court, with the blaze of rank and beauty flashing all around her, with the smile of a queen beaming upon her face, while a coronet, that tells the ancestral glories of a thousand years, rests brightly upon her brow!

"Dora Livingstone, wife of Livingstone, the merchant prince; that sounds well, though prince that word merchant as you may, it still retains—ha! ha!—a wonderful taint of the shop! But there is a title, written on the very clouds that tint over my future, which would sound much better, and that title—but hold, my brain grows dizzy; I seem to glide on air—that title is——"

"Dora Lyndeswold, Countess of Lyndeswold!" said a deep voice at the shoulder of the beautiful woman.

She turned hastily round, gazing upon the intruder, with a glance of mingled surprise and anger.

Fitz-Cowles, in all the elegance of his fashionable attire, stood before her, with his conical hat in one hand, his gold-headed cane in the other, while a smile of peculiar meaning lighted up his dusky countenance.

"Ha, ha! Dora, you are surprised to see me! The truth is, old Artichoke your gardener, attracted my eye as I passed through the hall. He wanted me to examine some of his favorite plants. While his attention was turned another way, I stole up the back stair-case, reached the conservatory, and here I am! Yes, yes, Dora, notwithstanding your incredulous smile, it is in your power to be Countess of Lyndeswold."

"Algernon, it can never be—" exclaimed Dora, fixing the gaze of her brilliant eyes, upon his countenance, with a glance of strange meaning.

"But it can be, Dora, and it must be—" answered Fitz-Cowles, in a careless tone, as he gently balanced his gold-headed cane, on the palm of his right-hand, with a see-saw motion.

Dora silently laid her hand on his shoulder, and gazed into his eyes, with a glance of deep interest.

"By what means, you would ask? By flight! Yes, by flight! Next Tuesday the Great Western sails from New York. Let us arrange all our matters, take passage on board the steamer, and in fifteen days we will be in London. It is but a day's ride from London to Lyndeswold."

"Lyndeswold—" echoed Dora, and the name seemed to act like a spell upon her—"Ah, ha! England boasts an aristocracy, founded on high deeds, whose records we trace in the history of a thousand years. The aristocracy of his land, and ha, ha, ha, this city, is founded on—what? Can you tell, Algernon."

"I've been trying to find out for the last three months. I flatter myself that I know something about the peculiar merits and glories of Quaker City aristocracy."

"An aristocracy founded on the high deeds of dentists, tape-sellers, quacks, pettifoggers, and bank directors, all jumbled together in a ridiculous mass of absurdities. Your dentist, whose proper coat of arms should be a 'tooth and pincers on a field gules,' sends to the Heralds' college, in London, and asks the heralds to trace back his pedigree to the conquest! And so with all the classes of the Philadelphia *ton.* Now could we establish a Heralds' college

LIVINGSTONE ALARMS FITZ-COWLES BY PRESENTING A LOADED PISTOL AT HIM.

in the state house, I would make the profession of every man the rule by which to fashion his crest or coat of arms! To the quack—a pill-box! To the pettifogger, three links of a convict's chain, with the penitentiary in the distance! To the bank director a widow's coffin, with a weeping orphan on either side by way of heraldic supporters! Pah! There is no single word of contempt in the whole language, too bitter, to express my opinion of this magnificent pretension—the aristocracy of the Quaker City!"

"You are quite animated, Dora! I never trouble myself about such small matters!"

"Do you know what was the profession of my grandfather?" exclaimed Dora, as with a smile of bitter sarcasm playing on her proud lip, she again confronted Fitz-Cowles. "Why, ha, ha, ha! He was—guess what?"

"A merchant perhaps? or a member of one

of the oldest families of Pennsylvania,' to use the slang of the day, or—or ——"

"A shoemaker!" shrieked Dora, with a burst of laughter, as she strode hurriedly up and down the room. "Yes, yes a shoemaker!"

"A cobbler!" muttered Fitz-Cowles, with a look of silent disgust.

"Yes, yes, a toil-begrim'd cobbler, who sate working all day long on an old bench, mending other people's old shoes? Am I ashamed of this? Ha, ha! Not in the least! The cobbler's grand-daughter moves in the first circles of the aristocracy of Philadelphia! And what is something to her credit, she is not ashamed of her ancestry! She does not conceal it with some sounding pretension to high birth, but at once, and without reserve, horrifies the tape-and-bobbin nobility of the Quaker City, with the plain declaration, that Dora Livingstone, wife of the merchant prince, is a cobbler's grand-daughter!"

"Deuce take me, if I can understand you Dora; you are not ashamed of having a shoemaker for your grandfather, and yet you reverence the spirit of ancestral pride!"

"You have given my opinions with remarkable precision! I tell you, Algernon, that I respect the mechanic, at his bench, though his hands be rough, his face begrimed with toil, his manners uncouth and destitute of polish! But for the pretty aristocrat; the Duke Thimble-and thread, the Count Soap-and-candle, the Baron Peddle-and-cheat, for all these, I do entertain the most sovereign contempt! Give me the honest mechanic at the bench if we must have a nobility for your true republican nobleman : not the dishonest bank-director at the desk! But if you pass the mechanic aside—whose honest vote, sustains your republic—if you pass him aside, when you form your aristocracy, then I say, give us the titles and the trappings of an English nobility! Let us at once have a throne and a court a king and courtiers!"

"Ha, ha, ha! Dora—you grow philosophical! Decidedly so! But you have quite forgotten my proposition. Flight, Dora, sudden and successful flight."

"And do you think Fitz-Cowles, that I would fly with you as an—it is a sweet word and a true one—as an adulteress! As an adulteress, forsaking her husband? No—no! By my life; no!"

"Once in England, we could be united in marriage, without the slightest difficulty. You would become the Countess of Lyndeswold on the death of my father, when I would succeed to the earldom. During his life, our title would merely be, my Lord and Lady Dalveny, of Lyndeswold."

"Countess of Lyndeswold, and my husband living in America! Ha, ha, ha! This is like some probable history in the Arabian Nights!"

"And how do you propose to overcome the—the difficulty?"

"Which is but another name for a—husband, after all—" muttered Dora in a tone inaudible to Fitz-Cowles.

"You know, Dora, that we must arrange our plan of action without delay. A solitary word of suspicion, whispered in your husband's ears by some officious friend, and our schemes are blown to the—gentleman in black."

Dora approached Fitz-Cowles, and laid her hand on his shoulder, while her dark eyes, flashing with a deep and meaning glance, were fixed upon his countenance.

"Suppose Livingstone should die," she said, in a low whisper, while her eyes became intensely brilliant and her face grew suddenly pale.

"Why," replied Fitz-Cowles, with a slight start, "why, you would then be the widow Livingstone, with a fortune of some two hundred thousand in your possession. But you know, Dora, Livingstone bids fair to live at least half a century from the present moment."

"Livingstone may die and that suddenly," said Dora, in that same low tone, while the hand resting on Fitz-Cowles' shoulder trembled like a leaf.

"Egad! Dora, you're white as snow in the face! One would think you meant something by the glance of your eyes. Do speak out, and let us hear the news."

"Listen, Algernon, and I will tell you a secret. Strong and vigorous man as he looks, Livingstone has been for years the victim of a secret and insidious disease. It is that disease which slowly and quietly, almost without pain, ossifies the main arteries of the heart. The victim may live for years, with the flush of health on his cheek and brow, while this insidious disease is closing up the avenues of his life. He may live for years with all the outward signs of health and vigour, when a sudden excitement of mind would lay him down a lifeless corse; aye, in an instant, without a single pain to warn him of his danger, he would fall a lifeless corse."

"Yes, yes, I remember. Mc'Torniquet, the queer doctor, who talks of Henry Clay, the statesman, and Henry Clay, his blood horse, all in the same breath—took the trouble, one day last week, to explain this disease to me. However, he did not tell me that Livingstone was its victim."

"This doctor, who is our family physician, called here but an hour ago, and asked me when I expected Mr. Livingstone back from New York. I answered, of course, next week. He then told me that the main arteries of my husband's heart were now almost entirely ossified; that I must take every care in the world of him, for any sudden excitement would kill him in an instant."

"What a pity! Poor fellow! To think of a man going about with such a bad heart in his bosom!"

"You understand me, then? Livingstone may live for twenty, nay, for thirty years longer, and he may die in a year, a month, a day, or it may be—in an hour."

"I appreciate his position, Dora. To say

the least, it's a very ticklish one. Jove! The idea of a man having red cheeks, bright eyes, and a firm step, while his heart is turning to bone—the idea of such a state of affairs, I say!"

Dora drew nearer to Algernon's side, and suddenly grasped him by the wrist. There was a wild light gleaming from her dark eyes as she gazed fixedly in his face, and a slight wrinkle indented the surface of her fair forehead, between the eyebrows. Her voice was utterly changed in its tones, when she whispered these words to the listener's ear.

"Algernon, give me your advice on a point of the deepest interest. When my husband returns from New York, I will seize the earliest opportunity to press upon his attention the importance of having his will prepared without delay. Poor man! His life hangs by a slender thread—the most trifling chance may sever that thread, and precipitate him into eternity. It is important, therefore, that he should hold himself prepared for death. Justice to his wife comands that his will, making a final disposition of all his fortune, should be executed with all possible haste."

"By Jove, Dora, you look quite wild. To what tends all this? Hush! did you hear a footstep in the conservatory?"

"Suppose, Algernon, that my husband should make his will. Suppose he leaves his fortune to his wife. These suppositions made, I wish you to imagine a scene. Livingstone and myself are seated in the parlour on a winter's evening, beside the cheerful fire. His face is lighted up with a pleasant smile, as, displaying the unfolded will in his hands, he gazes upon the beaming countenance of his wife. And that wife, mark you, Algernon, at the very moment when the husband reaches forth his arms to clasp her to his bosom, falls on her knees at his feet, and in broken words, shrieks forth the story of her guilt, and his dishonour! Yes, yes, to his ear, to the ear of the man who loves his wife as man never loved wife before, that young and *innocent* wife, tells the dark story of her shame! Even while his face beams with affection, she tells him that he is dishonoured, aye, dishonoured! That she has been false to his bed, recreant to her plighted faith! That she is polluted in person, corrupt in soul! That this young wife, whom he loves so well, is—ha, ha—an adulteress! This she tells him with tears of repentance, with prayers for mercy, with groans of anguish! And he, how think ye Livingstone would hear this confession from the wife whose very image he now worships? Ha! Algernon! Think ye not it will kill him, even before his frantic wife had done with her tale of guilt? Even as he sate, without a moment's delay, he would fall from his chair, a stiffened corse? Would he not, Algernon?"

A blasphemous oath escaped from Fitz-Cowles' lips, and in a sudden start, which shook his frame, he suffered his hat and cane to fall on the floor.

"By G—d, Dora, I don't think you're a human being!"

He said this in a low-toned voice, and turned away from the merchant's wife, as she stood in the centre of the room, her stature dilating to its fullest heighth, while with a panting bosom and a flashing eye, she awaited his answer to her momentous question.

"And this," she cried, gazing upon Fitz-Cowles, who stood near the window with his face averted from her glance. "And this, after I have sacrificed all I possess on earth, all I hope in heaven! and sacrificed for you!"

"Hush! Did'nt you hear a footstep in the conservatory? Really, Dora, you are very imprudent," exclaimed Fitz-Cowles, in a sullen tone, as he gazed vacantly through the window-curtains.

"Would to God there had been a footstep in the conservatory when I first resigned myself to shame!" said Dora, with biting sarcasm.

"When a lady agrees, makes up her mind to part with her virtue, and a gentleman makes up his mind to accept the gift, all is fair and satisfactory, and nobody but an injured husband has a right to complain. But, murder, Dora—murder."

"Murder! Madman that you are, who spoke of murder? Fitz-Cowles, I beseech you do not force me to change my opinion, with regard to you. I thought you were a man; one of that class, in fact, who looked rather to the end that is to be accomplished than to the delicacy of the means."

"But Dora, this experiment of yours has ten chances to one of failure, to one of success. Livingstone might recover from the shock, occasioned by your confession."

"Then it is the chance of failure, not the experiment itself, which turns your face to the hue of ashes."

"D—n the thing, Dora, Livingstone never wronged me. And I can't see that he has done you any injury sufficient to warrant such a return."

"I perceive Algernon," said Dora, crossing her arms, with a calm gesture. "You do not understand me. Livingstone never did me a wrong; on the contrary, he has bestowed wealth upon me, almost without bound, and lavished affection upon me, until amounts to idolatry. You never gave me wealth, you never gave me love. Then what is the tie that binds me to you? You have it in your power to grace the—the—ha, ha!—the cobbler's grand-daughter with a title! Livingstone is the 'bar sinister,' ha! ha! between me and hereditary rank! Who spoke of murder? Not I, by my life! Livingstone may die; he *may* die. That was all I said."

"He may die, that is true," said Fitz-Cowles, turning away from the window. "By-the-bye, Dora, you are remarkably ambitious, for a sensible woman. Your very soul seems absorbed in this ambition to rise."

"There is a leaf of my heart, Fitz-Cowles, which you have never read. I loved once; loved with all the intensity of my nature, and sacrificed my plighted love, for wealth and Livingstone. Did you never read in books, that the first love of a strong-minded woman, when diverted from its proper source, turns to the gall and bitterness of worldly ambition? I feel in my inmost soul, that I was destined from my birth to rank and station, to the sway of hearts and the rule of power. In my early childhood, when forced by penury, my mother, a widowed and a friendless woman, sought a home, in the outskirts of the city, the prophecy was whispered in my ears, that one day, I should wear a coronet, and walk a titled lady among the grandees of a royal court."

"And some old crone, I suppose, with a cup sprinkled with tea-grounds in her hand, was the oracle ?"

"It matters not, for the prophecy, come from whom it might, found its echo in my own heart. Does it not often chance, that a casual word, uttered by an ignorant mechanic, strikes a mighty chord in some statesman's heart, and originates a new and magnificient scheme of state policy ? So a chance word, from vulgar lips, may arouse a prophecy which has been hidden in our souls, since the hour of our birth. Why did the creole, Josephine, credit the withered hag, who foretold that her brow would one day be encircled with the crown of France? Because the old crone was gifted by Heaven with especial power ? No—no—no ! She might have foretold a thousand incidents, and not one would have impressed the heart of Josephine, with even a passing sensation.

"On the heart of this same creole, Josephine, from the hour of her birth, had been written down by God's own hand, the high destiny for which she had been born, and the chance words of the old crone aroused the prophecy into life !"

"Hush ! Dora, there is a footstep on the stairs," exclaimed Fitz-Cowles, with a sudden start.

"My God ! It is Livingstone's footstep !" and as she spoke, Dora's face grew suddenly pale. "Ha ! The note, which I left last night on the centre table was gone when I looked for it this morning. Could he have returned in the night ?"

The door leading into the main building of the mansion was suddenly opened, and a red-faced servant in grey livery, turned up with velvet, entered the boudoir.

"Mr. Livingstone, ma'am !"

And in an instant Livingstone appeared in the doorway, and entered the room.

"Ah, ah ! My dear, I've stolen a march on you, have I ? Back from New York sooner than I expected, you see ! Ah—ha ! Colonel, is that you ? How do you do ?"

"My God ! Livingstone ! How pale you are !" was the involuntary exclamation of the wife, as her eyes were rivetted to his countenance. "Have you been ill ?"

"Egad ! You look as if you had been sick a-month !" exclaimed Fitz-Cowles. "Why Livingstone positively you're turning grey !"

Calm and smiling, Livingstone advanced, and gathered his right arm round the waist of his beautiful wife. His face was very pale, and his blue eyes had an unnatural brilliancy in their glance, which in the mind of an acute observer might have aroused a suspicion as to the sanity of the merchant.

"One kiss, my love !" exclaimed Livingstone, as he pressed his lips to the full and pouting lips of his wife, while his face brightened with a look of pleasure. "You must excuse these little matrimonial attentions, Fitz-Cowles. We married men are apt to be fond of our wives; especially after a long absence. And how's your poor sick friend, my dear ?"

"You have my note, then ?" exclaimed Dora, as a slight tremour was visible on her lip.

"To be sure, my dear, to be sure. I returned from New York in the night, found your note on the centre table, and having read its contents, I retired from the house without alarming the servants. I spent the night at the counting-house, examining my books and papers. How did you say your poor sick friend was, Dora ?"

"Alas ! She is dead !" and Dora turned away as if to conceal her agitation.

"Well, well, it can't be helped. 'Debt we've all got to pay' as the old women at a funeral have it. By-the-bye, Fitz-Cowles, I've got some traces of the forger at last !"

The merchant laid his hand playfully on Fitz-Cowles shoulder and gazed smilingly in his eyes, while his unoccupied hand toyed with his watch-seals, in a careless manner.

"The deuce you have ?" answered Fitz-Cowles with a stare of surprise—"By Jove !" he muttered to himself, "there is a strange look about Livingstone's eyes, that doesn't exactly please me !"

"I tell you how it was, my boy," continued Livingstone, still toying with his watch-seals. "While I was in New York, the head clerk of the Charlestown house arrived in town. He recognised the forger one day in Broadway, strutting it among the finest bucks in the city."

"And you arrested him ?"

"Not exactly. We had evidence enough for suspicion ; but conviction you know is a different thing. You'll laugh when I tell you how I managed it with the fellow. He was one of my most intimate friends in New York, and was wont to frequent my rooms very much during the day, manifesting his familiarity by calling me 'jolly old fellow'—'Old Lin,' and all that kind of thing, you understand. Before the head clerk arrived from the south, I did not ever dream of suspecting this perfumed gentleman of the forgery. Why, colonel, do you know, that I'd just as soon suspect you as him ?"

"Curse me Livingstone these kind of comparisons, are deuced unpleasant," observed Fitz-Cowles, growing very uneasy under the merchant's gaze.

"What do you think we did when we found that we had'nt evidence sufficient for conviction? Why, ha, ha. It's too good! We dressed up a decayed police officer like a southern planter, and introduced him to the forger as a gentleman of immense fortune from the south. The forger promenades New York, with the disguised police officer at his elbow, showing the pseudo-planter, all the lions of the town, and making himself agreeable in a general way. Now the joke of the thing—"

"Yes," echoed Fitz-Cowles, "The joke of the thing.'

"Is simply this. The southern planter has a warrant in his pocket, for the arrest of the forger, the moment he shall attempt to leave the city. Ha, ha, ha! Capital."

"Capital! capital! ha, ha, ha!" roared Fitz-Cowles.

"Is'nt it too good?"

"Ha, ha, ha! It is too good! A warrant in his pocket for the arrest of the forger all the while—did ye say? Capital—ha, ha, ha! Capital."

"Why Fitz-Cowles, your ladylove has been making free with a lock of your hair!" exclaimed Livingstone playfully, "look here, Dora, what a space there is near Fitz-Cowles right temple! A large lock severed close to the skin—why, Dora, I declare you too, have been making somebody a present of a lock of your hair! A large tress severed from the hair, near your right temple too! Singular coincidence oh, Fitz-Cowles."

With the same involuntary gesture, Fitz-Cowles and Dora, both raised their hands to their right temples, and both discovered that a large tress was missing from among the clustering locks of their raven-black hair.

"Curse that barber! I shall have to flog him," muttered Fitz-Cowles. "How deuced careless in him."

"Positively Albert, I can't tell how this occurred," said Dora approaching her husband, "I must have cut it off in my sleep. How extremely odd."

"Or somebody may have cut it off, to save you the trouble, while you were asleep!" said Livingstone with a kindly smile, as turning from his wife he approached one of the windows, and looked out upon the sky.

Meanwhile Dora stood silent and thoughtful, her bosom heaving upward with sudden pulsations, clashing for a moment convulsively together, trembled with the agitation that quivered through her whole frame.

"Now," she murmured as a slight pallor overspread her beautiful countenance. "Now, is the moment of my fate. The disease gathering round his heart manifests its progress already in his countenance. I will confess all, ha, ha, I will throw myself at his feet and beseech his pardon."

Fitz-Cowles turned pale as ashes. He did not hear the whispered words of Dora, but he read her fixed and desperate purpose in the lines of her countenance, now moulded into an expression, as unrelenting as death. While his brain whirled round in wild confusion, he resolved to delay or at least to thwart the accomplishment of her purpose.

"Aid me now, Great Father, before whom, I shall so soon appear!" were the murmured words that broke from the white lips of Livingstone, as with his face turned from his wife and her paramour, he made a pretence of gazing upon the clear and blue winter's sky—"I feel that fit of madness coming over me again. Oh, for a little strength to go through the mockery! To pretend affection to the wife; friendship to the paramour! There is frenzy in my veins; I know it; I feel it; but I will command my soul!"

And yet as the words escaped from his lips, he felt that same feeling of mocking frenzy, which had given its impulse to his actions in Monk-Hall, the night before, rushing like a torrent through his veins. Conscious that he was acting like a madman, he drew a pistol from his bosom, and making one stride across the floor, held it to the heart of Fitz-Cowles.

"A handsome pistol, colonel! Silver mounted, with a hair trigger! One touch of my finger and you're a dead man! Ha!—ha! How you step backward, how you recede to the wall. Zounds, man, but I believe you're afraid!"

"For Heaven's sake, Livingstone, put the thing away—" cried Fitz-Cowles, as with the pistol at his heart, step by step he retreated to the wall. "You might, you know, pull the trigger by chance! It's loaded you say, and—"

"The ball might lodge in your heart!—Ha! ha! ha! So it might! Suppose we try!"

As he spoke he pulled the trigger. Dora uttered an involuntary shriek as the "clicking" of the pistol broke on the air, and then covered her face with her hands. When she again looked around the room, she beheld Fitz-Cowles standing in one corner, pale as ashes, while Livingstone, with a bitter smile writhing his white lips, still held the pistol presented at his breast.

"Confound those 'caps'—not worth the having!" exclaimed Livingstone, with a pleasant smile—"Why, colonel, ha, ha, ha! You look as frightened as if, ha, ha, ha! I had intended to shoot you!"

"The pistol was loaded," hesitated Fitz-Cowles, as he averted his eyes from Livingston's flashing glance.

"Loaded? Nonsense man—I was merely trying some new percussion caps."

"The disease has affected his reason," muttered Dora, as she advanced to her husband's side; "Now for the confession and the—result!"

"You dropped your handkerchief, Mrs. Livingstone," exclaimed Fitz-Cowles, as starting hastily forward, he presented the snow-white *mouchoir*, with a low bow—"Not on the peril of your soul!" he hissed the whisper between his set teeth, as his dark eyes were fixed upon her face, with a malignant yet frightened glance.

She returned his glance with a look of scorn.

She advanced to her husband's side, she seized his arm with a convulsive grasp, while his dark eyes flashed with an expression of the deepest emotion.

"Livingstone," she shrieked, with all the pathos of voice and gesture at her control, "I have much to tell you."

In another instant she lay panting upon his breast, with her arms flung round his neck, while the convulsive sobs which heaved her bosom, broke silently on her husband's ear.

Fitz-Cowles saw that his fate hung in a balance, which the weight of a feather might turn.

"Ha!" cried Livingstone, with the same strange glance which marked his wandering intellect, flashing from his clear blue eye—"Ha! what means this agitation—this sudden emotion—these sobs and tears?"

"Why the fact is, Livingstone, your wife is anxious—that is to say—deuce take the thing! Mc Torniquet was here this morning, and, and, dropped some strange hints about a disease to which you are subject—and—and—your wife is alarmed for your health."

"Fools!" They think to deceive me!" thought Livingstone, as his wife lay sobbing in his arms, "they do not dream that I overheard their ingenious plans, as I stood in the conservatory, not five minutes past! Ha! ha! I will be even with them! Oh, with regard to the disease of the heart," he continued, aloud, "which has threatened me for so many years, I forgot to mention a slight circumstance—Mc Torniquet, this morning assured me that he had long mistaken my symptoms. I am no more in danger from any malady of this kind than you are, my dear. There, Dora, don't weep—I can well appreciate this affectionate regard for my health, but you mus'nt weep."

As Dora lay with her head buried in his bosom, a quick and sudden tremor shook her frame from head to foot. She was deceived for once in her life, and after having betrayed her husband—in the very hour of his madness—became his willing dupe. With one start she raised her head, and her face pale and ghastly, from the effect of the sudden revulsion of feeling, was disclosed in the morning sunlight.

"Oh, Livingstone," she said in a voice tremulous with emotion, "I am so glad to discover that all my apprehensions are groundless."

She walked to the window, as if to hide the agitation, the joyful agitation which Livingstone's unexpected disclosure had aroused in her soul. As she passed Fitz-Cowles, she darted a look in his face, full of dark and fearful meaning. For a moment her countenance was convulsed by an expression, hideous as it was resolute, and then like a sunbeam gleaming from a cloud, all was calm and smiling again.

"By-the-by, Dora, I had nearly forgotten an important circumstance, connected with our celebration of the Christmas holidays. You know my country seat of Hawkwood, in Jersey, some twenty miles from Camden? It is the old family mansion of the Livingstone's, was built in fact long before the revolution. Full of secret passages, solemn old rooms, with wide fireplaces, lofty halls, and wainscotting without limit—you know?"

"I have often heard of this strange old family seat," replied Dora, without turning from the window, "and have as often felt a desire to see the place."

"You shall see it, my dear, within two days. I have this morning despatched servants to the place, in order to arrange the old hall for the celebration of Christmas in the old English style. To-morrow morning we will start for Hawkwood and spend the holidays there. Fitz-Cowles, I hope you will favour us with your company: You nod assent. Well, that is settled; and now I must away to the warehouse: You will excuse me, Fitz-Cowles. I'll be home to dinner my dear."

Livingstone left the boudoir as he spoke.

Dora turned from the window and faced Fitz-Cowles. Their eyes met in one deep and meaning glance.

"Well," said Fitz-Cowles drawing a long breath, "we're out of that d—d scrape, any how!"

Dora smiled, but did not speak. Her attention was attracted by a loose slip of letter paper, which lay on the carpet, near her feet. With a manner of easy *nonchalance*, she picked this paper from the floor, and examined it with a careless glance.

In a moment, quick as a lightning flash, her dark eyes shone with sudden fire, her stature dilated to its full height, and her bosom rose and fell beneath the folds of her morning gown, with an impulse of the deepest agitation. She stood in the centre of the room, in all her beauty and loveliness, regarding the paper which she held in her trembling hand, with one intense and flashing glance, while her face, was crimsoned over by a sudden flush of excitement. There was an expression of scorn mingled with triumph on her curving lip; and her high forehead was impressed with a slight, yet meaning frown.

"Why Dora—you are agitated!" exclaimed Fitz-Cowles advancing, "what can there be in that slip of paper to move you thus?"

Her eyes gleamed like flame-coals, as the answer broke from her lips in a slow and deliberate whisper, rendered most wild and thrilling by the sudden huskiness of her voice:

"Leave that to me and to the future."

CHAPTER V.
THE GOLD WATCH.

"Luke, you know how liable we are to accident and sudden death? If I should die suddenly, I wish you to open this packet and execute the commission which it names. Consider this as the last request of a dying man. Will you promise me?"

"I will, and do promise you," Luke replied

grasping the hand of Livingstone—"As soon as you are dead, I will open this packet, and at every peril, at all hazards, execute the commission which it names. Egad!" he muttered to himself—"he seems to have recovered from his mad fit! A precious tramp I've had, up and down this beautiful city ever since daybreak, in order to cool him off!"

"Now, Luke, I must go home to my family," said Livingstone, with a faint smile, as they emerged from the Exchange. "Here we part, Luke, at least for a little while. It is now nine o'clock. At noon, I will meet you at my house on especial business. Good morning!"

They parted. Livingstone pursued his way up Walnut street, while Luke Harvey remained standing at the corner of Walnut and Third.

"I don't suppose anything peculiar will take place between this and sun-down—do I? Very likely I don't. Possibly I do! Well, well, let matters take their course. When a woman adorns her husband's forehead with horns she ought to remember that these ornamental branches may be turned into dangerous weapons. Stags gore people sometimes!"

Half an hour afterwards Luke stood in front of a three storied dwelling, which, remarkable for its old and desolate appearance, stood among a cluster of pawnbrokers' shops, like a decayed gentleman surrounded by pickpockets and thieves. Thick masses of rank green moss grew over the steep roof, and the garret window was stuffed with an old straw hat and bundles of rags. The shutters on the first story were entirely closed, through the windows of the second floor, faded green blinds of a damp and mouldy aspect were visible, while the glasses of the remaining windows, in the third story, were concealed by rough boards, nailed loosely to the window frame on the outside. The solitary front door, was one of your old fashioned front doors with massive posts and heavy cornices. The old brass knocker was covered with a thick crust of verdigris, and all along the door and frame some industrious nand had driven innumerable nails and spikes of every size and pattern.

Becky Smolby lived in this ancient house. Becky Smolby and an Irish female servant were the only tenants of the old time mansion. Who Becky Smolby was, or what were her sources of livelihood, was a question often asked, but by no means frequently answered. Becky was old, penurious and avaricious; every body knew that. Didn't she keep the female servant for one entire week on stale gingerbread and sassafras beer? Becky was queer and whimsical; this point was never doubted. Did she not keep candles burning all the day long in the old mansion, even when she was starving herself for the want of generous onion-soups and broiled steaks? Becky was rich—aye, aye, old rooms lumbered with antique but costly furniture, mysterious caskets standing upon picturesque sideboards of black mahogany, great monsters of chests, stowed away beneath canopied bedsteads, ribbed with brass bands, and corded with thick

ropes, all bore witness of Becky's hidden plate and doubloons; Becky was capricious to a fault; had she been a little younger, and worn blue stockings and talked dictionary, she would have been termed a genius, and her whims would have assumed the shape of amiable eccentricities peculiar to a gifted mind. Becky had four cats and a parrot by way of agreeable companions, on whom she was wont to bestow her daily investments of good humour, which, as the reader may judge, were sometimes remarkably limited in their nature; while she kept her Irish female servant as a sort of safety valve for all her vapours spites, animosities, and what was worse than all, her reminiscences of her five husbands, Buddy, Crank, Dulpins, Smolby, and Tuppick.

"Well, well," cried Luke, as he gazed upon the front of the old house. "The old lady has always passed for my aunt—the man in the moon knows whether I'm related to her at all! At all events I'll go in and see her."

He gave a slight tap with the knocker.

* * * * *

In a large room furnished in an old fashioned style, sate the ancient lady, bending over a small table, on which was placed two lighted candles, flinging their glaring light full in her withered face.

Opposite the old lady, sat a gentleman of some forty-five, resting in a capacious arm-chair; his corpulent form clad in glossy broad cloth, while his round face of oily sweetness was strikingly relieved by the snow white cravat encircling his neck. The sharp features of the old lady, all their harshness of outline thrown out into the light by the tight-fitting black silk cap which covered her head, were impressed with peculiar and distinctive characteristics. A long aquiline nose, hooked like an eagle's beak, thick grey eyebrows meeting together and shooting up into the forehead at either extremity like two sides of a triangle; small dark eyes, quick, piercing, and brilliant in their glance; a wide mouth, with thin lips much sunken from the absence of teeth; a pointed chin and high cheek bones; all gave a stern and decided expression to the countenance of the aged dame, which was in strong contrast with the oily sweetness of the round face, whose large grey eyes were gazing in her own.

The Reverend Dr. Pyne, who sat opposite, —commonly called Fat Pyne from the initials of his name, or his peculiar disposition to blaze up in his sermons—was a fine specimen of a well preserved dealer in popular credulity. A red round face, with thick lips, watery grey eyes, and lanky hair, of a doubtful colour, mingling white and brown, and hanging in uneven masses around the outline of his visage, formed the details of a countenance very sanctimonious and somewhat sensual in its slightest expression.

"Trouble, brother Pyne, nothin' but trouble in this blessed world," said the widow Smolby, bending over the small work-stand which separated the parties. "Only to think o' it! This very mornin' I was sittin' up stairs in the back room, with Wes on one side and Nappy on t'other, when I heard a knock at the front door. D'ye mind? Ike was a sittin' in one corner; Washy was cardin' wool near the fire; Abe was hanging up against the winder, when I hears a knock at the front door."

"I didn't know that the old lady's family was so extensive!" muttered the Rev. Dr. Pyne. "Ike, Washy, Nappy, Wes and Abe! Hired men I suppose."

"Peggy Grud—that's the young woman who lives with me, you know? She goes to the front door, and lets in a little humpbacked Jew, who wanted to sell me a gold watch. Ike was a spinnin' near the fire, as I heered the Jew's voice below, and Abe was a hollerin' murder with all his might, when I comes down stairs. Now you know, Brother Pyne, that a poor lone widow like me, ought to turn an honest penny whenever she can, and so 'cordingly, I buys watches whenever opportoonity offers."

"He that provideth not for his own house is worse than an infidel," said brother Pyne, with great oiliness of manner.

"Considerable. Well, the Jew hands me the gold watch, and I goes up stairs to compare it with some time-pieces I has on hand. Abe was a hollerin' murder all the while, and Washington carded wool with all his might. Napoleon looked in my face as I compared the watch with another one, jist as if he'd say'd 'take care, old woman, somethin's wrong about this house, I do say.' Down stairs I comes, considerin' the price o' th' watch over in my mind, when I diskivered that the Jew was gone! I say," she cried, elevating her voice into a shriek, "I diskivered that the Jew was gone!"

"And left his watch with you? Surely sister, this was not the act of a Jew."

"D'ye see that little drawer, in the old sideboard yonder? D'ye see the keys a-hanging in the keyhole? When I went up stairs I left the keys in the keyhole, jist as they are now—when I came down, the keys was jist the same as ever, but five thousand dollars in gold, which I, a poor lone woman had saved up from five husbands was—gone! The Jew took 'em! I'm ruined! Oh, Lor! Oh Lor! And Abe a hollering murder all the while."

"He cried murder, did he? What could have induced Abel——"

"It ain't Abel," said the old woman sharply, "its Abraham. I named him arter the first patriarch. Washy I named arter Washington; Nappy, arter Napoleon; Ike, arter Isaac son o' Abraham, which was the son of Heber; and Wes, arter the great and good Wesley."

"Bless me, sister, what a numerous family! Your grandchildren, I perceive?"

"Grandchildren! Och, pelt me to pieces wid thimbles! They ain't no grandchilder; only four cats an' a parrit——"

"Now, Peggy Grud, who told you to put in your sixpence?" said the old woman, turning sharply round to the new comer, who stood in the doorway—"Bless my soul, if you ain't more pervokin' nor bad bank-stock!"

"Put in my sixpence, indade. And you sellin' your soul to the devil for your cats and yer parrit! Twist the necks ov 'em! Wouldn't I, if I had my will o' th' creeturs!"

Peggy Grud, who had suddenly appeared in the doorway of the room, was a tall, stout Irishwoman, coarsely clad, with large hands, and a withered face—looking as though it had been scorched in some fire and hardened to the dryness of an Egyptian mummy—surrounded by an immense cotton night-cap, adorned with colossal ruffles.

"And Abe was a-hollerin' murder all the while——"

"I say, Aunty, let's have a look at that watch," said a voice proceeding from the doorway, occupied by the form of Peggy Grud. "Let's see the trinket any how."

Luke Harvey advanced toward the light, his jaws enveloped in a kerchief of burning red, which gave a singular and flaming effect to his entire appearance

"My nevey, brother Pyne——"

"Bah!" ejaculated Luke, in a whisper intended for the reverend gentleman's ears. "You can't come it, Fat Pyne."

"Have you a small sum about you, say five dollars, or ten, which you would like to invest in a Heavenly Bank?" said the Rev. Doctor, in a remarkably bland whisper.

"Heavenly Bank!" echoed Luke. "Monk-Hall for instance."

"Monk Luke!"

The reverend gentleman turned aside and spritualized a whistle; or in plainer English puckered up his mouth as though he was about to perform a lively air, while a faint sound, like a sigh, was all that escaped his lips.

"I say, aunt," exclaimed Luke, "this Jew must have had an accomplice in the house. Otherwise how could he know, that you had five thousand dollars in yonder drawer?"

"Troth and so he must!" said Peggy Grud. "He must have had an a complish—shure!"

"That's jist what I was a goin' to tell brother Pyne," exclaimed the old lady rising to her feet. "Three days ago, there comes to my house a poor girl, without cloak, bonnet, or shoes, a beggin' me to take her in for God's sake, for somebody was pursuin' her, and a goin' to murder her, an' what not! I took her in, though she would not tell me her name; I took her in, gave her bread to eat, and a bed to sleep on—here's my thanks I say, here's my thanks!"

"Ha! This is singular!" exclaimed Dr. Pyne, his red face turning suddenly pale, "has the girl dark, very dark hair, and dark eyes? I merely ask from curiosity?"

"Black as your hat!" vociferated the Widow Smolby with vehemence, "black as your hat."

"Very pale in the face?" said the worthy Doctor in a suggestive tone.

"A freshly white-washed wall ain't no paler!" responded the Widow Smolby

"And you suspect that this girl was a spy, introduced into your house by the Jew in order to accomplish the robbery of your five thousand dollars?" asked Luke in a quiet tone.

"Don't I? Ain't I a-going to give her up to justice in an hour? Havn't I penned her up in the room, which hasn't been opened these seventeen years? The ghost-room, as Peggy Grud calls it! To think that I should outlive five husbands, Buddy, Crank, Dul—Dul—I say Peg, what was my third husband's name?"

"Dulphins, av'it plase ye, ma'am!"

"Ye see, brother Pyne, I hadn't that one more than three months, so I sometimes forgits his name. Buddy, Crank, Dulphins, Tuppick, and Smolby; five husbands in all. To think that I—I—should—what was I goin' to say, Peg?"

DR. TORNIQUET POINTS OUT TO LIVINGSTONE THE TREATISE ON POISONS.

"To think that you should outlive five husbands, and be robbed afther all in this murtherin' manner!"

"Jist so. And afore an hour goes over my head, this girl shall be placed in the keer of Alderman Tallowdocket, that she shall. I'll have justice!"

"Could I see the young lady for a few moments alone?" said Dr. Pyne, with his usual bland smile. "It would be such a comfort to tell her, that in the next world, she'll be burned up for ever and ever. It would, indeed."

"I 'spect you can't see her, brother. I'd rather not. Come this way, Luke, and I'll show you the watch."

The old lady led the way up two pair of dark stairs, followed by Luke. In a few moments they stood in a large room on the third floor, whose outlines, Luke might dimly discern by the glimmer of the candle, which the old lady grasped in her hand. It was wide and spacious, the floor covered with carpet of an ancient though costly pattern, while the ceiling was emblazoned with a picture in fresco, whose gorgeous hues had been softened down by time. Massive velvet curtains hung along the three windows, which, facing the street, were hermetically closed by the boards outside the sashes. A bed with a lofty canopy, was in one corner; and an antique dressing bureau, surmounted by a circular mirror, stood in the space between two of the windows! a wide hearth, with ashes and loose pieces of half burned wood scattered over the bricks, extended along one entire end of the chamber, while the wall above the mantel, was concealed by a large picture, set in a gorgeous frame. It was the picture of a fair and lovely girl, remarkable for the brilliancy of her eyes, and the midnight blackness of her hair.

It was a singular circumstance, which did not escape the notice of Luke, that the carpet was covered with thick dust, as though it had not been opened for years, while the velvet of the window curtains, the gilt of the massive portrait frame, and the hangings of the bed were all obscured by the same thick, grey dust, and hung with heavy spider webs.

"Ghost room, indeed!" muttered Luke; "why look here, aunt, the carpet is covered with dust, and the air is damp and unwholesome as the grave vault. What's the meaning of all this, any how?"

"It has not been opened since she died, until this day!" said the widow Smolby, as her features, withered and wrinkled as they were, glowed with an expression of strange feeling. "She died in yonder bed. I held her in my arms. Her child lay dead upon her bosom. Yon hearth—d'ye see it, Luke? The fire went out when she died—it has never been lighted since!"

"What mean you?" cried Luke, amazed at the agitation of the old woman. "Ha!" he shouted, ere she could answer his question. "Here is the watch on the dressing bureau! It is Fitz-Cowles', by my life! The Jew must have stolen it from him! Fitz-Cowles once told me, that his name was inscribed within the case. Hold the light while I open it, aunt. Ha! What is this! A memorandum on a slip of paper, in Fitz-Cowles' hand, inserted between the case and the body of the watch! 'In Charleston,' on such a date—'Must be in Philadelphia,' on another date. 'Ellis Mortimer,' ho, ho, ho! We've tracked the fox at last! Ellis Mortimer and the hump-backed Jew are one! Fitz-Cowles is the master villain! Before to-morrow night, I'll have him, ha, ha, ha! where patchoully can't sweeten him!"

"Why, Luke, what in the world's the matter with you!" cried the widow Smolby, in utter wonder. "You go on like mad. Howsomever, here's the Jew's accomplice, sleeping in the bed! Don't she sleep sound for such a guilty thief!"

Leading the way along the floor, the old lady pushed aside the cobweb-hung curtains, and gazed upon the sleeper's form.

"Ha! The dead have come to life!" She shrieked, starting backward. "It is not the stranger; it is my daughter, just as she looked nineteen years ago, when she was pure and innocent! Look, Luke, look, I say! That pale face, that long dark hair, that lily-white hand! I'd swear it was my daughter come to life!"

Advancing to the bedside, Luke gazed upon the sleeper's form, as it lay dimly disclosed by the light of the flickering candle.

The face of a fair young girl, relieved by long tresses of jet-black hair, broke like a dream upon his gaze. True it was, the young form, thrown along the bed in an attitude of slumber, was clad in a dress of tattered rags, yet the outline of a figure ripening from the bud of maidenhood into the bloom of beauty and womanhood, might be discerned, beneath the disguise of mean apparel ; true it was, the face, pale as death, bore the traces of a long life of sorrow, yet were the features regular, the dark eyebrows pencilled and arching, the brow was calm and white, full of the silent grandeur of intellect, while the rounded outline of the checks, the fulness of the pouting lips, and the dimple of the chin, all bespoke the youth and loveliness of the sleeper.

"Thus nineteen years ago, she lay upon that bed ! My only daughter! Seventeen years ago, upon that bed breathed her last ! Since that hour, the light of day has not shone within the walls of this house! Since that hour I have not stepped beyond the threshold of my home! And now—now, she has arisen from the dead!"

"And this," cried Luke, gazing in silent wonder upon the pale yet beautiful face of the sleeper, "this is the accomplice of the Jew."

Luke's exclamation aroused the old woman from her waking dream. Her daughter, for whom she had mourned so long, was forgotten when she remembered the five thousand dollars stolen from her house that very morning by the Jew, whose accomplice lay sleeping on the bed.

"The huzzy !" she cried, shaking her fist at the form of the unconscious girl—"To steal my hard earnings, and arter I'd given her a home and a bed, without so much as axing her name! But I'll have justice! That I will, Luke! To jail with the trollop !"

"I tell you what it is, aunt," exclaimed Luke, with his gaze rivetted to the face of the lovely girl, "promise me that you will not consign this child to the care of the police until to-morrow morning, and I give you my word, that before sunrise your five thousand dollars shall be safe in your hands again."

"You never yet broke your word to me, Luke! You've got my promise. But mind you keep yours. Hush! She wakes!"

The lids of the sleeper, fringed with long dark lashes, slowly unclosed, and her eyes large, dark and brilliant, gazed wonderingly around. In a moment the glance of wonder changed to one of the deepest terror.

"My father!" she shrieked, starting up in the bed, and gazing fixedly, over Luke's shoulder.

Luke turned hastily around. The Rev. Dr. Pyne stood by his side with his smooth face all radiant with an expression whose doubtful meaning of malignancy and triumph Luke found it difficult to fathom.

"My father!" again shrieked the girl, crouching up in the bed, with her limbs huddled together as though she anticipated a violent blow.

"My child, you please me," said brother Pyne, mildly. "You recognise your parent. You repent your late flight from his roof? You will return to your home?"

"To the prison!" shrieked the girl; "to the cell, to the gibbet, anywhere you please, but not to him. For God's sake, good woman, do with me what you will, but save me from his power! He is my father, but sooner than return to his roof again, I would drag out the life of a convict within a dungeon's walls, I would beg my bread on the highways, I would, I would. Stand back from the bedside! back, back, I say or you will drive me mad. Ah, ah, I see it all again. That scene—the night I fled from your roof! Oh, God, oh God!"

She fell prostrate on the bed, her limbs writhing in a convulsive spasm, while her cheek grew like death, and the white foam hung on her livid lips.

CHAPTER VI.

THE POISON OF CATHERINE DE MEDICIS.

"This, you see, is my museum. My museum, Livingstone! A little of everything from all parts of the world. In that jar a negro child with two heads. Preserved in spirits. Capital specimen of a double-headed negro. Ought to have been at hall this morning; cut off a poor fellow's arm. Took it quite lively."

"By-the-bye, doctor, what erroneous notions have come down to our time, with regard to poisons! Now, some credulous historians would have us believe that in the time of Catharine De Medicis, the art of poisoning was carried to such perfection that a feather, a glove, or a perfume, impregnated with a chemical preparation, would send the victim quietly to his long home. All fudge—isn't it, doctor?"

"Fudge!" echoed Doctor McTorniquet, raising his tall form to its extreme height, while his long black morning gown floated loosely round his square limbs—"Fudge! Let me tell you, Livingstone, that I have devoted some small portion of my time to the study of chemistry. Its very well to encourage the idea that these legends about Catharine De Medicis' poisons are all fudge—for, were the truth known, there would be an end of all civilized society. Do you know that there are poisons so stealthy and subtle in their operations, that the minutest particle infused into a drink, mingled with food, laid gently on the victim's lips, will produce instantaneous death?"

"But such a death will be attended with marks of violence?"

"Not a bit of it, Livingstone! No mark of violence, no sign of murder attests the manner of the death. The victim lays as though he (or she) had but fallen asleep. What d'ye suppose would be the consequence, were these chemical secrets made known?"

"Very disastrous, I presume."

"Just fancy what a world it would make! A lawyer picks a quarrel with a judge, and sends him to heaven with a whiff of a perfume.— Two clergymen disagree on matters of controversial divinity—one makes the other a present of a pair of gloves! W-h-ew! He's gone! A lady jilts her lover—he sends her a magnificent Bird of Paradise, tipped with poison!— The lady jilts no more lovers! Two candidates are running for office—one puts a pill in t'other's brandy, and kills him off, on th' eve of th' election. Delightful world it would make! Tom poisons Dick; Dick poisons Harry; Harry poisons his wife, and his wife poisons—the devil knows who!"

"You've a very poor opinion of human nature, McTorniquet?"

"You've hit it! Its a way we doctors have. God Almighty trusts us with very little knowledge of the grand mysteries of nature, for fear we'd abuse our gift. Why Livingstone, d'ye know that were this secret and most subtle poison generally known, half the men in town would give their wives an eternal leave of absence? And *vice versa*. Precious world we'd have! Would you like to see a manuscript volume of mine, on the theory of poisons? Here it is in this cabinet. Just take a peep at it while I run round and have my horse brought to the front door. Put it back in the cabinet when you've gratified your curiosity. Back in a minute, Livingstone!"

Livingstone took the small volume of manuscript in his hand and eagerly turned over the leaves. He was alone. He stood in McTorniquet's museum, surrounded by shelves piled with surgical curiosities, preserved in jars, or hanging by parti-coloured strings, or, yet again, huddled carelessly together. The very air was reminiscent of the scalpel and the tourniquet. Dead men in fragments, in great pieces and little, in all shapes and every form, were scattered around. In the full light of the window, fashioned in the ceiling of the room, stood a grisly skeleton, one hand placed on his thigh-bone, while the other, with the fingers struck in the cavity of the nose, seemed performing the stale jest common with the boys along the street. "You can't come it, mister, by no manner o' means!" that gesture said, as plainly as a skeleton's gesture can say.

" 'In the days of Catherine de Medicis,' " murmured Livingstone, reading from the manuscript volume—" 'there was prepared by her command, a poison, combining in its nature, the most deadly chemical attributes. This poison laid its victim down in the sleep of death without a mark of violence, without the slightest sign of murder, to tell the tale of an untimely death. Subtle and penetrating in its nature, most fearfully opposed to the principle of life, in its mildest form; this poison was prepared by the alchemist Ellarbin D'Zoisboigne, after the study of years, passed in searching for the Grand Secret, the Water of Life. The alchemist sold the poison to the queen, for the price of one of her royal jewels. Secure of the deadly preparation, and aware of the manner in which it was to be used, the queen determined that the secret of its composition should rest with her alone. The alchemist was her first victim. Among various strange legends of medical lore, the poison, its various qualities, and the secret of its preparation, have descended to modern times. It is prepared thus——' "

Livingstone paused. The terrible idea which had rested upon his brain, since the scene of the past night, now began to take form and shape. He saw the horrible path which he was doomed to tread, more clearly and distinctly in its minutest windings.

He listened intently for a single moment. There was no sound of the doctor's returning footstep. The Museum was still as the grave. And yet, as the fatal idea rose blackening Livingstone's brain, with all it's details of horror, the very air of the room grew stifling, and he could distinctly hear the beatings of his own heart.

Ere another moment had passed, seizing a lancet, which lay on an adjoining shelf, with a calm and cautious movement, Livingstone severed the leaf, which he had just read, from the manuscript volume, and folding it in letter form, placed it within the breast of his overcoat.

"Close to the keepsakes—next to my heart," he grimly smiled, as he placed the manuscript volume in the cabinet again. "Three days ago, I little dreamed that Catharine De Medicis would become serviceable to me!"

He quietly passed from the room and from the house.] Hurrying along the crowded street, in the course of fifteen minutes he arrived before his stately mansion. At the very door he was met by Luke Harvey; who had just returned from his visit to the widow Smolby's house.

"It is noon," exclaimed Luke, with a quiet smile. "Here are the fruits of my morning's labours."

He placed in the merchant's hands the memorandum which he had taken from the stolen watch.

Livingstone started, but in an instant re-

covered the fearful composure which ha marked his demeanour since the fatal scene Monk-Hall.

"I bear it well? Do I not, Luke?" h calmly exclaimed. "So, so! He is not onl the—the adulterer, but the swindler an forger. We can settle both accounts once."

"There is enough in that slight memoran dum to excite suspicion," exclaimed Luke "but not enough to produce conviction. Leav the matter in my hands, and before Friday nigh —that's to-morrow—the fellow will be in th hands of the police."

"To-morrow morning, Dora, and I start fo Hawkwood," replied Livingstone, with a sligh smile. "By-the-by, while you are procurin the necessary documents for the conviction the forger, we must be sure that he does no leave the city. Ha, ha! I have it! Let u walk down the street while I let you into m plans."

They were walking down the street, whis pering earnestly together, when a hand was lai upon Livingstone's shoulder.

"Look here, curnel, you don't forget ol friends, do you?" said a bluff voice, whicl sounded very much like the deep bass of a oysterman.

"Why, Larkspur, is that you! Why what' the matter with you?"

"Nothin' much. Only there was a change i the admineystration, and Easy Larkspur wa turned out.

Easy Larkspur, as the new comer was styled was a short, stout man, with broad shoulders and a tolerably corpulent person. His face wa remarkable for its crimson hue, and its immen sity of jaw, or cheek, as the reader pleases His costume was at once picturesque and simple A short grey roundabout, exhibiting glimpses o a saffron shirt at the elbows, and buttoned u] to the neck across his muscular chest; cordu roy trowsers, reaching to the calf, agreeabl variegated with patches of various colours, an a pair of shoes, rather the worse for the wear with the heels worn away all at one side, an picturesque crevices near the toes. Easy Lark spur wore no stockings. Such things as stock ings had been invented long after man ha departed from his primitive simplicity of man ners; Easy Larkspur was above wearing stock ings. The hat which surmounted Mr. Lark spur's broad face, was quite a curiosity in it way. In material it was rather flimsy, being fashioned of common straw; in shape it wa singular, bearing a strong resemblance to nothing in heaven above, or on earth beneath or in the waters under the earth. Speculative people would have called it a shocking bad hat You might have fallen down and worshipped it without any violation of the commandment The picturesque appearance of the hat wa rather increased by a glimpse of a dingy red handkerchief, which peeped from the cre vices of the crown, like a quiet observer.

taking a view of the world, from a favourable elevation.

" Why, Larkspur, where have you been all this while ?"

" Two years ago I was turned out of the police. Since that time I've been perambulating the continent. Part of the time, as a tuppygraphical ingineer ; I carried the chain on the railroad. Part of the time, I was ingaged in the mercantile marine service ; drove the horse on the canawl. I attributes the present depression of my funds to the cursed whig tariff of '42. It must be that ; for deuce take me, if I know what else it can be !"

" Larkspur, would you like to earn a hundred dollars ?"

" Jist try me. I'm putty desp'rate now, I tell you. I might accept."

" Could you assume the manners of a southern planter ?"

" What d'ye mean ? Swear a few big oaths, carry a bowie knife, and talk about my niggers ? I jist could do that, and nothing else."

" Go down to my store, in Front-street, Larkspur, and wait for me." said Livingtone, turning towards his mansion again. " Luke, attend to the accomplice of the forger, in the den of Monk-Hall. I'll see that the forger himself does not leave the city."

It was in this state of mind, with his plans of vengeance fully matured, and his soul determined upon the prosecution of those plans, that Livingstone sought the presence of his wife, and passed through the scene in her boudoir, which we have already described."

" The girl is beautiful," Luke soliloquised as Livingstone and Larkspur passed on their separate ways, leaving him alone in the street. " Beautiful as a dream ! Pshaw, Luke, this folly ought not to move you again. Jilted once, and again in love ! and with whom ? A nobody, who coming from nowhere, knocks at old widow Smolby's door, and begs admittance, but won't give her name ! Fat Pyne, her father too—hum, that's suspicious, to say the least. Aunt Smolby promised that the girl should not leave her roof until she heard 'from me. There's mystery about the thing, take it as you will, and so as I said last night when hurrying down this very street, I say now—to Monk-Hall."

CHAPTER VII.

'THE COUNCIL OF WAR.

LORRIMER sat in the rose chamber. The light of the candle fast waning to the socket, streamed in fitful flashes over his wan and pallid face.

" I say, Monk Gusty, what shall we do with the feller ?"

" With Byrnewood," muttered Lorrimer, turning his head slowly round and gazing upon the form of Devil-bug, who stood at his side,

with his usual hideous grin, " with Byrnewood, you mean ?"

" With Byrnewood or the feller, jist as you like ! About these times I konsiders him a putty disagreeable feller, I does that ! He's a layin' on the floor of the walnut room, half dead with opium, and all sorts o' drugs ! He won't come to his senses for hours yet. But Gusty, what shall we do with him when he does come to his senses. That's the pint which I wants to argur !"

" And the gal, what shall we do with the gal ?" interrupted a voice proceeding from the other side of the room. " She's been sleepin' in the painted chamber ever since daylight. At fust she took on considerable, but a drop o' laud'num in her coffee settled her business ! What shall I tell her ven she vakes ?"

Mother Nancy, with her sharp features and colloped cheeks twisted into an expression of sneering malignity, approached Lorrimer and laid her withered hand upon his shoulder.

" What do you propose ?" exclaimed Lorrimer, as his face, changing to a death-like pallor, was illumined by a sudden glare of light.

" I perpose to keep a tight hold on the gal !" said mother Nancy, with a pleasant smile. " Nothin' like bein' on the safe side ! And then, Gusty, you can have a little bird to yerself, all in this old cage of Monk-Hall, and nobody be the wiser !"

" And as for Byrnewood," suggested Lorrimer, turning to Devil-bug.

" I perpose to keep a tight hold on him, too !"

The face of the doorkeeper of Monk-Hall was crossed by a hideous smile. His solitary eye glared with sudden intensity, and the muscles of his countenance were agitated for a single moment, by a violent and convulsive movement.

" Cuss it, how that light flickers in the socket !" Devil-bug calmly answered, raising his hand to his protuberant brow and smoothing the matted hair to one side. " What do I mean ?" he continued gazing at Lorrimer through the outspread fingers of his hand. " Nothin' o' konsekence ! Only the young feller will not come to his senses till long arter dark, and then—and then—cuss the light, it's gone out !"

The libertine and his minions were enveloped in sudden darkness.

CHAPTER VIII.

MAJOR RAPPAHANNOCK MULHILL.

ARRAYED in all the paraphernalia of his walking costume, Fitz-Cowles was threading his way among the crowd of loiterers, who daily occupy the pavement in front of Independence Hall. His brow was clouded by a frown, and once or twice, as he walked along, he allowed his gold-headed cane to fall on the hard bricks with a ringing sound. It was evident that the gallant colonel, in all the glory of his origin' hat, his tight-fitting overcoat, his long dark hair, his white kid gloves, and gold-headed cane, was still somewhat ruffled in temper, and disturbed in soul.

"This woman!" he muttered. "'Gad I never knew her match! Bold, reckless, and dangerous! I must take care! Dora, with her imprudence may frustrate all my schemes, and scatter my fortune to the wind! I stand upon a dangerous height! A step higher, and I arrive at the object of my desires, unlimited wealth and safety! A step lower, a single misplaced movement, and—ugh! The prison, the convict's cell, and—it makes my flesh creep—the lash, are mine!"

"Ah, ah! Fitz-Cowles! I've just been seeking for you!"

"Is that you, Livingstone! Which way are you bound! Up Chestnut-street or down?"

"Colonel Fitz-Cowles, allow me to make you acquainted with Major Rappahannock Mulhill, of Mulhill Plantarion, South Carolina. A planter from the south, colonel," suggested Livingstone, in a whisper; "rich as Girard. Lands without limit, and a gold mine!"

"I am proud of your acquaintance, sir," replied Fitz-Cowles, graciously extending his hand to the stranger. "Queer specimen of a planter," he muttered to himself. "Wonder if he's keen at the cards? I must try him at faro!"

"Sur! Happy of the honour! I like you—you're of the right stripe—'the real pig,' as we say at Mulhill," observed the southern planter, clapping Fitz-Cowles on the back. "May I be cussed, curnel, if I don't think you've got the real alleygator eye, which gives sich wiwacity to the phizzes of us bloods, from down south!"

Colonel Fitz-Cowles had seen many queer specimens of the southern planter, but this gentleman was decidedly the queerest of all. Rappahannock Mulhill was a stout, thickset, gentleman, with a round red face, and a corpulent paunch. His dress was at once singular and effective, as the playbills have it. A broad-brimmed hat, of raw felt, with a round crown, and a long blue cord, to which was appended a tassel that hung drooping to the major's shoulders. A deep crimson velvet waistcoat, double-breasted, and buttoned up to the throat. Pants made very full and wide, and striped like fancy bed-ticking; a sky blue coat, with glaring metal buttons; yellow buckskin gloves; tight boots of patent French leather, and a check neckerchief, tied in an enormous bow, and affording free play to the colossal shirt collar, which rose to the major's ears. Had you seen the major thus attired, walking along Chestnut street, you would have said that there was only one thing wanting to complete the general finish of his appearance; a cane of the proper style and dimensions. This want was supplied by an enormous stick or club, which the major grasped in his right hand. Bending in a dozen ways, all twisted and curled, and knotted, it looked as though it might have been the root of the

tariff, which politicians have been endeavouring to find for years.

"How did you leave all the folks down south, major?"

"Lively," replied the major, pulling up his shirt collar. "Lively! Roasted an abolitionist the day afore I left, for tryin' to steal my niggers. Lynched a Yankee, the day afore that, for sellin' me some Jersey cider for shampane! Things is werry lively in our diggins, jist now."

"I suppose you've been in a few knockdowns in your time?" observed Fitz-Cowles condescendingly.

"Can't say much for my skill in that line, curnel," replied the major, still tugging away at his shirt collar, while he grew suddenly red in the face, "Killed four or five fellers in a duel. Took 'em one after another. Had to pay their funeral expenses. Very low business. The sheriff had the impoodence to get a warrant out, for me. There it is—I've preserved it to this day as a coorosity!"

"Why it looks quite fresh," observed Fitz-Cowles, looking at the document which Mulhill held in his extended hand. "Very fresh, indeed."

"Oh, that's because I have kept it in spirits : a warrant 's sich a coorosity down south."

"Colonel, if you'll excuse me, I wish to speak a word with the major, before I resign him to your care. Major will you walk this way a moment."

He led the major beyond the hearing of Fitz-Cowles, and glanced quietly over his shoulder at the millionaire as he spoke,—

"Larkspur, how can you be so hazardous!" exclaimed Livingstone. "His name on that very warrant, and the signature of the mayor at the bottom!"

"Werry true," replied Easy Larkspur, *alias* Rappahannock Mulhill, "werry true. The ma'or swore me in as depitty polesman. He, he! The idea-r! My comin' the southern planter over him, when I've got a warrant in my pocket for his arrest!"

"Remember, Larkspur!" whispered Livingstone, in a deep and hurried tone. "Remember the injunctions which Mr. Harvey gave you. At three o'clock you leave this civet cat, and with a dozen policemen at your back, hasten down town to *the house*—you know the rest? After that business has been settled, you are to hang on to Fitz-Cowles, until all our plans are matured; you understand?"

"Don't I? Good mornin', Livingstone," he added aloud, as strutting to Fitz-Cowles' side, he waved his hand to the merchant, "call and see us at the Ton House when you've time."

"What a monster!" muttered Fitz-Cowles, "red vest and blue coat! However, there's money to be made by cultivating this creature. Walk up to the Ton House, major and smoke a cigar," he added aloud, in the most insinuating tone imaginable.

"I always carries my appeyratus with me,"

said the major, taking a box of lucifer matches from one pocket, and a large German pipe from the other. "Nothin' like bein' pervided with these things in case of accident. 'Tain't fashionable to smoke a pipe in Chestnut-street, is it curnel? Never mind—we 're the real alleygaters—we are."

And taking the colonel's arm within his own the Major strutted down Chestnut-street, his immense pipe attracting the attention of all by-standers, while Fitz-Cowles regarded both pipe and planter with a look of smothered disgust.

"Ha, ha, ha!" chuckled Livingstone, as he gazed after the retreating pair. "The handsome millionaire arm in arm with a police officer!"

CHAPTER IX.

THE DEAD-VAULT OF MONK-HALL.

THE beams of the lantern flashed over a wide cellar, whose arched roof was supported by massive pillars of unplastered brick. Here and there, as the flickering light glanced fitfully along the dark recesses of the place, fragments of wood might be discovered, scattered carelessly around the pillars, or thrown over the floor in crumbled heaps.

Every moment, as the light of the lantern shifted from side to side, some new wonder was discovered. Now the solid plastering of the ceiling, now the massive oak of the floor, now the uncouth forms of the pillars with loose bricks and crumbling pieces of wood scattered around, and now, as a gleam of light shot suddenly into the distant recesses of the cellar, a long row of coffins might be discovered, with the lids broken off, and the bones of the dead thrown rudely from their last resting place.

The extent of the cellar might not be ascertained by the uncertain light of the lantern. It may have been a hundred feet in extent, or even two hundred, but whenever the light flared up, it disclosed some dark recess, filled with crumbling coffins, or laid bare some obscure nook, where ghastly skulls and fragments of the human skeleton were thrown together like old lumber in a storehouse.

Even where the lantern stood in a square, described by four massive pillars which, arising from the oaken floor, supported the arched ceiling, its light gleamed over a skeleton, with the various bones separated by time, and the jaw, with its bristling teeth, falling apart from the blackened skull.

The sound of a footstep rung echoing among the arches of the cellar with a hollow sound, and in a moment, ere the figure of the intruder might be seen, the murmur of a human voice mingled with the echo of the footstep.

"Ha, ha, ha! While the broad-cloth gentry of the Quaker City guzzle their champaigne two stories above, here, in these cozy cellars of Monk-Hall, old Devil-bug entertains the thieves and cut-throats of the town with scorchin'

Jamakey spirits, and raw whiskey! Hark how the fellers laugh and shout in the next cellar!"

And the chorus of a rude drinking song, chaunted first by a single voice, then echoed by a score, came faint and murmuring through the thick walls of the adjoining cellar.

"Let the Bank D'rector swill his sham-pane,
 It's pisoned with orphan's tears—
Raw Jamakey we'll drink and drink again,
 For d—l 'a beak we fears!"

"That's what I likes," said Devil-bug, as he came shuffling onward into the light of the lantern, dragging the remnant of a coffin at his heels.

"The genelman as used to inhabit this konwenient winter and summer residence has soffened into dust. His coffin 'ill sarve me for a scat. Turn it over—that's right—now let me think. Hum—hum! Musketer, I say——"

"Yes massa," muttered the voice of the negro, from a distant part of the cellar.

"If any one wants to see me, tell Glowworm to show 'em down, and—d'ye hear, you brute? Do you show 'em in when they are down. Devil-bug's at home for wisiters."

"Yes massa!" muttered the negro from the darkness of the cellar; and then all was silent again.

Devil-bug was seated upon the coffin, with his elbows supported by his knees, and his swarthy cheeks resting on his thick and heavy fingers.

"My life's been a purty quiet one," he soliloquised. "Not many incidents to tell; passed my years in the comfortable retiracy o' domestic fellicity, as Parson Pyne would say! Yet there was one adventoore in my life: queer one, that. One stormy night, 'bout seventeen year ago, there comes to Monk-Hall, a rale bully of a feller, with a purty gal on his arm. He struck her a blow with his fist: I knocked him down. Gal liked me from that hour—ha, ha, ha—the thing makes me smile! A purty gal in love with a han'some man like Devil-bug! And yit, and yit, many's the night I've laid at her door, a watchin' her—and a keepin' harm from her, and ——ho! ho! ho! She used to say she loved me 'cause I did'nt deceive my looks. For one year, me and that gal was man an' wife! The year passed—one night she quit Monk-Hall—I ain't never heerd on her since. And, what is a werry rimarkible circumstance, I never think o' that gal, without my heart gittin soft, and the water comin' in my eyes! If any other man would say that o' me, I'd sue him for libel!—hallo! who's there?"

"Monk Baltzar, massa," answered the voice of Musquito, from a distant recess of the cellar.

"That's Parson Pyne's slang name," muttered Devil-bug. "Show him in, Musketer."

And in a moment, there came hurrying from the darkness which enveloped the distant portions of the cellar, the figure of a man wrapped up in a long and drooping black cloak.

"I say, Abijah, what are you doing down here?" he muttered, in a surly tone, from the folds of his cloak, as he approached Devil-bug's lanthern. "Very odd taste, this!"

"Draw a cheer, parson," exclaimed Devil-bug, smiling blandly; "or now that I think o' it, there ain't no cheers. Draw a coffin, parson, and let's have a talk."

"I've no time to stay," muttered the new comer, as he allowed the folds of his cloak to fall from his face, and discovered the full and beaming visage of the Rev. Doctor Pyne. "One word, and I'm gone."

"And that word about the gal you've been seekin' for three days?"

"At last I've lured her to Monk-Hall! This morning I discovered her hiding place; and, notwithstanding her tears and cries, forced her in a carriage, quieted her with threats, and but five minutes since, smuggled her into Monk-Hall,"

"More work for me, I see. What was the kontract?"

"You were to give her a potion in her drink, in order——"

"That she might be prepared for your wishes?"

"See that it's done before ten o'clock to-night, and the hundred dollars are yours?"

He disappeared in the darkness, and Devil-bug was alone once more.

"Yes, yes," he muttered, falling into the same soliloquising mood which had come over his soul, before the entrance of the Rev. Mr. F. A. T. Pyne. "Yes, yes, she was a purty gal, an' I sometimes thinks she's a livin' yit! She never told me nothin' but her first name, an' that's on the goold bracelet which she gave me. I've got it fast—fast—under lock and key!"

Devil-bug was silent. The shouts of the revellers in the adjoining cellar grew more loud and uproarious, yet he heeded them not. Deep in the heart of this monster, like a withered flower blooming from the very corruption of the grave, the memory of that fair young girl, who, eighteen years ago, had sought the shelter of Monk-Hall, lay hidden, fast entwined around the life-cords of his deformed soul.

"She was a purty gal, and whenever I think of her, as I said before, my eyes grow watery! I struck the feller who had laid his hands upon her—I struck him to the floor. I b'lieve my soul she liked me from that hour! Hullo—who's there?"

"A little nigga, massa," replied the voice of Musquito, still speaking from the distant nook of the cellar.

"Fitz-Cowles' nigger!" muttered Devil-bug.—"Wonder what he can be wanting with me?"

"De High Golly!" cried a voice echoing from the darkness of the vault. "Dis de deb-bil's own den, and dare's de debbil hisself!"

Dim, the creole, in his neat blue round-jacket and trousers, came stealing cautiously towards the lantern.

"You're a purty boy, ain't you? What d'ye want down here, hey?"

"Dare's a lettaw from Massa Fitz-Cowles," observed Dim, approaching Devil-bug with a cautious glance. "De High Golly! I wonder if dat ting hab got a tail!"

"Here, young indoovidooal, read this letter. There wasn't no free schools when I was young. Konsekence was, my eddycation was neglected."

"And he hab got two feet!" muttered Dim. "Bress my soul, I t'ought one foot was a hoof. Oh, massa, you can't read dat letter, may be you kin read dis ring!"

"Hullo! the ring!" cried Devil-bug, with a start. "I remember well, that when Fitz-Cowles first rikvested me to hide the Jew, he told me to mark this ring. 'Mark it,' ses he, 'and whenever I send this ring to you, cause the Jew to retire!' Ho, ho, that's what's in the wind, is it? Hurray, charcoal, an' read that letter!"

Bending slowly over the light, Dim read the letter which we have already laid before the reader.

"To think a nigger like that should read, and my eddycation neglected! Ten thousand dollars about his person! Recompense meself for the keer and trouble I've had with him! Won't I? You can go, young genelman—yet hold up a minnit! Why didn't you bring this ring and letter sooner than this? You've been playin' pitch-penny with some other nigger, I'll be bound?"

"Ha, yah!" laughed Dim, to himself—"Dat mus' be de debbil, sure 'nuf. I say, massa, how did yer know dat? I jis was doin' dat same t'ing. A party ob us young bloods went down to see de Navy Yard, and den we tuk a shine roun' town!"

"Re-tire young genelman!" said Devil-bug, severely, "re-tire and re-port yesself to head-quarters, forthvith."

"Ha-yah!" laughed Dim, as he hurried from the cellar, "Dis chile know a little more dan most folk! He seen de debbil—ha, yah—once in his life, anyhow!"

Devil-bug was alone again. Shifting the lantern from its position, he carefully examined the oaken planks of the floor. The outlines of a large trap-door were discernible, with the bolt, which held it to the floor, inserted in the worn and rusted socket.

"Trap-door 'bout ten feet square! There's a well below it, a deep well, a dark well; the d—l knows how deep! Any individooal gettin' a fall through that trap-door, might stand in danger of bein' eat up by rats and all sorts o'wermin, in case the fall didn't hurt him! Ten thousand dollars! Buy a snug little farm out west."

"Massa," exclaimed the voice of Musquito, from the darkness, "Dat ar Jew is a-comin' down stairs."

"Let him come," answered Devil-bug. "It

don't cost nothing. And, hark ye, the minnit he passes the cellar door, do you dig off."

Having thus spoken, Devil-bug hastily took a lamp from within the lantern, and poured some oil over the rusted bolt of the trap-door. In an instant the bolt yielded to the impulse of his hand, and moved quietly along the socket.

"All right! I'll jist leave the bolt a-clingin' to the socket by its end. The slightest touch from my hand won't unloose it? Redikulus! I must get a cheer for my friend—tain't nice to give a party without cheers!"

Disappearing behind a brick pillar, he drew the fragment of another coffin from its resting place, and laid it down on the floor, some six feet from the spot where the lantern stood.

"Any genelman a-sittin' on that cheer, will

THE WIDOW SMOLBY PREPARING TO DEFEND HER TREASURES FROM DEVIL-BUG.

have the hinges of the trap-door directly at his back, with some six feet o' the trap a-twixt me and him. The bolt will be right under my foot, so it will. Suppose I was to git thinkin' on some subject, and forgit myself? My foot might unlodge the bolt from its socket in the trap-door. K-u-sh-ew-bang!" he continued, producing a strange hissing sound, by suddenly forcing his breath through his clenched teeth.

"K-u-sh-ew-bang! The trap-door 'ud fall, and 'melancholy to re-late,' as the newspaper sez—some body 'ud git their brains knocked into shad-roe right off!"

"Massa Von Gelt am here, Massa 'Bijah," cried Musquito, from the distant extreme of the vault.

"Show the genelman in, and tell him to walk mighty keerful, or else he might fall through some o' them cussed holes, in the floor !''

In a moment, a cautious footstep was heard, and the dim outline of the Jew's figure became visible, as he advanced along the vault.

"Good eveningsh !'' was his salutation, as he approached the lantern, "Fader Abraham ! vot you dosh in dis place ?''

"Good afternoon,'' exclaimed Devil-bug, grinning hideously, "sit down, an' take a cheer !''

With a slight shrug of disgust, the hump-back, seated himself upon the coffin opposite Devil-bug, and quietly folding his arms over his fragment of a body, gazed fixedly into the hideous face of the door-keeper.

The two figures would have made an effective picture. The lantern placed at the feet of the Jew, threw a strong light over his person, while the form of Devil-bug was wrapt in a sort of lively twilight. The calm visage of the Jew, rendered even more quiet and contemplative by the segar which he smoked, the unnatural length of his face, and the absurd disproportion of his small and hump-backed body, which looked more like a shapeless lump, dressed up in man's attire, than the frame of a human being, all presented a vivid contrast to the visage of Devil-bug, his solitary eye glaring through the obscurity of the vault, like a flame coal, while his short, but stout and muscular frame, with the heavy body, knotted into uncouth knobs at the shoulders, with the long arms and bony fists, the slim legs and massive feet, all gave you the idea of a Sampson stunted in his growth ; a giant whom nature had dwarfed from the regular proportion of manly beauty, down into an uncouth image of hideous strength.

Around the twain, extended the death-vault of Monk Hall, its distant recesses, wrapt in heavy shadow, while the arched ceiling directly overhead, the oaken floor around, and the four pillars of massive bricks were now disclosed in strong light, as a sudden gust of wind, agitated the lantern-flame, or yet again veiled in a dim shadow, which gave a dark and dreary appearance to the place.

"I wash to see Vitz-Cowle dis morningsh,'' exclaimed Gabriel, with a calm decision of manner, that indicated the man of business.

"You wos, wos you ?'' answered Devil-bug, playing carelessly with the bolt of the trap-door. "And arter you'd seen him, what happened ?''

"You knowsh de widow Smolby ? She has de goldt plate. and de monish ?''

"Know her ?'' cried Devil-bug, still playing with the bolt. "The old woman's as rich as Girard ! You wos to see her, was you, Gabr'el ?''

"I vos, and soldt her a goldt watch. Dat ish to say, I made her a presentsh ov de watch.''

"Do I look like a werry young infant ?'' exclaimed Devil-bug, as bending his face down between his knees, he passed his fingers along

the floor, with a quick movement. "A Jew give anybody a watch !''

"Vot you scratch your fingersh on te floor ? Hey ? I doesh not like dat noise ! I am so nervous ! I gives te watch to her, but I takes five thousandt dollars in goldt from the house for my watch !''

"Five thousand dollars in gold, where is it, Gabr'el, where is it ?''

"Up stairsh, in your room. I put it in te closetsh, near te firesh. Vot you scratch your fingers on te floor ?''

"Gabr'el are you good at 'rithmetic ? How much is five thousand dollars and ten thousand dollars ?''

"Fifteen thousandt tollars. Vot you asksh for ?''

"Why,'' replied Devil-bug, as with his face still bent down between his knees, he played with the bolt of the trap-door. "Why—why, in fact, Gabr'el, you can re-tire !''

The word had not passed his lips before the bolt flew back from its socket ; there was a creaking noise, succeeded by a crash—and the whirring sound produced by the falling trap-door echoed around the death-vault. Devil-bug listened. All was darkness and silence. With the last gleam of light he had beheld the Jew tottering on the brink of the chasm, and now he listened for the sound produced by the mangled body, as it went sweeping through the air, to the bottom of the well. Another moment passed. A sound arose from the depths of the well. It was the sound of the lantern as it struck against the sides of the chasm. Bending over the well on hands and knees, Devil-bug listened with an intensity that forced the cold sweat from his forehead. No sound came echoing up the chasm, not even a murmur or a groan.

"He's gone home to his daddy,'' muttered Devil-bug, as rising on his feet again, he turned in the darkness, from the edge of the trap-door "He'll never refuse fat pork agin', I warran ye !''

"I say, vot te teffil you cuts dem capersh for ?'' said a clear bold voice, resounding through the darkness of the vault. "Got-tam ! I might have fell town and hurtsh meself ! Vot for you actsh like a crashy man ?''

Devil-bug started. So certain had he been of the Jew's death, that when he heard his voice echoing through the darkness, it struck him with a feeling of supernatural awe. In a moment, however, he recovered himself and began to crawl around the edge of the trap-door in the direction from whence the voice had issued.

"He got off, did he ?'' he muttered to himself. "Ha ! I won't seize him by the throat and pitch him into the well ? Jist trust me with him, a minnit, somebody ! Why you see, Gabr'el,'' he added aloud, in his blandest tone. "I happened to put my foot on the bolt of that cussed hatchway, and it come loose ! Where are you, Gabr'el ? I've got something pertickler to say to you.''

"No toudt, no toudt,'' responded Gabriel

"Put I vill keepsh my dishtance! Fader Abraham! vot a man it ish!"

Creeping along the floor on hands and feet, Devil-bug approached the pillar from whence the voice proceeded.

"To sarve me sich a trick!" he muttered. "But I'll bruise him for it, I'll bruise him!"

"I vos a-goin' to tell you dat I drop mine pocketsh-book in de woman Smolby's house. Ten tousandt tollars in it, too!"

"What's that you say?" grunted Devil-bug. "Dropped your pocket-book in widow Smolby's house? You are a precious pork-hater, to give ten thousand dollars for five!"

A shrill whistle echoed round the vault, ringing through nook and crevice with a piercing sound, like the winter wind shrieking down a chimney.

"What are you up to?" growled Devil-bug, as his outspread hands grasped the brick pillar. "Jist let me have a feel of your hand, Gabr'el."

As he spoke the glare of a lamp flashed over the vault. Devil-bug beheld the face of the Jew thrust from the opposite side of the pillar, with the keen and piercing eyes fixed upon his countenance.

"Where did that light come from?" he shouted. "Hey, Gabr'el?"

Turning suddenly, he beheld the form of a stranger advancing from the distant door of the vault, with a lighted candle in his hand.

"I vos jist a-goin' to tell you," exclaimed Gabriel, as Devil-bug was occupied in watching the stranger, who came hastening over the floor of the vault. "Tat we can rop te widow Smolpy's house. Dosh dat pleash you? I can git into te house tish very afternoon."

"Now mister, may I axe, who you are, and what the d—l you want here?" cried Devil-bug, as the new comer, light in hand, stood in front of the pillar which separated the doorkeeper from the Jew. "What's yer name anyhow?"

"Brick-Top," responded the stranger in a snuffling voice, "Brick-Top, at your service, sir. My daddy was a scavenger, and my mammy sold rags. Now you know all about me, and my family into the bargain. How d'ye feel, old cove?"

"You're werry familiar, young man; you are!" exclaimed Devil-bug, as he gazed upon the new comer, with a suspicious glance.

Brick-Top, was a tall, thin personage, clad from head to foot in rags; not ragged clothes, nor damaged clothes, nor shabby genteel clothes; but absolute and unconditional rags. His thin face, with its aquiline nose, was spotted all over with large freckles, and a great bunch of fiery red hair hung over his forehead, down to the very eyes. The lower part of his face was hedged in by a thick beard, of the same fiery red as his matted hair; while his eyes, keen, dark, and brilliant, presented a strange contrast to the vacant and unmeaning expression of his freckled countenance.

"Yer daddy was a scavenger, and yer mammy sold rags? It's my opinion, young man, that yer mammy must a-dressed you up in her

rag shop, and that yer daddy got mad with you won day, and cleaned some werry dirty alley with yer carcase! Wot a jail bird! It must a-been a dirty alley, anyhow! Who is the chap, hey, Gabr'el?"

"A person I got dis mornin' to help us to rob te widow Smolpy's, house. He can git into te house, easy as nothinsh! Dis young man vill help!"

"The widow Smolby's house?" exclaimed Devil-bug. "Stores o' plate, chests o' yaller boys, closets full o' walleyables? We kin get into the house easy as nothin', kin we? That 'ud be a haul; the widder Smolby's jewelry! Why didn't ye say this at fust, Gabriel? I wouldn't a-played any jokes on you then—no more I wouldn't!"

"Tem jokes ish very tampdt' bat," said Gabriel quietly; he little dreamed that this pleasant joke had been prepared by Fitz-Cowles, for his especial benefit.

"Vot a set o' wretches ye are!" exclaimed Brick-Top, snuffing the candle with his fingers. "To stand here gabblin' about nothin', ven the old widdey's house is a-waiting to be robbed. Didn't that servant wot's a-goin' to betray her missus, tell us to be on hand afore three in the arternoon!"

"So we kin git in that way, kin we?" exclaimed Devil-bug, with his accustomed delightful chuckle; "come along, pork-hater, come along, bundle o' rags; this is kon-siderable better than 'Nited States bank stock!"

And the three pleasant companions hastened from the death-vault of Monk-Hall; Devil-bug and Gabriel Von Gelt, conversing together in subdued tones; while Brick-Top, following at their heels, manifested his exuberance of spirit, by various strange gestures and mysterious expressions.

"Can we trust that are loafer? Werry low fellow he is!" exclaimed Devil-bug in a whisper.

"Very despirit fellersh!" replied Gabriel. "Toes not care for tanger, and ish goot mit a knifesh?"

"Hurray for Tippeycanoe!" shouted Brick-Top, cutting a caper in the air; "lots o' gold and walleyables we're a-goin' to lay hold of! All in che arternoon, ven the Quaker City has had its dinner, and all the Aldermen is a-strugglin' with boat loads o' terrapins and basket of oysters! Hurray for Tippeycanoe!'

CHAPTER X.

THE GHOST-ROOM.

"It's about seventeen years this day!" muttered Mrs. Smolby, quietly seating herself in a capacious arm-chair, placed in front of the fire place! "Seventeen years since she died— seventeen years since I have had a fire made in this room! Hum—hum! So brother Pyne was that gal's father! The trollop, to run away from her own father's house! Howsom

ever, he tuk her home agin this mornin'!
Wonder if Luke won't swear when he hears it?
To think that I should outlive five husbands,
Buddy, and Crank, and Dul—Dul— Peg, I say,
what was my third husband's name? Oh, she
aint here. Dulcombe—or Dulman, or, yes
that's it, Dulpins, and——what was I a-goin'
to say?"

The old lady glanced around the room, with
a puzzled look. The ghost-room was perfectly
still and quiet. The faint wood fire, flickering
over the hearth, every now then, flared up
in a sudden flash, dispelling the dim shadows
which rested upon the corners of the chamber.

The picture above the mantel, as the light
trembled over its surface, assumed the appearance of reality, and for a moment, ever and
anon, it would seem animated with a sudden
life. The deep, lustrous dark eyes, the pale
face, blooming with a rose-bud freshness in the
centre of either cheek, and strikingly relieved
by the long black hair, twining around the
neck, and falling over the bosom in glossy curls,
seemed warming into life, while it gazed with a
melancholy gaze upon the wrinkled visage of
the old woman seated by the fireside.

"Murder—mur-der!" screamed the parrot,
from his cage, which hung beside the portrait.
"Murder—Fi-er!"

"Now, Abe," cried the widow Smolby,
starting from her reverie,—"That's a lie! I was
not a goin' to say murder nor fi-er! But I was
a-goin' to say that it was a strange thing that I
should outlive five husbands, Buddy, and Crank,
and Smolby, and Tuppick, an' one whose name
I dis-remember; and be robbed, arter all, by a
plunderin' Jew; not at all mentionin' Peggy
Grud's filling the hopper brimfull o' nine cent
coffee!"

The old lady gazed fondly into the faces of
her four cats, grouped around the fire-place,
like pieces of Dutch statuary, as though she
awaited their answer to her lamentations.

"I feel very heavy, now that I come to think
of it. I b'lieve I'll lay down a bit."

She moved towards the bed, with the cats,
following at her heels, and in a moment disappeared within the curtains.

"I've never laid in this bed," her voice resounded from within the hangings, "since the
day afore *she* died. Be still Ike—don't stick
yer claws into me, in that way! Down Wesley,
I say get off my head—Wesley how dare you tear
my cap to pieces in that way! Nappy, ye
black snake ye, will you be quiet?"

"Abe wants a pe-ta-ter!" screamed the
parrot bustling about in his cage.—"Abe wants
a hot pe-ta-ter! Fi-er! murder, mur-*der!*"

"I'll get up and choke you, Abe! I will!"
screamed the old woman turning over in bed.
"Yer a perfec' pack 'o wretches! To think
that I should outlive five husbands, Buddy,
Crank, Dul—Dul—I say Peg, what's that one's
name? Dul—Dul—."

The old lady was asleep. The parrot in a fit
of violent misanthrophy laid his head between

his wings and muffled himself up in those very
wings, like a traveller in his cloak. The room
was perfectly quiet; the silence unbroken by a
sound save the purring noise made by the cats,
as they clustered round the sleeping widow.

This entire quietude continued for the space
of ten minutes or more, when it was disturbed
by the opening of the chamber door.

The withered face of Peggy Grud was thrust
through the aperture.

"Aslaape, is she? An' cut me aff wid a
shillin'? The likes on her to thry that game
wid me, a'ter my long sarvice! Wait till three
o'clock comes; jest wait!"

Closing the door, Peggy hurried down the
dark stairway.

Peggy had not disappeared more than five
minutes, when the front door of the mansion
creaked harshly on its rusty hinges, footsteps
were heard in the entry, and the door leading
from the entry into the front room, swung
slowly open.

"Dish is de plashe!" exclaimed a voice in a
deep whisper, and the diminutive form of a
hump-backed man, clad in a threadbare cloak,
with an immense white hat concealing his face
from view, strode softly into the room. "Dish
is de plashes. Now for mine pockets-booksh,
vich," he added in a tone of quiet glee, "Vich
I nefer did lost."

Ere another moment passed, two other
figures, wrapped in threadbare cloaks, like the
first, stole cautiously into the room, and approached the light, which burned dimly on
the small table in the centre.

"I say, Gabr'el bolt the door," said the
stoutest figure of the three, "Let's have a
quiet time to ourselves! Ho, ho, ho! Robbin'
a house in broad daylight! It tickles me, it
does! Now gentlemen to your posts—two of
us must go up stairs, while the 'tother one
watches below. Will you watch in this 'ere
room Gabr'el?"

"Fader Abraham! Viles you has te privi-
liges of looking over te oldt lady's cash-pooks up
stairsh. Not I, py no meansh!"

"What d'ye say, Brick-top? Will ye keep
watch down stairs?"

"Jist as this 'ere convention of the sovreign
people may decide," replied the gentleman addressed, quietly taking his seat by the table.
"But fair play ye mind? 'I'm to have my
thirds out o' this estate,' as the Irish widder
said, when she fit with fourteen children for
thirteen potatoes, and a salt mackerel. Go up
stairs, boys, and remove the deposits. We're the
rale dimmycrats—we are!"

They hastened from the room, and in a
moment were heard ascending the stairs, while
their companion, the contemplative Brick-top,
remained seated beside the table in the front
room.

"This is lively! They go up stairs; they
commence rummaging the front room. Meanwhile, there is no one on the look-out for them?
Oh, no: dont think of such a thing. Having
plundered the front room, on the third story,

they try the back room door, and find it locked. This excites their curiosity. They break open the door, and—find themselves in the arms of Easy Larkspur and twelve police officers!"

It was singular to note the change which came over Brick-top's voice and manner, as he sate by the table muttering mysterious words to himself, in a tone of quiet satisfaction. His voice suddenly lost all its vagabond hoarseness, and his manner was utterly unlike the manner of the devil-may-care loafer, whom Devil-bug and Von Gelt had left in the front room as their sentinel.

Suddenly rising from his seat, Brick-top turned his face from the light, as he bent over a small wash-stand, in an obscure corner of the room.

In a moment he turned towards the light again, and passing his hands rapidly up and down his person, stripped his costume of manifold rags, entirely from his tall figure.

"Faugh! How that red wig stinks!" he cried, flinging his head of hair to the other side of the room, "I flatter myself I did the 'loafer' rather genteely! Ha, ha, Luke, it wasn't so bad for you! 'My name is Brick-top, gemmen, my daddy wos a scavenger, and my mammy sold rags!' Ha, ha, ha!"

Luke Harvey, dressed in his usual costume, with the paint and the freckles washed from his face, stood disclosed in the light!

"Dressed myself in a small rag-shop this morning, and prowled about the avenues leading to Monk-hall. Met the Jew—introduced myself as a ruffian out of business—closed the bargain with him to help to rob this house. Went to the police office, engaged twelve fellows with red noses and agreeable complexions. Gave their leader, Easy Larkspur, the pass key to the small door at the back of this house, which opens into the private staircase, leading up into the back room on the third story. The old lady sleeps there in the afternoon. The police were to warn her of her danger. And the old lady and the girl, I suppose, are safe in the garret, while Devil-bug and Von Gelt are being trapped in the midst of their plunder. At all events, the police are close at hand! They are there at this moment waiting for their prey! Ha! Let me listen."

Advancing to the foot of the stairs, he listened with silent intensity for a single moment. Not a sound came echoing down the dark staircase. All was silent as though no robber's foot pressed the floors of the old mansion.

"Let me once have the Jew in my power, and then Fitz-Cowles is a doomed man! Was not that a shriek? Ha! the police are upon them! I hear them fighting up stairs. As for Devil-bug, it rather pains me to bring the old fellow to harm's door. Egad, but they're at it up stairs! No doubt he has commited crimes enough to sink a ship, even if each separate crime weighed no more than a pebble on the sea-shore. But he's an honest old rogue for all

that, and—the oath of our club prevented me from betraying the haunts of Monk-hall to the police, so I had to lure the Jew from its cozy old nooks and cells! Pity that Devil-bug came with him. Ha! Was that a shriek? Another shriek—a groan—and the tramp of footsteps. Devil-bug fights hard! He is scuffling with the police—I'll hurry up stairs and see the fun!"

Luke rushed up stairs and gained the head of the stairway; all was dark as the tomb. No light glaring from an open door served to illumine his way. Standing at the head of the topmost stair, Luke held his very breath as he listened. A dark and horrible suspicion flashed over his soul. Not a sound struck his ear, not even the breathing of a man, or the rustling of a passing footstep.

"This is strange," muttered Luke, "but a moment ago the house rung with shouts and shrieks, and now—Ha! This must be the door of the ghost-room."

He entered the dark chamber, his hands outspread, while he listened with painful intensity for the slightest sound. He passed over the carpet, he was moving in the direction where he supposed the bed was fixed, when his foot slipped from under him, and he fell to the floor.

"The floor is wet," he muttered, with an oath, as he endeavoured to regain the floor. "Curse the thing, who has been flinging the furniture about the room?" he continued, as an object—a piece of furniture, or perhaps a chest, or a bundle of clothes arrested his progress, and flung him headlong to the carpet. "The police must have had a d—l of a scuffle! But what has become of the old woman and the girl?"

Arising hastily to his feet, he rushed down stairs, in order to procure a light. Entering the front room once more, he extended his hands to grasp the candlestick, and in the very action, started back with a feeling of horror, that chilled him to the inmost heart.

His hands, which he raised in the glare of the light, were crimsoned with thick red blood.

CHAPTER XI.

DEVIL-BUG IN THE GHOST-ROOM.

"Cuss the stairs, they creak as if they had the roomatiz! Keep close to my heels, Gabr'el."

"Yes, I dosh!" whispered the Jew, in reply. "There ish a light, take keer now, take very goot keer."

Ascending the dark staircase with a hushed and cautious footstep, Devil-bug stood on the landing which gave entrance to the back and front rooms of the third story. A ruddy gleam of light flared out upon the passage from within the ghost-chamber, as the door hung slightly ajar. Devil-bug advanced a step and listened. All was silent. He pushed the door wide open, and with Gabriel following at his heels stood within the confines of the ancient chamber. The candle was still burning upon the table, and the wood fire flickered fitfully on the hearth.

"The old woman's a sleepin' on that bed," muttered Devil-bug. "She snores like a trumpet! We must be keerful! Have you got the keys—them false keys."

"Here tey ish, te trunksh under te foots of te bedt."

Devil-bug took the keys in one hand, the candle in the other, and advanced to the foot of the bed. In a moment, placing the candle upon the carpet, he swept the bed-hangings aside, and drew from under the couch, with a slow and careful movement, a small chest of dark wood, with a keyhole of peculiar shape.

"Bi-Gott!" cried the Hebrew, who ever made use of this favourite oath when very much excited. "I smellsh te gooldt already!"

"H-u-sh!" whispered Devil-bug, fixing one of the keys, which he grasped in his hand in the keyhole of the chest. "Be still, or I'll damage you so the d—l won't know you! Ha, ha, there's the yeller boys! The rale giniwine mulatters!"

"Gott! Toubloonsh! Toubloonsh!" muttered the Jew, thrusting his hands eagerly into the chest.

"Are ye a nateral born fool?" muttered Devil-bug, in a surly tone. "The clink of the pewter 'ill wake up the old woman. Be quiet while I konsiders the pecooliar circumstances, under which we are placed."

And as they bent lowly over the chest, their eyes feasting on the rich store of doubloons, the bed hangings were agitated by a slight movement, and in an instant, a worn and withered face, whose sharp features were rendered painfully distinct, by the tight-fitting cap of black silk, was thrust between the purple folds, within striking distance of the robbers' heads.

It was the face of the old woman, aroused from her sleep by the clinking of her gold. With the presence of mind that would have done honour to a general in the battle-field; she noticed the movements of the robbers, without so much as a cry of surprise, and in that instant of silent observation, she resolved upon her plan of action. Beneath the side of the bed, nearest the side of the wall, was a small chest, in which a pair of pistols had been always kept by her last husband. Could she slowly drag her form along the massive couch, to the opposite side of the bed, and extending her hands, raise the lid of the chest, and seize the pistols, she had no fears for the result. While the robbers bent over the chest, whispering to one another in hushed tones, she withdrew within the curtains, and commenced dragging herself slowly and cautiously along the bed.

"I tells you vat it ish," whispered the Jew, "dish is too mosh monish to take away leetle by leetle! Sompody may come and take it afore we come agin. Let ush put down the lid; and carry off te chest at wonsh!"

"Was that the old 'oman moanin' in her sleep?" whispered Devil-bug, holding his breath to listen,—"Hush! The bed's a creakin' like blazes. Let me go round an' take a look at the old lady."

Arising from the chest he strode cautiously around the bed and gazed within the curtains. All was dark as midnight. He could hear a sound like the hissing of an enraged cat, mingled with a slight creaking noise.

"The light Gabr'el!" he whispered.

"I'll give it to you, you ornery scound'l— to rob a poor lone woman in this 'ere vay," screamed a woman's voice from within the curtains, and the light of a pistol caused by the powder flashing in the pan, flared up in Devil-bug's face. By that momentary gleam of light he beheld the form of the old woman; crouching on the bed in the attitude of an enraged tigress preparing to spring, a pistol extended in each outstretched hand, while a gleam of superhuman malignity shot from her small grey eyes.

"Rob a poor lone woman, will ye? Take that!" she cried, pulling the trigger of the remaining pistol. It flashed in the pan, but missed fire.

"Them pistols is old fashioned like yerself— ought to have the rale percushions, ha, ha, ha!" laughed Devil-bug, but his laughter was of brief duration.

With a wild yell, gathering all her strength for a desperate effort, the old woman bounded from the bed, and in an instant came plunging at the throat of Devil-bug, her arms outstretched, and her long skinny fingers clutching him by the face and hair. She hung upon him like a living night-mare; her arms gathering convulsively round his neck, while her long nails dug into his cheeks like the talons of a vulture.

"Help me Gabr'el," muttered Devil-bug, struggling fiercely with the old woman, "give me a lift, and I'll choke her in a minnit."

Gabriel looked up in surprise, mingled with terror. His course was taken in a moment. Closing the small chest heaped with doubloons, he gathered it in the embrace of his long arms, and winding his dingy cloak round his shoulders, made towards the door.

"Down de back staircase," he muttered, hurrying through the door, "I vill make my tracks."

The old widow still clung to the robber's neck, gathering him to her withered form in an embrace more pressing than maternal. With a violent effort Devil-bug raised his arms, and poising her a moment in the air, dashed her to the floor. In an instant she was on her feet again; in another instant her arms were round his neck, with one hand gathered in his hair, and the other clutching him by the face.

"What an old critter! Not to pare her nails," muttered Devil-bug, as his face and hands were wet with his blood. "I'll give ye a lesson ye'll never forgit, I will."

"I'll larn ye to rob a poor lone woman," shrieked the widow.

Then commenced a contest which, but a minute or two in duration, was characterized on both sides by all the malignant energy of wild beasts fighting for their prey. Again and again Devil-bug raised her in his arms and dashed her to the floor; again and again she sprung to her feet, and with the bound of the rattlesnake darting on its victim, gathering her hands round his throat. Along the floor Devil-bug dragged her, upsetting chairs and tables in the struggle; from one end of the room to the other, with the celerity of lightning, the combatants passed, the old woman muttering a suppressed shriek all the while, as the hand of the robber was pressed upon her mouth. Now around the bed, now along the hearth, scattering ashes and firebrands in the air, now against the wall, this desperate fight was continued, the old woman struggling with supernatural strength for her life and her gold, while Devil-bug, with all his muscular vigour, his arms of iron sinew, and his fingers, whose grasp was like the shutting of a vice, found, for once, he had encountered an antagonist as determined as himself.

"Murder, mur-*der*!" shrieked the parrot, aroused from his nap by the sound of the contest.

"Ye'll cry murder, will ye?" cried Devil-bug, mistaking the cry of the parrot, for a shriek of the old woman. "I'll settle that business for you, I will!"

His teeth were fixedly compressed, as with one desperate effort he unloosed the arms of the old woman from his throat, and grasped her firmly by the middle of the body. He fixed his eye upon a massive knob surmounting one of the brass andirons before the fire, and, as a blacksmith raises a hammer in his arms, he swung the body of the old woman suddenly on high. She uttered a loud and piercing shriek—it was her last! As the blacksmith with his muscular arms, braced for the blow, brings the hammer whirling down upon the anvil, so Devil-bug, with his hideous face all a-flame with rage, swung the body of the old woman wildly over his shoulder, with every impulse of his strength gathered for the effort, struck her head—her long grey hairs streaming wildly all the time—full against the knob of the brass andiron.

He raised her body in the air again to repeat the blow, but the effort was needless. The brains of the old woman lay scattered over the hearth, and the body which Devil-bug raised in the air, was a headless trunk, with the bleeding fragments of a face and skull, clinging to the quivering neck.

"B'lieve o' my soul, the old 'ooman's nurt," muttered Devil-bug, with a ghastly smile, as he flung the body, yet trembling with life, to the floor. "Ha! ha!" he shouted, standing as still as though suddenly frozen to stone. "There's that feller at my side with the jaw bruk and the tongue stickin' out! There he is, just as he fell through the trap, and there, by his side, is the old woman, with the brains a-pourin' out from the empty skull! There's two on 'em now—and they'll always be with me—ah! ah!

I'll not stand this, I won't! Why can't a feller kill his man or woman and have done with 'em? But to have 'em this way, always with you—— He, he, he! I begin to b'lieve in hell now, I do!"

He stood before the fireplace, with his back to the portrait. The corse of the old woman, the mangled fragments of a face and skull, resting in a pool of blood, lay at his very heels along the hearth. In front of him, at some distance along the floor, beside the bed, stood the candle, now flickering in its socket, and flinging a waning light around the room. The face of Devil-bug was pale as ashes; his lips were tightly compressed; and his solitary eye glared out from the shadow of the overhanging brow, like the eye of a war-horse, with the death-arrow in his heart. His hands hung stiffened by his side; his entire appearance was that of a man whom some wierd enchantment is transforming to lifeless stone. The cold sweat in big and clammy drops, streamed over his tawny visage, and his eye grew more vivid and intense in its burning gaze.

"I hear the critter groan," he muttered, without moving the fraction of an inch from his statue-like position. "Somethin' evil is goin' to happen to me! Just as he fell through the hatchway, his jaw broke and his tongue out—he lays afore me! And he moves his bloodshot eyes and waggles his tongue, and groans and groans! And the old woman's there too! She's layin' at my back. I know, but there she is, at my side—the brains oozing out from the hollow skull!"

For a moment the murderer trembled from head to foot.

"By God!" he muttered the oath with deep emphasis—and this was a singular thing for Devil-bug to do, for he scarcely ever swore by the name of the Almighty. "By God! I do—I do begin to b'lieve that there is a hell!"

And around his feet, and over the hearth, silently and slowly the blood of the murdered woman began to flow and spread, while the ghastly corse, with the hollow skull oozing with clotted flesh and brains, lay huddled in a shapeless heap, the hand contorted with the spasm of death, and the stiffened limbs flung along the bricks, in the crouching position peculiar to a violent and a bloody death.

Murder was in that room in its most awful form. Like a terrible presence, it seemed to darken the very air of the room, and chill the strong heart of the murderer. The light flickered dimly in the socket, and then sank down, after a sudden glare, and all was dark as midnight.

"It's gone out," muttered Devil-bug as his heart gathered a strange courage from the darkness which took the sight of all outward objects from his view. "It's gone out! Why should'nt I fill my pockets with some o' the old woman's plunder? Ha, ha, ha! Why not? Devil-bug ain't so easily skeered, I tell ye."

He turned towards the fireplace as he spoke.

He was about to prosecute his researches in the darkness, when the light, which he had fancied extinguished, flared up from its socket, and lit the room with a sudden glare. That glare was but for an instant, and yet by its red light, Devil-bug, with his face turned to the hearth, beheld the dark eyes of the portrait gazing fixedly upon him. He had not observed this portrait before. But now as the pale cheeks glowed in the momentary glare of the dying candle, as the dark eyes grew suddenly brilliant, and the hair seemed to wave and float in the ruddy light, while the back ground of this picture, the frame and all its minor details were wrapt in thick darkness, Devil-bug thought he beheld not a portrait, or a mere piece of inanimate canvass, but a breathing and living woman, whose look was fixed upon his face in terrible reproof.

"Nell!" he shrieked.—"The gal come to life agin' jist as she was seventeen years ago! Ho, ho, ho! I do believe there is—a God—that's a fact!"

The light went out, and all was darkness. Devil-bug with a wild yell fled from the room, his footsteps echoed through the next chamber, and in a moment resounded from a private stairway leading into the yard. Again and again that wild yell mingled with a woman's name broke upon the air, and then all was still.

Silence and darkness and murder were the only tenants of the ghost-room, while the oozing blood began to harden over the cold bricks of the fire-place.

BOOK III.

THE SECOND NIGHT.

CHAPTER I.

LUKE HARVEY IN THE GHOST-ROOM.

LUKE raised his blood-stained hands in the light, and stood chained to the spot with horror In a moment he mastered the dead and icy feeling of awe which began to change his very heart to stone. He seized the candle, rushed up the stairway, and stood before the ghost-room. The light which he grasped flashed through the open door of the back room. It was silent and untenanted by human being. The door, opening on the private staircase, hung slightly open. Luke gazed through the doorway of the back room again and again, but his gaze, never for a single instant wandered into the ghost-room, whose opened door laid its secret bare to his glance.

He stood at the door with the light in his hand, trembling with a strange fear, but he dared not enter the room.

Even as he stood, footsteps, hushed and softened, came echoing faintly from the private staircase, and in a moment, through the doorway at its head, there stole the figure of a stout man, wrapped in a thick overcoat, with a pistol in one hand, and a thick knotted mace in the other. One by one at his heels, there followed twelve muscular men, dressed and armed like their leader. Luke neither heard nor saw them, but stood as if frozen to the floor, with his head turned away from the door of the ghost-room.

"Why, Harvey, is that you?" cried the leader of the band of twelve. "Has them fellers been here, hey? Or am I too early? Easy Larkspur is generally too early. Why what's the matter with you, man? Where's the old woman and the gal? Strike me stoopid, if you haint struck dumb!"

Luke silently pointed to the ghost-room.

Larkspur seized the candle and followed by the twelve police officers, hurriedly rushed into the chamber.

There was a pause for a single moment, and then from every man there yelled one involuntary and awful shriek of horror.

"By G—d we're too late!" muttered Larkspur, in a voice whose emphasis of horror was in fearful contrast with his usual devil-may-care tones. "The party has been here afore us, and finished their job!"

"Didn't I tell you," cried a police officer, "that the feller whom we saw shinnin' it down the alley, as we came in the gate, was one of the party from this house?"

"May I be hung for stealin' a tooth pick from a match boy, if this aint a leetle a head of my time!" exclaimed Larkspur; and Luke could hear him walking hurriedly up and down the room. "Too late, boys, too late, by G—d!"

Luke gathered nerve for a sight of horror, and slowly advancing into the room, pushed through the band of police officers, and ~azed upon the mangled corse.

"Here's some of the fruits of my d—d plot to catch the thieves," he said in a husky voice, as he gazed upon the shapeless mass, which but five minutes before had been a living and breathing creature. "Larkspur, I thought that you were hidden in the back room, when I first entered the house; but no matter. It's all over now."

His face was white as the death shroud, and his upper lip trembled with an involuntary movement.

"Larkspur," he said in a voice which did not rise above a whisper; "search this room, and see—and—see—if there is not another—another—corpse!"

"Och, Whilaloo! Ochone! Ochone! Murtherin' th-a-aves in the house of me misthress! Ochone!" a voice came echoing from the main stairway of the mansion. "Ochone! We're ruinated and kilt intirely! Heard ye iver the likes o' this?"

Peggy Grud came rushing into the room, her hair flying about her head in wild disorder, while with her clasped hands upraised, she rent the air with a succession of vivid shrieks. The police officers were between her and the fireplace, and the fearful object, laid along the floor, did not meet her eyesight.

"Will ye git out o' this, ye murtherin' blag-

gards? Where's my misthress? Ochone—ochone! Th-*a*-aves! I'll riz the nabor'ud on ye. Where's me mistress?"

Luke silently pushed the police officers aside, and taking Peggy Grud by the hand, led her forward.

"There," he cried, fixing his snake-like eyes upon her, with a glance which she dared not face, "there is your mistress!"

"Murder, mur*der*!" cried the parrot, rust-

ling about in the cage above the mantel-piece.

Peggy Grud looked down upon the corse, and then leaped into the very air, with a start of unfeigned horror. Uttering shriek after shriek, no longer feigned by shrewd hypocrisy, but wrung from her bosom, by the horrible sight of the ghastly corse, combined with her own guilty fears, Peggy Grud, sank in a kneeling

position, with her face averted from the dead body, while she tore her hair in very madness.

"Who sez I did the murther?" she shrieked, "it's a lie! it's a lie! Who ses I did the murther? It is a lie as black as hell! Och—ochone!"

"Yer a purty pictur' aint you?" cried Lark-spur, advancing from the throng of police officers. "Yer a purty thing, aint ye? You'll be in all the papers, now won't you? Oh, ye'll become a public karacter ye will!"

"Ochone—Ochone!" screamed Peggy Grud, "what have I done? Jist tell me anybody what have I done?"

"Murder, murder!" screamed the parrot from his cage, "murder!"

CHAPTER II.

STRANGE VISITORS IN MONK-HALL.

"'Genelmen, my daddy vos a scavenger and my mammy sold rags!' On my travels again, ha, ha! A pretty mess I've got myself into, with all this planning and plotting! The old woman murdered, the Jew and Devil-bug escaped, and all my work to do over again! Peggy Grud, however, is safe: and the 'proper authorities' have promised to leave the arrest of Devil-bug to me; I'll manage him before to-morrow night, or my name is'nt Luke! And that pale-faced girl, with the soft eyes and dark hair.—Parson Pyne's daughter, is she? I'll know more about her, *too*, before I'm many hours older!"

Attired in the rags of Brick-top, with the red hair falling over his eyes, and his face all smeared with paint and invested with huge crimson whiskers, Luke was hurrying down Third street, his hands in his pockets, and his body thrown forward, while his walk that of a genuine loafer, being made up of an Indian's tramp when on a war-path, and a Highlander's characteristic trot; a sort of half-walk and half-run, with a slight sprinkling of a lazy lounge.

To say that Luke did not relish these excursions, for the adventure's sake alone, would be doing him rank injustice. He found as much pleasure in pursuing the thread of a difficult enterprize, which combined danger, romance, and mystery, as the most indefatigable novel-reader finds in the pages of a book, where the attention is, from first to last, rivetted and enchained by one passage of breathless interest succeeding another, in transitions as rapid as the changes of some well-contested battle.

"Here's a new mystery," muttered Luke, as he struck into a bye-street. "Mary Arlington missing, and her brother in the bargain! Egad, this will be an eventful Christmas, if things keep on this way."

The beams of a small lamp, of rusty iron, standing on the table near the fire, gave a faint and dusky light to the doorkeeper's den. Devil-bug was seated beside the table, with his elbows resting on its rough oaken surface, while his hands grasped his tawny cheeks, the long finger nails sinking into the flesh like the talons of an eagle, and spotting his face with drops of blood. His teeth were fast clenched, but his lips hung apart, shrivelled with a fixed and grotesque grin; like the smile of a fiend, frozen into marble.

Watching him with his snake-like eyes, sat Brick-top.

"And not to git the chest o' doubloons arter all!" said Devil-bug. "Kin ye read, feller; I say, kin ye read?" he exclaimed in a fierce tone, as he laid his hand on Brick-top's arm. "Or are ye a stupid jackass as don't know nothin'?"

"Shut me up in a coal-mine all my life, and make me chaw dirt for a livin'! Kin I read? I wish my daddy could hear you say that! He'd show my school bills, old chap, with a wengeance to ye!"

"Here's a package o' papers, which I picked up on the stairs o' th' widow's house. Sit down on t'other side o' th' table and read 'em to me."

Brick-top sat down on one side of the table while Devil-bug resumed his seat opposite.

"Papers!" cried Brick-top, pulling his lank red hair down over his brows. "Egad!" he muttered to himself, "the very packet entrusted to me by Livingstone this morning! The seal broken too!"

"Read, will ye? And mind yer eye, feller. If I ketch you playin' the fool with me, and readin' any stuff what isn't there, I'll make no bones of hurtin' your body so no doctors wont buy ye arter yer a corpse!"

"Talk that way to the Wolunteers, will ye! Howsomever, here goes into the doc-y-ments."

In a low toned voice, still marked by his vagabond accent, Brick-top began to read the contents of the package.

At first Devil-bug leaned over the table with a look of the deepest interest, but soon the details of the package seemed to tire him, and he leaned listlessly to one side, with his eye fixed vacantly upon the ceiling. Brick-top read on. A name attracted Devil-bug's attention, and then a date, and an incident. He leaned over the table, his solitary eye blazing with the most intense interest.

"Look here, youssir—you ain't a-foolin' me are ye? Ellen—did ye say?"

"The werry same," replied Brick-top, burying his face in the unrolled package. His attention also seemed rivetted to the paper and its contents, for his glittering and snake-like eye grew more brilliant in its glance, while the outlines of his countenance became fixed and compressed. Brick-top pulled his red hair farther over his brow, until it almost concealed his eyes, and then resumed the reading of the paper.

Devil-bug listened with every power of his soul, enchained by an overwhelming interest. His solitary eye dilated and flashed with excitement, and the nails of his talon-like fingers were thrust into his tawny cheeks with a movement of involuntary agitation.

"Christmas-eve?" he echoed, repeating the words of the manuscript as they fell from the lips of the reader, "Christmas-eve, eighteen hundred and twenty-four? Hallo, youssir. Is them the words?"

"The werry same!" replied Brick-top, raising the paper before his face. "Left her mother's house on that date——"

"Read on, will ye? Don't ye see how I'm a quiverin'? I want to know the rest—read on!"

Brick-top again turned his attention to the manuscript. Devil-bug was utterly absorbed in its details. He held his very breath, as he drank in each word, and date, and incident.

"The *second child* died, did it?" he shrieked, starting wildly from his seat. "Now look here, feller, if you've got the feelin's of a common human bein' don't make a fool o' me! Read it agin—be sure that it's the second child; jist be sure o' that!"

"The second child—born Christmas-eve, eighteen hundred and twenty-four," exclaimed Brick-top, reading from the manuscript, while a slight tremor was observable in his voice.

"That's the date, too, that's the date!" cried Devil-bug, in a voice of the deepest agitation. "Look here, feller, d'ye see that arm? The night arter she left this house, I got a sailor-chap to print this here with Injin ink."

And as he spoke, Devil-bug bared his right arm, and thrust it forward into the full glare of the light. Brick-top gazed upon it in surprise. On its brawny skin, in rough characters, was punctured this brief name and date: "Christmas-eve—1824—Ellen."

"And so ye know'd her, did ye?" exclaimed Brick-top, gazing in Devil-bug's face with a piercing glance, while his lip trembled with some unknown emotion. "Werry singular that!"

"Know'd her?" responded Devil-bug, in a tone of sudden anger. "Don't axe no questions, feller, but read on!"

Brick-top again resumed the manuscript. A name, once more, started Devil-bug from his feet.

"Dick Baltzar?" he echoed. "Sure that's the name?"

"The werry same. Here it is:—'The second child was buried by a man named Dick Baltzer, who with his wife, resided in the widow's house. The first child——, howsomever, let me read on!"

The manuscript drew near its close. His brows woven in frown, his teeth clenched, his hands clutching his cheeks with a convulsive grasp, Devil-bug listened to the closing words with breathless interest.

"The whole of his fortune?" echoed Devil-bug, repeating the words of the manuscript.— "Luke Harvey entrusted with the commission? Hey, hey? is that it?"

Brick-Top nodded, but said nothing. Well was it for him that Devil-bug occupied with his own strange thoughts, had no eye for his companions demeanour. A tear stole from Brick-top's eyelid and rolled down his freckled face. His hand trembled as he grasped the manuscript, and his lips quivered with a tremulous motion.

"Luke Harvey!" muttered Devil-bug.— "He's a wild fellow, and one of the devil's disciples, who hold their meetings in this house! A purty chap to have sich a matter in his charge! He'll be here some time to night, and I'll have a talk with him! Gi' me that paper —will ye?"

"I say, old feller, come now and uncork this mystery! Let a body know all about it— that's a conwivial old devil!"

Devil-bug turned towards him with a lowering brow, but as he turned a knock was heard at the front door.

"Dig off—*feller!*" said Devil-bug, with great emphasis.—"'Taint for sich as you to know what quality comes to this house! Dig, I say!"

Brick-Top lounged lazily toward the doorway of the mansion-hall, while Devil-bug, unbarring the front door, gazed through the crevices of the green blinds upon the form of the newcomer.

"Who's there?"

"Monk Baltzer," answered an assumed and artificial voice.

"What had you for dinner to-day?" asked Devil-bug, repeating the first part of the countersign of Monk-Hall.

"Fire and brimstone!" answered the voice.

"Come in!" said Devil-bug, "All right! The gal's up-stairs in the room—I'll be up d'rectly."

And as he spoke the Reverend Parson Pyne strode silently across the floor of the den, and with his face muffled in the folds of his cloak, passed through the doorway, and along the hall, and up the stairs; and in a moment disappeared into one of the rooms on the right side of the massive staircase, on the second floor of the mansion. As he disappeared, a tall figure rose upward from the darkness, which hung round the banisters of the staircase near the floor.

"Parson, I think I've tracked you to some purpose!" said a deep-toned voice. — "The girl *your* daughter and you in Monk-Hall! I'll drop Brick-Top for a little while and assume Luke Harvey again, in order to be ready for all accidents! My game is a desperate one, but I'll play it with a cool head and firm hand!"

With these words he disappeared into the door of Luke Harvey's room; and in a moment the sound of the key turning in the lock, echoed faintly round the hall.

Meanwhile Devil-bug, standing near the table, in the centre of his den, with his arms crossed over his breast, and his right hand grasping Livingstone's mysterious packet, seemed utterly absorbed in the contemplation of the disclosures which it had revealed.

The sound of voices, mingling confusedly together, came echoing suddenly from the stairway leading to the banquet-room of Monk-Hall. And then a rude burst of laughter, resounded.

through the hall, mingled with the hurried tramp of footsteps,

"Ha, ha, ha! And so you drugged the brother with opium!" exclaimed a voice familiar to the reader. "That was an odd mistake of mine, Gus., about the fellow's name."

"To think Silly should introduce him to you by the name of Byrnewood!" cried another voice. "And then—ha, ha, ha!—the bridal scene! Oh! Lord, that was too good, wasn't it Gus. ?"

"Very good, no doubt, very good, gentlemen," exclaimed a third voice, "but there are some jokes which cost a mint of money. I rather suspect that this amusing adventure is one of the costly class!"

Ere the words had ceased to echo in the air, Lorrimer, followed by Petriken and Mutchins, lounged into the doorkeeper's den. Their faces were slightly flushed by the kisses of that long-necked giant, the champagne bottle, and their entrance into Devil-bug's private parlour was heralded by clouds of smoke issuing from the segars which the trio carried between their lips.

"Come on, fellows!" exclaimed Lorrimer, who had been gazing quietly at Devil-bug, as he stood unconscious of their presence. "Let us out, and make a night of it!"

As he spoke, a hand was laid upon his shoulder, and Long-haired Bess stood before him, her jet-black tresses hanging dishevelled along her white neck, while the peculiar brilliancy of her eyes, with a dark circle of discoloured flesh beneath each eye, gave indications of deep and powerful agitation.

"Well, Bessie, what's the matter now? How is the girl, that is to say, how is Mary?"

"She has lain unconscious all day long, until within a few minutes past," answered Bess, in a low-toned voice. "She has now recovered her reason. She does nothing but wring her hands as she paces up and down the room; nothing but wring her hands and shriek your name. Lorrimer, you had better see this girl before you leave the house."

"Not to-night, Bessie, not to-night," cried Lorrimer, moving towards the door. "Any time but to-night; as for Byrnewood—"

"That 'ere patient is in the hands of the doctor." exclaimed Devil-bug, advancing. "I give him a leetle opium to begin with; arter a-while I'll per-scribe somethin' more coolin'—a leetle hard steel for instance. Wonders how that 'll work?"

As he spoke, Lorrimer and his companions disappeared through the front door, with a loud burst of laughter.

"He is gone!" cried Bess, folding her arms across her bosom. "Oh, God of Heaven! The shriek of that ruined girl is ever in my ears, its accents of despair freezing my soul with a horror I never felt before," as she left the room.

"That gal is a born devil," said Devil-bug, in a whisper, as he wiped the cold sweat from his forehead. "Ha! There's the feller agin-his jaw broke, and his tongue lollin' out! Ha! And the old woman too; her holler skull drop, pin' blood on the floor! But I'll not be trou-bled this way much longer," a ghastly smile crossed his visage. "It seems to me I've got to wade through blood up to my neck! I'm only ancle-deep jist now, arter a while a swim in blood, I'll float, I tell ye I'll float."

CHAPTER III.

PARSON PYNE AND HIS DAUGHTER.

"COMFORTABLE range of apartment's" mut-tered the Rev. Dr. Pyne, as he entered a small chamber on the second floor. "This is my study. A nice little room, with a coal fire in the grate, a lamp on the table, a cupboard in the corner, and a bed in the other. This is what I call comfortable," he smiled pleasantly, as standing with his back to the fire, and his hands under his coat-tails he warmed his respectable person, and surveyed the room at the same time. He cossed the room, and quietly opened a small door, leading into the adjoining chamber. A cheerful smile overspread his round face, and his watery eyes twinkled with glee. There was something very meaning in the energy with which he smacked his large red lips together,

"She sleeps!" he muttered, and then with a quiet manner and cautious footstep stole into the chamber, closing the door carefully behind him.

It was a wide and spacious chamber, with lofty ceiling, and wainscotted walls. A small lamp burning on the table near the fireplace, gave a clear cold light to the hearth-side, while the other parts of the room were wrapt in shadow.

Near the fire, a fair girl dressed in spotless white, was sleeping as she reclined in a massive arm-chair, whose high back thickly cushioned with dark velvet, afforded a gentle repose to her maidenly form. The light fell mildly over her countenance, disclosing its pale hues and regular features, strikingly relieved by the long black hair, which half unbound, fell waving over her cheek, down to her shoulders. Her hands small and delicate, and death-like as the whitest marble, were clasped in front of her person, and the light folds of the robe which enveloped her form like a death-shroud, were softly agitated by the faint motion of her bosom heaving gently upward as she slept.

"Mable is quite beautiful!" muttered the oily-faced parson, gazing upon the girl with his watery eyes distended by an expression of animal admiration. "It's most a pity to awake her! However Brother Devil-bug will be here directly with the potion! Mabel," his voice assumed its blandest whisper as he applied his mouth to the sleeper's ear. "Mabel, look up, my child!"

"It is night, it is night!" muttered the

sleeping girl, "Back father, I say, back! Heaven's vengeance will strike you dead, if ye but attempt this crime! Back I say, or with this lamp I will fire the window curtains, and in an instant this house which you have for ever polluted by this attempt at crime, never to be named to human ears, this house will arise to heaven in flames! Each spark of flame, a witness before God of the horrible crime! Back I say—I will to the door—back, or I fire the house! Ha, ha! I gain the door, the entry is past, and the stairs! Ha! ha! I am in the street, the night is cold and the flinty stones rend my feet, but I am saved, I am saved!"

"Mabel, girl, I say you hush this nonsense!" exclaimed Parson Pyne, in an angry tone, as he shook the maiden roughly by the shoulder.

The girl slowly unclosed her eyes, and gazed in his face with a bewildered stare.

"Oh, do not hurt me, father," she exclaimed clasping her hands beseechingly in his face.

"Hurt ye, girl? Who talks of hurtin' ye?" exclaimed Pyne, betrayed by his excited feelings into an harshness of dialect which spoke of the habits of his former life, when he was not precisely a saint. "What d'ye set there dreamin' about such stuff and nonsense? Havn't I provided you a home, where you might recover from the unfortunate state of mind which has possessed you of late? Dismiss that unhappy dream, now and forever!"

Brother Pyne drew a chair, and sat down by his daughter's side.

"And then, father, you think it was a dream?" she exclaimed, with an expression of rapture warming over her face.

"To be sure it was, my dear," replied Dr. Pyne, taking his daughter's hand within his own.

"Did you not seek my chamber, did you not—oh horror, horror! My tongue cleaves to the roof of my mouth, when I endeavour to picture forth that scene in words!"

"Tush, tush, this is all nonsense!" and as he spoke the doctor gently wound his arms around her waist. "Have I not always been a kind father to you? Have I not rented this house for your especial comfort? You see, my child, your solitary way of life has slightly, very slightly, affected your mind. A few weeks of quiet, with the change of scene afforded by this old mansion, the perusal of wholesome books, together with the cheerful conversation of your father, will bring you right again. Have your attendants brought you any refreshments, my child?"

"Yes, father. An hour ago, just as I had lain down upon the bed to rest myself for a few moments, a servant entered the chamber, and set food upon the table before the fire. He did not observe me, father, but I saw him and was chilled with horror at the sight of his hideous countenance. Why, do you employ such a hideous monster, father?"

"What, Brother Abijah? Oh, he is a fine fellow, a christian, my daughter, although his face is not precisely handsome. What are you thinkin of now, Mabel?"

And brother Pyne patted the palm of her fair white hand, while his arm gathered more lovingly around her waist.

"Of my mother! She has been dead long, very long, has she not, father? Many and many an hour, in the daytime, when abroad in the street, and at night when resting in bed, have I endeavoured to recall the memory of her face, or a tone of her voice, or a smile wreathing her lips, but in vain! All is dark with me, when I think of my mother."

"The fact is she died when you was a mere babe, Mabel. Think, my child, what a care you have been to your father, how he has reared you. Think of this, my child, and then think of your conduct in leaving that paternal roof which had sheltered you from childhood!"

"Forgive me, my father, forgive me!" cried the girl.

"Father!" echoed a hoarse voice, and Devil-bug, holding a waiter in his extended hands, glided from the doorway, and advanced towards the light. "I say, brother Pyne, here's the hot coffee which you called for, and hot cakes in the bargain."

As he spoke he advanced towards the table, and arranged the contents of the waiter upon the white cloth, which he spread over its surface.

"Ho, ho, ho! So the gal puts her arms around his neck, does she? There won't be much need of the drug in that case!" he muttered to himself, as he arranged the supper equipage upon the table. "'Father' indeed! Could I'ave heered my own ears?"

The girl raised her head from her father's shoulder. At the same moment Devil-bug, turning on his heel to leave the room, caught a glimpse of her face for the first time. He started backward as though he had received a death-wound in his very heart. The waiter fell clattering on the floor, and with another start backward, Devil-Bug raised his hands and gazed upon the face of the young girl. Never in his life had Devil-bug been seized with an agitation terrible as this. His face grew white as a sheet, and his solitary eye glanced forth from its socket with one wild and absorbing gaze. Once or twice he essayed to speak, but the incoherent words died on his tongue.

"I say, brother, what's the matter?" cried Parson Pyne, gazing upon the doorkeeper with unfeigned astonishment. "Going to have a fit, brother?"

"No, nothing," replied Devil-bug, with his usual grunting tone of voice. "Only that gal looks something like a gal I used to know; that's all."

And he strode hastily towards the door.

"Devil-bug," cried Fat Pyne, in a whisper, as he hurried after the retreating doorkeeper. "is the coffee drugged?"

"Yes it is, parson," growled Devil-bug, with his hand on the door.

"Soh, son! All's right then. Devil-bug, you will lock all the doors after you if you please," he added, in a whisper. "You understand? I don't want to be interrupted, and mark ye, if you should hear a shriek or a groan, you needn't mind it."

"Devil a mind!" replied Devil-bug, as he stepped through the door-way. "You're a jolly cove, you are!"

And Parson Pyne caught the strange gleam of Devil-bug's solitary eye, and laughed merrily as he closed the door, while Devil-bug echoed his laugh with a hollow sound, more like the groan of a dying man who struggles with death and madness at the same time, than the echo of a cheerful laugh.

"He's alone with the gal!" he muttered. "And she called him father!"

That peculiar expression which had been gathering over his face, while conversing with the parson, now manifested itself in a look of fiend-like hatred, which convulsed every line of the doorkeeper's countenance. He shook his large hands wildly on high, and clenched madly at the air with his talon fingers.

"Ho, ho, ho!" he cried, as the idea, which absorbed his soul, rose before him like an embodied thing of flesh and blood. "Ho, ho ho! I wonders how that'll work!"

CHAPTER VIII.

THE PIT OF MONK-HALL.

"MUSKETER," cried Devil-bug to his negro, "jist go down stairs, and git a few strands o' thick rope. We shall want it in this room arter a while. And look ye, Glow-worm, keep your ears picked, will ye? If you don't I'll pick 'em with a hot fork. If you hear a cry, or a groan, or even a moan from that gal in the next room, jist run up stairs and call me! I'll be in the Walnut-room; d'ye mind, ye black devil?"

Seizing the lamp in his right hand. Devil-bug hurried from Monk Baltzar's ante-chamber, as it was styled, and in a moment found himself hastening along the dark corridor, which traversed the second floor of the mansion.

He entered the Walnut-room. The glittering floor gave back the reflection of the light which he held in his hands. The place was silent and desolate, with nothing but the bare walls, the dark ceiling and the glittering floor of polished mahogany. In the centre of the room, lay a shapeless mass which moved slowly to and fro, while Devil-bug advanced, and as the light flashed over its outlines, resolved itself into the form of a human being.

"Ha, ha, ha! Not more than twelve hours ago, this lump o' flesh an' blood an' broadcloth was a fine young gentleman, who cut all sorts o' capers in the next room. Cussed like a trooper and swore like a preacher! A little bit o' opium mixed in his drink, and here he lays, a perfect bundle o' sleep and stupidity! A werry contemptible thing is human natur'."

He flung the blaze of the light full over the face of the unconscious wretch, who lay prostrate on the floor, his knees huddled up against his chest, and his outstretched hands clutching the polished floor, with an involuntary and ineffectual grasp. Long locks of curling black hair fell streaming aside from a young face, which seemed to have grown permaturely old in the compass of a few hours. The skin was yellow and discoloured, the lips wore a livid hue, and the dark eyes, glared upon the ceiling with a cold and glassy stare. A thin, clammy foam hung around the white lips, and there were spot of blood upon the cheeks and hands of the unconscious man. He had torn the flesh from his cheeks in very madness. As Devil-bug gazed upon him, his limbs moved with a faint motion, like the last sign of departing life, and his outstretched hands grasped feebly at the smooth boards of the floor. The light flashed over his fixed eyeballs, but they gave no sign of life, no quick flashing glance that might betoken consciousness.

"Ha, ha, ha! I'll try it!" screamed Devil-bug with a wild shriek of laughter, "I've heard many stories about that same thing, but I never saw it done!" I'm jist the man to do it, and jist in the humour to do it now!"

He knelt beside the insensible man, and allowing the light to play over his fixed eyeballs he applied his mouth to his ear.

"Hel-lo! Yous sir, I say look here. I am a going to bury you alive: D'ye hear that? I'm a-goin' to bury you alive! God—how the feller wriggles! D'ye feel the cold clods fallin' on your breast a ready! Ho, ho, ho! I'm a-goin' to bury you alive!"

A slight tremor, a quivering shudder passed over the frame of Byrnewood Arlington. Was he conscious of the meaning of the words whispered in his ear? God alone knows, but his limbs were agitated for a moment by a convulsive motion, and the muscles of his face worked as with a spasm.

"Come my feller," he cried, raising the unconscious form of Byrnewood upon his shoulders. "You an' me has got a little business to transact, which ought to be done in private."

Unheeding the muttered groan which escaped from Byrnewood's lips, he raised him on his shoulder, as though he had been a mere bundle of merchandise. In a moment he left the walnut room, and was descending the stairs, with the unconscious man on his shoulders, while his extended hand grasped the flickering lamp. With a quiet smile on his lip, Devil-bug descended the stairs, and in a few moments stood on the floor of hall, opening into the banquet room. The echo of shouts mingled with laughter rung around the place. Devil-bug grimly smiled, and passing the doorway of the banquet room, stole cautiously along the damp floor of the hall, and in a moment the glare of the lamp flashed over the grand stairway of stone, leading far down into the vaults of Monk-Hall.

And far, far down, over massive steps of granite, with solid arches above, and thick walls on either side, far, far down, with the rays of the lamp flashing over the void beneath, with a faint yet gloomy effect, like a light darting its beams along the darkness of some hideous well, Devil-bug pursued his way, his strong right arm supporting the insensible form of his victim, flung like a bundle over his shoulder, while his distorted face grew animate with that grimace of habitual cruelty, which gave his visage the expression of an incarnate fiend, and developed all the hideous moral deformity of his nature.

At length he stood at the foot of the stairway, before the massive door, with timbers of oak, and bands of iron. Time had rusted away the lock, and the timbers in various places, between the intervals of the iron bands, were crumbling to decay. Devil-bug fixed his foot against one side of the door, and it fell before him with a crushing sound, whose echo swelled upward like thunder.

Another moment, and advancing over a floor of hard clay, he stood in the pit of Monk-Hall.

It was a vast and gloomy place, all full of oaken beams, rising from the floor to the ceiling far above, with pillars of dark brick, massive and uncouth in their outlines, towering at irregular intervals on every side.

Devil-bug, holding the light on high, with the unconscious Byrnewood on his shoulder, picked his way among the heaps of rubbish and advanced along the cellar. He paused in the centre of a vacant space, extending between a massive brick pillar, and a rising piece of ground, which shooting upward at the distance of a few yards, closed all the floor of the vault beyond from view. On either side were heaps of crumbling lumber and rubbish, and near the sudden elevation, thick dust, the accumulation of years of decay, had gathered ancle deep.

As Devil-bug laid down the lifeless form of Byrnewood, placing it on the hard clay beside the lamp, which burned dimly under the pressure of the foul atmosphere, he growled—

"Cuss the thing, I forgot the spade!"

He glanced at the form of Byrnewood with a mocking laugh.

"Ha, ha! Don't be *dis*-patient, young man," he exclaimed, as turning away from the light he moved towards the door. "I'll be back d'rectly. 'Pon my word I will!"

He disappeared in the darkness, but in a moment stood beside his victim, holding a rusted spade in his hand.

"Reether old fashioned this." You see my friend, we used it some years back to bury a gal wot died reether sudden, as one might say. It's been a standin' against yonder pillar ever since. A little bit rusty but it'll do!"

Devil-bug coolly proceeded to dig the grave of the unconscious, though living man, chuckling merrily to himself, as sticking the spade into the earth, he paused for a moment and spat in his hands, like a labourer preparing for his day's work.

"I've hung a man in my time, and I've killed a man by the trap, and I've buried some few, and I've stole corpseses for the doctors, but I never did bury a man alive! That's a fact. Not meaning any harm to you, but only waiting to see how it 'll work, I'll jist lay out the grave."

Devil-bug proceeded with his task. Plying the spade with all the vigour of his lusty arms, he soon stood in the square pit reaching to his knees, while the heap of clay at the side of the grave increased in size. Now humming a catch of some dismal gallows-bird song in his grindstone voice, now muttering gaily to himself, now filling the old vault with the echo of a deep and piercing whistle, which he emitted from his large mouth, puckered together like the end of a purse, and now glancing slily aside at the form of his victim, while that same devil's-grin distorted his inhuman face, Devil-bug made speedy progress in his work. He soon stood up to his middle in the grave.

As half-concealed in the grave, he bent down to his labour, a slight shudder, like the faint indication of a spasm, agitated the form of Byrnewood. Then his hand clutched suddenly against the hard clay, and in an instant, while his chest heaved with convulsive throbbings, he arose into a sitting posture, and with his long dark hair falling wildly aside from his wan and ghastly face, he gazed around the vault with an agonized glance that betrayed a fearful consciousness of his awful situation. Devil-bug turned from his task, and beheld his victim. He shrieked forth a horrible peal of laughter, more like the howl of a hyena, than the sound of a human laugh.

"Ho, ho! Hurray! So ye begin to diskiver yer sitivation? It's all werry good that you should know what's a'goin' to be done with you, 'specially when ye can't help yerself! How ye sit there, a starin' round the cellar, as though you wos about to buy the primises! Pound me to death with pavin' stones, but this is a jolly sight!"

Laying down the spade he advanced toward Byrnewood. The half-conscious man shuddered as his torturer approached.

"Hope ye'll excuse my not havin' prayers at the grave!" he exclaimed as he laid his hands upon Byrnewood's shoulder with a hideous grin convulsing his features. "You may shudder young feller, but into that grave you've got to go, alive and kick in'."

Laying his hand upon the shoulders of the shuddering victim, he dragged him slowly towards the grave. Byrnewood's lips parted, he essayed to speak, but the effort was vain. An incoherent sound, like that uttered by an enraged mute, was all that came from his lips.

Devil-bug dragged him along the floor and held him over the verge of the grave, when a deep groan awoke the silence of the cellar. Devil-bug started as though a dagger had entered his heart.

"It's him," he muttered, dropping Byrnewood heavily on the floor. "It's that or'nary feller who's been hauntin' me for these six years! He always groans when anything evil's a goin' to happen to me. It's him, it's him! Ha! There he is, with his jaw broke, an' his tongue out, and ha! ha! There's the old woman with the blood oozin' from the edge o' her broken skull! He rises from the floor—his bones rattlin' against one another, and his broken jaw droppin' blood! I say you devil, dont touch me, dont ye, dont——Ah!"

His soul fired with the sight of the terrible phantom, aroused into life by the spectacle of the skeleton of the murdered man, Devil-bug retreated backwards, with his face turned towards the light, while raising his hands high, he aroused the silence of the vault with another yell of horror. As the yell broke from his lips, he fell backward, and was lost in the grave which he had dug for another.

No sooner had he disappeared in the pit, than the form of a man sprung from one side of the brick pillar, at the same moment that the figure of a woman advanced from the other side.

"Quick, Bess, quick, I say," shouted the man, seizing the spade. "The antidote, quick, or all is lost! Apply it to Byrnewood's lips, while I keep this monster in his grave!"

Luke Harvey, his snake-like eyes blazing with excitement, and his slender form raised to its extreme height, stood beside the grave, while long-haired Bess, her face flushed, and her dark eyes sparkling with animation, bent over the unconscious form of Byrnewood, and applied a small phial to his clammy lips.

"Hello feller, it was you that groaned, was it?" shouted Devil-bug, as his hideous face, appeared above the edge of the grave. "What the devil d'ye mean by them sort o' capers, any how?"

"You infernal monster," shouted Luke Harvey with an oath. "Make but an attempt to get out o' that grave, and I'll crush your skull with this spade! Quick Bess—the antidote! Apply it to Byrnewood's lips, and lead him from the cellar, while I hold this devil at bay!"

"Joy, joy, he revives!" shouted Bess, gently raising the form of Byrnewood from the floor. "The antidote has taken effect. Keep back the monster another moment, Luke, and we will escape from the vault."

"Ye will, will ye?" cried Devil-bug, grasping the edge of the grave with his talon fingers. "Jist wait till I get out o' this!" His eye glared with a ferocious gleam, as placing his knees against the side of the grave, he began to crawl from its confines.

"Back devil! You have made the grave and you shall sleep in it?" shouted Luke, as raising the spade above his head, he hurled it full against the skull of Devil-bug. "Back devil; you have met your match this time!"

Stupified by the blow, Devil-bug reeled backwards into the grave. Luke turned round, and beheld Byrnewood standing erect on his feet, with the arm of long-haired Bess gathered round

his waist, while her shoulder supported his head.

"Lead him from the vault, Bess!" exclaimed Luke. "In a moment old Devil-bug will recover from the effects of the blow, and Byrnewood may again fall into his hands."

"The antidote has restored him physical but not mental strength!" exclaimed Bess as her cheek grew deathly pale with the war of conflicting emotions. "Ha!" she muttered to herself as she disappeared into the darkness of the vault with Byrnewood walking unsteadily by her side. "Ha! It was in the vault that Paul Weston fell, when the trap-door sunk beneath him. Yonder his bones lay uncovered to the light; and his murderess beholds them, and lives."

Luke stood beside the grave holding the spade in his hands, while he gazed upon the retreating figures of Bess and Byrnewood.

"If I believed in any particular saints, I think I'd call in their aid just now! A cursed scrape I'm in again, all from my disposition to meddle in other folks affairs. There I stood in front of my room, where I had just left my character of Brick-top, together with the rags and the wig, when who should tap me on the shoulder but Bess! 'Byrnewood Arlington's in danger—Devil-bug has just now borne him to the vaults of Monk-Hall,' quoth the maiden, and without stopping to tell me the particulars she hurries down stairs like wildfire! I hurry after her—Devil-bug is seen far below with a man on his shoulder, and a light in his hand—we creep along stealthy as cats, close at his heels. He enters the cellar, places the light on the floor, and commences his infernal orgies. We steal behind the brick pillar, and watch his movements. Bess tells me about the poison and the antidote; I select my time for my melo-dramatic groan, and here lies the result of that groan! Old Devil-bug in the grave which he dug for another."

A deep groan resounded from the depths of the grave.

"Oh, you're there, are you?" cried Luke, as his face darkened over with an expression of mingled hatred and rage. "Suppose I try your own game with you? How would you like to be buried alive?"

With a mocking sneer playing over his features he struck the spade into the loose earth, and threw several clumps of hard clay into the grave. Another groan came echoing from the pit, and Luke turned his jest into serious earnest, by throwing one spadeful of earth after another, into the grave.

"Oh groan by all means, it will do you good!" cried Luke, plying his spade with renewed energy. "An elderly gentleman like yourself, who whiles away his leisure time in burying folks alive, should hold himself prepared for any little contincies like the present. How are you off for clay — eh, Devil-bug?"

As he spoke, the spade rose and fell in his active grasp, and his face warmed with excitement. The beams of the light fell over his slender figure, and around the grave, while all beyond was impenetrable darkness. As Luke stood on the verge of the grave, occupied with the use of the spade, which he plyed so rapidly, a swarthy hand stole quietly from the edge of the pit, and moved as quietly over the hard clay, as though feeling for some object, and in an instant another hand, with talon fingers, appeared by its side. Luke did not behold these hands moving so quietly beside his very feet, but absorbed in his occupation, continued to shower the hard clods into the grave.

"Ha, ha!" he laughed, as his dark eyes gleamed with excitement. "Old Devil-bug little thought of this when he dug the grave! It was his turn awhile ago, it's my turn now, and——"

"It's my turn agin!" shouted a hoarse voice, and the grim face of Devil-bug, all streaming

with blood, was thrust from the edge of the grave. "There's such a thing as playin' possum young man!"

He seized Luke by the ancles, and with all the strength of his iron-sinewed arms gathered for the effort, flung him to the earth. In another instant he had leaped from the grave, and stood over the prostrate form of Luke, with his iron hand upraised, while his eye blazed with rage.

"Take that, feller!" he muttered, with deep emphasis, as gathering all his strength for the blow, he struck Luke on the head near the right temple.

Luke saw the blow descending, and tried to ward it off, but in vain. The blow descended, and in another moment, with a faint tremor quivering through his frame, Luke lay senseless as a stone.

Bending over the unconscious form of Luke

Devil-bug extended his hands and fastened the talon-like fingers around his throat, with the grasp of a vice.

"I would'nt give much for yer eyes, my feller!" he muttered, tightening the grasp of his fingers, until the face of the prostrate man grew purple, and the lids of his eyes, slowly unclosing, revealed the bloodshot eyeballs starting from their sockets. "It's my opinion you'd make a bad subject for a dissectin' table!"

A deep booming sound like distant thunder, echoed through the vaults and chambers of the mansion. Devil-bug released his grasp on the throat of Luke and sprang to his feet. It was but the labour of a moment to seize the lamp and rush towards the door of the cellar. With his muscular right hand he raised the fallen door from its resting place, and placed it against the door-frame.

The incarnate sneer which had played over his countenance suddenly gave place to that peculiar expression which had agitated his visage an hour before, in the presence of Parson Pyne and his fair daughter. What was the meaning of this expression it was difficult to tell, but it drew the eyebrows down from the protuberant forehead of Devil-bug, until the sockets were nearly hidden by their thick and uneven hair; it compressed his wide mouth with an expression as grotesque as it was determined, while his solitary eye grew alive with a deadly and glaring light, like the white heat on a bar of iron. There was revenge in that expression, and memory and love! The heart of the monster suddenly became a chaos, over whose tumultuous clouds of storms and darkness, a single ray of light, streaming from the far distance, revealed a gentle form, with arms outstretched in mercy, and a fair face animated with a smile of love.

"Nell!" muttered Devil-bug, between his clenched teeth. "It's werry long ago since I saw yer face—" he paused suddenly, while some dim memory seemed struggling from the chaos of his soul. "I don't know much about it now, but if it is—if it is, I say, then he shall die by inches, or there is'nt no sich person as Devil-bug!"

He closed the door of the vault, and all was darkness. Close beside the grave, cold and stiffening, lay the form of Luke Harvey, with the rats, who were so soon to hold their revel on his flesh, already crawling around their prey, and snuffing their banquet in the tainted air of the vault. Close beside the grave lay the skeleton of the murdered man, mouldering to dust, in darkness and silence, as it had lain for years, and the sullen stream of the vault still rolled moaningly onward, its sluggish waves chaunting a rude death-song for the slain. The nooks and crannies of the vault took up the echo of the flood, and on all sides a low, muttered murmur, swelling to the arching roof above, seemed but the whispered tones of fiends, chuckling with glee as they spoke of the murders done in the pit of Monk-Hall.

CHAPTER V.

THE RESCUE.

"Drink your coffee, my love, drink, it wil do you good!" said the Rev. Dr. Pyne, with an unctuous fatness of voice. "Nothing like coffee to raise your spirits, 'specially,'" he added in a cheerful whisper. 'Specially when it is spiced with a drug or two."

"I feel so strange, father," exclaimed Mabel, passing her white hand over her brow. "There is a burning sensation on my forehead, and my eyes pain me. Oh father, can I indeed be going mad! The room is filled with strange forms, and I feel as though an invisible hand were dragging me over a frightful precipice."

Her dark eyes suddenly assumed a wild and unearthly light. In an instant the lids seemed to have shrunken away from the eyeballs, and each eye, dilating to an unnatural size, assumed a strange lustre, rendered more apparent and striking by the utter paleness of the countenance with a single vivid spot of red, crimsoning the centre of each swelling-cheek. Even the lips of the maiden assumed an unnatural hue. Suddenly their moist vermilion changed to a warm and unhealthy purple.

"Father, father," she cried, "I am going mad! For God's sake, save me, save me! The room sinks from beneath my feet, the air is filled with horrible phantoms, and—oh save me, save me!"

She fell back into the chair, and covered her face with her hands.

"This is the first stage of the potion," blandly whispered Dr. Pyne, as his red face, with its rubicund cheeks, flushed all over with deep crimson, assumed an expression of the most decided character. "At first she will be frightened, then she will fall into a gentle doze, and then, ah then!" He took her fair white hand within his own, and platted it playfully against his oily cheek. "No one shall hurt you my child. Your papa is with you. Go to sleep, that's a dear Mabel."

"I gave Devil-bug three potions sometime ago," muttered Dr. Pyne, as he drew his chair to the side of the bewildered girl. "One kills, the other makes crazy, the third makes love; or rather disposes a young girl for the exercise of that delightful sentiment."

Mabel's head dropped lightly on her shoulder, and her eyelids slowly closed. Her long dark hair fell showering over her shoulders. Her arms sank stiffly by her side. She lay silent and motionless, as though suddenly stricken by the hand of death.

The Rev. Doctor Pyne rose slowly from his seat. He smacked his lips with unctuous fervour, and then taking his watch from the fob, he strode quietly up and down the room.

"This is the second stage of the potion," he whispered, looking at the watch. "The third stage is the most delightful of all. That paleness will give place to the peach-like bloom, that stiffness of limb will be overcome by a voluptuous languor, that closed eye, when its lids again unclose, will fire with passion and flash with all the bewitching softness of a woman's love! It now wants ten minutes of twelve o'clock. At twelve she will be in my power. The care and trouble of seventeen years will be well repaid.

The ten minutes passed. Alas for Mabel now!

"Come kiss your father," said Dr. Pyne, extending his arms towards the girl. "That's a good child. Kiss your papa."

Mabel gazed upon him with a wandering glance. It was evident that while her animal nature was roused into full development, her intellectual powers were for the moment crushed, if not utterly broken. The glance which rested upon Dr. Pyne's face was humid with passion, but it was the glance of an idiot.

"The potion works like a miracle!" murmured the parson, as his rubicund face warmed with a ruddy glow, while his watery eyes, with the veins of each pupil filled with discoloured blood, stood out from their very sockets with a look of gloating admiration. "Come and kiss your papa, Mabel! It was a good girl, that it was, and it must kiss its papa."

Like one arising from their sleep, Mabel arose from the chair, and extending her arms, advanced to her father's side. She extended her arms and kissed his lips.—Faugh! Those lips were gross and sensual, though they *were* a parson's lips! She kissed his lips again, and yet again. She laid her soft cheek against his face; she encircled his neck with her round arms; he felt her tiny fingers playing with the thin locks of his hair. The parson's face grew more crimson, and his arms gathered more closely around his daughter's waist.

"What a blessed thing it is, to possess, a knowledge of medical science, however slight!" And Dr. Pyne kissed the red lips of the girl with fervour. "Here she was, an hour ago, full of intelectual energy! Now, ho, ho! her mind is laid to sleep for a little while, and all the animal portion of her nature is aroused into active life. Quite active! A good potion that! A-h!" the good Dr. Pyne tasted the freshness of her lips again.

"Ha, ha, ha!" Dr. Pyne started with a sudden thrill of horror, as that maniac laugh broke on his ear.

"Ha! ha! ha!" The girl started to her feet, and while her swelling cheeks flushed with animation, and her dark eyes seemed to swim in liquid fire, she stood erect upon the floor, her extended hands pointing at his face, with a maniac guesture.

"Mabel, my child," the Doctor began, as he rose from his feet.

"Ha, ha, ha!" shrieked the girl, as with that same unearthly look she gazed steadily in the face of the good parson.

"What can all this mean? Certainly the child has gone mad! Mabel, my dear, come to your pa-pa!"

Still the girl stood erect, her form raised to its full height, her eyes gathering new fire every instant, her cheek blooming unnatural freshness, while her extended hands, with the long fingers trembling in the light, pointed fixedly in his face. Oh how beautiful the picture—a vivid impersonation of beauty, mere animal loveliness, yet still bewitching loveliness, utterly deprived of intellect! Oh beautiful as a dream, and yet more terrible than death!

"Ha, ha, ha!"

Dr. Pyne turned pale. The laugh sounded like the shriek of his evil angel.

"Come girl, no more of this!" He advanced fiercely toward the maiden. His hands were clenched, and his brow was darkened by a frown. "No more of this! Your shrieks will arouse the neighbourhood. I have trifled too long?"

"Ha, ha, ha!" Louder and more terrible arose that shriek of maniac-laughter.

"Now for the reward, for which I have waited seventeen long years!"

Maddened with lust and rage he advanced, he gathered the quivering waist of the girl within his vigourous arm. She struggled, and writhed and leapt from her very feet in the effort to tear herself from his grasp. He raised his clenched hand, and—oh villain and dastard! He struck her to the floor!

She lay prostrate upon the floor, her breath heaving with convulsive gasps, her form quivering like a leaf, her cheek white as marble. He knelt by her side. He knelt before the crazed girl, he gathered her form in his arms, he kissed her death-cold lips. One more effort, sweet Mabel! With one convulsive bound she sprang from his embrace, again sunk kneeling on the floor, and raised her hands and eyes to heaven.

"Oh mother," she cried, in tones that would have melted the heart of the fiend in hell, "oh mother, save your child!"

"Your mother can't save you now! You must come to your pa-pa, my love!" He bent down and gathered her form in his arms.

"Save me, mother," shrieked Mabel, "oh save me mother!"

"You are mine! You are—" began the parson in tones of exultation, when his arms suddenly relaxed their hold, and his fat form rolled senseless on the floor.

"G-a-l you called yer mother, and that call saved ye!" said a rough voice. Mabel looked up, and shrieked. Devil-bug in all his hideous deformity stood at her side. His face was convulsed with an expression of fearful hatred, and his long talon-like fingers worked as with an epileptic spasm.

"Here Glow-worm—here Musketer," he cried "drag this old porpis'into the next room."

The negroes came stealing through the small doorway of the apartment. They seized the unconscious form of the Rev. Dr. Pyne, and bore him into the ante-chamber. Devil-bug was alone with the fair girl.

He stooped slowly down, while she shuddered in horror, at the sight of his hideous visage.

He gathered his rough arms around her tender form; he raised her from the floor. She shrieked with affright. Devil-bug trembled from head to foot. Stepping softly over the floor, he bore her to the bed, and laid her gently on its coverlid. Mabel's dark eyes grew lustrous with terror.

Devil-bug stepped backward from the bed. He gazed upon her face for a moment in silence. His huge mouth was fixedly compressed, and his large nostrils quivered with a nervous movement. His solitary eye glared upon the face of the girl. with a fearful intensity. She was thrilled to the very heart with a strange awe.

A wild cry burst from his lips. It was like the howl of an enraged beast holding the hunters at bay. Again that cry! He rushed fiercely toward the bed. Mabel started up in involuntary affright. Devil-bug struck his huge hands violently against his forehead, and uttered that terrific howl yet again. Then turning on his heel, he fled madly from the room.

CHAPTER VI.

PARSON PYNE HAS A GOOD LAUGH TO HIMSELF.

THE portly form of Parson Pyne lay on the carpet of the ante-chamber, with a huge negro watching on either side.

Devil-bug rushed madly into the apartment and stood beside the form of the unconscious preacher. His solitary eye glared with all the malignity of a devil, and its glance rested upon the round and rubicund face of the parson.

"Here, yo' niggers," he shouted; "d'ye see that couch? Strip off the bed an' the bed-clothes and lay the parson on the sackin' bottom! That's right, that's right! Now, Musketer, tie one leg to that bed-post, and Glow-worm, d'ye hear? You tie his t'other leg to this bed-post! Sarve his hands the same way! Ha, ha! He looks like the letter X in the primer books!"

The fat form of the parson was extended on the sacking bottom, with each leg tightly pinioned by the ancle to the bed-posts at the foot, while his extended hands were tied in the same manner to the posts at the head of the couch. He certainly looked like a very corpulent representative of St. Andrew's cross. His round paunch stood out from the sacking bottom in painful prominence, and his large lips hanging apart, affording an interesting anatomical view of his mouth and palate.

"Where am I?" said Parson Pyne, faintly, as he unclosed his eyes.

"Why you see, parson, I wanted to axe you a few questi'ns, and bein' afeer'd you wouldn't answer 'em quite easy, I jist tied yo' to that bed."

"Villain, d'ye mean to murder me?"

"No, not 'xactly. I only wants to axe ye a few questi'ns."

"What are your questions?" he asked.

"Is that gal in the next room your darter?"

exclaimed Devil-bug, bending his head down to receive the answer.

"She is," responded the parson, in a firm tone.

"That's as big a lie as ye ever did tell," growled Devil-bug. "I see we can't git no truth out o' you' without the lawyers. Take off his shoes an' stockin's, Glow-worm!"

"Monster, you shall pay for this!" cried the Reverend Pyne, as his fat face was distended by an expression of surprise. He evidently gazed upon the movements of Devil-bug with some considerable wonder.

"Now, parson, for the questi'ns! And fust o' all, I'll tell you what I know mesself. Pick yer ears, parson! About Christmas Eve, eighteen hundred an' twenty-five, a man named Dick Baltzar, with his wife, Sarah Baltzar, hired rooms in the house of widder Crank, livin' in —— street, near —— street."

"Ha!" the involuntary cry of surprise was forced from the parson's lips.

"Wos yo' that man, Dick Baltzar, or wos yo' not?"

"Go to the devil!" roared Parson Pyne.

"Oh, wery well, wer-r-y well!" exclaimed Devil-bug, as he gently touched the soles of the parson's feet with the tips of his talon fingers. "I'll tune you up my pianey fortey, I will! Ho, ho! How d'ye feel, parson?"

"Ha, ha, ha!" roared the parson, with an outburst of spasmodic laughter, the result of the titillating movement of Devil-bug's fingers along the soles of his feet. "Ha, ha, ha! Ho, ho, ho! Oh-oh-oh! Hi, hi, hi! Oh for God's sake don't—d-o-n-t! Hoo, hoo, hoo!"

And the fat form of the parson wriggled, and strained, and heaved, as with an epileptic fit.

"Ha, ha!" roared Devil-bug, executing another flourish.

"Hah! ya-hah!" shouted Glow-worm.

"Ya-hah-ha-yah!" echoed Musquito.

"Go it my pianey fortey!" cried Devil-bug, with a most effective flourish. "Jist see how my fingers go over these white soles! Ha, ha! parson, you save souls; I tickles 'em! 'Gently over the stones, driver!' E-a-sy, I say!"

"Ha, ha, ha-a-a!" roared the parson, as he grew black in the face, while his watery eyes started from their sockets. "Ho, ho, ho! Oh, for God's sake—hoo, hoo, hoo! Don't ye tickle—ha, ha, ha! Tick-l-e, tick-l-e me! Hi, hi, hi-i-i!"

"Wot a spektikle. Ha, ha! Jist see the Parson wriggle! Wos there ever sich twistin' as that! How black he grows in the face! His eyes as big as Delawar' bay oysters—ha, ha, ha! Come on, my pianey fortey—I'll tune yo' up!

Yankey doo-del is the tune—"

"Ha, ha, ha!" interrupted the parson.

"An' nothin' comes so han-dy!
As yankey doo-del doo-del do-oo—"

"Hoo, hoo, hoo!" roared Parson Pyne.

"An' yankey doo-del dan-dy!"

Screamed Devil-bug, executing a delicate

flourish on the soles of the tortured parson's feet.

"Ya-hah-hah," roared the negroes, holding their sides as they beheld the preacher's agony.

Wriggling and twisting along the bed, Parson Pyne made the most superhuman efforts to extricate himself, but in vain. Still the finger-tips of Devil-bug ran softly, oh how softly, along his feet, still he was forced to rend the air with unwilling laughter. Tickle, tickle, tickle! Ha, ha, ha! His face had now assumed a dark livid hue, and as his eyes hung out from their sockets, the white surface of each eyeball assumed a fearful prominence. Tickle, tic-kle, tic-kle! Ho, ho, ho! The veins stood out from his forehead like cords, and his chest heaved and swelled as though moving under the impulse of a small steam engine. Softly moved the finger tips, oh softly, soft-l-y soft-l-y! Tic-k-le, tic-k-l-e, t-i-c-kle! Hoo, hoo, hoo!

"Oh, God, God, God!" yelled the parson, as the tears rolled down his livid cheeks. "Mercy, ha, ha, ha! Ho, ho, ho! Hi, hi, hi! Mercy, H-o-o! Ah-a-a-ha-a!"

A wild unearthly shriek burst from the parson, and the white foam frothed around his lips.

"Do yo' give in?" shouted Devil-bug, executing a brilliant flourish with his finger-tips.

"Ho, ho, ho!" roared the parson. "Ye-s, ye-s! Hoo, hoo, hoo! Curses—ha, ha, ha! curses! D—n! Hi, hi, hi, hi-i-i!"

"Did'nt I tell yo' my feller, that ye'd better not perwoke me?" calmly exclaimed Devil-bug, walking round the foot of the bed. "Now will you answer them questi'ns?"

Parson Pyne lay silent and speechless. Poor fellow! He looked quite pitiful. He lay gasping and panting for breath, while his livid cheeks and starting eyes, bore traces of the awful agony which he had endured. Had Devil-bug continued his musical experiments a moment longer, his congregation would have lost their preacher, and the devil gained a soul. As he lay there, pinioned to the bed, his starting eyes glaring vacantly around the room, he looked for all the world like a man who has been precipitated over some awful height; he lay so silent, so motionless, so utterly blank and speechless. Had the Pope of Pagan Rome have seen his foe, he would have pitied him. Even the four-and-twenty cardinals would have wept. The Vatican itself, that deplorable edifice, would have shed tears. St. Peter's church, that object of the parson's hate and scorn would have been convulsed with pity. Alas, for the foe of Pagan Rome! To think that he, the daring and high-souled Pyne, who had stood up so often in his pulpit, and defied the pope and the devil, who had electrified the old women with his eloquence, and convulsed whole churches-full of bigots with his matchless zeal, to think that he should have been tickled into submission.

For ten long and weary minutes Devil-bug awaited the recovery of the parson. Never

was whipped dog more completely cowed by the lash than was Parson Pyne by the finger-tips of old Devil-bug.

"Was you Dick Baltzar, or was you not? Answer old porpis!"

"I was," faintly responded the parson.

"You rented rooms at the house o' the widder Crank, on Christmas Eve, eighteen hundred an' twenty-five?"

"I did."

"The widder Crank had a darter?"

"She had."

"Her name was——"

"Ellen," faintly chirped Parson Pyne. "I'll tell you all about her. She had been seduced two years before I came to widow Crank's house. Her seducer was a young merchant named Livingstone. On Christmas Eve eighteen hundred and twenty-four, she gave birth to a female child. It was called Ellen. A few days after the child was born, her mother in a fit of rage drove her from the house. The child remained with the widow Crank. It seems that Ellen and Livingstone had quarrelled soon after the birth of the child; and the mother's harshness resulted from her daughter's confession that she was not married to her lover. For one year no intelligence whatever was heard from the daughter."

"Ha!" shrieked Devil-bug. "Are yo' sure o' that?"

"Why as myself and wife only came to the widow's house a year after Ellen had disappeared it's hard for me to tell!" murmured the Rev. Dr. Pyne. "I never yet have been quite certain, but that Livingstone knew of the girl's whereabouts all the while."

Devil-bug smiled grimly to himself.

"Ho, ho!" he muttered. "Then I'm the only human bein' as knows where Ellen was during her absence from her mother's home."

"As I said before I came to the widow Crank's house, on Christmas Eve eighteen hundred and twenty-five. That very night Ellen Crank returned home. She was in a very sad condition you see, and her mother welcomed her back with tears of joy. That very night she gave birth to another child."

Devil-bug leaned slowly forward, and applied his mouth to the ear of the parson.

"And that 'ere last child, died?" he muttered in a whisper that thrilled the parson to the heart.

"Livingstone always thought so," said Dr. Pyne in an evasive tone.

"No lyin,' parson. One child died that night I know. Was it the first or second?"

"It was the first," answered Dr. Pyne.

Devil-bug buried his face in his hands, and the parson heard him groan. The negroes looked on in mute astonishment. Their master affected by any thing like a human feeling. Ha, ha! The thought tickled them, and they chuckled quietly together.

"And the *second* child, parson, whatever becom' of it?" said Devil-bug, looking at the preacher through the outspread fingers of his hands.

"I don't know," answered Pyne in a faint voice.

"You lie!" shrieked Devil-bug. "You lie! You stole that child, parson, you and your wife trained it up with the idea-r of havin' a hold on Livingstone, when he came into his father's property! Don't I know ye, ye fat dog?" he rose from his seat and seized the parson fiercely by the throat. "Yer wife died, and you turned parson! Ho! ho! am I right? Tell me quick, or I'll choke ye!"

"You are—you are!" cried Pyne, as he felt the talon-fingers of the deformed wretch gathering round his throat.

Devil-bug started up with a wild howl, and rushed madly into the next chamber.

CHAPTER VII.

THE SAVAGE ALONE WITH THE MAIDEN.

His teeth grating together, and his hands outspread, while his eye blazed with a madman's glare, he rushed towards the bed whereon the girl was sleeping. Mabel started up in affright, and clasped her hands over her bosom as she beheld him approach.

"Oh save me now, my God!" she shrieked and held her breath in very terror.

"Come g-a-l, come!" cried Devil-bug, as gathering his arm around her waist, he bore her quickly along the room. "Come, I say, come!"

He stopped before an antique mirror of circular shape, which depended from the wainscotted walls. He placed Mabel on her feet, and rushing from her side, seized the light from the table near the fire. In a moment he stood by her side again, and as she started backward, in utter horror of his hideous countenance, he flung the matted hair aside from his right temple.

"Look gal, look!" he cried pointing to the reflection of his loathsome countenance in the mirror. "D'ye see that red mark along my right temple? That red mark like a snake? D'ye see it, d'ye see it? That mark was born with me!"

Mabel gazed upon him with an expression of blank wonder, mingled with terror.

Devil-bug wound his rough arm round her neck, and swept her thick tresses aside from her right temple.

"Look, look, g-a-l, look!" he shrieked, as he pointed to the reflection of her beautiful countenance in the mirror. "I don't want you to look at them black eyes, which are like her's, nor the lips, nor the cheeks! But the right temple, g-a-l—the right temple!"

Mabel involuntarily gazed within the mirror. She started back with a strange feeling of surprise as she beheld a slight, thin and discoloured streak, marring the beauty of her face, near the right temple. It was a faint and delicate copy of the deep red mark near the swarthy temple of Devil-bug.

"That was born with you, g-a-l, that was born with you g-a-l!" shouted Devil-bug. "An you're my—yes, yes, you're my——"

He paused suddenly and fell on his knees He placed the light on a chair, and then looked up into her wondering face, with his hideous countenanc distorted by a strange emotion.

Then, bending to the very floor, he clung with his huge hands to the skirt of her white dress, and pressed his thick lips upon the shoe of her tiny foot. Then big tears stole from the lids of his blazing eye, and from the shrivelled socket which was destitute of an eyeball. Then his lips became fixedly compressed, and as he raised his clenched hands he uttered a yell, like the howl of an enraged hyena.

"Oh, mercy, mercy!" shrieked Mabel, gazing upon the monster at her feet in utter alarm.

Devil-bug seized her fair white hands and looked up into her face in silence. It was a strange and fearful picture. The savage kneeling at the feet of innocence!

"Do not, do not harm me!" cried Mabel, all other feelings absorbed by the terror which she felt for the strange being at her feet.

"Harm ye?" growled Devil-bug, as he rose from his kneeling position and forced her gently into a chair. "Gal, who is it that talks to me of harmin' ye?"

He seated himself on a chair opposite the maiden. The light standing on another chair, flashed its beams over the outlines of their faces, so strangely contrasted to each other.

A wild hope fluttered over the heart of the maiden, as she beheld something like human feeling in the solitary eye of the monster.

"He may aid me to escape from this house!" she murmured.

"G-a-l, had ye ever a friend?"

And as he spoke he took her fair white hand within his talon fingers.

"Never!" answered Mabel, as her heart warmed with a strange sympathy for the being before her. "My father has given me food, and clothes, and shelter, but I never yet looked upon the face of a human being whom I could call friend! No mother ever smiled upon me, and as for my father—oh, for God's sake do not place me in his power again!"

"The g-a-l's been edicated!" muttered Devil-bug. "You never had a friend, then? You don't remember your mother. I do, g-a-l, I do!"

"You!"

"Yes, g-a-l, I was your mother's servant, a good many years ago. I used to kiss the very ground she stood upon. Don't mind me, my dear, if I talk a little wild. I'm a poor one-eyed devil, and nobody cares for me! But I'll be your friend g-al—I, that never yet was friend to a human bein' save one—I will be your friend!"

"You!"

"Yes, gal, me! I'm ugly as the devil—I

know it! But for you, gal, for you, my heart feels warm! Ask me to hold my hand in that fire for your sake, jist ask me!"

He reached forth his hand toward the light as if to carry his words into action, when a spot of thick red blood crusting the swarthy skin, attracted the gaze of his solitary eye.

"Ha! It is her blood," he shouted, starting from his seat. "The old woman's blood! The blood of Ellen's mother! Ha! There she lays with the red blood droppin' from her holler skull! There—there—" he pointed fiercely to a vacant spot of the room.

"Don't ye see her, gal? And here, gal, here, by my side, his jaw broke and his tongue stickin' out, he lays—jist as he fell through the trap?"

He rushed wildly towards the door, as the terrible phantoms, in all their horror, broke anew upon his gaze.

"But I'll be yer friend, g-al!" he shouted, turning suddenly round. "I, I, old Devil-bug will be your slave! You shall roll in wealth, g-a-l! Parson Pyne ain't yer father—not a bit o' it! Yer father has gold enough to buy ye a row o' houses! I tell ye, gal, old Devil-bug is yer friend! The man that tries to injure ye will have a wild beast to fight—that's all!"

He rushed into the next room, where Parson Pyne still lay pinioned to the sacking bottom of the bed. The Herculean negroes watched by the bedside.

"Put on this feller's shoes an' stockin's an' let him clear out!" shouted Devil-bug. "And look ye, Parson Pyne! it 'ud be better for you to crack jokes with an angry tiger than to dare touch that gal ag'in! Go home, Parson Pyne, and mind yer business, and put down the Pope o' Rome! The g-a-l shall go to her father, the rich merchant, Livingstone! Her face is proof enough that she is Ellen's darter! And mind ye, Parson Pyne," he cried, as he stood in the doorway, his face darkened by a scowl of rage. "If yo' ever lay a finger on that g-a-l ag'in I'll have my revenge on you, if I have to drag you from yer pulpit! I'll have yer blood if I have to spill it in the sacrament cup!"

He closed the door and rushed madly down the stairway of Monk-Hall.

"To the vault, to the vault! An' let me think these things over! My brain feels kind o' crazy like, and my blood biles in my viens! Ha! ha! ha! Old Devil-bug's darter shall ride in her carriage, and wear silks an' satins—that she shall!"

And as he went down to the vault of Monk-Hall, his wild and discordant laughter broke upon the air with a sound of strange and savage joy.

CHAPTER VIII.

THE FLIGHT FROM MONK-HALL.

THE negroes were alone in the ante-chamber. Glow-worm stood on one side of the fire gazing into the face of his comrade, who leaned against the mantel on the opposite side.

The door leading into the hall of the second story opened suddenly, and long-haired Bess entered the chamber. Her large dark eyes flashed with a clear and brilliant expression, and her jet-black hair streaming wildly over her shoulders gave a strange relief to her deathly countenance.

"De Lor Jimminy! It am de gal!" muttered Musquito, with an expression of idiotic surprise.

"Quick, I say, quick!" exclaimed Bess, approaching the fire-place. "I want the keys of the house—old Devil-bug is waitin' for 'em! Where are they? Quick, I say!"

"Dere dey are, missus!" exclaimed Glow-worm, with a mock bow, as he pointed to the bunch of keys resting on the small table near the light. "What de debil yo' want 'em foh?"

Bess seized the keys and rushed into the adjoining chamber, where Mable was imprisoned.

"I say, niggar, what all dis mean?" exclaimed Glow-worm, gazing in Musquito's face.

"I 'spect dar's some fuss down sta'rs!" responded the other negro.

As he spoke, Bess re-entered the room with the form of Mabel, supported by the embrace of her right arm, while the pale face of the young girl, lit by her large and lustrious eyes of midnight blackness, wore an absent and bewildered expression.

"Come, this way, this way," whispered Bess, moving towards the door which led out into the hall. "This way and you shall be saved!"

"What foh you do dat foh?" muttered Glow-worm, fiercely, as he turned toward Long-haired Bess with a threatening look.

"Hush, h-u-s-h!" whispered Bess, as she glanced meaningly at the half-conscious face of the girl who hung on her arm. "You see, Glow-worm, there's a rumpus kicked up down stairs, and Devil-bug wants to have the gal removed to the tower-room. Open the door, quick, let me hurry up stairs with her. You are so stupid, Glow-worm—quick, I say!"

The look which animated the face of Long-haired Bess, dispelled all the doubts which the negro had entertained. With a mechanical gesture he flung open the door.

"Now, Glow-worm close it after me," she said, gazing in his hideous face, while her tone was that of a confidential whisper. "And if anybody should come up here and ask after the gal, you must swear that she was never in the house."

"Yes, missus."

"Ha! ha! ha! We know how to manage these things—don't we, Glow-worm?" laughed Bess, as, standing in the doorway, she gathered her arm more closely around the waist of the girl who lay half-fainting, in her embrace. "It takes us don't it, Musquito?"

"It jist does dat!" chuckled the negro, and Glow-worm, joining in his laugh, carefully closed the door.

Bess stood in the darkness of the hall. A

smile of triumph flashed over her proud face. She felt the heart of the girl throbbing against the hand that held her form to her side.

"The plot of the parson and his tool shall be scattered to the winds! I will save the wronged girl, save her from the hands of her *priestly* father! This way, fair girl, and we will escape together!"

"Whither are you leading me?" murmured Mabel, in a bewildered tone. "Oh save me from my father! Do with me what you will, but do not hurry me to his roof again! I will work my fingers to the bone, beg in the streets, or starve, but—oh! Do not place me in his power again!"

Bess silently led the way down the stairs. Crouching on the steps, about half-way down, was the form of a woman, attired in floating robes of white.

"Mary, arise; we will escape!" exclaimed Bess in a whisper. "Take my arm, and cling to me with all your strength—we will escape from Monk-Hall!"

The fair girl rose in the darkness, and clung to the arm of the fallen woman. No word escaped her lips; no sigh heaved her bosom; she was silent as the grave.

Bess seized the trembling girls, one in each arm, nerved for the effort by a hallowed hope that now began to brighten over her soul, she gathered a fair form in each arm, and hurried down the stairs.

"The key, the key!" she shouted, in a wild delirium of joy. "A moment longer and we are saved. A moment and we escape from Monk-Hall!"

Meanwhile Devil-bug ascending the stairs, stood before the door of Monk Baltzar's ante-chamber.

"I'll see the gal once agin," he muttered. "I'll look on her purty face agin; she shall roll in gold; she shall! Old Devil-bug's darter shall have the money—ha, ha, ha! Sich lots o' money!"

He entered the ante-chamber, and passed along without heeding Glow-worm and Musquito, who stood by the fire. Gently unclosing the door of the next apartment, he stepped within the chamber where he had left the girl. He closed the door and advanced towards the light.

"She's a sleepin' on that bed, the darter of Ellen!" he muttered, folding his arms. "Many and many's the night I've laid at Ellen's door, watchin' her while she slept, and keepin' her from harm. There wasn't never a human bein' as didn't cuss me, except one! That was her—Ellen—the gal whom I'd 'ave died for! And this is her darter—ha, ha! And she shall ride in her carriage, and have goold pieces thick as flies in a molasses jug."

He advanced a step nearer to the bed, his head inclined to one side, as if in the act of listening. He listened for the low, soft sound of a woman breathing in her sleep.

"She sleeps wery softly!" muttered Devil-bug. "An' I'll go to Livingstone, an' I'll tell him the story, and I'll tear that Parson's heart from his carcase, if he dares say that she ain't the merchant's darter! I hate and cuss the whole world; the whole world hates and cusses me—but the g-a-l! I'll skulk along the street, and see her ridin' in her carriage; I'll watch in the cold winter nights and see her—all shinin' with goold and jewels—as she goes into the theatre, with the big folks round her, and the rich merchant by her side."

He drew a step nearer the bed.

"And then I'll skulk down into the pit, and hide my head, but keep a look out on her with my one eye. When I sees the folks makin much of her—the jewels shinin' on her dress, the bracelets round her wrists, and the goold band around her white brow, then I'll stick my face in my hands an' laff! Ho, ho, ho!—*There*, I'll cry to myself—there is old Devil-bug's darter among the grandees o' the Quaker City!"

He drooped his head on his breast, while his eye blazed, and his thick lips parted in a grotesque grin.

In a moment, however, a strange mood of thought seemed to pass over the distorted intellect of this monster.

He stood with his head drooped low on his wide chest, while his hands hung extended by his side. His solitary eye, which contracted and dilated like the eye of a tiger, grew large and lustrous. His teeth were clenched, while his thick lips receded in a convulsive grimace. He stood motionless as the aged walls of that old house, of whose wide rooms and dreary vaults he seemed the living soul.

In that moment of silence, what a world of thought passed over the soul of the monster!

First came a vision of the fair woman, who had loved him. Loved the outcast of mankind, the devil in human shape! Could you have seen Devil-bug's soul at that moment, it was agitated by this memory, you would have started at the contrast, which it presented in comparison with his deformed body. For a moment the soul of Devil-bug was *beautiful*.

Then the scorn of the world crowded upon his soul. His ignominious birth, his lonely life, the hatred was felt for him, and the loathing which he felt for man, his distorted face and deformed body. Like a black cloud it gathered upon him. Had Devil-bug's soul assumed a tangible shape, his body in comparison, would have grown beautiful. It was terrible to note the malice of his soul flashing from his eye, and trembling on his lip.

He approached the bed, and his mood changed. His child lay sleeping there; *his child!* The darkness, which shrouded the corners of the chamber, lay thick around her couch, but she was *there!* His heart beat with a strange feeling of joy as he approached the bedside, and from his heart, through every vein, that strange joy darted like lightning.

He extended his hand, he passed it over the bed-clothes. A shudder ran over his frame. Again he extended his hand, again passed it ervously over the white coverlid. He started backward with a cry of horror.

He stood for a moment silent and immoveable. Then running from one corner of the room to another, he shrieked the name of Ellen, again and yet again, while the muscles of his face worked as with a death-spasm.

"Ellen," he shrieked, in his frenzy, confounding the mother with the child. "Where have they tuk yo'? Ellen—did I not watch yo' in the winter nights? Did I not fight for yo'? Say, Nell, was there sich a sarvant as old Devil-bug? Nell—Nell! Answer me, Nelly; don't play 'possum with Devil-bug, I know you're hid somewhere; I know it! You'd not leave me, Nell!"

Again he shrieked that name. He listened for a moment—no answer came to his call. He

THE PERILOUS SITUATION OF MABEL WITH PARSON PYNE.

rushed hurriedly into the ante-chamber; he seized the negro, Musquito, by the throat with a giant's grasp.

"Tell me, yo' scoundrel, where did you take that gal?"

"Massa," replied the negro, speaking with difficulty as the talon fingers encircled his throat, "Missus Bess took de keys and de gal,—dat's all, Massa."

"Nigger, I'll have you roasted alive!" shrieked Devil-bug, with an ominous scowl of anger. "Bess took the gal and the keys did she? Niggers, I'll tell you what it is, if that gal escapes, I'll have your black flesh torn off with hot pincers—I'll—"

He rushed through the doorway, and was heard descending the stairs.

* * * * *

Meanwhile, with the fair form of a trembling woman on each arm, Bess pursued her way.

"Cling to my arms, girls," she said, "and ere an hour passes over my head, I will place you in a quiet refuge, where no wrong can assail you, no dark passion mar your peace!"

"Any where Bessie, to the lowest hovel, to the abode of rags and misery and want, but for God's sake not to that home—the home which I left only last night for the mansion of Lorraine. I have had my dream, Bessie—God alone knows how terrible has been the awaking from that dream!"

As Mary spoke, her voice grew tremulous, and Bess turned her face away from the gaze of the ruined girl. That wan countenance, those eyes of liquid blue dilated with a frenzied glare—the vision blasted the very eyesight of Long-haired Bess.

Mabel clung to the arm of the tall woman, and in a whisper besought her to fly from the spot.

"Let us away," she cried. "My father, I fear him worse than the grave."

Bess silently gathered the arms of each girl within her own, and then as the moon shone upon the wan, yet beaming face, with blue eyes and golden hair, on one side, and the pale countenance, with dark eyes and midnight tresses on the other, she raised her gaze to the moonlit heavens above, and for the moment her dark orbs grew lustrous with a strange eloquence.

At that moment, as standing at the corner of the gloomy street, with a ruined girl on one side, and a wronged maiden on the other, her face once so beautiful, and now lovely to look upon in its very ruins, was imbued with an expression holy as that which mantles over the face of the dying mother when blessing her first-born child.

Up to the throne of the pure and merciful God, from the heart of the courtezan there ascended a vow, a holy vow! She was degraded, steeped to the very lips in pollution, cankered to the heart with loathsome vice, yet at that moment she was a holy thing in sight of the angels; for before the altar of Almighty God she swore to protect the ruined Mary to her death, she vowed to guard the stainless Mabel from the shadow of her wrong. And the vow went up to God, and the moon rising higher over the roof-tops, seemed to shed a more kindly light as if to crown that vow with an omen of success.

And the three sisters, the fallen, the betrayed, and the innocent, wandered forth along the streets, on their gloomy way.

They were passing a house, when Mabel uttered an exclamation of suprise.

"This is widow Smolby's house, from which my father dragged me twelve hours ago!" exclaimed Mabel, as she beheld the gloomy walls of the old house rising in the moonbeams.

"The widow Smolby!" muttered Bess, as though some strange memory had flashed over her brain. "Ha! We may obtain shelter here—I'll make the attempt at all events!"

She knocked at the door It receded slightly, and a rough voice from within demanded her errand.

"Ha! Larkspur!" she exclaimed, "is that you? Long-haired Bess asks you to give her shelter for the night—she has some important facts to disclose with regard to the late murder."

"Why, Bess, my duck, is that you?" cried Easy Larkspur, opening the door. "Two young ladies with you—oh, oh! Up to some new caper, I 'spose! Come in, my dear!"

For the first time a wild suspicion darted over the brain of Mary Arlington, that Bess was a courtezan, that she had been betrayed through her means. That thought, so wild and vague, and yet so terrible, smote poor Mary to the soul. The familiar manner with which a rough looking gentleman like Easy Larkspur, greeted Bessie, first aroused this suspicion in the mind of Mary.

"Walk in ladies, walk in! You see I was jist enjoyin' a glass of whiskey punch by the fire, with a prime hawanner! And whiskey punch, ladies, as you may have had occasion to know, is a werry good drink, an' goes down quite e-a-s-y! Ladies, I'd always adwise yo' to marry a gentleman, as knows how to make good whiskey punch, but you must be keerful he don't make it too weak. Weak punch," continued the red-faced gentleman, with an anti-total-abstinence smile, "Weak punch, in my opinion, is the most dispisable thing as is."

"Larkspur, I have one word to say to you. From an accomplice of the murderer I have gained some knowledge of the murder committed in this house yesterday afternoon. This knowledge I will place in your keeping on one consideration. Give these ladies and myself shelter for the night; this is all I ask of you."

"Why you see, Bessie, I was app'inted after the crowner's inquest had sot upon the old lady, to stay here all night, in case the thieves might take a notion to repeat their wisit. My fellers is a-sleepin' in the back room. You wouldn't like to try a leetle of this punch, would yo'? You may stay here all night; no doubt o' that! But as all the other rooms was locked by the Ma'or, you'll have to sleep in the room where the corpse is."

"Oh, heaven!" whispered Mabel. "Is the old lady dead?" and her dark eyes grew lustrous with fear and awe.

"Dead, my darlin', as a door nail!" observed Larkspur, with whisky punch beaming from every line of his face. "And a deader thing than that I don't know; it's about the deadest thing as is; that's a fact!"

Bess silently led the girls up stair. The same shudder thrilled through every heart as they entered the ghost-chamber. Two formal wax candles gave a dim light to the place. The massive bed, with its thick curtains, still stood in one corner, the high-backed chairs had been replaced in their positions against the wall; the mirror between the windows still flashed back the light of the candles. The room was the same as in the morning; the furniture still wore the same antique and ghostly air ; and the portrait above the mantel still gazed around the place, with its pale and beautiful countenance relieved by sweeping tresses of long black hair, and enlivened by the gleam of lustrous dark eyes.

The ghost-room was the same, and yet not altogether the same. There was a crust of hardened blood congealed along the cold bricks of the fireplace ; the very air seemed tainted with the smell of human blood, shed in violence and murder.

In the centre of the chamber, in the full glare of the light, rested a coffin, covered with a plain cloth, and placed upon tressels of sabel wood. The glare of the light flashed over the details of the cold white shroud, the stiff hands carefully crossed over each other, the feet thrusting the death robe slightly upward, all were painfully disclosed, but the face was covered with a loose piece of snowy linen. Mangled, and shattered, and crushed, it was too fearful a sight for the eyes of the living to behold, and yet was it not tenfold more horrible to see that white cloth thrown over the face, leaving the vivid fancy to depict the loathsome reality, than to look upon the palpable reality itself ? To fancy the cold blood falling drop by drop upon the bottom of the coffin, from the hollow skull!

There she lay, her gold forgotten, her blood cold and icy, her limbs stiffened as marble. And as the light flickered with an uncertain glare, and as the wind moaned through the crevices of the chamber, and as the hangings of the bed and the windows rustled to and fro, while from the frame of the portrait, the face of a beautiful woman gazed sadly upon the scene, it seemed as though an awful and invisible fiend had infected the very air with a curse. That fiend was Murder ; in the rustling curtains, in the moaning wind, in the flickering light, in the sad gaze of the portrait, in the spectacle of the coffin and the corse ; in all these he spoke with a voice that froze the blood in its career, and stilled the heart in its beatings.

"Behold your mother !" cried Bess, in a tone of wild agitation, as seizing Mabel by the hand, she pointed to the portrait. "Behold your mother ! You are the child of Livingstone the merchant ; this house and all its contents are yours ! Yours by the will of yon murdered woman, who rests cold and icy in her coffin. Behold the face of your mother, gazing upon you in kindness and love. Kneel, Mabel, kneel, and thank your God, that after the long night which has darkened your life, the day has dawned at last !"

And while Mabel stood stricken dumb with astonishment, while her brain whirled in wild confusion, and the very room seemed to reel round her, Bess turned aside and took Mary by the hand.

"Now hear the dark confession which I have to whisper to your ear," she shrieked, falling on her knees. "I was the cause of your ruin ; I was the accomplice of the seducer ; I took his wages ; and earned them by selling myself, body and soul into his hands ! I, it was, that lured you from your home ; I, it was, that led you on to ruin—my soul is blackened by the foul guilt of a crime than which hell can name no deed of darker horror.

"Hear this confession, and hear my fixed resolve ! Spurn me from you, trample on me, curse me, oh, curse me, but from your side living I will never depart ! You do not wish to return to your father's house. I will slave for you, work for you, beg for you ! Let me wash out some portion of my crime by a life-long devotion to your service. Curse me, Mary, spit upon me, Mary, spurn me, as the base thing I am should be spurned, but I am your slave through life—my crime shall be washed out in tears of blood !"

Vain were the power of language to paint the horror which paled the face of Mary Arlington as this dark confession fell shrieking on her ear. She looked vacantly in the face of the kneeling woman, she even toyed playfully with her long dark hair, and then she gave utterance to a wild and maniac laugh.

"Lorraine," she cried, "Lorraine, ha, ha, ha! He will return at last, he will yet be mine! Lorraine ! Lorraine !"

CHAPTER IX.

SLOWLY and silently Devil-bug ascended the staircase of Monk-Hall. The lamp, which he held extended at arm's length, cast a flaring light over his distorted face, now rendered tenfold more hideous by the tokens of some terrible emotion. He had bitten his upper lip until the blood trickled over his clenched teeth, down to his pointed chin. There was a glassy light in his solitary eye, and a lowering frown full of omen, upon his protuberant brow.

Slowly and silently, with the light in his hand, he ascended the massive staircase of Monk-Hall. He uttered no word, but fearful thoughts were working at his heart. One hour ago, his heart had softened into something like human feeling —a very child might have led the savage, and ruled him with a word. That word, a word of kindness to the child of Ellen. Now—they had stolen the child, they had torn the fair girl from his arms, and Devil-bug was a savage once more. Like a black cloud arising from the stagnant waters of the Dead Sea, so the feeling of fierce malignity to all the human race, arose hideous and terrible from the depths of the monster's soul.

"Ha !" he cried, as he suddenly paused upon the stairway. "The corpse o' that man Harvey, is a-layin' beside the grave in the pit o' Monk-Hall ! I must go down and bury it. Yes, yes, snug under the airth, snug, snug I'll put it out o' sight."

He turned round and descended the stairway,

and soon stood over the form of the prostrate man with a light in his hand. He regarded the pale face of Luke with a scowl of fierce malignity. His distorted countenance assumed an expression of savage hate.

"Soh, soh, mister, yo' helped them to dig off, did yo'?" he muttered, placing his foot upon the breast of the insensible man, "I've a notion to knife your wizzin'—wonders how you'd look with a small air-hole in your throat?"

He drew an old-fashioned Spanish knife from the breast of his coarse garment as he spoke. The blade long, pointed, and glittering, flew open with a touch of the spring. Stooping over the form of the insensible Luke, he applied the knife to his unbared throat, and with a wild grimace distorting his features, he moved it gently along the skin.

"I on'y wants to see how near to the skin I can go, without cuttin' his wynd-pipe! Ho, ho, ho!"

There was a great deal of the philosopher in Devil-bug. Never a doctor of all the schools, with his dissecting knife in hand and the corpse of a subject before him, could have manifested more nerve and coolness than the savage of Monk-Hall. Slowly and gently along the throat of the insensible man, he moved the glittering knife, holding its keen edge within a hair's breadth of the skin. Then as if to show that his spirits were not depressed by the solemnity of the operation, he laughed merrily to himself, and hummed the catch of some dismal song.

Suddenly his protuberant brow grew heavy with a scowl. He clenched the handle of the knife with a grasp of fierce resolution, and in a moment the blade glittered in his upraised hand.

"I'll put an end to this," he muttered hoarsely. "I'll give him a taste o' this piece o' hardware. Crack me over the skull did he?"

For a moment the knife quivered in the air above his head, and the scowl grew darker over his brow. The next instant, as if some strange thought had suddenly taken his soul by storm, the frown cleared away and the knife fell from his hand and stuck upright in the oaken floor.

"Nell," he slowly muttered, "yer only hope lies *here*!" He pointed to the body of the insensible Luke. Here lies yer hope, and yer fortin'—this man can make all matters straight. He can place yo' afore the proud folks o' this town as the daughter o' Livingstone; and nobody else can do it! I'd rayther burn myself alive than to hurt a hair of his head."

Stooping to the floor, he raised Luke on his shoulder, he bore him from the den up the stairs, and into his room and laid the form of the insensible man upon the bed.

*   *   *   *   *

The day was breaking in the east, when a pale man came trembling up the marble steps of a mansion in South Third-street, and leaning against the stone pillars of the door buried his face in his hands, while every fibre of his frame shook with emotion.

The day was breaking, and red gleams of morning shot up into the sky, cold white clouds, sailing slowly through the heavens caught the first kiss of sun-rise on their bosoms.

The man who leaned for support against the heavy door pillars, raised his face from his hands, after a moment of silent agony, and tossing his dark hair aside from his brow, looked fixedly at the vacant air with set teeth and flashing eyes.

He stood at his father's door again. In the strange oblivion of soul which succeeded the drugged potion, he fancied that only a night had passed since he left his father's threshold.

The key was in the lock; he turned it, and after the lapse of a moment stood in the dark entry and closed the door at his back.

He advanced along the hall, while an awful presentiment flashed over his soul. Dim memories of the scenes in Monk-Hall rushed upon him.

"I will seek my sister's room," he muttered. "If she is there, then all is right, and these presentiments are but folly."

He was passing by the parlour door, when the sound of voices talking in low tones, arrested his attention. Gently opening the door, he started back in surprise, as a blaze of light rushed out upon the darkness of the hall. He entered the parlour with a softened footstep, and looked around in vague wonder. The astral lamp stood lighted on the centre-table, and the remains of a coal-fire mouldered in the grate.

Two figures were seated upon the sofa, an old man and an elderly dame. They sat with their hands clasped on their knees, and their eyes fixed vacantly upon the carpet. So deep was their reverie, that they did not look up, or manifest any knowledge of the intruder's presence.

Byrnewood stood chained to the spot, by a silent horror. Scarce might he recognize his father, in the careworn old man, who sat silent and withered before him; scarce might he know his mother in the hollow-eyed old woman, whose dark hair, slightly silvered by age, fell carelessly over her shoulders.

He advanced a step, and beheld that his mother's dark eyes were red with weeping; his father's lips trembled with an incessant movement.

They looked like people who have been watching long days and weary nights by the sick-bed of some loved one, without once changing their apparel or taking an hour's repose.

Byrnewood advanced another step; they beheld him, and started to their feet with a half-muttered cry. Oh, there was a volume of hope and fear and agony in that involuntary shriek!

For a moment there was silence. The father and mother gazed in the face of their son, with the same look of horrible suspense. Byrnewood returned that look, and the three stood like statues of some unspeakable agony.

"*Mary*"—gasped the father, and then all further words died on his tongue. He stood with his hands extended, and his lips trembling as with a spasm.

"Mary!" echoed Byrnewood. "Father, there is some dark mystery here. Is she sick? Or —or—" and his lips grew white—"Or it may be that she is—*dead!* Keep me no longer in suspense; tell me the worst at once."

"Know you not Byrnewood that your sister has been missing since the night before last?" slowly asked the old merchant.

"The night before last!" echoed Byrnewood. "Surely father that cannot be. Last night when I left home, she was in your arms."

"Last night?" echoed Mrs. Arlington in vague astonishment.

"Why Byrnewood you have been absent from home for the last thirty-six hours," exclaimed the merchant, sharing the wonder of his wife.

Byrnewood made no reply, but tottering to the sofa, he buried his face in his hands, and was silent for a single moment. With all the force of his soul concentrated on one point, he endeavoured to remember the events of the last thirty-six hours.

"Did I ever think of this!" cried the father, clasping his hands wildly together. "Did I ever think of this, when I toiled day after day over the desk, labouring like a slave at the galley, to build up a fortune which my children might enjoy, when I was dead and gone. Did I ever think that Mary—Mary for whom I have toiled and toiled for years, should be torn from me in this way? My God! This suspense is tenfold more horrible than death."

"Don't you remember her light laugh as she sprang over that threshold two nights ago—'I'll be back, I'll be back to-morrow.'"

The mother paused and burst into tears. There are some things which can be written down in language, but not a mother's love, nor a mother's fear. What was Mrs. Arlington thirty-six hours ago? A blooming matron, with a healthy cheek, and a dark eye, speaking affection and tenderness. What is she now? An old woman, with a withered cheek and a hollow eye-socket, a brain fired by a thousand mingling emotions, and a heart cankered by the gnawings of care. A mother's love does not manifest its tenderness in words, but in the gleam of the eye, or the smile of the lip; a mother's fear is written down in the wrinkled brow, the faded cheek, the eye darting unnatural light and the lip quivering with a tremulous motion, that speaks the helplessness of the agony that is eating into the soul.

"Father—mother," cried Byrnewood starting from his seat. "There is a strange mystery pressing on my brain! I am either the victim of an awful delusion, or else there is in store for me, for you, for us all, a reality worse than death! Even while I speak to you, there are passing before me, shapes and forms and visions, whose mystery I dare not—oh dare not —speak to you! You know father that I love Mary, that I always loved her. You know that I would give my life for her. Trust the mystery of this matter, with me! A few hours will bring her back to this threshold in safety and honour, or confirm these horrible suspicions which are working through my brain—"

"Yet stay, Byrnewood," cried Mr. Arlington as his son moved towards the door. "Where have you been during the last thirty-six hours, where—"

"Ask me not, ask me not," shouted Byrnewood with a start and look full of frenzy. "Ask me not for the sake of Mary, ask me not! In a few hours I will return to you—then you shall know all!"

With these words he rushed from the room, and assuming another hat and cloak in the place of those which he had lost at Monk-Hall, he went slowly down the stairs and from the house.

CHAPTER X.

THE State-House clock struck nine, and the carriage of the merchant prince stood waiting in front of his door. The coachman in grey livery turned up with black velvet, sat on the box, and the footman attired in like costume, stood beside the carriage door which was flung wide open. The burnished harness of the dark bay horses glittered in the sunbeams, and the panels of the coach, emblazoned with the merchant's coat of arms, shone like mirrors in the light.

It was nine o'clock, and from the front door of the mansion, the merchant and his wife came forth. Attired in a splendid travelling habit of dark green cloth, which developed each queenly outline of her form, Dora hung lightly on her husband's arm, while her eyes shone with unusual lustre, and her cheeks glowed with the hues of the damask rose. As she stepped down the marble steps, she was peerlessly beautiful. Every look, each gesture and grace of her faultless limbs and imposing countenance, bespoke the Queen, whose throne was in the hearts of all beholders.

It was observable that as the merchant led his wife toward the carriage, his face, half-buried in the shadow of a fur travelling cap, was turned away from hers, and once or twice as her gloved hand touched his arm, he shrank with a slight but involuntary start, as if there had been pollution in the contact.

Their eyes met as they stood before the carriage door. The merchant's face was almost hidden from the sight, by his fur cap, and the upraised collar of his great coat, but his blue eyes dilated to an unnatural size, gazed in the beaming face of his wife, with a cold impenetrable look that sent a strange awe to her inmost heart.

"The day is beautiful, Albert," said Dora, with one of her winnihg smiles.

"It is indeed beautiful!" replied Livingstone, as his lips parted, not with a smile, but with a spasmodic contraction of the muscles of his face. "We have seen many such beautiful days, Dora; may we live to see many more!"

There was a singular gleam in his large blue eyes as he spoke.

"Have you invited our friends to meet us at Hawkwood?" asked Dora, as she entered the carriage.

"Trust me Dora, we shall have a pleasant company at the good old place," said Livingstone in a tone of affected lightness. "Bye the bye my dear, you will have to travel alone, for an hour or so. I have some business to transact, which will detain me a short time in town. I will join you on horseback in an hour."

Without waiting for her reply, he softly closed the door, and waved his hand to the coachman. The carriage whirled away over the echoing stones of the street, and Livingstone stood alone in front of the mansion.

"Let me see, let me see," he muttered, pressing his hand against his forehead, "What author is it that tells the story of an English lord, who world-worn and heart-sick, used to amuse his leisure hours by rehearsing his own funeral? Ha, ha! There are scarcely twenty-four hours of life left to me, and yet I while them away in digging my grave, and—another grave beside my own!"

That cold spasm, which mocked a smile, played round the merchant's lips, and he went slowly up Fourth-street, in the direction of his warehouse.

The State-House clock struck nine, and two little men were walking up and down the broad walk of Independence Square. All around them arose the giant trees, whose massive trunks had been young sixty years ago, when the proclamation of independence rang from the steps of the ancient hall. Their leafless limbs shot upward into the cold blue sky, and between their intricate branches, the white clouds might be seen, sailing slowly through the winter heavens. At one end of the walk was Walnut-street, with a line of splendid building towering in the place of the old gaol; at the other, through the vista formed by opposing lines of trees, was seen the ancient State-House, with its steeples rising into the full glow of the sunshine.

And up and down this walk, paced two little men, engaged in an interesting conversation, as might be seen from their linked arms and rapid gestures. One little man wore a high hat and frock coat, which was buttoned so tightly around his thick body, that it gave you the idea of a mammoth Dutch pudding, stuffed and crammed until the skin was ready to burst. Beneath the skirts of this frock coat appeared a pair of legs which once seen might never be forgotten. With a thick piece of cord reaching from one calf to the other, they would have described the letter A, they rubbed together at the knees, and were separated by the space of a foot between the boots. Bury a man eighty years in a coal mine, and show him those legs after he is brought out into the light again, and show them to him, apart from the pudding body, and if he had ever seen them before, he would know them on first sight. Who could ever forget Buzby Poodle's legs?

The other little man was dressed in a grey over-coat and a shiny leather cap. That pale, square, Dresden-wax-doll-face would have been known among a thousand. Who could mistake the large oyster-coloured eyes of Sylvester J. Petriken.

And there they walked, the editor of the "Daily Black Mail," and the Magazine proprietor. Poodle's face reminded you of a grimacing ape, making mouths at a magpie; Petriken's was the visage of a solemn old baboon, wrapt in deep thought. The one fattened on the garbage of the town; the other lived on stolen literature. One was a scandal-monger, a bravo on a small scale; the other a plagiarist, a very Jew, who lived by clipping the coin of the wide realm of intellect. There they walked, the one living on the murder, suicide, and bloodshed of the town, the other thriving on the fruits of various adroit literary robberies; there they walked arm in arm, alike the boon companions of blackguards, and the loathing of all honest men; these Courtezans of the Press. Poodle was the pander of the whole town; anybody could buy him, body and soul, for three dollars, a bottle of wine, a Bologna sausage, and a few crackers; Petriken was the hireling of but one libertine, Gustavus Lorrimer, and his price varied from a two dollar subscription to his magazine, up to the value of a second-hand steel engraving.

"And so you see we'll have a great magazine!" exclaimed Petriken with one of his sickly smiles, "To-morrow morning all the Intellects of the land meet at my office in order to talk the matter over. I, Sylvester J. Petriken will become the focus of American literature."

"Won't the name of Busby Poodle be known all over the country? Posterity shall reverence the name of Poodle, and millions yet unborn will write it on their hearts. Is'nt there something in that? The name of Poodle inscribed on the pillar of Immortality, alongside the name of Shakspeare! And then the name of Petriken!"

"Let us mingle our names together!" cried little Sylvester, striking an attitude. "We will go down to posterity as Petriken and Poodle!"

"The Petriken and the Poodle! Huzza! A sort of Siamese-twinship of genius! *Ensemble de chose*—decidedly the cheese—as we say in domestic French!"

The little men then shook hands and stood

erect, like proud representatives of the outcast literature of the Quaker City.

Suddenly Petriken started.

"I vow there's Lorrimer and Mutchins!" he exclaimed, looking towards the State House; and ere a moment had flown, the magnificent Gustavus stood by his side, with the round-faced Mutchins hanging on his arm.

"Ha, ha, Pet, my boy, how d'ye do!" cried Lorrimer, as a gleam of laughter broke over his manly visage. "Silly, who is this fellow?" he continued, arranging his moustache as he glanced at the Black Mail man with somewhat of a supercilious smile. "Who is the gentleman in the big hat and the duck legs?"

"He, he, he, you're quite jocular this morning!" exclaimed the little editor, who had heard this aside speech. "Why, I'm Poodle, sir, Buzby Poodle of the——the Daily Black Mail!" And the little fellow advanced with a spring.

"Oh, you are Buzby Poodle?" exclaimed Lorrimer, with a glance from his half-shut eyes. "Come on, Petriken, come on, Mutchins; I've something to say to you. And so that is Poodle of the Black Mail, is it? Jove! He looks for all the world, like a monkey dressed up to dance on the top of a street organ!"

And taking the arm of each gentleman within his own, he strode down the broad walk, leaving Poodle to his own delightful meditations.

"Well," muttered Buzby, "w-e-ll if I don't cut that fellow up some day my name ain't Poodle! And as for that Petriken——damme I'll go right to the office and abuse his Western Hem. People that insult Buzby Poodle must look for a Poodle's vengeance. I'm a perfect Injin; I am!"

"Boys I've a capital joke for you," exclaimed Lorrimer, as they hurried along the broad walk. "You see Mutchins, ha, ha! It's capital, capital! And d'ye hear, Pet—by Jove, man!" he cried, starting suddenly. "You are as white as a cloth in the face!"

Petriken stood transfixed to the spot by some unknown horror.

Not a word escaped his lips, but standing motionless as one of the trees along the walk, he pointed with his outstretched hand towards Walnut-street.

"Look! Look!" cried Mutchins, pointing in the same direction. "There's a sight for you, Lorrimer."

Lorrimer looked towards Walnut-street and at the same moment, a cold shudder darted through his frame. He was dumb with astonishment. Could he believe his eyes? Yes, yes, there, there before him, advancing slowly and leisurely along the walk, was the form of Byrnewood Arlington whom he left the night before in the hands of Devil-bug, whom he never dreamt to behold among living men again! Lorrimer's expressive face grew pale and red by turns; for a moment he gasped for breath.

"Leave the matter to me," he muttered to his companions, who stood silent, "and mark ye—deny everything, d'ye hear?"

He had scarcely time to whisper these words to his frightened panders, when Byrnewood approached. Lorrimer started as he beheld the wild light gleaming from his dark eyes.

"I have a few words to say to you, sir," Byrnewood began in a low deep tone like a voice from a sepulchre.

"I beg your pardon, sir!" cried Lorrimer, with a haughty inclination of his head. "You have the advantage of me. I do not know you sir!" And his face was wreathed in a polite and insinuating smile.

"Not know me?" echoed Byrnewood. "Was I not in your company last night?"

"Decidedly not!" And Lorrimer dropped the arms of his minions, and placed the head of his gold-mounted cane to his lips in an easy, devil-may-care manner, characteristic of a Chestnut-street lounger.

"Why, sir, Mr. Petriken here, introduced me to you; and the introduction took place at this gentleman's rooms." He pointed to the red-faced Mutchins as he spoke.

"Pet, did you ever introduce this gentleman to me?" exclaimed Lorrimer, with a meaning look.

"Nev-er!" faltered the white-faced pander.

"And damme, sir, I never saw you in all my life, sir," blustered Mutchins, buttoning the front of his white coat in a pompous manner.

Byrnewood placed his hand to his forehead for a single instant.

"I remember the introduction;" he said in a slow deliberate tone, "I remember being in the streets with you; and beyond that all is darkness!"

"Depend upon it, sir," exclaimed Lorrimer, laying his hand pleasantly on Byrnewood's shoulder. "You are the victim of some strange delusion. I give you my solemn word of honour that I never saw you in my life before!"

"And your name is Lorrimer?"

"Egad! you've hit it! Bye-the-bye, my dear fellow, is'nt that a bald eagle sailing among the clouds yonder!"

With an air of languid nonchalance he pointed upward with his cane.

"Will you give me your word of honour, that you never saw my sister?" exclaimed Byrnewood, as the images of memory darted over his brain.

"Your sister!" echoed Lorrimer, with a vacant stare. "Oh, ho! My dear fellow, you're too hard for me! Upon my honour, I never saw your sister, nor any member of your family, to know them by name. Your name is——"

"Arlington," responded the brother, with a steady look, "Byrnewood Arlington."

"Have heard the name, but never knew any member of the family. By Jove! That must be a bald eagle yonder!"

Byrnewood advanced a step nearer, and looked silently into the dark hazel eyes of Lorrimer.

"Now for the last trial!" he muttered, and then repeated in a slow and solemn voice, the words of the prophecy.

"'On Christmas-eve, at the hour of sunset, one of you will die by the other's hand. The winding sheet is woven and the coffin made.' Tell me, sir," he added, in a voice full of emotion. "Did you ever hear these words before?"

Lorrimer's cheek did not blench, nor his eye quail. He raised his cane languidly to his lips, and then replied, in a careless tone—

"Never! Yet stay—I think I've read them somewhere in Dickens or Bulwer."

"Oh, madness! madness!" muttered Byrnewood, pressing his hand forcibly against his forehead. "I am indeed the victim of some dark delusion. Excuse me, gentlemen, for this intrusion," he continued, in a tremulous voice. "It is all a dream, a horrible dream!"

With these words he darted down the walk, his head bent on his bosom, and his eyes fixed upon the ground.

"Well, Lorrimer, that was neatly done!" cried Silly Petriken, approaching the master-libertine, who stood in the centre of the walk, gazing upon the retreating form of Byrnewood.

"You did him brown," laughed Mutchins. "But, boys, we must be careful — there's a devil of a stir made about this baby-face!"

Lorrimer made no reply. A strange glow brightened over his face, and his hazel eyes gazed sternly on the vacant air.

"I say Lorrimer," began Petriken, but a fierce scowl on the brow of the libertine silenced him.

Without a word, Lorrimer strode slowly away from his companions, and passing through the State-House, hurried rapidly along Chesnut-street.

His manly form, his handsome face, attracted many a look, many a gaze of admiration. But that heaving of the chest, that flashing of the hazel eye! Little did the fair dames who gazed upon the handsome libertine, dream of the hell that raged within his bosom.

Christmas-eve, the river and the death, glided like a warning from Eternity before his dilating eyes. Dim and shadow-like, yet terrible, the vision rushed upon his soul.

That day as Fitz-Cowles walked along the street, these thoughts passed through his brain.

"All is safe. This morning I sent the hair trunk, and all my other baggage to New York, under an assumed name. Public curiosity is still alive with regard to the—forgery—and yet no one suspects me! I stand as clear as the day among the aristocracy of the Quaker City! Von Gelt is gone; no accomplice can now mutter treason with regard to his master, Dim, my Creole slave, has orders to have two of the best horses to be had in this town for love or money, ready saddled and bridled to-night, in the wood beyond Camden. With these horses, Dora and I will escape from Hawkswood; by-the-bye she must take care to have all her jewellery with her. I must make something by this woman; must turn her fancy for a coronet into Fitz-Cowles' gold. All therefore is fair day with me, and what should I fear?"

"What should I fear?" he muttered aloud, and ere the words had died on his lips, a dark presentiment crept through his blood. "While I stand here, this man Harvey may be laying some infernal plot to blow all my schemes in the air! That would be a pretty spectacle. As I am about to leave the city to-night, to feel an officer's finger on my shoulder, 'you are my prisoner, sir'—ugh! I have not seen Harvey to-day—this silence annoys me. Poodle gave me a hint that Harvey was on the track of the Jew yesterday—Zounds! Could he have seen that rascal before his—death!"

Fitz-Cowles was troubled. His lip was compressed, and his swarthy face grew darker with a settled frown.

"I will go to Monk-Hall," he muttered. "I will spy out the secrets of the den, and if the Jew made any communication to Harvey before his death, I will know it, ere this day is gone by. Ha! Here is that fool Mulhill!"

And with a smile on his red visage, the redoubtable Major Rappahannock Mulhill came lounging lazily along the street, twirling an enormous crooked stick in one hand, while the other was inserted in the capacious pocket of his pantaloons.

The costume of the major, you will remember, was striking and peculiar—a broad-brimmed felt-hat, with a blue cord and tassel; a white blanket over-coat, which was thrown open in front, revealing a sky-blue coat with metal buttons, a deep red velvet vest, and a pair of pants made very full, and striped like bed-ticking. Brimstone kid gloves and patent leather boots, completed the costume of this dashing gentleman.

"How do, curnel? Fine day," wobbled the major, lounging to the side of the millionaire. "Cussed dull this! Not a man shot down in the streets to day, I vow!"

"Your humble servant, major. May I request your services in an affair of great delicacy? I have an enemy. He has resorted to mean practices to injure me. I have determined to put him down. In order to do this, I must visit one of the vilest dens in the Quaker City. I want a friend to go with me, stand by me, and fight for me. Will you be that friend?"

"Where is the den of thieves?" drawled Mulhill with a sleepy look.

"Did you ever hear of Monk-Hall?"

"There's my paw," said the classic Mulhill. "But mind ye, if there aint a man killed I shall account the affair low, d—d low!"

"Thanks, major, thanks," exclaimed Fitz-Cowles, taking the proffered hand. "Meet me an hour from this time, at the corner of Fifth and Chestnut streets. Till then good bye."

"Da-day!" drawled Mulhill, "I will not fail you. A-doo?"

And Fitz-Cowles hurried up the street, with a frown on his brow, while Mulhill lounged in an opposite direction, with a broad grin on his red visage. Fitz-Cowles placed his gold-headed cane to his lips, and muttered wildly to himself, while Mulhill drew from his pocket a slip of paper, and rattled it against the tip of his nose with a broad grin.

"A love letter from a g-a-l!" he muttered, and then went laughing on his way, chuckling over his trick on the forger.

CHAPTER X

An old man, leaning upon a spade, stood on the gentle eminence, with the beams of the setting sun falling over his wrinkled face.

He stood in front of a massive gate, whose posts falling to decay, were in strong contrast with the solidity of a thick stone wall, which extended along the eminence, until it was lost to the view in the hollows on either side.

Behind the wall grew a thick grove of pines, with the steep roofs and grey walls of an old-timed mansion, dimly visible through their evergreen boughs.

In front of the aged man lay a wild and broken tract of country, plains of dreary sand, varied by sombre forests of pine, or here and there an orchard of peach trees, with the bare and desolate limbs waving stiffly in the winter air, or a solitary farm-house rising from some bleak waste of brown earth. The distant western horizon was one dim and dreary wall of pine forest, with the broad disc of the setting sun, seen half above the dark barrier, while his level beams fell with a red lustre over the wintry landscape.

The whole tract of country, in view of the old man, who stood on the brow of the eminence, wild and dreary as it was in summer, was now rendered fearful as some night-mare dream by the absence of the scanty foliage, which served to hide some of its most hideous features.

The setting sun-light streamed over the sides of steep ravines, sunken in the bosom of the sandy wastes, like colossal graves, or along the surface of black pools of water, visible through the intervals of pine forests, or over the side of some barren hill, which shot up suddenly from the surrounding plain, with its bleak sides covered with the trunks of burnt and blasted trees.

The eye of the old man was fixed upon the road, which made one straight track through the landscape, from the distant horizon, until it terminated at the gate of the mansion. Frequently crossed by streams of water, or again rising into slight eminences, this road was all one dreary path of sand. A sight more barren can scarcely be conceived.

Within the compass of a mile from the spot where the old man stood, arose three gentle hills, and on the summit of each of these, his eye was rivetted with peculiar interest.

On the nearest hill a carriage was visible, drawn by two noble bay horses, whose harness glittered in the sun.

On the next hill, like some enormous beetle, creeping forth from its haunts, ere the day was done, a black and gloomy hearse, came rapidly onward.

On the last hill, the form of a horseman, bestriding a gallant grey steed, rose up between the eyes and the setting sun,

"Man and boy, for sixty long years, I've lived in this old place, and yet I never see'd sich a sight as that afore. For the last half hour I've watched 'em, and still they come on, the carriage fust, the hearse next, and the horseman last! An' they will drive at the same pace; the hearse keeps little over a quarter-a-mile from the carriage, and the horseman keeps the same distance from the hearse! Well, well, if it ain't the queerest sight, and reether the solemn'est, I'll never strike spade into airth agin!"

As the old man muttered this rude soliloquy, an aged woman clad in a petticoat of coarse linsey, hobbled through the gate, and took her place at his side, her grey eyes dilated with wonder, as she gazed upon the road beneath.

Meanwhile the carriage, the hearse, and the horse came hurriedly onward.

We will descend for a moment from our eminence at the mansion gate, and take a glance at carriage, and horse,

In one corner of the thickly cushioned carriage, sat a proud and peerless woman, whose tall form enveloped in a green riding habit, was also muffled in the warm folds of a dark cloth cloak. Her hands were folded across her bosom, and her face drooped down, until her chin rested on her fingers. There was a volume of thought in her full dark eye, and a strange meaning in the steady frown which indented her queenly brow.

"To give up all, a coronet, and a title, for virtue and Livingstone! The thought is galling! and yet it shall be so!"

As these thoughts flashed over the soul of Dora Livingstone, she leaned slightly forward, and looked through the opened carriage window.

"How strange! A journey of only thirty miles, and yet it has consumed the entire day. First the carriage breaks down—it takes the servants at least three hours to repair the accident. Then, at noon, I am overtaken by Albert; he tells me, that the doctor has forbidden him to ride in a close carriage, so he will follow me on horseback. Then, with one delay after another, we are detained on the road, and now, as the night is coming on, we approach the old domain of Hawkewood."

As she fell back on her seat, her soul became engaged again in the fearful contest which had convulsed it the entire day. Virtue and Livingstone or a coronet and murder!

*   *   *   *   *

The noble figure of the horseman and the form of the gallant grey steed which he rode, rose up in the light of the sun, from the summit of the last hill.

Pausing for a moment on the brow of the hill, the horseman bared his brow to the setting sun. The thick corded veins stood out from the bronzed skin, and the blue eye, deep sunken beneath the dark eyebrow, glared with an unsteady and wandering light. For a single moment as the light of the sun shone over that face and brow, it presented a sight of fearful interest.

For a single moment, the muscles of the face, the veins of the forehead, the livid lips, worked and writhed, like crawling lizards. The blue eye, so strangely contrasted with the dark eyebrow, dilated until the pupil absorbed nearly the entire surface of the eyeball. It was but for a moment, and then all was calm again, but it was a calmness like sunset over the black waters of the Dead Sea.

A deep husky sound like the mingling of a death-rattle with cheerful laughter, shook the broad chest of the merchant, and then with a set smile on his lips, he gave the rein to his steed, and dashed along the road.

He had not gone ten paces, when another horseman, dressed in plain black, riding a brown horse all whitened with foam, attained the summit of the hill, and shouted to Livingstone at the top of his voice.

"Hello, you sir, hello," he cried. "Can you tell me which is the way to Hawkewood?"

Turning his head over his shoulder, Livingstone gazed upon the stranger.

"Yonder building among the trees, is the place you seek," he calmly answered.

"Dev'lish glad to hear it," exclaimed the stranger, who was a man of some thirty years, with a face of no particular meaning. "Never in all my born days, have I had such a ride as to-day! You see, sir, I landed at New-York, yesterday, from the steam-ship, and came post haste to Philadelphia, where I found that I'd have to ride a matter o' thirty miles before I could see the genelman I was seekin' after. Couldn't tell me sir, whether I'd be sure to find Mr. Livingstone at that old place yonder?"

"My name is Livingstone," coolly responded the merchant.

The stranger gave a start, which he communicated to his horse by a violent twitch at the reins.

"What, Albert Livingstone, Esq., Philadelphia, Pennsylvania, 'Nited States o' 'Merica?" he shouted in a voice of unlimited astonishment.

"The same, sir," replied the merchant.

"Well, sir, I'm a clerk of your father's lawyers—Messrs. Billings, Smith, & Charmley, London. I'm a special messenger, sir, sent over to see you. There's the package, sir, that is to say, my lord——"

The excited special messenger had thrown himself from his horse, and hat in hand approached the stirrups of the merchant, holding a large packet, in his hand, sealed with enormous red seals.

"I guess its purport," said Livingstone, with a slight smile. He took the packet; placed it within the breast of his overcoat, and then drew forth his pocket-book. "Here is something for your trouble," he exclaimed, handing the special messenger a roll of notes.

Then putting spurs to his steed, he rode forward, leaving the gentleman standing in the centre of the road; a very well executed picture of blank astonishment, with its hand crammed full of paper money.

In a few minutes Livingstone dashed by the hearse, and speeding rapidly forward he reached the eminence in front of the mansion gate, at the same moment that his wife stepped from the carriage. Dismounting from his steed, the merchant received the salutations of the servants.

"Welkim to Hawkewood, Mister Livingstone; welkim to Hawkewood ma'am," exclaimed the old gardener and his wife, as they hobbled forward.

Mrs. Livingstone greeted the old people with a cordial bow, while the merchant took them each by the hand, and spoke cheerfully of the good old times, when his father was living, and he roamed the deep woods, an idle and free-hearted boy.

Livingstone now approached his wife. She stood erect in the centre of the knoll with every outline of her magnificent form, displayed to advantage by the green riding habit which she wore.

While the merchant's horse and the travelling carriage were led or driven toward the out-buildings of the mansion, Livingstone and his wife stood on the summit of the knoll gazing in silence upon the setting sun. The aged man and woman, like statues of extreme old age, leaned against the crumbling gate posts, and gazed steadily upon the beautiful form of the merchant's wife.

"Wot a han'some couple!" muttered the old woman.

The beams of the setting sun streamed over the proud form of the merchant, and over the figure of his beautiful wife. Behind them lay the thick grove of pines, with the massive outlines of the old mansion, seen through the darkening boughs. In front of them swept the wild track of broken country, now blending into one mass of darkness, under the gathering gloom of twilight, while far away, the last glimpse of the sun was stealing over the thick horizon of pine forests.

Dora gazed upon the scene, and felt a strange feeling of awe steal over her soul. Turning to Livingstone, she began an observation on the thoughtful quietude of the hour, but it died half-uttered on her lips.

"It is a solemn sunset, Albert—" she whispered, when she caught the gleam of his calm blue eye. There was something so unnatural, so fearful, in the expression that flashed from the eyes of Livingstone, that Dora felt a thrill of horror dart through every vein.

"It is indeed a solemn sun-set," answered Livingstone, in a calm and even tone. "But the morning will be bright, Dora, bright, my love!" He turned his head aside to conceal a frightful grimace that distorted his face.

CHAPTER XI.

DORA LIVINGSTONE GAINS THE CORONET, FOR WHICH SHE PERILLED HER SOUL.

A FINE old-time mansion, Dora!" exclaimed Livingstone, as he crossed the threshold of the chamber. "That was a solemn hall thro' which we passed, with its gloomy pictures and quaint carvings in dark stone, and then the stairway, Dora, with its steps of massive oak—by my life, I like this mansion of Hawkewood! It has a wild baronial look."

"And this chamber, with its old-time furniture, and antiquarian appointments," exclaimed Dora with a smile, "has it a characteristic name?"

"It is called the oak chamber of Hawkewood; you see the walls are concealed by huge panels of dark oaken wainscot, and the floor is covered by an old-fashioned carpet. In yonder corner, stands a bed with dark purple hangings, and here, from this lordly hearth, the glare of a cheerful wood fire flashes round the place. I like it Dora!"

"And then this round table, of dark walnut,

standing in the centre of the room, with a Gothic arm-chair on either side! Certainly the place looks like the den of some old monk, half wizard, half antiquary!"

"In that chair my father breathed his last," whispered Livingstone, with a sudden sternness of tone. "And on that table words have been written, which were followed by deeds of blood.

With a kind of gesture he pointed to the arm-chair on one side of the round table, motioning his wife to a seat, while he sat down on the opposite side.

"We'll have a cup of coffee, before you change your travelling-dress, my love," said Livingstone, with marked kindness of tone. "I forgot to inform you, that by a careless mistake, I dated the invitations to our friends, for to-morrow instead of to-day. You will have to endure the solitude of this place until the morning, when old Hawkewood will put on a face of smiles. By the bye, my dear, I have despatched all the servants to town, in order that my various preparations for the Christmas festival may be completed. Old Davidson and his wife will wait on you until the morrow——"

There was something so natural and common-place in all this, that Dora forgot the strange wildness of manner which Livingstone had once or twice manifested within the past hour; and her own dark thoughts were, for the moment, silenced by his calm tone and composed look.

"Ha, ha," cried Dora, with a laughing smile, "I can endure the solitude of Hawkewood for a single night, unless, indeed, yon bed, with its gloomy hangings, should chance to be haunted by pale ghosts or hideous dreams."

"Oh, your dreams will be sweet and undis-turbed. I pledge my life for it," said Livingstone, with a peculiar look, which escaped the eye of his wife.

The face of the merchant was deadly pale, yet an expression of immovable calmness lingered on every feature. The massive brow towering above the dark eyebrows, was full of silent thought, and the slight smile, playing round the expressive mouth, gave his face a mild and benignant look, which was in fearful contrast with the discoloured circles of flesh beneath each eye, or the sunken outlines of each bronzed cheek. The eyes of Livingstone wore a look never to be forgotten. Large, azure, and calm, they shone in a strange light, which seemed to flicker around each eyeball, like rays around a lamp.

Her form flung back in the arm-chair, in a position of grace and ease, Dora's face af-forded a vivid contrast to the countenance of her husband. The dark eyes swam in a mild, melting light, the smiling cheeks were flushed with warm rich hues, the high forehead was full of soul, and the small mouth with its lips of deep voluptuous red, was curved in a winning smile.

"Dora, my wife, you are very beautiful," said Livingstone in that deep-toned voice, which sounded from the depths of his chest. "We have now been married one year. You

have been to me, a faithful, true, and affectionate wife. As a slight tribute of my love, let me place in your hands this Christmas gift."

He drew from his breast a small casket of gold, richly set with jewels. Dora received it with an exclamation of delight.

"A gift like this would not shame the bride of an emperor!" she murmured, as her delicate fingers enclosed the princely gift.

"That casket encloses a gift, yet more pre-cious than the jewels that glitter on its ex-terior," said Livingstone as he rose from his seat. "Excuse me one moment, my love, I have some trifling orders to give to Davidson. In an instant I will return with the key of the casket—"

He advanced to the door of the chamber, and passed out into the spacious landing, at the head of the stair-way. The dim beams of the stars obscured by clouds streamed through a solitary window in the southern wall, giving a faint light to the oaken floor and massive walls. Closing the door of the oak chamber, Li-vingstone stood with his back towards the window, gazing down the dim stairway, with folded arms and compressed lips. Pre-sently the sound of footsteps was heard; a slight tremour ran over Livingstone's powerful frame, and the next instant, the form of Da-vidson was seen through the dusky shadows, ascending the stairway with a waiter in his hand.

"I will take the coffee, Davidson, while you hurry down stairs, and have my horse brought to the hall-door. Business requires my immediate return to Philadelphia. Lose no time, my good fellow, but let it be done without an instant's delay."

Taking the waiter from the astonished ser-vant, he advanced to the window, and laid it down gently on the oaken sill. In an instant the form of Davidson was lost in the shadows of the stairway, and soon the faint echo of his footsteps sounded faintly from the hall below.

Livingstone stood in the faint light of the stars, gazing steadily on the waiter, whose dark surface was relieved by two large cups of white porcelain, smoking with fragant coffee.

For a moment the merchant stood silent as the grave. His chest heaved, and his lip qui-vered with emotion. With a muttered groan, he drew forth from his breast a small phial of glittering silver.

He raised it in the dim light, and the fingers which clasped it, trembled like dry leaves in the storm. Then his blue eyes were fixed upon it with a gaze of horrible intensity, and a single large and scalding tear, starting from the hot eyelid, rolled slowly down his bronzed cheek.

"My wife!" he groaned, and still absorbed by an awful effort to control his reeling intellect, he stood for a moment regarding that silver phial with the same wild and intense stare. He soon recovered himself.

"Here is the coffee, my dear," said Living-stone, in a careless tone, as he entered, and placed the waiter on the round table. "It is a long while since I tasted coffee in this house, but I can commend old Hannah's coffee, above all other's, for its delicious flavour. Is'nt it singular, my dear, that so few people in the world know how to prepare, even tolerable coffee?"

Seating himself beside the table, the merchant raised one of the porcelain cups to his lips, and sipped its fragrant contents.

Reclining in the arm chair, her beautiful face glowing in the mild beams of the light, and her rounded limbs disposed in an attitude of careless languor, Dora followed the example of her husband, and raising the other cup to her lips athirst from the fatigue of travel, she drank profusely of the smoking coffee.

At this moment, Livingstone's blue eyes did not glare, nor shine, nor glisten; they seemed to blaze with a glassy lustre, as deadly as light emitted from the eye of the rattle-snake, ere it kills its victim.

"By-the-by, my dear, I must mention a singular piece of news, which overtook me on the road to Hawkewood this evening. I have spoken to you of the noble descent of my family. I have told you that Livingstone was an assumed name, that my grandfather left the broad lands of his barony in the hands of distant kinsmen, when he sought the solitudes of the new world——"

The words of the merchant had a strange interest for Dora. Half-starting from the chair, she listened with flashing eyes and parted lips, to the whispered tones of her husband.

"During my father's life, the last of the race of kinsmen died, leaving the old barony without a lord. My father hastened to England, and placing his claim to the lands and title in the hands of able lawyers, awaited the result with an impatience that clung to him until his dying hour. Here was the difficulty—our ancestor had left England, having first circulated the rumour that he was dead, and dead without an heir. He wished to bury his name, and the dishonour which the treachery of a woman had brought upon it, in eternal oblivion. My father's lawyers found it almost impossible to prove the identity of our ancestor, with the self-exiled lord. That impossibility has now been overcome. While my father's ashes rest in the family vault of Hawkewood, side by side, with that ancestor, who exiled himself from his native soil, I hold in my hand the packet which informs the Philadelphia merchant, that restored to the lands and title of his race, he is now——"

"Yes, yes," muttered Dora, as her face grew ashy pale. "Speak on, for God's sake, Livingstone. Yes—you are now——"

"Lord of Longford!" said Livingstone in a clear, deliberate tone.

Dora rose to her feet with a half muttered shriek.

"A title, and in England!" she murmured, "the fulfilment of my wildest dream! Lady of Longford—ha! Already I behold myself the mistress of broad lands, already I move in the throng of a royal court, already I feel the coronet encircling my brow!"

"Dora, shall we look at your Christmas gift?" said the merchant with a calm smile.

Dora's eye grew suddenly glassy. Was it from the overwhelming emotion which followed Livingstone's announcement?

"I will move among the proudest nobles of the British court! Rank, title, power! The prophecy is fulfilled! The boon is mine, without the crime. How my head swims—I feel giddy—my heart—ah! I am too much affected by this joyful intelligence."

As these words fell wild and trembling from her lips, while her cheek grew crimson and ashy by turns, Livingstone sat regarding her with the same look that glares from the eye of the tiger, ere he crushes the victim at his feet.

Dora started from her seat; she pressed her hands on her forehead; the glassy film which veiled her eyes was succeeded by a wild and flashing lustre.

"Why, Livingstone," she cried in a strange whisper, "the room is filled with strangers. Ha, ha," she laughed, resuming her seat again with a look of calm loveliness. "The suddenness with which you imparted this unexpected news, has given me a violent head-ache."

"Down," muttered Livingstone, in a tone inaudible to his wife. "Fiend, be still! A little while, and I am yours!" Was he speaking to the devil that lay couched near his heart——the devil of madness?

"Come, Dora, look at your Christmas present," he exclaimed in a calm voice, as he opened the casket.

Dora leaned forward until her beautiful countenance well nigh touched the face of her husband.

"Ha, ha," she laughed, "why, Livingstone, what child's play is this? You promise me jewels, and here is but a lock of hair—mine, I do believe—enclosed within this casket."

"Two locks of hair, my wife," spoke the deep voice of Livingstone. "Your's and Fitz-Cowles' !"

"Mine and Fitz-Cowles'!" echoed Dora with a look of vacant wonder. What mean you!"

Livingstone replied with a single word. Leaning forward, his blue eyes flashing with a glance of fearful meaning, he looked like a fiend blasting a guilty soul with a single look.

"Monk-hall !"

Dora looked steadily in his face, but her senses whirled in a delirium that lasted for a single moment.

"Monk-Hall?" she echoed—and her face was like death. "What means this jest?"

Jest?" echoed Livingstone in a husky voice. "Vile adultress! Call you this a jest? Two nights ago bending over the bed in which you and your paramour lay reposing in your shame, I severed these glossy locks of hair, as witnesses of your damning guilt—"

Livingstone's voice was fearfully calm as he spoke these words.

"Is it a jest, now?" the sneer quivered on his lips, and his blue eyes glared with an expression of ferocious hatred.

Vain is the power of speech to picture the horror which convulsed the frame of poor Dora Livingstone, as this awful discovery rushed upon her soul, like an ante-pest of hell.

Sinking in the chair with her hands clasped quiveringly together, for a moment consciousness, reason, and mind, were gone.

"Am I awake, am I dreaming? My brain whirls * * * * all, all discovered * * * * oh shame, eternal shame!"

Such were the ravings that fell from her trembling lips.

"And you must die," shrieked the frenzied voice of Livingstone. "You must die! Ere the hand of this watch tells the hour of seven, you will be a lifeless corse.

"Poisoned * * * Poisoned* * * I see it all now!" muttered Dora as with her head resting on her shoulder, and her eyes closed in a dreamy half consciousness, she lay thrown helplessly in the chair.

Did you ever see a chained tiger glutting its fierce eyes with the agonies of the helpless victim, whom the keeper's hand has thrust into its cage? So Livingstone sat, with his glaring eyes fixed upon the frenzied face of his wife.

"The hand of the watch is on the hour of six; in one hour she will be a lifeless mass, over which the worms will crawl and revel! This is my revenge! No gushing blood, falling from the white bosom, tells the story of my wrong and its punishment. But the soul bleeds—yes, yes—I hear its life drops falling from the ghastly wound—I feast upon its quivering agonies; the soul of my victim bleeds, ha, ha, ha!"

Pale, mute, motionless, sat tearless Dora Livingstone. Her eyes half closed, her hands gently clasped, her bosom faintly throbbing, while her soul became the victim of a thousand frenzies.

"Dora," shrieked Livingstone in the ear of the dying woman. "The hand of death is upon you, but I can save you yet; I have an antidote to the poison which you sipped in your coffee—"

"And you will give it me!" shrieked Dora, starting from her seat and seizing him by the hand. The touch of those icy fingers thrilled him to the heart.

"Give it you?" his voice sounded as though every syllable was torn from his heart. "Three nights ago, I bent over the bed in which you lay, lapt in the arms of shame. I listened for a word of repentance, nay, I tried to catch one lingering syllable of regret! Not a word, not a sound of penitence. You had sold yourself unto shame, and shame in its most polluted shape. In that hour, woman, when my heart was breaking, when my soul was torn from thought and reason, when all the hopes of my life were gone, and but one awful prospect lay before me, a madman's cell, through whose barred windows I beheld the grave of a suicide yawning for my corse, then woman, oh then, I coined my existence into a vow! By the majesty of God, by the doom of hell, by the awful desolation of my soul, I swore to make you feel every throb of the agony whose fangs quivered through my heart! I matured my revenge in silence. I madman that I am, through the course of two fearful days, laid every snare to trap you into the power of the man whom you have dishonoured, *dishonoured*! I lured you to Hawkewood, I gave you the poison, and now, while death darkens horribly over your soul, I dash you from me, scorn your prayer for mercy, glory in your last agonies, and shriek in your freezing ear, Dora, Dora, my love, my wife, I can save you, but I will not! I can save you, but still you must die!"

"Livingstone," faltered Dora, with a look of perfect consciousness. "It is hard to die—I am guilty but you will not, cannot kill me. Spare me, Albert, for your own sake, oh spare me!"

She knew that she was dying. Guilt, shame, reproach, all were forgotten; all she craved was life! Could she have fallen dead on the floor, she would have hailed death without a murmur. But to count each pulsation of her freezing blood, to feel a separate agony in each throb of her bursting heart, to meet death while her brain was reeling in a delirium, that left her still conscious of her doom, oh merciful God, this was a hell, far beyond the rude fancies, with which superstition goads her crouching victim.

"Life, life." she shrieked, "spare me Albert, —*Life!*"

"Could every throb of your dying heart take voice and form, and shriek for pity, I tell you, woman, that still my answer would be, Dora, you must die."

He turned away from her, as in a voice of deliberate tone, he spoke these final words of fate.

There was silence for a moment. With the last impulse of her failing strength, Dora sprang forward, she flung her arms around his neck.

An awful convulsion distorted Livingstone's features.

"Oh God!" he groaned.

Those arms—they had encircled his neck in the by-gone time of faith and peace. That bosom, heaving against his own—so it had heaved and throbbed in the days of his love. But that beautiful face, those eyes flashing super-natural lustre, that long black hair showering down over the queenly form!

Livingstone trembled; he made an effort to unwind her arms from his neck, but in vain! She kissed him, yes, with those ripe lips, which had called him husband one year ago, smiling like heaven all the while, she kissed him, and he shuddered. Her lips were like flame coals.

"Life!" she whispered, in husky tones, "only *life!*"

Now was the awful moment. Now man of iron will, is the instant of your fate. This moment is destiny, eternity, heaven or hell, to you.

An expression of pity smiled from his livid face, but in an instant his fixed determination called an awful frown to his brow.

"Woman," he shrieked, "I have sworn it. You must die."

He dashed her from him as he spoke. Her magnificent form swayed to and fro for a moment, then with a look of terrible despair, she fell backward, into the arm-chair.

"Ha, ha, ha!" she screamed, with a burst of maniac laughter. "Ha, ha! These are brave steeds, Fitz-Cowles! Away away! With the night we leave all danger behind. How softly the morning breaks, oh beautiful! H-u-s-h My mother is dying. H-u-s-h! That was her last groan! Livingstone claims me as his bride, over the corse of my dead mother. Heaven will bless our nuptials, yes, yes—Ah! How cold. how dark, how drear! We are in the death-vault now. I am not dead, yet they bury me—oh, God, oh God! Will no one burst this coffin lid—how it presses on my bosom, close, close, close! Oh for one gleam of God's light again, oh for one breath of God's free air."

Her dark eyes rolled in their sockets. and with her white hands she dashed the tresses of her raven hair aside from her brow.

Livingstone gazed upon her, with folded arms he gazed upon the face of his wife. Paint me, the agony of a lost soul, and I will picture for you the awful resolution that distorted every feature of his face. The cold sweat on the brow of the dying woman was not more clammy than the beaded drops on the forehead of the husband.

"Oh, God!" Livingstone groaned, as a feeling of mercy came stealing over his heart. He was afraid that he might relent.

Dora rose once more upon her feet. She rose in an attitude of fearful sublimity. Her tall form towering in all its beauty and pride, she dashed the dark hair from her clammy brow, she raised her hand on high, with a gesture of command. Zenobia on her throne, with the spoils of all the nations scattered round her feet, could never have looked more sternly beautiful.

"Livingstone," she shrieked, with that upraised hand quivering in the air, while the cold sweat glistened in beads along her cheek and brow, Livingstone you *must* save me! *I cannot, will not die!*"

There was an awful will beaming from that woman's face. Her eyes were painfully compressed, and her dark eye glared with a fierce light, wild as madness, and as determined as death.

"*I will not die!*" she shrieked, clenching her white hands in agony and despair. Ere the words died on her lips she fell heavily on the floor. She lay with her head pillowed on the hearth, with her limbs flung stiffly over the carpet, while her cheek was cold and pale as marble. Her lips—they had grown suddenly

white—hung gently apart, and her dark eyes, gazed steadily on the ceiling. A glasty film was on each eye, She was dead. The proud and peerless Dora Livingstone lay on that floor a lifeless corse.

"There," shrieked Livingstone, in a voice choked by despair. "There, there is all that was my wife!"

He fell on his knees beside her coffin. At this moment, a thin stream of blood stole from her lips, and trickled over her face and bosom, marking its progress, with a line of ghastly red. She had died within the hour; her mighty heart had burst its channels, and that blood, whose every pulsation was a thought, now stained the whiteness of her bosom.

The madman knelt beside his victim. For two long days and two weary nights, he had anticipated the scene. With his reason tottering all the while, he had prepared the accumulating agonies with which to torture her closing hour. The journey to Hawkewood, planned with such cool deliberation, the poison of Catherine de Medicis, these were alike the work of a madman.

He knelt beside his victim. Was it a drop of death sweat, or a tear that trickled down her face?

Not a word passed from his lips, but while his blue eyes shone with one fixed expression, he tore aside the robe from the breast of the corse. The light shone on her bosom, so beautiful and yet so white and cold. And over its alabaster skin, marring the beauty of the blue veins, trickled the thin stream of blood, mingling with the tears that fell from the hot eyeballs of the murderer.

The light from the table, and the warm glow from the hearth-side, streamed over the musular form of Livingstone, kneeling beside the coffin, with the form of his dead wife resting on his arms. The contrast was full of terrible interest. His bronzed face with the livid lips and the glaring blue eyes; her pale countenance, with the parted lips stained with blood, and the dark eyes, glassy with death. The Lord of Longford with his lady in his arms!

"You have won your coronet, Dora, but it is of worms! You have won your empire, but it is a narrow grave! Here, here, lies all that was my wife!"

Laying her gently down, he silently arose. One look at the dead body, and he passed from the room into the darkness of the stairway. It was but a moment ere he stood in the large hall of the mansion, where a small lamp, suspended from the ceiling, flung a dismal light around.

"Davidson," he cried in hasty and impatient tones.

The withered figure of the old man emerged from a side door.

"Your horse is saddled at the door Squire Livingstone."

"He calls me squire," muttered Livingstone with a mocking smile. "squire and I am a *lord!* Look ye Davidson, I must return to town on business. Do not disturb Mrs. Livingstone before morning, she is tired, and would have a long sleep."

Grasping the fur cap which he had worn to Hawkewood, from a side table, he strode through the hall door. In a moment, the clatter of a horse's hoofs echoed from the road leading to the mansion gate, mingled with a wild hurrah.

In the early dawn of the morning, a noble horse, with the saddle on his back, covered with dust, and the bridle thrown loosely over his neck, was seen wandering without a rider along the public highway. It was the steed of Livingstone.

For one hour the light burned merrily in the oak chamber, and the cheerful glow of fire, gave warmth and comfort to the place, but the corse of the woman was gone from the floor, while a box of glittering gold gleamed among the hearthside ashes.

CHAPTER XIII.

SUNSET ON CHRISTMAS-EVE.

THE warm glow of the setting sun, gleaming through an opening in the clouds, streamed down the hill of Walnut-street, over the wharf, and along the broad bosom of the Delaware.

Some few idlers were lounging round the doors of the hotel; here and there stood a vagrant, along the edges of the wharf, gazing indolently at the form of the retreating ferry-boat, which some hundred yards from shore, was ploughing its way, through the waters of the Delaware, towards the dim shores of Jersey.

Suddenly the sun disappeared behind a cloud, and two figures came hastening down Walnut-street, rushing hurriedly through the snow, towards the wharf. In a few moments they attained the edge of the wharf, they stood upon the ferry landing, and gazed upon the retreating steamboat, while an expression of deep chagrin spread over their faces.

"Curse the thing," cried the tallest of the twain, whose manly form was enveloped in a tight-fitting white overcoat. "We are too late for the boat!"

With an oath on his lips, he then gazed nervously along Walnut-street, and paced the wharf, with a wild and hurried footstep.

His companion, a little man, wrapped up in a large cloak, with a well-polished glazed cap on his head, also cast an eager look along Walnut-street, and then gazed at the retreating ferry-boat, with a deep muttered curse.

"Gus, we're too late for the boat," he exclaimed, in a hurried whisper. "Had'nt we better go up home again? I don't exactly like the idea of standing here in this public place——"

"I will leave this town to-night!" exclaimed Lorrimer. "Aye, leave the Quaker City, if I have to swim to yonder shore. Tell me, good fellow, is there no way of crossing to Camden?"

He spoke to a weather-beaten man, whose broad shoulders, and brawny chest were enveloped in a stout pea-jacket, while an old tarpaulin hat shadowed over his sunburnt brow.

"That's the last ferry-boat, mister," said the fisherman, "but I've got a boat layin' alongside the wharf, there, that would take you over in a jiffey."

"Quick—there's a dollar for you," cried Lorrimer, in hurried tones. "Row us over in time for the New-York cars, and I'll make it five!"

Ere a moment passed, Petriken and the fisherman, were seated in the boat, while Lorrimer lingered on the edge of the wharf.

For a single instant he stood with his handsome form raised to its full height, while the wind played with the curls of his dark brown hair. His hazel eye gleamed with light, while his mustachioed lip was compressed with some deep emotion.

"Christmas Eve!" he muttered, "Farewell to the Quaker City, and farewell for many a day!"

He leaped into the boat, and seated himself by Petriken's side, in the seat nearest the bow.

"Trim boat," cried the fisherman, as he sat in the central seat, with an oar grasped in each sturdy hand, "trim boat, an' I'll make the crittur fly!"

He was about to urge the boat into the stream, when his attention was arrested by a voice from the wharf. Two persons stood soliciting a passage to the opposite shore. One was a tall quaker, whose broad brimmed hat shadowed a fine venerable face, while his ruddy cheeks contrasted with his snow white hair, presented the tokens of a green old age. He was dressed in dark brown attire, shaped after the peculiar fashion of his sect, a capacious great coat, reaching to his heels, thrown open in front, revealing the under coat, and voluminous waistcoat, all of the same respectable hue.

"Friend," he said in a calm even voice, "I will be much obliged to thee for a place in thy boat, in case thou art bound for Camden?"

"And I," said a harsh and shrill voice at his side, "will give you five dollars, if you will row me over in time for the New-York Cars."

The person who last spoke was clad in an over-coat of coarse grey, buttoned up to his throat, with a fur cap drawn down over his head, and a large black kerchief tied round his cheeks and mouth. From between the upraised collar of his coat, and his dark fur cap, a few locks of snow-white hair fell waving on the wind.

"Come on, gentlemen," said the old fisherman, in his bluff, hearty tone. "Jump in the boat, an' I'll spin you over like a top! Take that seat in the stern! Now then, trim boat, and away we go!"

The boat darted from the wharf, with the old fisherman seated in the centre, while Lorrimer and Petriken, occupied the front seat, and the quaker sat beside the old man in the stern.

For a few moments all was silent, save the sullen dipping of the oars. One thick mass of clouds lay over the city, and along the western horizon; a dense gloom covered the face of the waters, not a ray shone over the surface of the rippling billows, not a single golden beam lighted on the crest of a rolling wave. Lorrimer turned his face over his shoulder, and glanced vacantly at the other occupants of the boat; there was a calm smile on the face of the quaker; but the man in the grey surtout sat with his head drooped on his folded arms, while his long white hair lay floating on his shoulders. One

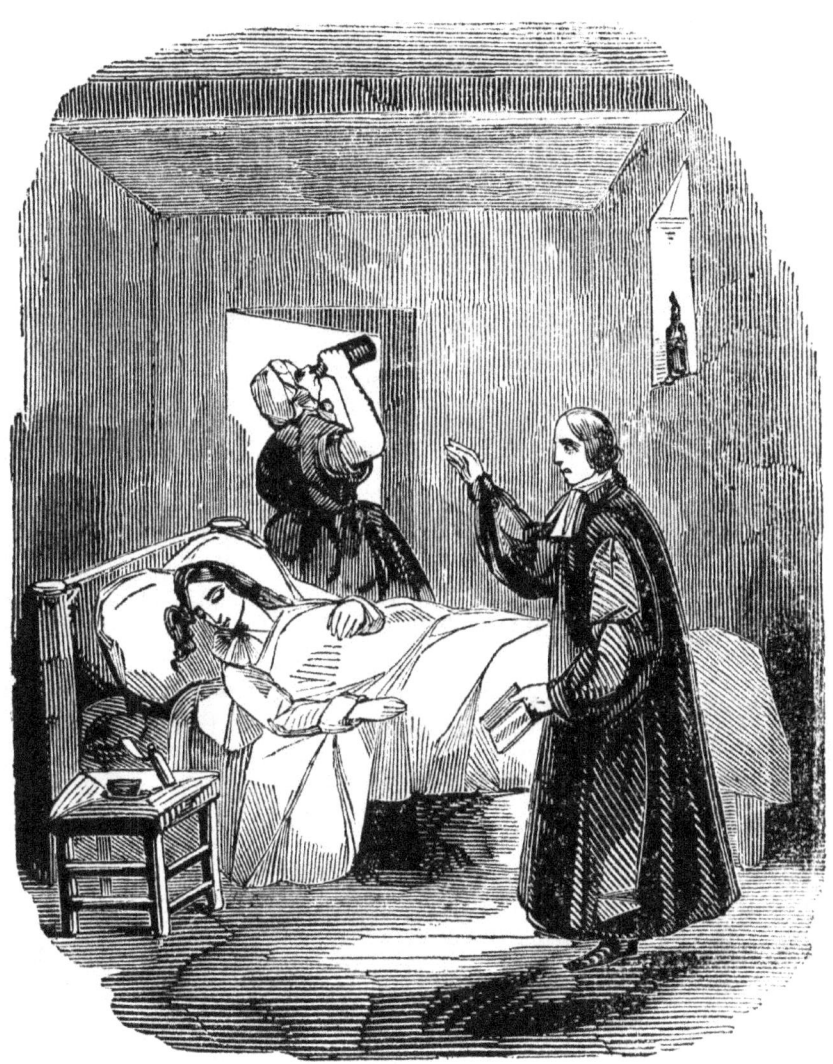

eager glance at the sky, and Lorrimer gazed in the pallid face of Petriken, who sat like a statue by his side. He was about to speak to his minion, but the strange gloom, which fell from the clouds upon the waters, cast its shadow on his soul.

"It is a cold wind, my friend," said the quaker, to the old man in the grey surtout. "A bitter cold wind; and look yonder, surely those are snow flakes, tossing in the air?"

"Yes, it is cold," was the reply of the old man by his side, as he sat with his head drooped upon his folded arms.

There was something so harsh and repulsive in the manner of this man, that the old quaker, apparently baulked in his effort to start a conversation with him, addressed his next remark to the boatman.

"Can thee tell me, friend, whether this darkness is caused by the clouds, or is it sunset indeed?"

"Sunset?" echoed Lorrimer, turning in his seat, and gazing over the boatman's shoulder into the quaker's face. "Who talks of sunset? Ah, excuse me, sir," he continued, as if startled by his own abruptness, "I thought the remark was addressed to me. But tell me, my good fellow, has the sun gone down, or is this sudden darkness but the shadow of yonder wall of clouds?"

"It wants five—p'rhaps ten minutes of sunset, young gentleman," was the answer of the boatman.

Lorrimer turned his face to the Jersey shore with an expression strange and doubtful in its character. True, his dark hazel eyes gleamed with a steady glance, true, his manly cheek glowed with a ruddy hue, but there was a gloom on his brow, as vague and undefinable as the shadow resting on the bosom of the Delaware.

"Pshaw!" he muttered. "The boat creeps along with a snail's pace. Would I could feel my feet upon the solid ground again—would—Why Silly, you sit there like a stone. Why don't you say something, man?"

"The fact is, Gus, my spirits are rather low," returned the man, with clattering teeth. "It's cursed cold on the river, too; that wind cuts a fellow like knives!"

There was silence in the boat again. She darted over the waves with a light careering motion, while the dipping of the oars into the sullen waters struck the ear with a wild and mournful sound. The dark atmosphere was whitened with falling snow-flakes, which came down with a fluttering motion, and sunk into the waves, like birds dissolving all at once into thin air.

In silence the boat approached the island which arises in the lordly Delaware. She entered the canal, which divides this bank of land in twain; the sound of the dipping oars broke on the air, mingled with the hoarse murmurs of the waves, as they dashed against the oaken planks which line the shores of the channel. Still all was gloom upon the waters, still the flakes of snow came gently down, still all was silence within the boat.

This channel was soon cleared; the city lay on the west like a black wall of houses, roofs, and mast-heads; the boat darted towards the Camden shore.

Lorrimer's head was bent on his breast. Thoughts of his home came gathering around his heart like dear hopes and sad farewells. He beheld the parlour, lighted by the Christmas Eve fire, he saw the form of his mother, the angel-face of his sister. And then the thought of Mary, the betrayed, the dishonoured, came over him, grim and ghastly as a pall flung over a bed of roses.

"Would to God, we could reach the Jersey shore!" he muttered. "My foot once on that soil, all these gloomy thoughts will vanish."

The clouds broke in the west, in glorious piles, and towers, and pinnacles, and the red sun poured a flood of glory over the water, as their rolling subsided to a soft and undulating mosion. Every tiny wave was gold, every ripplet quivered in floods of voluptuous light.

Lorrimer glanced over his shoulder. The aged Quaker was gazing round in calm delight, while the old man in the grey coat, still sat with his head drooped on his folded arms. With a murmur of admiration, he gazed upon the distant city, as its steeples rose in living light. The river was a sheet of floating gold; the western horizon was filled with a gorgeous world of clouds, rising pile on pile, with the light of the setting sun streaming over the spires and roofs of the city, while the white snow-flakes floated in the air like birds, whose hues were beautiful as the rays of a star.

Never had the sky looked so gorgeous, the river so lovely, the city so much like home.

With a murmur of delight, Lorrimer rose on his feet, gazing towards the west with dilating eyes.

The full glory of the sun poured over his manly form as it rose in all its towering height; it shone gladly over his face, with its handsome features, the curving lip darkened by a mustache, the glowing cheeks, the open brow, with the brown locks tossing in the air. His eyes were full of life, his brow grew radient with the deep joy of existence quivering through every vein. He stood the incarnation of manly glory and pride.

"Ha, ha," he muttered in a half audible tone, "'On Christmas Eve, at the hour of sun-down, one of ye will die by the other's hand!' Ha, ha! The shadow is gone from my soul. It is Christmas Eve, and the prophecy is false!"

He gazed towards the massive edifice of the Navy Yard, and then as he stood with outspread arms, his eye was attracted by some object floating in the water near the boat. It was a fur cap, half concealed by a mass of waving grey hair—while a syllable of wonder trembled on his lip, he turned his gaze to the boat, and the life-blood at his heart grew cold.

There, there, right before his face, at the back of the old boatman, stood a quivering form, there his eye met the gaze of a dark eye, flashing incarnate hate—there his sight was blasted by the vision of a livid face, with long dark hair, streaming wildly aside from a brow like death. The stranger, whose hair was white, had vanished. In his place towered the form of the avenger, Byrnewood Arlington!

Lorrimer gave but a single look, and then, frozen with a strange horror, he beheld the arm extended, he saw that pale hand, he saw the pistol pointed to his heart.

"Back!" he shrieked. "You dare not murder me. The prophecy is false——hah!"

"In the name of Mary Arlington—die!" was the awful and deliberate sentence of the avenger.

There was the sudden report of a pistol, there was a cloud of curling blue smoke. In a moment it cleared away. His clenched hand raised stiffly in the air, his chest heaving with an awful agony, his parted lips disclosing his gnashing teeth, his hazel eyes bulging from their sockets, Lorrimer stood for a single instant and then with a faintly-muttered name, he fell.

"Mary!" the word gurgled upward with his death groan, as he lay with his back against the hard plank of the seat, while his head sank to the bottom of the boat. A thick stream of blood gushed from his chest, and stained the hands of the boatman; Petriken's livid face was red with the life-current of the libertine.

With one simultaneous cry of horror, the quaker, the boatman, and the minion started to their feet. The boat quivered like a child's toy, on the agitated waves.

That cry of horror shook the air again.

Byrnewood Arlington knelt on the bottom of the tossing boat, the dead man's head upon his knees.

His face was the face of a maniac. Every feature quivered, every lineament trembled with a joy more horrible than death. His black eyes stood out from their sockets; his dark hair waved in the beams of the setting sun.

"Ha, ha!" the shout burst from his lips. "Here is blood, warm, warm, aye warm and gushing. Is that the murmur of a brook, is that the whisper of a breeze, is that the song of a bird? No, no, but still it is music—that gushing of the wronger's blood! Deeply wronged, Mary, deeply, darkly wronged. But fully avenged Mary, aye to the last drop of his blood! Have you no music there, I would dance, yes, yes, I would dance over the corse! Ha, ha, ha! Not the sound of the organ, that is too dark and gloomy! But the drum, the trumpet, the chorus of a full band; fill heaven and earth with joy! For in sight of God and his angels, I would dance over the corse, while a wild song of joy fills the heavens! A song—huzza—a song! And the chorus, mark ye how it swells! Huzza!"

"This, this is the vengeance of a brother!"

CHAPTER XIV.

THE CONCLUSION.

In a deep forest wild, a maiden form bent over a spring of clear cold water, which bubbled upward from among a mass of green leaves, near the foot of a giant oak. She bent down on the velvet moss, while the green leaves of the shrubbery encircled her on every side, and the thick branches of trees, meeting over-head in a canopy of verdure, made the place seem like a fairy bower of some olden story.

She bent down over the spring, not with a cup or a goblet in her hand, but with a white lily, trembling in her delicate fingers, as its petals dipped gently into the waters. Those waters, so clear, so cold, so tranquil, reflected the outlines of a fair young face, the gleam of

two mild blue eyes, the graceful flow of light brown hair, tossed gently on the summer air. As she gazed into this living mirror, a single ray of sunlight fell quivering from the canopy overhead, and trembled on the bosom of the spring, while a smile stole over the maiden's face. It was a smile, but sad and mournful as a knell; it was a smile, but gloomy as a sunbeam falling over the grave of youth and beauty.

Suddenly the maiden uprose from her kneeling posture. She placed the lily on her bosom, and with a light step threaded the mazes of a winding path that led around the trunks of colossal trees, over the softly turfed moss, and beneath the shade of leafy branches. Now the strain of some wild and melancholy song burst from her lips, and now with her blue eyes upturned, she gazed vacantly upon a glimpse of the blue heavens, murmuring strange words to herself all the while. Again she bounded on her way, until dashing a mass of green leaves aside, she stood on the brow of a gentle hill, with the summer wind playing among her dark brown tresses, while her blue eyes shone with a calm and holy delight.

A calm sheet of water, embosomed in the crest of the mountain, with banks high and rugged, clothed with forest trees, or gentle and sloping, crowned with soft and luxuriant shrubbery, a calm sheet of water, with its stainless depths resting in the smile of a summer sky, like a sleeping child beneath its mother's gaze! Such was the vision that burst on the delighted eye of the maiden, while her ears were soothed by the melody of the wood-bird's song, mingling with the murmur of a brooklet, echoing from the bosom of the shrubbery around the foot of the knoll, as it sank gently into the waters of the mountain lake.

The maiden gazed upon this scene of calm loveliness, while a mournful expression stole over her face, as though some memory of the past came sadly to her soul.

Arising from the centre of a fair garden that bloomed over the slope of a glade, declining gently to the water's brink, a cottage, over-shadowed by a grove of forest trees, with vines trailing round its arching windows, and winding walks leading down to the lake, broke on the maiden's eye like the vision of a happy home, reared by the hands of love in the solitude of the wilderness. The cottage, two stories in height, with arching windows and a steep, gabled roof, arose from a flowery knoll, not more than a hundred yards from the spot where the maiden stood.

The faint yellow hue of the cottage walls, was in beautiful contrast, with the verdure of the vines trailing round its windows, the deep green of the branches waving above its roof, the brown gravelled paths of the garden, or the beds of flowers scattered all around, with the sunbeams gleaming over rose and lily, as they waved gently to the summer air.

Suddenly the sound of footsteps came faintly to the maiden's ear. Turning toward the forest, she beheld two forms advancing along a wide gravelled walk, which sloped down toward the knoll, with the interwoven branches forming a verdant arch overhead. A fair girl supported the arm of an aged woman, whose tall form, clad in deep black, was in strong contrast with the light figure at her side, also attired in robes of sable. They came slowly along the walk; they perceived the form of the maiden clad in light robes; in a moment they reached her side.

"We have lost our way in the forest, miss," cried the aged, lady gazing upon the beautiful face of the girl, with an expression of wonder mingled with admiration. "In company with a party of our friends, we left the valley of Wyoming this morning, with the intention of enjoying the free air of these mountains. But having missed our friends, we are forced to ask you to direct us to the wood which leads from the forest."

The maiden in robes of white made no reply. Her blue eyes were enchained by the face of the maiden who accompanied the aged lady. With slow footsteps she advanced to her side, she laid her hands gently on her shoulders, and with a wild gaze perused each feature of her beautiful countenance. She was indeed beautiful as a dream. Waving tresses of auburn hair mingling the purple dyes of sunset with the deep black of midnight, relieved a fair countenance, whose pale brow was impressed with an expression of deep sadness, whose dark hazel eyes were full of thoughtful sorrow.

There they stood gazing in each other's faces, these two images of youth and loveliness, while the aged dame looked from countenance to countenance, with an expression of mute wonder.

*   *   *   *

The free sunbeams and the glad summer air came through the windows of the cottage. In a small room furnished in a style of neatness, combined with taste, sate a man in the prime of early manhood. His form was thrown listlessly in a large arm chair, while his arms were lightly folded across his chest. His high forehead was rendered deathly pale by the ebon blackness of his hair, which fell in thick masses down to his shoulders. His dark eyes dilating with an expression of intense thought, glared steadily in the air, while his nether lip quivered with a tremulous motion. His countenance was pale, yet it was not the pallor of disease, but of long, deep and absorbing thought. And as a stray sunbeam fell over his brow, or as his black hair was tossed aside from his face, by an occasional breath of wind, low-muttered words broke from his lips, words fraught with many a bitter memory, or dear hope of the by-gone time.

While he sits there, in that silent room, wrapt in strange thought, we will glance at the contents of a newspaper, that lay among some books and letters, on the table by his side.

It was dated, Philadelphia, June —— 1843.

* * "Among the passengers in the steam-ship, Great Western, which sailed from New-York yesterday morning, was our respected townsman, Luke Harvey, Esq., of the firm of Harvey and Arlington, late Livingstone, Harvey and Co. His bride, the daughter of the late Albert Livingstone, Esq.—who, with his wife, was destroyed in the conflagration of the country mansion of Hawkewood—accompanies our friend to Europe, where, it is said, an immense fortune, if not a title, has fallen to her, through the due course of law. Many of our readers will remember the romantic story of Miss Livingstone's former life. Stolen in her infancy from her father's arms, she was, after a lapse of seventeen years,-recognised and restored to her home.

* * "Abijah K. Jones, convicted of several atrocities, evaded the public execution that awaited him, by hanging himself in his cell yesterday morning.

* * "Peggy Grud, convicted of murder in the second degree, was yesterday pardoned, by our truly merciful governor * * * * Mrs. Nancy Perkins, a respectable widow lady, who lives retired, in an ancient mansion, situated in the southern part of the city, was yesterday tried on a scandalous charge, originated by some designing enemies. She was acquitted by the jury, without leaving the box * * * *

* * "The dead body of a woman was found on last Thursday, in the graveyard of L—— in this state. The corpse when discovered, was lying beside the grave of Mr. Walraven, once a highly respectable citizen of the town, but now some years deceased. The unknown female was dressed in deep black, her hair was very dark, and her face retained some tokens of former beauty. Having no friends to claim her corse, she was buried in the graveyard of the county poorhouse."

"The villain who perpetrated the wholesale forgery on several houses in New-York, Charleston, and New Orleans, was arrested last night, just before our paper went to press. He was taken to New York, under care of the police, heavily ironed, in order to baulk any effort to escape. He proves to be no less a personage than the notorious Algernon Fitz-Cowles, who has been displaying himself in Chestnut-street, for a year or two past." * * * *

"We also learn, from the best authority, that one of our first clergymen has been guilty of a most atrocious act of perfidy. As the case will shortly be brought to trial, we refrain from giving the particulars. Suffice to say, that the victim is the daughter of one of our wealthiest merchants, the heartless seducer, none other than the Reverend Doctor F. A. T. Pyne, author of several works on the Iniquities of the Pope, &c."

While the record of human weakness, wretchedness and crime, lay fluttering on the table, the head of the young man drooped slowly down, until his face rested on his folded arms. There was a world of meaning in the steady gaze of his dilated eye, which glared beneath his woven brows.

The silence of the room was scarcely broken by the opening of the door. A beautiful woman advanced with a softened footstep and stole gently to the back of the chair. Her clustering hair fell in thick tresses of gold, aside from a mild countenance, on whose fair outlines were written the tenderness of a mother, the deep and abiding love of a wife. In her extended arms, she held a sweet and laughing child, whose tiny fingers wandered playfully through the dark locks of the father's hair.

And there in that quiet parlour sat the man of the pallid brow, with his face drooped on his folded arms, wrapt in deep and terrible thought, while at the back of his chair, leaning over his downcast head, was the form of a fair and lovely woman, with a laughing babe in her extended hands.

"Byrnewood!" whispered the soft voice of the wife.

He raised his head; he beheld the beaming countenance of his wife, the laughing face of his child.

"Annie!" he whispered, while a smile of pleasure warmed over his pale face.

He rose from his seat, but that smile was gone. The dark thought was on his soul again! he turned from his wife and child towards the door of that chamber, from which he never emerged without a flashing eye and gloomy brow.

"Oh, Byrnewood, do not enter that chamber to-day," said the soft pleading voice of his wife. "I have never sought to know the secret of that dreary place, I have never crossed its threshold. But this I know, that you are always dark and gloomy after you have spent but a moment within its walls. Do not enter the chamber to-day, Byrnewood, do not, I beseech you!"

"This day, Annie, for the last time!" said Byrnewood, as he took the key from his pocket, and inserted it in the lock. "After to-day, that room shall never make me sad or gloomy."

With a melancholy smile he opened the door, passed into the chamber, and closed it again. It was a small and narrow room, with a plain carpet on the floor, a table standing in one corner, and an arching window opening on the lake. Through the half closed curtains of this window came the warm sunshine, the cool air, and a glimpse of the clear waters, the deep forests, and fragrant flowers.

In the centre of the wall opposite the door, a long curtain of dark velvet hung drooping from the ceiling to the floor. Byrnewood stood opposite this curtain, with his arms sternly folded on his breast, while a fearful agitation convulsed each lineament of his expressive countenance.

"Ha! I remember it well," he muttered, "I remember it well! There, there I stood, with the gaze of the callous mob fixed upon my face, the stern visages of the jury, and the iron

countenance of the judge, these were all before me! I stood in the presence of my fate.

"There too were the lawyers, full of craft and cunning. They had anticipated long speeches, ingenious pleas, knotty points of law, ha, ha! How I baulked them all! I remember it yet. "Plead not guilty," whispered my lawyer. I smiled in my heart. I knew his plan. He would clear me from the gibbet or the gaol, by the paltry plea of insanity! I insane! when my soul was firm as its own despair, when my hand was true as the weapon it grasped! "Guilty or not guilty?" whined the clerk.

"'Guilty!' I shouted, rising to my feet, while my lawyers started up with dismay. 'Guilty in the sight of God! I am charged with this man's murder; I did murder him! Yes, yes, as a dog should die, he died! I had a fair and stainless sister, gentlemen, my grey-haired father had a pure and innocent daughter! On that daughter's happiness hung the life of a true-hearted mother. Yes, yes, your honour, that daughter was the hope and joy of three persons, a father, a mother, a brother; and each of these would have given their life for her!

"'A libertine came; he lured this girl from her home; he perjured his soul that he might betray her! He did betray her! Betrayed, polluted, dishonoured, she returned to her father's house.

"'And think ye that there was no brother to avenge her wrong? Ha, ha! There was a brother. He pursued the libertine. He overtook the craven in his guilty flight! Calling on the high God to nerve his arm, and send the bullet home, he shot the libertine, as, in the flush of triumphant guilt, he stood glorying in his crime. Not guilty? Ha, ha! I am guilty, I am the murderer, I shot the libertine, and would shoot him again! Now, gentlemen, convict me if you can! Now, your honour, pass sentence of death upon me, if you can!

"'Here I rest my defence; on this I peril life and honour! He wronged my sister and he died!'

"How that glad shout rung through the court-house! Not guilty! I was free!"

As this wild soliloquy trembled from his lips in broken murmurs, he tore aside the velvet drapery, and a portrait was revealed. It was the portrait of Gustavus Lorrimer! Strolling into the studio of a celebrated artist, Byrnewood had seen the picture, and having ascertained that it was a copy of a portrait ordered by Lorrimer a month before his death, he purchased it, and took it to his mountain retreat among the wilds of Wyoming. There was the same appearance of manly beauty, the same dark hazel eye, the scornful sneer, the curling moustache, the flowing locks of dark brown hair. There it hung aloft, gleaming in the light of the sun, while the handsome Gus Lorrimer was rotting in his grave, six feet below the glad earth.

The avenger knew that he was right in the sight of God, in the execution of the fearful deed which had been death to the libertine, but still there was one thought never absent from his soul. At his board, on his pillow, in the walk through the wild wood or the crowded city, the face of Lorrimer was ever with him. He found an awful pleasure in contemplating the portrait of the libertine. He had avenged his sister's wrongs, but the memory of the scenes he had witnessed in Monk-Hall, in the parlour of his father's house, in the streets of the Quaker City, or on the broad river, dwelt like a shadow on his soul.

While Byrnewood Arlington stood gazing upon the portrait, the door slowly opened, and three figures entered the room. His reverie was deep and absorbing; he did not hear the sound of the opening door, nor the tread of footsteps. An aged dame, clad in deep black, a fair young girl in robes white as snow, and a maiden attired in sable, with auburn hair floating along each youthful cheek—these all, unknown and unperceived, stood at the brothers side.

" Ha !" he cried, with a sudden start as he perceived the intruders. "Mary, have I not told you never to cross that threshold ?"

His words were drowned in the wild shriek that quivered on each lip. They beheld the portrait ; they sank kneeling on the floor.

"My child !" shrieked the dame, and she clasped her hands in silent agony.

"My brother !" cried the maiden in black, and she buried her face in her bosom, while her auburn hair floated over her trembling hands.

The girl in robes of flowing white, knelt on the floor with her eyes so full of unutterable feeling, centered on the portrait, her cheek flushed with strange emotions, and her clasped hands raised on high. A single word burst from her lips, a single word uttered in a whisper, like the sigh of a broken heart—

" LORRAINE !"

THE END.

London : Printed by E. Lloyd, 12 Salisbury-Square, Fleet-street.